Steel and Sorrow

Book Two of the Blood and Tears Trilogy

Joshua P. Simon

Steel and Sorrow: Book Two of the Blood and Tears Trilogy

A Warleader proves his worth, a High Mage seeks revenge, a Commander overcomes his past, and a Queen solidifies her rule.

On the continent of Hesh, Tobin has finally gained the two things that have always been out of his reach—the respect of his clan and a woman's love. He now seeks to finish what his father began. When Tobin faces an enemy he never knew to suspect, he is left questioning not only his ability to rule, but also his sanity.

A High Mage has been humbled, but he has not been defeated. After spending his time devouring the history of Hesh, he's discovered a way to return home and reclaim what was once his. But before he exacts revenge on his enemies, he fulfills an obligation to his one remaining friend.

In the aftermath of great tragedy, Kaz has taken the role of commander, and with it, a mountain of headaches. He expected threats from his enemies. He did not expect the largest headaches to from within his own ranks. To make matters worse, the faded memories of Kaz's previous life are returning and what he sees haunts him.

Copyright © 2012 Joshua P. Simon

All rights reserved.

ISBN- 978-1-4791783-0-8

These stories are works of fiction. Names, characters, places, and incidents are either products of the author's imagination or used fictitiously. Any resemblance to actual events, locales, or persons, living or dead, is entirely coincidental.

No part of this publication can be reproduced or transmitted in any form or by any means, electronic or mechanical, without permission in writing from Joshua P. Simon.

Visit the author at www.joshuapsimon.blogspot.com

Contact joshuapsimon.author@gmail.com with any comments.

Cover Design by Brooke White with Sprout Studios (Houston, TX) brooke@sproutstudio.us

Editing by Joshua Essoe (www.joshuaessoe.com)

WORKS IN THE BLOOD AND TEARS WORLD

Warleader: A Blood and Tears Prequel Short Story

Rise and Fall: Book One of the Blood and Tears Trilogy

Walk Through Fire: A Blood and Tears Prequel Novella

Steel and Sorrow: Book Two of the Blood and Tears Trilogy

Hero of Slaves: A Blood and Tears Novella *Forthcoming*

Trial and Glory: Book Three of the Blood and Tears Trilogy *Forthcoming*

NORTH LINCOLNSHIRE

Library items can be renewed online 24/7, you will need your library card number and PIN.

Avoid library overdue charges by signing up to receive email preoverdue reminders at http://www.opac.northlincs.gov.uk/

Follow us on Facebook
www.facebook.com/northlincolnshirelibraries

---

www.northlincs.gov.uk/libraries

SLUM ISLE
CADONIA
OLD QUORON EMPIRE
GHAL
THURUM
TRIBAS SEA
EULOR SEA
MYTARCIS
BYZERNIAN ISLANDS
THE WORLD OF HYRON
PARITIA OCEAN
HESH

THE KINGDOM OF CADONIA

1. ITHANTHUL
2. LYROSENE
3. FLOROSON
4. NAMARIS
5. CATHYRIUM
6. NOROCOVA
7. ASATRYA
8. BOLYSIUS
9. LUCARTIAS
10. SEGAVONA
11. ARCAS ISLAND
12. ESTUL ISLAND
13. TRIBAS SEA
14. ASYCIUM RIVER
15. TYRESEOS RIVER
16. THE HIGH PASS
17. CATARIC RANGE

THE CONTINENT OF HESH

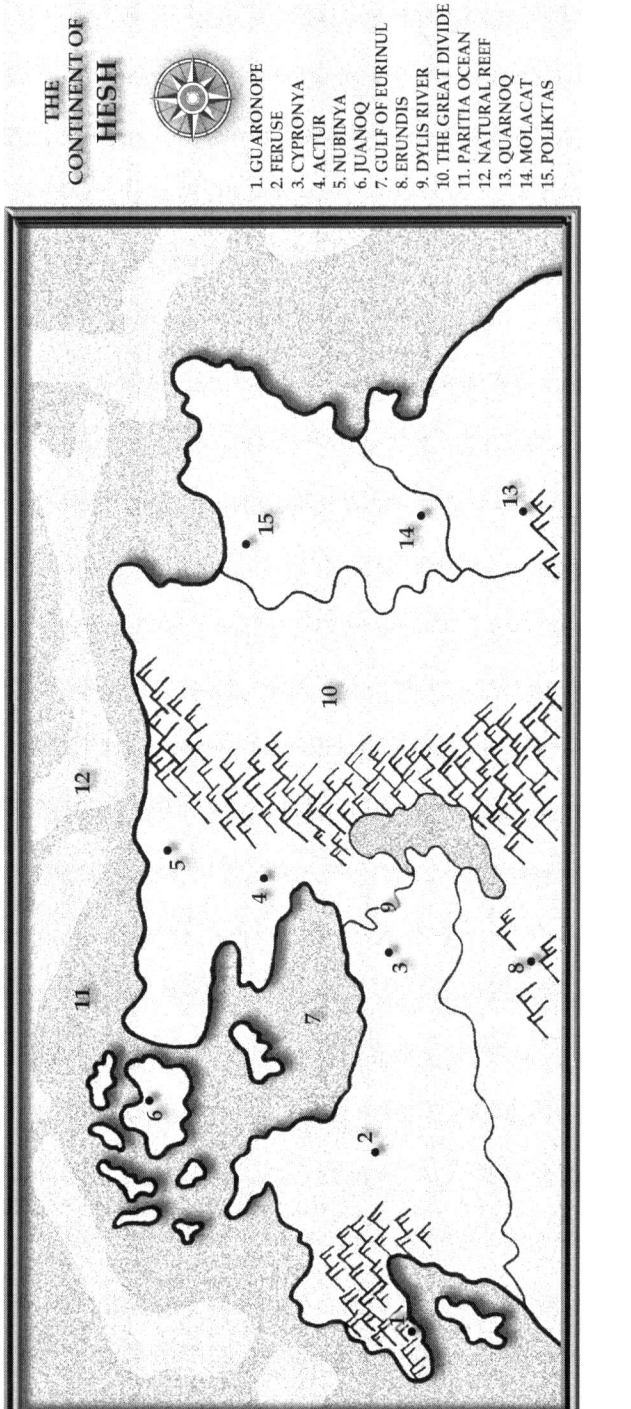

1. GUARONOPE
2. FERUSE
3. CYPRONYA
4. ACTUR
5. NUBINYA
6. JUANOQ
7. GULF OF EURINUL
8. ERUNDIS
9. DYLIS RIVER
10. THE GREAT DIVIDE
11. PARITIA OCEAN
12. NATURAL REEF
13. QUARNOQ
14. MOLACAT
15. POLIKTAS

DEDICATION

For Leah

PROLOGUE

Charu paced the quarters given to him that morning. The plush surroundings befitted his station as an emissary for the Red Mountain Clan, yet the ornate woodwork of the Green Forest Clan failed to impress him. Each clomp his boots made on the oak floors only increased his anger, causing him to focus more on the time of night than the impending meeting.

The warchief rubbed at his smooth face with an open hand. He cursed, wishing he walked the granite floors of his home in Guaronope. "Do they not know how to work stone at all?"

Melat spoke in her calm tone. "Feruse's walls are made from stone, as are many of their buildings' foundations."

Charu threw up his hands at her. "Yes, and what walls! Barely eight feet. How do they expect to defend something a man could scale without even the use of a ladder?"

Melat shrugged. "I didn't say they were good at working stone. Just that they could do it." One side of her mouth turned up into a lop-sided grin. Instantly, Charu forgot his anger, enthralled by the woman's ever-seductive allure. He drank in her curves and smooth, brown skin. Her smile grew wider. "I know that look. You need to stay focused for when Jolnan arrives."

Charu frowned, remembering the true focal point of his anger. He started pacing again. "He's kept me waiting for over an hour. If we were in Guaronope, it would be different."

"But we aren't," said Melat. "Though it wounds your pride, you need to remember that. We need Jolnan to win over the council." She walked over and placed a hand on his arm.

Charu sighed. After becoming warchief of the Red Mountain Clan, he had planned to invade the Green Forest Clan with his army, and then move on to the other clans until all of Hesh bowed to him. But the Blue Island Clan had acted first.

"You're right," he admitted.

A knock sounded at the door.

"Be strong, but be respectful," said Melat.

"Let him in."

Melat opened the door and Jolnan strode through with chin high. Lamplight danced off his bare scalp. Dark green trousers and a white shirt hung loosely from his thin frame. He wore an odd smile that reminded Charu of someone recalling an old joke.

Jolnan gave a slight bow that Charu begrudgingly returned. "I apologize for my tardiness, Warchief. Duty called."

Charu gestured to a couple of chairs and the two sat across from each other. "Yes, especially in such troubling times."

Melat came over with cups of wine for each. Jolnan's gaze lingered on the woman's figure before accepting the cup.

After a long swallow, Jolnan set his drink down. "So, what did you wish to see me about? It's unusual for a council member to meet in private with an emissary the day before he is to speak before them."

Charu remembered Melat's warning. He set his own cup down and leaned forward, elbows on his knees with hands clasped. "How about we forget the formalities and get right down to it? I know the power you possess among the council and I need your help."

Jolnan raised an eyebrow. "I'm listening."

"Despite our differences, the Red Mountain Clan has always held a great deal of respect for the Green Forest Clan," lied Charu. "I hope the feeling is mutual."

Though Jolnan gave a slight nod, Charu noticed the lie it also held.

"Our clans must unite against a common enemy. The Blue Island Clan. They conquer the Orange Desert Clan. They form an alliance with the Gray Marsh Clan. Their warleader mysteriously disappears and his successor, his own brother, kills his father and gains command over the people." He paused. "If not for the change in weather and the mobility of the nomadic Yellow Plain Clan that delayed Tobin's victory over them, I have no doubt his armies would already be on your land."

"We've considered these things and have begun retooling our forces. There are also plans to raise our walls."

"That's not enough. You can't afford to sit behind the insignificant walls of the capital and wait for Tobin to come for you."

"You're talking about becoming the aggressor?"

"Together, we would hold a significant advantage in numbers."

"They hold other advantages. Armor and weapons."

"Yes," admitted Charu. "But it isn't like our blades will be useless against them. Besides, let's not forget the advantage the Green Forest Clan has in terrain or our advantage with shamans."

Charu could see Jolnan weighing his words. He did not seem convinced.

"What about Nachun?" asked Jolnan. "Reports say he is more powerful than anyone since the Elder Age."

Charu clenched his fists at the shaman's name. "Nachun's abilities are an exaggeration, I assure you. You remember when his father sought aid from you some time ago?"

"Yes, we respected your wishes not to admit his family into our clan."

"And for that I'm grateful. His family wronged me and the Red Mountain Clan."

"The rumors are that you defiled his sister."

Charu grimaced. "Lies." He refused to elaborate, the truth was not for Jolnan to know. "But, I knew Nachun's family well. The shaman was weak. If he had shown any real ability, wouldn't his father have used that as enticement for you to accept them? No shaman is as strong as the stories say."

"Then how do you explain those stories?" asked the councilor.

Charu shrugged. "He must be a figurehead for Tobin. His shamans are probably focusing their power through him. From a psychological standpoint, it is far more intimidating for it to appear as though one man can wield power on that scale rather than a collective. As an outsider, Nachun's story adds to his mystique among the Blue Island Clan." He paused. "If we face Nachun, we will destroy him."

"So, you want our armies to join forces. You could have made this argument before the council yourself. There has to be something else you're interested in."

Charu quickly glanced at Melat who gave a slight nod. "I'll be blunt. My army is better trained and better prepared. I want complete command over our combined forces. Someone must have final say otherwise our chances of success will be drastically reduced."

Jolnan snorted. "That will be a hard sell to the council." He looked down and played with the hem of his sleeve. "I've recently learned of your own plans of conquest."

Jolnan reached forward and grabbed his cup of wine. He had not asked a question. He made his accusation and waited to see how Charu would respond. The warchief grew angry at the man's arrogance and angrier still that he had learned such information.

Melat passed between them, jarring Charu from his thoughts. She sat on Jolnan's lap and threw her arm over his neck. Jolnan froze, eyes widening. "Councilor, would you really consider spreading such an awful thing to others? Something like that could harm both our causes."

Jolnan cleared his throat as if intending to speak. Yet he failed to find the words as Melat grabbed his hand and placed it on her leg. Jolnan began to sweat.

Melat continued. "I know something about you too. I know that you've wanted to do away with the council and rule Feruse outright for some time. So much so, that an assassination attempt you orchestrated against one of your rivals failed less than a month ago. If word of that got out, I'm sure it would be just as damaging to you as your news would be to us."

Jolnan took his hand away and stirred uncomfortably in his seat. "It would still be your word against mine," he muttered.

Charu heard the lack of confidence in his voice. Melat stood and gave a wink as she walked to a side door. Though Charu hated to see her flaunt herself to others, he could not deny its effectiveness.

"Convince the council to put me in command," said Charu. "After we've defeated the Blue Island Clan, I want your help solidifying my rule. I admit that I did plan to conquer the Green Forest Clan, but I'd much rather do so peaceably. Do this for me and I'll see that the council is eliminated and you are put in charge of managing Feruse in their stead. It may not be exactly what you wanted, but you'd have a great deal more power and wealth than what you have now."

Melat opened a side door and two women, barely into their womanhood, entered the room. They wore very little.

"What is this?" asked Jolnan. He tried to appear upset, but could not hide his interest.

"Two virgins," said Melat. "They are a gift for you. I thought it a more enjoyable way to seal the deal than a handshake."

Jolnan's eyes finally left the teenagers and drifted to Melat and then Charu. He chuckled. "We have a deal." He shook his head. "You have a remarkable woman."

"Yes, I do," said Charu.

The two young women left with the councilor. Melat locked the door behind them. She turned with a smile. "You did it."

Charu scowled. "I didn't do anything. You convinced him. How did you know about the assassination attempt?"

"It was a hunch based on other information whispered about the city, especially in the local bathhouses where I bought the two girls." She giggled. "They aren't really virgins, but I doubt the old coot can tell the difference."

"And what if you were wrong about your hunch?"

"I would have thought of something." She frowned. "You aren't upset with me, are you?"

Charu didn't answer. Melat came over and wrapped her arms around him. Her familiar lavender smell drowned out the faint traces of pine from the furniture. "Look, you're a brilliant man and a great military leader, but you aren't a politician. That's why I'm trying to help you. I'm not overstepping myself, am I?"

"I don't know."

"I'm sorry. I promise I won't be so direct in the future." She pulled a letter out of her dress and handed it to him. "Perhaps this will change your mood."

Charu furrowed his brow as he opened the letter and began reading. He stopped and looked up. "These are details about Tobin's army, including possible locations of attack."

She smiled. "Yes. I made a friend."

"Who?"

She gestured to the letter. "See for yourself. He contacted me. What do you think?"

Charu continued to read. "It seems legitimate. And he has good reasons for helping us."

"So we can trust him?"

"For now."

"Good. Because I already sent a reply. I expect the next letter to contain more details regarding Tobin's plan for invasion."

Charu stared at Melat, thinking of where he had been two years ago. His wife, Nachun's sister, had cheated on him and embarrassed him before the council. He had lost standing with the Red Mountain Clan council as a result.

He met Melat a short while later after literally running into her on the streets of Guaronope. They had been inseparable since. Within a month, Melat managed to recover not only what standing Charu had lost, but also helped him rise higher than ever before.

And the entire time she asked for nothing. "It is enough to know I have you. What more do I need?"

"Stop looking at me like that. It's embarrassing." Melat cast her gaze downward. "What are you thinking about anyway?"

Charu snatched her off her feet. "Just how remarkable a woman I have."

* * *

Duke Conroy sat in his study, thumbing through a book that chronicled the exploits of a general from the Quoron Empire named Victas. Centuries ago, Victas had conquered most of the known world.

Conroy felt a close connection to him.

During Victas' early years, Quoron's emperor had been the victim of an assassination. Victas seized control of the empire rather than supporting the heir to the throne. Scholars claimed that the young general did so out of necessity rather than selfish ambition.

He saw that the emperor's son didn't have the skills to keep the empire intact and therefore took the burden upon himself. His love for his country was too great to allow it to fall apart.

Historians agree that without Victas' intervention and subsequent rule, Quoron would not have lasted.

What will historians write about me?

A knock at the door preceded the creaking hinges. A servant stuck his head in the room and bowed. "I apologize for interrupting, my lord. Duke Bronn has arrived. He's insisting to speak with you right away."

Conroy's eyes peaked over the top of the book. "Send him in."

The servant bowed again before quietly closing the door.

Conroy rose from his seat and strode to one of the large bookshelves lining the walls of his study. His most prized possessions, his library's completeness and wealth of knowledge was second only to the collection on Estul Island.

Books had always been a passion of his. He had read his family's collection several times over before reaching adulthood, and collected countless volumes since.

Hurried footsteps echoed from the hallway behind the study's door. The door flung open and slammed into the stone wall. Unsurprised, Conroy did not turn around.

"What are you doing in here?" said Bronn. "I thought you would be marshaling your forces. It's time we showed Jeldor and that black devil who should rule Cadonia."

Conroy paid little mind to the urgency of the man's tone as he carefully found the spot for the ancient text and replaced it. He slowly turned and gestured to the study door that hung half open. "In the future, you will treat my home with more respect."

Bronn gave Conroy a confused look. "Are you that upset about a door?"

"I'm upset that you would barge into my private study like a child and then presume to order me around like one of your servants." The edge in his voice cut through the air.

Bronn frowned and began to apologize. "You're right, I was only—"

"Close the door and sit down." Conroy told him, finding his chair once again. He could see Bronn's frustration, but the young duke wisely bit his lip and did as instructed. "Now, why are you here?"

Bronn took a deep breath, gripping tight the arms of his chair. He cleared his throat. "As I was saying, we must mount an offensive. They embarrassed our armies in the north."

"No," said Conroy. "They embarrassed your army. Mine remains behind my borders, waiting for the right moment, just as we previously discussed."

"Jeldor was susceptible for an attack after having come to Cathyrium's aid. My commander took the initiative to act. Orenthal didn't expect Kaz to redistribute his forces so quickly when he had Tomalt on the run."

"Your commander is an imbecile."

Bronn managed to control his emotions. "My father trusted him and he is well-liked among the men."

"Well-liked means nothing. I care little if my men like me, only that they respect and trust me to lead them. They fight for me because I don't make stupid mistakes. You should remove Orenthal from command."

"It's not his fault entirely. There were circumstances—"

"Circumstances you caused by seizing Arcas Island. That was not what we discussed. That act alone probably pushed Duke Jeldor to side with Elyse. If not for that alliance, her army would be a fraction of what it is now." Conroy watched Bronn's arrogant face twist with anger.

"How was I to know she'd be able to convince Jeldor to come to her cause? She had never shown the ability for such things before."

"It was all tied to Jonrell arriving. Gone for twelve years and then he shows up when she needs him most."

Bronn laughed. "I almost cried in joy when I learned he was shot by a boy with a crossbow. Just imagine, you fight the battle of your life only to have some foolish child put a quarrel through your heart."

"He deserved better," said Conroy.

"Hmm?"

"I never liked Jonrell, but what he pulled off at Cathyrium with the resources and time he had was impressive. And to retake Namaris at the same time? Incredible!"

Bronn grunted. "Pure luck."

"Luck comes from wise decisions."

"Is that how you explain Elyse's decision to make that animal her commander after her brother's death? Wise?"

"It depends. The reports say most of Kaz's men would follow him to hell and back. Others, especially the nobles, are eager for the foreigner to meet his demise."

Bronn's eyes widened. "You admire him, don't you?"

"You would have to be close-minded not to. Despite so many things working against him, he's still managed relative success."

"Listen to you. It's almost as if you plan to bow before him rather than the other way around."

Conroy's eyes narrowed. "He and everyone else he commands will pay homage to me when I take the crown."

"You say that, but then you refuse to attack. I could understand your hesitancy if Elyse still had the scepter. That would certainly change things. But Amcaro must have destroyed it before he died. Otherwise, she would have found a mage to use it against us by now."

Conroy shook his head. "True, but I won't leave the High Pass undermanned prematurely. Aurnon the Second bestowed its defense to my family centuries ago. I won't throw my duty away to seek personal glory."

"Why not at least remove Olasi from the field then? His lands are close enough. We wouldn't have to travel so far from the High Pass to reach them."

Conroy smiled. "I already have plans for Olasi." He refused to elaborate further. "I'll continue to let Elyse wear down her resources against Tomalt for now. When they are at their weakest, then I'll crush them. Not a moment sooner."

CHAPTER 1

Raker lay on his back, staring at the ceiling. He downed the last of the whiskey bottle's contents in one large gulp. Despite his position, he didn't spill a drop. Years of practice made him an expert in drunkenness and he had become nearly perfect in the craft since Jonrell's death. So caught up in war, few had noticed his recent mastering of the art.

Speaking of the art. Raker pressed the glass to his lips. He guzzled air and cursed.

Where's that kid when you need him? Oh yeah, off with Kroke and Krytien on some assignment for Kaz.

"Hey!" he called out. "You wanna throw me a bottle?" His voice echoed in the stone room. He and Drake, like most of the other officers, stayed in rooms away from the main barracks. Since returning to Lyrosene for the winter, an old place in the back of the armory had become their home.

"I know you're there. You gonna answer me or just skulk in the shadows?"

A lithe figure emerged from the far corner of the room, stepping into the pale moonlight from a high window. He drew back the black cloak concealing his face and figure. He looked young, barely a man.

I hate kids.

In his right hand, the kid held a knife. "How long have you known I was here?"

"I heard you come through the window." Raker allowed himself a grin as he watched the young man's eyes betray his surprise.

"I expected you to be asleep at this hour."

Raker spat and a glob of tobacco landed between the young man's feet. "I don't sleep much these days. I just drink."

The kid looked at the mess near his feet then up again, disgusted. "So, I noticed."

"You gonna hand me that bottle I asked for?"

After a moment the kid grinned. "Why not?" He walked over to a nearby table, picked up a full bottle, and threw it across the room.

Raker fumbled the toss, but the bottle thankfully landed in his lap. He popped the cork and took a drink. "Much obliged." He took another swallow and put the cork back in. "I gotta say I'm flattered that I'm the one to get taken out. I thought you'd have gone after someone else. Kaz perhaps?"

The kid grinned wider. "Don't worry, you're not alone. Our entire guild was hired to take out everyone in the Hell Patrol. A few others as well."

Raker whistled. "That's gotta be a pretty big payday. I'm guessing the queen too?"

The kid nodded.

Raker heaved a sigh and turned his eyes toward his mace a few paces away. "Well I hate to tell you, but that knife ain't gonna do much for you."

The assassin widened his stance. "You really think I'm gonna let you get that thing? Not that it matters. You're probably too drunk to wield it."

Raker smiled a mouth full of stained teeth. "Aye, you're right. I've never been quick on my feet. But that's the problem with you kids. You get distracted and focus on the wrong things."

Raker raised the arm he had moved beneath his sheets. It came up holding a rope that he yanked across his body. A missile sailed across the space and impaled the kid through the chest. The impact threw the assassin across the room, pinning his body against a wooden post.

Raker took another drink as he watched the light go out of the kid's eyes. Then he cursed, realizing the thing worked. He kept telling Drake that firing a ballista with a rope wasn't important, but the boy had pushed the issue.

Good thing he ain't here. I'm in no mood to hear him gloat. He cursed again. *I'll have to get someone to clean this mess up tomorrow though.* He sighed. *I probably should get up and tell someone what's going on.*

He looked down at his bottle. *Gotta finish paying my respects first.* He eyed the kid whose blood dripped all over his floor. *Besides, if all the guild's assassins are this sorry, there ain't much to worry about. Good thing Kroke ain't here. He'd be floored at what they're passing for a killer these days.*

He raised his bottle to the ceiling.

We miss you, Jonrell.

* * *

Zorik opened his eyes, but saw nothing in the pitch-black. He tried to move his hand to his head, hoping the simple touch would lessen the incessant pounding that echoed in his skull. But his arm wouldn't move and neither would his other. He looked down and saw they had been tied to his sides. Thick rope also bound his legs. He panicked.

What happened? How did I get here?

He struggled, but to no avail.

Though the giant hearth had burned down long ago, the stone near him still emanated heat. Coupled with the stacks of pots and pans off in one corner and several sacks and crates of foodstuffs in another, Zorik remembered he was in the kitchen.

The rest of his memories came flooding back.

The guild had received a big contract, employing all its members to eliminate the Hell Patrol. He wanted a crack at one of the main officers, but since he had botched the last two assignments, they gave him the task of taking out some old woman and her lover.

This was my last chance.

And somehow he blew it. He had snuck easily enough into the building, locating the kitchen soon after. The two targets shared a room adjoining the kitchen's eastern wall. He had been inching toward a door when something struck him in the back of the head. A low cackle had followed as he hit the stone floor.

A hushed murmuring of voices caught his ear. Hinges squeaked and a small patch of light fell into the room.

"I told you its fine. I killed a rat. That's all," said a raspy voice.

"Well, then let me help you dispose of it," said another, more gentle than the first.

"I think after all these years I know what to do with a dead rat. Now go to sleep. You'll need your rest when I'm done," said the first voice. Zorik noted the playful tone.

The door shut before the second voice could respond. The light remained in the room, growing stronger with the approach of shuffling footsteps.

A squat figure with long stringy hair appeared by his feet brandishing a cleaver in one hand and a candle in another. The glow of the flame danced across her face. When she smiled, a low cackle pushed itself out from the back of her throat. Zorik's spine crawled.

She gestured with the cleaver to his crotch. "Scream and I start there." The ugly grin grew wider. "I know what you're thinking," she said. "You're wondering how an old woman could possibly take you down, right?"

He nodded, eyes on her weapon.

"All you fools are overconfident. Like someone has to be a member of your guild to understand the nuances of sneaking up on someone and the thousands of ways to kill a person. You see me and think I'm an easy target. But I've done more wicked things than you could ever imagine and I take offense when someone tries to harm me or my man."

"It's not personal," he whispered, feeling as helpless as a newborn babe.

The old woman chuckled. "Oh, it's about to get real personal."

* * *

Terk gestured at the two men flanking his left and right. Never before had the Assassin's Guild assigned three men to take down one person, but considering the giant's size, the master saw it fitting to send three of his best. Terk understood the reasoning once he saw Crusher up close.

Terk had been told the Ghal could sleep through anything, including his own snores, which had pushed the giant to an isolated part of the barracks, away from other soldiers.

He sounds like a wagon barreling down an uneven cobble road.

Overwhelmed by the strong smell of musk, the three men inched toward the bed. One moved to the Ghal's feet, the other his head, and Terk took the middle. He breathed through his mouth trying to ignore the odor turning his stomach.

The other two cocked their heads confused. He felt it too. Something seemed off. Yet, the giant slept soundly, mouth catching flies while his snores rattled the room.

I've been doing this long enough to know when someone's faking it. And he's not faking it.

He scanned the giant's length and noticed how odd he slept, rigid as a board with arms at his sides and covers pulled up to his chin.

You'd think the man was dead if not for the echoing in my ears.

The assassin to Terk's right waved a hand in a silent question. Terk blinked and then nodded.

We don't have time to waste.

They raised their knives together, one meant for the throat, the other for the chest, and the last for the lower abdomen. Terk counted off with a slight bob of his head, feeling the watchful eyes of the others.

At the third nod all three blades plunged down. Knives clanked against metal and skidded to the sides, throwing each of the three figures off balance.

What the . . .

The snoring stopped and in a roar covers came off. A massive arm lashed out. The one motion sent the three assassins sprawling. Terk watched the Ghal climb out of bed.

One Above, he's huge.

The man wore full plate, including a gorget around his neck.

Who sleeps in full armor?

The Ghal reached down and grabbed one of them with his bare hands. Bones popped as the giant closed his grip about the man's throat.

Crusher threw the body at Terk as he pushed back to his feet. He heard a scream cut short by a sickening crunch and then the heavy plodding of footsteps.

The Ghal stood over him, eyes filled with hate, pronounced brow furrowed. He sneered and raised his boot above Terk's head.

Three wasn't enough.

* * *

Leo, the Shadow of Cadonia and Master of the Assassin's Guild, worked his way down the long corridor with a silent proficiency that none could match. He wore thin black silk, wrapped tight about his body and head, so not even the rustle of fabric would make a sound in the drafty hallway. Stepping lightly on the dark marble floors, he had already slipped by a half dozen royal guards, passing within inches of them while alerting none.

Pathetic.

The palace guards, though well-trained, were below what he considered a worthy challenge. He could have killed them with ease.

Leo had ordered his men to take down the rest of the Hell Patrol, one assassin per target with the exception of the Ghal. He also sent four of his best to kill the queen. Normally, he would have taken the queen himself, but that wasn't what the job called for.

Their employer had been adamant that only the Shadow of Cadonia could be trusted to take out the Hell Patrol's leader, Kaz, since none could stand before him on the battlefield. Leo had laughed at his employer's warning. "I will take him in the shadows. And in the shadows, I have no equal."

His employer seemed satisfied with his response and smiled, breaking the lid on a large chest of gold. Half the payment for the job. He would receive the rest upon completion, when the troublesome mercenary group and the queen were no more.

And once this is done, I will be set for life. Perhaps I'll move to Thurum and carve out a small kingdom for myself.

He edged ever closer, ducking in and out of the shadows cast from oil lamps positioned in wall sconces. A half-open door stood at the end of the corridor. Instinct caused him to freeze and he slid twin blades from oiled sheaths. Then he remembered the odd detail about his target. Informants had told him that the foreigner felt more comfortable with the door and windows open.

Something about being less confined. Barbaric is what it is. No matter. I won't have to double-check the hinges before I enter.

The open window of the room brought cool air into the hallway, reminding Leo that winter still struggled mightily against the inevitable spring weather. He slipped into Kaz's room, hugging the stone walls to avoid the fractures of light cast about the space. He waited.

He had not become the greatest assassin ever to live, a man whose very name struck fear like an apparition in the stories of old, by being careless. As his eyes continued to adjust he saw the details of the simple room—a desk and chair in one corner, a chest and dresser in the other. A long bed rested in the center and the contours of a great form lay under the covers.

Leo took a deep breath and held it as he made his way to the bed. Kaz slept with the covers tight about him and his back turned to the door.

Leo had never been one to stab a man in the back. He obtained too much enjoyment from the shock in a target's eyes as he plunged his knife into their chest, that brief moment of clarity when they realized their end had come.

He yanked away the covers, expecting Kaz to turn, but to Leo's surprise saw only stuffed pillows and balls of clothing.

"Pathetic," said a deep voice.

Leo's eyes widened.

He wheeled with his blades, one slashing low, the other high. His target moved in a blur, easily dodging the blows. Leo kicked, but a meaty hand reached out and seized his foot in mid-air, wrenching him from his feet. He lashed out with his knives again, but Kaz's foot deflected one blow and before he could follow through, he had been tilted upside down.

A fist slammed into Leo's gut. He fought for air as the room spun. Panicked and trying to right himself, he dropped his knives, knowing he had others. He grabbed at Kaz, but his target's long arms kept him at bay.

Kaz carried him across the room.

The cool night air cut through his thin clothing. Moonlight shone in his eyes. He looked down and saw the ground below. He started to scream, but another fist slammed into his gut. The vomit had nowhere to go with the black cloth covering his face and the previous contents of his stomach sloshed around his mouth and cheeks.

Kaz held him by one outstretched arm like a toy.

"Am I the only one?"

Leo met the eyes of the dark foreigner. "Tell me how. Who told you I was coming?"

"Answer me first. Am I the only one?"

"No," he answered honestly, surprising himself.

Because he bested me. What else can I do with the man who brought down the Shadow of Cadonia like he was a common thief?

"Who else?"

"Everyone. All of your crew."

"And the queen?"

"Yes."

"Who hired you?"

"Our contract prohibits us from knowing the identity of our employer."

Kaz grunted.

"Please. Now tell me who warned you."

Kaz shook his bald head, a scornful look on his face. "No one. I needed no warning for an amateur."

Leo fell. He thought about screaming or shouting in protest as the ground rose up to meet him. But that word had been too great of an insult. It echoed in his mind, a word he had never remembered being called, even in his early days.

It was the last word he ever heard.
Amateur.

* * *

Kaz spun on his heels, grabbed his sword, and left his room. He raced down the hall half-dressed, cursing at the guards outside to follow him. They obeyed, but the clanging of heavy armor and labored breathing grew fainter with every step.

He refused to slow, knowing that every second counted against Elyse's life. The assassin had told him that the Hell Patrol had been targeted as well, but Kaz did not fear for their safety as he did the queen's. The Hell Patrol had lived this sort of life long enough to look after themselves.

The queen maintained half a dozen guards near her chamber door at all times. Yet, Kaz doubted their ability to defend Elyse any more than his had protected him.

A wide mass of stone, the queen's tower stood adjacent to the great keep. Kaz entered the tower on the third level through an enclosed walkway. Two guards near the entrance lay with blank stares and blue lips, a dart sticking from each of their throats.

Kaz bounded up the stairs, taking them four at a time. He discovered similar scenes on the next two landings. The last pair of guards had managed to eliminate an assassin before meeting their fate.

Blood trailed up the last remaining steps.

A small hallway at the tower's top led to three separate rooms. The queen resided at the end. A pile of bodies lay before the large, open double doors—five guardsmen and two black-cloaked figures. A scream sounded beyond the doors and Kaz sprinted toward Elyse's quarters, hurdling corpses and shouldering his way inside. The door slammed against the wall with a thud.

Elyse crouched behind a toppled dresser in her nightgown. Before her, a battered guardsman swung wildly as the last assassin dodged the sloppy blows. The assassin ducked under a tired thrust and plunged his blade into a gaping joint in the guard's armor. Crimson flowed from the wound as the guard crashed to the floor.

The black-cloaked figure flicked a glance at Kaz, acknowledging his presence for the briefest of moments. Elyse screamed in fear as she began throwing books at the assassin.

Kaz covered the room in a heartbeat. He leaped into the air and a guttural yell came from his throat. The assassin faced Kaz with his long knife raised in defense. Kaz's strike pushed aside the assassin's knife. His sword peeled away a layer of cloth and ear before carving its way down into the man's neck. Kaz wrenched his blade loose, turned it point down and plunged it into the man's chest.

Elyse wept in the corner. Kaz dropped his sword and bent down on one knee next to her. She looked up and lunged toward him, throwing her arms over his shoulders and squeezing his neck. She sobbed and he put his sweaty arms around her. He felt her limbs tremble.

"It's over," he said.

She took a deep breath. Her sobbing stopped. "You think I would be used to this by now. It isn't as if this is the first time someone's tried to kill me." She sighed. "Will it ever end?"

Kaz grunted. "Eventually. Don't give up."

"I know." She started to stand and Kaz helped her to her feet. "No matter how much the night has shaken me, I need to hide it from all prying eyes or others will use it against me." She smiled. "Or at least that's what Jonrell would say."

"He was a wise man."

"Yes, he was."

The clanging of armor told Kaz that the rest of the royal guards had finally caught up to him.

Elyse forced back her remaining tears and quickly wiped her face. Kaz admired the speed in which she composed herself.

Two dozen guards entered. The captain spoke. "Your Majesty, are you—"

Elyse cut him off. "I'm fine. Your men fought well and Kaz reached me in time."

The captain bowed. "We received word that there have been other attacks."

"My men," said Kaz.

"Go," Elyse said. "See to their safety. Come back when you're done and see me. I won't be sleeping any more this night."

He nodded, grabbed his sword, and sped past the guards and out the door.

* * *

Kaz ran through the dark corridor just as he heard a wet hacking sound behind a closed door.

I'm too late.

Rage took him as he shouldered into the room, splintering the door. His eyes darted frantically about.

An old woman appeared from behind a table. "What in the name of the One Above are you doing?" asked Hag.

She walked from behind the table, exposing a bloodied shirt. His stomach tightened and he took a step forward. "Are you alright?"

Hag looked down and cackled. "I'm fine. Some idiot tried to kill me and Wiqua. It's his blood. I was trying to get some information out of him, but I guess I got carried away." She scowled. "I had to keep him focused since all he wanted to do was babble about his poor childhood. Whined like a baby. Why can't people just take it like a man?"

Kaz felt a brief moment of relief. "Where's Wiqua?"

"Asleep. I haven't told him yet. You know how he is. He'd try to heal the idiot. Wait a minute. What are you doing here? Just before he died, he said there were others."

"I came to check on you first."

Hag scowled. "That's a stupid thing to do."

"You were on my way—"

Hag waved a hand. "One Above, you're an awful liar." She shook her head as she turned back to the body. "Get out of here before you make me blush. I've got to clean this mess up."

Kaz allowed himself a grin as he left the room.

* * *

He stood over the dead body and stared into its lifeless eyes. The young soldier had not even seen his twentieth year. The Hell Patrol had lost eighteen men from the attacks and though they killed over a hundred of the assassins, Kaz found little solace in those numbers.

It had been over a year since he had taken command of Elyse's army and in that time he'd lost thousands of men. Those who had died tonight shouldn't have affected him any more than the countless others, but they did. Each new death seemed to eat at him in a different way.

It's all this responsibility. It was much simpler taking command from someone else, having the death on someone else's hands. But now, every decision I make, everything I do, others must pay for.

He thought about the brief flashes of his old life that would sometimes visit him. He was no closer to learning who he was or where he had come from, but he knew that he had held some sort of command before. Kaz wondered if the loss of his men's lives had always affected him, and if so, how he handled it.

Is this what you went through Jonrell? All this worrying? Would you have made the same mistakes as I've made? Would you have lost fewer men?

Those questions, along with the brief glimpses of his past, kept him up at night when he felt the pressure of command. Cathyrium had earned him much of the army's respect and the battles that followed brought many others to his side. He knew some still didn't particularly like him, but they trusted him with their lives.

"What do you want me to do with them?" Crusher walked up and dumped three bodies at Kaz's feet—their features barely recognizable and limbs disjointed. "These were the ones that came after me."

"Cut off their heads and mount them on spikes outside the city's walls. Do it to every one of them. Let people think twice before trying something like this again."

"What about the one you dropped from the window? He ain't got much of a head left."

"Stick his whole body up there."

Crusher grunted. "I like it." A meaty hand slapped his shoulder. "You're taking this too hard. Stuff happens." The hand pulled away and the giant scooped up the three dead assassins before shuffling off.

It shouldn't.

"Commander," said a soft voice.

Kaz turned as Yanasi cleared her throat, eyes down. Rygar stood a step behind her, blond hair falling over his forehead. "Yes?"

"Rygar and I just made another round of the barracks and everyone else is fine."

"The armory?"

"All clear. Cisod was up working late and threw one in his forge. And despite being drunk, Raker still managed to kill one too."

Drunk again? Figures. "Good." He turned to Rygar. "Go tell Hag to wake Wiqua. I want him to double-check the injured."

"Aye, Commander."

Rygar pivoted and ran off. Kaz turned back to Yanasi. "Anything else?"

"No, sir. I think that's it."

"Then get some sleep. Training will be at the same time tomorrow. This is no time to become complacent."

* * *

The morning sun reflected off the melting snow, shining bright in Elyse's tired eyes. She struggled to walk on the wet ground, but drudged on nonetheless. She needed to be outside, away from the nightmare, only hours old. The dead bodies and frightful terror of the previous night reminded her of the atrocities inflicted by High Mage Nareash when he had slaughtered so many before her eyes. She still dreamed of that terrible day and the events surrounding it, doubting she would ever shake those helpless feelings or the dread that accompanied them. Her life had improved little since that day with court intrigue, spies, victories, defeats, and countless nightmares along the way.

Jonrell's death had become her most bitter memory, one that she thought of often.

One Above, I wish he was still here.

She let out a long puff of air that fogged before her face.

The stresses of running a kingdom weighed heavily. Less than a year ago, she had even wanted to hand the crown over to her brother.

But not anymore. I know I can do this.

Elyse walked through the army barracks and into the training grounds. She pulled her cloak tighter as a breeze sent a chill up her back. Spring approached, but winter had given the land one last memory of its wrath with a late snowstorm, the remnants of which still clung to the ground. In patches where the sun hit the frost more directly, Elyse saw the first shoots of grass peeking through.

It won't be long before fighting begins anew.

Elyse halted as she spotted Kaz on his knee talking to a young boy. A woman that looked to be the boy's mother stood at his side with an arm draped over the child's shoulder. Kaz leaned in while speaking to him. A moment later, he handed him a sword. The commander rose and took the woman's hand. He placed a pouch into it. Elyse saw the woman's eyes widen as she shook her head and tried to pull away. Kaz held her firm and said something that caused her to weep. After a few more words, the woman kissed Kaz innocently on the cheek and walked off with the boy.

Elyse came upon Kaz while he watched them leave through the gate of the training yard.

"Is everything alright?" she asked.

Kaz turned and bowed. Straightening, he nodded. "Yes. Fine. I was just about to make my rounds," he said, quickly changing the subject and walking ahead of her.

Before Elyse could press him, Kaz began talking about Yanasi's archers as they passed the castle's range. The young mercenary woman drilled her soldiers with admirable proficiency.

Elyse decided to drop her questions about the mysterious encounter for now. "It still amazes me how far they've come," she said as another flight of arrows hit their targets.

"Yanasi pushes them hard."

"And none resent being commanded by a woman?"

"Many did at first. But in time she earned their respect and trust. Now it's as if being commanded by her is a badge of honor. The last man from another division to say something cross about Yanasi had an arrow in his backside before he finished his sentence."

Perhaps I should learn the bow then, she mused.

As they continued on, Elyse heard heavy footsteps and turned. The Ghal strode behind them, in front of her personal guard. His gaze darted about them.

"Why is Crusher following us?" she whispered.

Kaz shrugged. "After last night, he appointed himself my personal bodyguard. He won't take no for an answer and I'm in no mood to argue."

Elyse shook her head, not understanding the connection the two men shared. "Gauge said there were over a hundred bodies found in the black cloth. The assassin guild was crippled, practically wiped out."

"Not enough of them died as far as I'm concerned. The Hell Patrol lost eighteen men," said Kaz solemnly. Elyse noted how well his accent had improved over the last year.

"It could have been worse. Gauge believes the man you threw from your window was the master of the guild, the Shadow of Cadonia. Without leadership in their ranks, it will be years before they're a serious threat again."

"So your enemies must find another way to kill us then."

She shuddered and changed the subject. "When do you plan to move out?"

"Another few weeks. It will all depend on Krytien's success on Estul Island. As much as I hate to admit it, our lack of mages has hurt us in battle. We've lost too many good men simply because we can't counter the sorcery Tomalt brings to the field." He scowled. "But even so, we nearly had him."

He still resents my decision. "I needed you to release Jeldor when Bronn entered his borders. In order to keep Jeldor's alliance we can't discount his concerns."

"I didn't need him to defeat Tomalt. I could have won without him," he said.

"At what cost?" she asked. "I saw the reports. I know you're a good strategist, but Tomalt had you greatly outnumbered. Even a victory would have decimated the army. Then what? Conroy would be free to finally make his move and we'd lack the men to face him."

He grinned at her.

"What?"

"You're growing into your role more each day. Jonrell would be proud."

Elyse blushed. Her hand wiped the tear streaking down her cheek.

"I didn't mean. . . ."

Elyse forced a smile. "It was only the wind in my eyes. Only the wind," she whispered.

* * *

"Oh my! I can't believe I almost forgot."

Elyse had just sat at her desk for a night of work when Lobella called out. The woman spun away from the door and glided toward her.

"What is it?" Elyse asked.

Though they were alone in Elyse's room, Lobella leaned in and whispered. "I learned the story of the woman and the boy you mentioned earlier today."

Elyse blinked. "You did? I didn't expect anything so soon."

"It was pure coincidence. My mother heard about it from one of her friends." She shook her head. "It's such a sad story."

"Tell me."

"The woman's husband, Sarex, had recently placed membership with the Hell Patrol a few days ago as an aide to Kaz."

"Yes, I know him. He didn't really look like much of a soldier to me."

"That's just it. He was never a soldier, but a scholar. With the war going on, people in Cadonia had cast aside such things and Sarex struggled to care for his family. He went to Kaz and offered to help him with research, cartography, histories, translations—that sort of thing. Kaz had thought it was a good idea to bring him on in that capacity."

"And?"

"He was one of the eighteen men killed by the Assassin's Guild. He was also the only one with a family. I don't know all the details of the exchange, but apparently the sword had been specially made by Cisod and Kaz had yet to present it to Sarex. He gave it to the boy in memory of his father. The pouch came from Kaz's own personal funds. The amount was enough to feed the woman and child for over a year. Kaz told them there would be more when that ran out." A tear streaked down Lobella's face. "Elyse, that is both one of the sweetest and saddest things I've ever heard. I never realized Kaz had that side to him."

Elyse's heart tightened. She had seen that side of Kaz many times.

CHAPTER 2

Nareash admired the handiwork of the ship gently rocking beneath his feet. The captain steered it effortlessly through the calm waters and the crew went through their duties with little fanfare. Though he hadn't lifted a finger in its construction, the design had been his and he couldn't help feeling a sense of pride at its success.

Well, mostly my design.

His fellow students at Estul Island often mocked him for the time he spent studying in the musty library. However, the knowledge he had obtained had been worth every moment of their ridicule. His recollection of Mytarcian shipbuilding techniques had been the catalyst for the designs he created with the Blue Island Clan's shipwrights. Nareash had followed a similar process with Juanoq's blacksmiths when introducing more sophisticated armor and weapons to the Blue Island Clan's military.

And look what my ideas have done for the Blue Island Clan.

His mind wandered back to his last couple of years in Cadonia, especially those last few months after discovering Sacrynon's Scepter. He opened and closed his hands in frustration.

All my efforts there ruined in one moment before they ever had a chance to come to fruition.

"Does something trouble you, Nachun?"

Nareash blinked and turned to Mizak. The old scholar's nose crinkled as he squinted against the sun, emphasizing the crow's feet at his eyes. "No. I was only thinking about how close we are to reaching the lagoon. It will be nice to see something alive above the water again."

When Nareash had spoken with Tobin about his desire to search out the ancient city of Quarnoq, he made it known he would not cross the Great Divide using the route through the wastelands as Hesh's ancestors had centuries before.

Yet even by ship, the High Mage could not escape the sight of the barren land as they sailed east along Hesh's coast, past both Nubinya and the Burnt Sands Desert. The rolling black sand and rock of the wastelands spanned a greater distance than Nareash had imagined. From the safe confines of the ship, he wondered how any of Hesh's ancestors managed to survive that journey.

Mizak pointed toward a cliff that jutted from the dry land. "I double-checked our best map. After we pass that point, it says the land completely changes. We should reach our destination before midday."

Nareash already knew, but allowed the old man to speak his mind in order to keep him enthused. He had obtained the scholar's services before leaving Juanoq, knowing that despite his studies on Hesh, Mizak held a fountain of knowledge the High Mage did not.

Mizak also offered Nareash intellectual conversation he couldn't find elsewhere onboard. Several warriors or members of the ship's crew would show flashes of intelligence, but none offered the insight Tobin had surprised him with from time to time.

I wonder how he's doing.

He shook his head, surprised at the thought. He never thought he would have developed a friendship with Tobin when they had first met in Munai.

Life has a way of surprising you.

Mizak had continued talking, though Nareash had stopped listening. The High Mage waited until the old man's words trailed away before speaking. "I'll be in my cabin reviewing notes. See that someone notifies me once we reach the lagoon."

* * *

Two hours later, Nareash stood at the bow of the ship. As incomprehensible as the ancient maps and texts seemed at times, his assumptions regarding them had been accurate.

The wasteland of the Great Divide ended as abruptly as if someone had drawn an imaginary line in the air. Lush, thick jungles rose to soaring heights, the likes of which unknown even on the Blue Islands. The water changed from a deep, dark azure to a light blue one could see through. The water played tricks on the eyes when trying to estimate depth, but after careful consideration, the captain dropped anchor in a small inlet.

A short while later Nareash, Mizak, two shamans, and three dozen warriors led by a Kifzo named Guwan, slid their ships onto white beaches. The pale sand made him feel guilty for intruding on the ground as if their crunching footsteps might tarnish its beauty.

He stared out over the wild land. Hills that looked like a staircase for the One Above disappeared into a distant mist that covered the highest peaks. All texts led Nareash to believe that the ruins of Quarnoq sat somewhere within that shrouded area.

And within the ancient city lies a means to counter Amcaro now that he has the scepter.

His gaze slowly drifted down the green landscape as he shielded his eyes from the sun, scanning the peaks of the lower hills. He read that smaller cities leading to Quarnoq had littered those hilltops, when mankind still inhabited the lands.

Nareash saw nothing.

"I have men scouting the shoreline to find the best place to camp for the night," Guwan said as he approached the High Mage. Naked from the waist up, the tall, lean warrior carried a long sword strapped to his back.

"We're not stopping here for the night," said Nareash.

"It's past midday. It would be wise to make use of the remaining light to get a lay of the land and formulate a plan for tomorrow."

"I did not travel weeks at sea only to arrive without a plan. We will leave now and make camp within the jungle when the day has abandoned us. Not a moment sooner."

"I don't want to risk the lives of my men."

Nareash eyed the warrior. "Need I remind you of your orders from Tobin?"

Guwan's tone hardened. "No."

"Then have your men search for a stone road leading into the jungle."

"A stone road? After hundreds of years, it would be impossible to find. It'll be covered in a foot of dirt and plant life."

"Not this road."

Guwan narrowed his eyes. "Do you have any other information about this road? It may help in locating it since you're in such a hurry."

"It's thirty feet wide and constructed from a variety of colorful stones. From what I gather, it's a breathtaking sight. I'm sure your men should be able to find something so unique." His voice dripped with sarcasm.

Guwan clenched his jaw and walked away.

Nareash chuckled. Tobin had insisted that one of his best Kifzo should command the regular warriors the High Mage requested for the trip. Guwan obviously did not appreciate his orders.

He found himself too filled with excitement about the journey ahead to care.

* * *

After an hour of searching, they found the road. Ancient descriptions did not do the legendary path justice. Slabs of white and black marble formed the base of the road while patterns of jade, jasper, and agate gave it a life all its own. Each step seemed more wondrous than the last, and Nareash had to keep reminding Mizak not to waste time studying the road when what they came for lay at the end of it.

Steel and Sorrow: Book Two of the Blood and Tears Trilogy

That first night and the two that followed, the party camped on the road. Guwan and his men scouted the jungle, but other than coming back with local animals and fruit to replenish their supplies, they discovered nothing of importance.

In the late afternoon of the fourth day, that changed. Low lying limbs and vines that hung over the road parted near the top of the first rise. Mouths hung agape as they took in the scene.

Less than fifty yards away, the remains of a limestone wall encircled the ruins of a city. White statues adorned the tops of the walls. Nareash assumed the figures had been important in their time though they meant little to him. Gray towers rose behind the walls, their architecture unlike anything he had seen before as the dull color still managed to shine.

"Which one is it, Mizak?" asked Nareash.

The scholar rode atop one of the pack animals. He cleared his throat. "Poliktas. 'The Beginning,' if I translated it correctly. The smallest and first city we'll pass through."

Guwan came up beside them. "A stupid name for a city. What does it even mean?"

"It means that as impressive as the shattered remnants of this deserted place are, it's nothing in comparison to what awaits us. Yet, this place in its glory would have made Juanoq seem like a cesspool."

"How dare you speak of my home? If Tobin were here—"

"If Tobin were here," said Nareash, cutting the Kifzo off, "he would concur with my assessment. Your ruler possesses enough depth to understand such things. Would you argue against that?"

Guwan ignored the question and started toward the arched entrance. "We're wasting our time."

Mizak lowered his voice. "I believe he doesn't like you."

"Few men do."

* * *

Poliktas may have been the smallest city the group would pass through, but it still took an hour to reach the far gate at the other side. The beginnings of dusk had touched the sky and though Nareash wanted to push on, he agreed to rest for the night.

They made camp in the ruins of an old bathhouse where fresh water still ran. To everyone's surprise the ancient pipes and wells flowed as well as Nareash assumed they once did centuries ago.

"It makes you wonder why our people ever left," said Mizak.

"Hmm?" Nareash had drifted off into thought.

Mizak nodded to one of the shamans. "Colan and I were discussing what we've seen so far." He tossed a piece of charred monkey into his mouth and followed it with a bite of copoazu fruit. "There is obviously still a great deal of food here and," he gestured to the fresh water, "we know our ancestors did not lack water. Why would they ever leave something so beautiful? History says that many died crossing the Great Divide before our ancestors settled in Nubinya and later branched out to the land we know. I can't find their reason for their decision anywhere."

Nareash faced Colan. Somehow the shaman had managed to keep his blue robes absent of any grime. "And what is your theory?"

Colan bowed as other shamans did when speaking to Nareash. Their fear of his power warranted respect. "I'm not sure I have one. The obvious guess is that they fled some enemy. Yet, there is no evidence in our history or in the remains of this city that would suggest that. Perhaps a great plague infiltrated their populace and the only way to escape it was to leave their sick and dead behind. But there haven't been signs of mass graves." Colan shrugged. "Of all the things we might learn in Quarnoq, the answer to that mystery is what I seek the most." He paused. "What are your thoughts?"

Nareash stood and brushed off the dust from his red robes. Though Poliktas still showed flashes of its brilliance from centuries ago, even the ancient people of this land could not stave off time from covering everything in a layer of grime. "I have theories, but none I'm ready to share. Though the answer would be interesting, it isn't my priority. If even half of what I've read is true, Quarnoq holds inventions and weapons that could forever change mankind. Think of what could be accomplished with those lost secrets. A people who would not only leave those things behind, but then forget their success, are a people I care little for."

Colan inclined his head in confusion. "But Nachun, these are your ancestors as much as they are ours."

No. Not mine.

"I'll leave you two to contemplate your questions. I have more pressing things to consider."

Nareash walked away from the crackling fire and into the ancient city. The light of the stars and a crescent moon illuminated his path. Venturing off the main road, he saw the plant life had worked its way through cracks in the stone. He stopped at a high tower where vines had crawled three quarters of the way up its side. A faint glow encircled his right hand, which he placed against the wall. The vines withered, exposing the chiseled carvings in the marble. Nareash recalled seeing similar work in his brief visit in Nubinya over a year and a half ago.

It would seem the people took something with them across the wasteland after all.

The sound of running water piqued his curiosity and he located the tower's doorway. He stepped through and canted a small spell that illuminated the space. In the center of the circular room, Nareash gazed upon a marble statue of a woman overturning a jug. Water dribbled into a pool at the statue's base. He strode to the pool, peered down, and his reflection stared back at him, or rather the reflection of Nachun. He allowed the glamour to fall away, thankful to look upon his real face once again.

"Nachun?"

The voice startled Nareash and he wheeled without thinking. Colan stood in the doorway. He wore a shocked expression. The young shaman assumed a defensive stance and found his voice. "Who are you?"

I lower my guard for the first time in months and it comes back to bite me.

Nareash sighed and returned the glamour to his features, darkening his skin, and smoothing out the hard lines of his face.

Colan's eyes widened. "It is you. But how . . ."

"Close your mouth. And cease with your nonsense." Nareash gestured to the shaman's hands. "We both know that you're no match for me. Now, come in before someone sees you standing in the doorway. Why are you following me?"

After a moment, Colan hesitantly lowered his guard and took several steps forward. "I just wanted to see if you could settle a debate Mizak and I were having."

Nareash waved a hand dismissively and began pacing.

"Is this your real face or is the other?" asked Colan.

"The other." Nareash gestured around his head. "This is simply a means to an end. A spell few even know about, let alone are able to master."

"I-I don't understand. Do you have some disease?"

Nareash chuckled. "I have no disease. I'm not from Hesh."

"But there is no other place than—"

Nareash threw up his hands. "One Above, Colan. I thought you were someone who could see past what's in front of him. It's ironic that the rest of the world thinks the lost continent of Hesh is a legend while Heshans can't fathom an entire world existing outside of them."

"Then where are you from?" asked Colan. "How did you get here? And who is this 'One Above?'"

"The One Above is the god of my people and I'm from a country called Cadonia. I'm not here by choice. A teleportation spell went awry."

"Teleportation is a myth," said Colan.

Nareash laughed, remembering his discussion with Tobin after Kaz's disappearance. "I still forget how far behind Heshans are. Believe me or not, I don't care."

Colan bit his lip as if in deep thought. "Is your name even Nachun?"

"It's an identity I assumed once I found myself without a way to get home. Teleportation is a risky and sometimes elaborate process. Without knowing more about the distance I need to travel, the results could be fatal."

"So everything you've done over the last year and a half has been a lie?"

Nareash shook his head. "No, not everything. Most of 'Nachun's' story is real. I simply borrowed it from a shaman dying in the Burnt Sands Desert after an attack by the Orange Desert Clan. I changed some facts to suit my needs, but the meat of the story is the same."

"Are you really trying to aid Tobin in conquering Hesh?"

"Yes. I want to see him succeed. Haven't I given the Blue Island Clan weapons, armor, ships?" He paused. "However, I made it quite clear to Tobin not long after we met that your people could help me accomplish my own goals too. Quarnoq holds the answers I seek in order to return to Cadonia and reclaim what was taken from me."

"So Tobin knows your secret?"

"No. As much as I like the man, I believe the truth would damage our relationship and I can't afford that to happen."

The young shaman's mouth formed in a thin line. Nareash heard his quickening breath over the constant flow of water from the ancient fountain. After a minute, Colan finally spoke. "You're going to kill me, aren't you?"

"Yes." Nareash shrugged. "But it's been some time since I've had the opportunity to speak truthfully. I rather enjoyed it."

"Then why kill me?"

"Because now you hold me at a disadvantage."

"Can I make a suggestion?"

Nareash raised an eyebrow.

"Let me live. I know your story, but what does that matter? No one would believe half of what you just told me, and it would be my word against yours. Plus you have Tobin's ear. Why would I betray you when you can dispose of me at any time?"

Nareash began pacing again. "What do you want?"

"Besides my life?" asked Colan. "Knowledge. I was sincere when we spoke earlier with Mizak. I volunteered for this assignment because of the chance to learn from our history but also from you. I want answers, and based on what you've told me, there are more questions than I even knew to ask."

Nareash grinned. "So you expect me to teach you? Perhaps then one day you will grow more powerful than me."

Colan shrugged. "It isn't likely. I'm a capable shaman, but I have to work twice as hard to put the theory into practice. My natural talent is less than others."

I know that feeling. It was that way for me before using the Scepter. Then things seemed to just open up.

Colan continued. "Hold back what you like from me. Even learning a fraction of what you understand would be more than what I could learn from anyone else in Hesh."

"And the benefit for me?"

"Just as you said. You haven't had the chance to speak freely with anyone for some time. That and my loyalty is what I offer."

Nareash considered the proposition. He had expected Colan to beg for his life, but the way the shaman handled the situation impressed him. In fact, he had reminded Nareash of himself.

He removed his hands from his sleeves. Colan flinched, obviously expecting an attack. Nareash smiled and scratched at his cheek.

"Your education begins tomorrow."

The young shaman bowed. "Thank you, Master."

CHAPTER 3

Bazraki had been dead for months. Yet at times, Tobin still felt the weight of his father's disapproving stare. He wondered what his father would say to the changes he had made to the Blue Island Clan.

No doubt he would criticize all of them. He was good at that, unless it meant evaluating his own actions. Otherwise, he would not have surrounded himself with so many incompetent people.

Tobin acknowledged each of his advisors entering the war room. Not one of the men had been part of his father's inner circle. Some suggested that his cleansing of Bazraki's advisors would result in them using their influence to cause discord among the populace to undermine Tobin's authority. Only one man had tried to test the mettle of the new Blue Island Clan ruler.

No one dared since.

Tobin created his council to include people who truly made the city work. He replaced those out of touch with the actual running of Junaoq with representatives from the various guilds. Tobin intended to complete the vision his father began and knew he needed the right people in place to help him accomplish those goals.

Walor and Ufer, his commanders, also joined the meetings.

"Everyone is here, Warleader."

Tobin nodded at Ufer. He would not stand for anyone referring to him by some ridiculous title like "El Olam" as his father had.

He gestured to the man on his far left, a blacksmith by trade. "Anun, you begin. But let's keep the updates brief. We need not rehash the details again."

Anun nodded and quickly gave Tobin a summary of his progress, noting any obstacles still to overcome. Each person after him did the same over the course of the next hour. Tobin listened intently until Odala slipped into the room and flashed a smile. He held back a grin as he watched her gracefully take a seat in the back of the room. Their relationship had blossomed, and the weight of being warleader became unnoticeable with her near him.

Ufer shook his head disapprovingly.

He glanced one last time at Odala before giving the person speaking his undivided attention.

The last of his advisors, a shipwright was speaking. ". . . we'll be testing the last of the vessels this week. And not a moment too soon. The bay is beyond crowded and we've raised the ire of the fisherman."

"We'll be out of their way soon enough," said Tobin. "Keep up the good work. That will be all." He gestured toward the door.

Each advisor offered a quick bow and filed out.

Walor stepped away from the wall as the door shut. "What do you mean by being out of their way soon enough?"

Tobin quickly glanced toward Odala and then faced Walor. Nachun had asked Tobin to wait for him to return from his expedition to Quarnoq before proceeding with the year's campaign. However, Tobin had reservations about waiting. Odala helped convince Tobin that starting without Nachun would not be a betrayal of their friendship since his focus would not be on the Red Mountain Clan. "We aren't waiting for Nachun. The longer we wait, the more advantageous it is for the Green Forest Clan."

Sorry, Nachun, but you told me to trust my instincts. If all goes well, you can return to my victory in time to exact your revenge on Charu.

"Good," said Ufer.

Walor began cracking his knuckles. "I agree. Even if he finds Quarnoq and comes back with the weapons he believes are there, I'd rather not rely on him. To me, his trip is another example of him thinking of himself first."

"The Yellow Clan all over again," muttered Ufer.

Tobin understood. Many felt that Nachun had left the Blue Island Clan in a poor situation as they finished the campaign against the Yellow Plain Clan. The shaman had returned to Juanoq shortly after the first victory on the Yellow Plain in order to oversee research for his journey to Quarnoq. Few doubted that Nachun's presence would have ended the conflict sooner.

"Nachun was not at fault. Blame my father for poor planning and not foreseeing the Yellow Clan's tactics." He paused. "Or blame me for not being more decisive. I had hoped to settle the matter in battle, but I underestimated the Yellow Clan's strategy."

After chasing the Yellow Clan's surviving forces for months across the expansive plain without success, Tobin's patience had reached its limit. He turned to Actur, their capital city. Mawkuk had captured the city earlier in the campaign so he faced no resistance upon entering. Tobin gathered up all the men, women, and children left in the city and separated them in three distinct groups. He sent word to the Yellow Plain Clan with his intentions unless he received their surrender. He would kill one man the first day, two the next, three the day after, and so on. Once the male population ended, he would move to the women and then the children. If the army attempted to retake the city, he'd kill everyone in one mass execution.

It took ten days and the deaths of fifty-five men before the army arrived. Tobin hated himself for killing innocents, but he rationalized that those fifty-five men had saved thousands from dying in battle.

"If Mawkuk would not have failed in his duties before the first battle, we would have beaten them more soundly and finished them sooner. It is his fault more than yours, Warleader," said Ufer.

"Mawkuk will have his chance to contribute greatly in our campaign against the Green Forest Clan. I feel confident he'll use the opportunity to redeem himself."

Tobin met Odala's eyes. She gave a slight nod. She worried about her father and he tried to do anything he could to ease her mind.

Ufer leaned forward and whispered. "I know you are fond of her, but I wish you would not allow her in our meetings."

"We've discussed this before," said Tobin in a low voice.

Ufer turned to Walor for support. "It isn't anything personal," said Walor. "We worry that she may say something in passing without realizing her error."

Tobin shook his head. "Look at her." Odala played with the hem of her dress. "Her motives for being here are to be near me. She knows that nothing leaves this room." He cleared his throat, raising his voice. "That's all for now."

Tobin caught the surprised expressions on Walor and Ufer's faces as he chose not to go over strategy. He had time for that later. After all, his men knew their responsibilities. They only needed the exact date of departure.

The door closed silently behind the Kifzo and Odala rose from her seat. She sauntered over to him and they met in the center of the room.

"I'm glad that's over with," she said in a voice that caused Tobin's heart to race.

He pulled her close. "I thought you liked to watch me work."

"I do. But I missed you." She wrapped her arms around him. "And I'd much rather be doing other things than simply watching you work."

Tobin gazed into her deep brown eyes. "Well, we're alone now."

The corners of her mouth turned up slightly. "I thought you had another meeting to go to before dinner."

Tobin shrugged. "I'm Warleader. I can afford to be late."

Her grin turned into a wicked smile.

* * *

Odala left the war room out of breath and weary. Yet, she wore a smile nonetheless. Since their relationship began, Tobin's passion had become infectious and she missed him during the day when his duties kept them apart.

At first the horrors of Tobin's past had frightened her, but she realized that he had little control over the things he had been forced to suffer through in his youth.

And despite those atrocities, he managed not to lose the good within him as other Kifzo had.

Even now when she thought about that night when Tobin had threatened her father in Cypronya, she understood it was a means to an end. Tobin may have threatened her father, but he did not kill him. And just like tonight when Ufer questioned her father's actions, he not only defended the Gray Marsh Clan leader, but also found a way to improve his standing.

She bit her lower lip while thinking about the hungry look in Tobin's eyes when they had made love.

Do I love him?

"There you are."

Odala jumped. She whipped around and saw her brother walking toward her.

"You nearly scared me to death."

"Perhaps if you were paying attention to where you were going, the sound of my voice wouldn't have startled you." Soyjid stopped a few feet from her and looked around the empty hallway. He lowered his voice. "We were supposed to meet half an hour ago."

"Sorry. I was busy."

Soyjid's eyes wandered over her body. He reached out and straightened her dress. "Yes, it's obvious what you were busy with."

Odala blushed, suddenly self–conscious of his gaze.

"Remember, that while you're enjoying yourself, I'm trying to look out for our clan. Or have you forgotten about Father?"

She scowled. "Of course not. In fact, Tobin said that Father would be given an important role in the upcoming campaign."

"Good. And how did Walor and Ufer react?"

"They didn't seem pleased. They still blame him for the problems in conquering the Yellow Plain Clan."

Soyjid sighed. "They aren't completely wrong. Father did make a mistake in his approach. However, Bazraki did little to help matters and Tobin should have ended things sooner."

"What's your point?"

"That the Kifzo will continue to blame someone other than Tobin for any failings. Bazraki is dead, so if anything goes wrong against the Green Forest Clan, I'm sure they will look Father's way again."

"Tobin will defend him," said Odala.

"But for how long? Tobin must act in the best interests of the Blue Island Clan. Otherwise, one of his men may do to him what he did to Bazraki."

Odala remained quiet. She hadn't considered that possibility.

Tobin will find a way. He is too smart not to.

Soyjid changed the subject. "What else did you learn?"

"Nothing new. His council droned on about the same boring updates and Tobin pushed back his discussions on strategy with Walor and Ufer until tomorrow because he wanted to talk to me."

Soyjid's eyes narrowed. "I see."

"Can I go now? I'd like to freshen up before dinner."

"No doubt. I have one more thing for you to do. When you see Tobin again tonight, I need you to convince him to let me sit in on these council sessions."

"What? Why?"

"Because your reports are growing more incomplete each day. I need more if I'm to continue helping our clan. Can you do it?"

"I don't know," she said, hesitant. "Tobin might—"

"So you would turn your back on your own family? I'm glad Father isn't around to hear this," Soyjid hissed.

"Don't say that."

"Why? It's true. But don't worry, I've kept a lot from him." He gestured to her dress. "He doesn't need to know everything, does he?"

The shift in Soyjid's voice as he spoke the question caused Odala to tense. "I'll talk to Tobin tonight."

Soyjid grinned as they started walking. "Cheer up Sister, at least now you won't have to attend the meetings."

* * *

Odala's head lay against Tobin bare chest. She watched his muscles rise and fall with each breath. Her finger drifted over to a scar near his stomach and she traced it to his hip.

He has every right to be an awful person, but he's only treated me with kindness. Soyjid is wrong. Tobin will protect Father. If for no one else, than for me.

She sighed.

"What's on your mind?"

She craned her head toward Tobin. His face wore a look of concern.

"I'm just thinking about Soyjid."

"Is he well?"

She smiled. Tobin always seemed concerned over her brother's health. "He's fine. Remember, he's just thin like our father."

"Then what's wrong? Is there something I can do?"

Odala tensed and after a moment made her decision. "Actually, yes. He wants to sit in on your council meetings."

Tobin sat up and Odala did the same. "Is he serious? You know I don't just let anyone into those meetings."

"You let me."

"That's different."

She saw the stern look in Tobin's face and knew she had to press. "I know. But, this would mean so much to him. He hopes that once you've united Hesh, he might be able to return to the Gray Marshes. He is in line to lead our clan when Father passes. He wants to be ready for that moment and wants to ensure that he won't do anything to offend you."

Tobin mulled over her words. "I'll think about it."

"Please do this, not only for him, but for me. He could become an assistant to you, not just sit in on your council. What better way to learn how to be a leader? Besides, you know he is wise beyond his years. He may surprise you."

Tobin shook his head and smiled. "Again, I'll think about it." He pulled her close. "But not now. Let's forget about everything else for awhile."

They kissed and Odala knew immediately that Tobin had made his decision.

CHAPTER 4

Krytien leaned against the railing at the bow of the galley as it sliced through rolling waves. In the distance, gulls circled Estul Island, diving for their meals. Krytien found peace in the mundane nature of the scene, a break from the worries of the task ahead of him.

His gray robes flapped in the cool wind, and despite the warm sunlight, goose-bumps sprouted across his skin. If he had half a brain, he'd be below deck and out of the crew's way, but his growing anticipation wouldn't allow it.

The school of Cadonia's mages held such a mythical place in Krytien's mind that he doubted it could live up to his expectations.

His shoulders bunched.

A short, wiry man came up beside him. Kroke whipped out a blade and picked at his nails. "You look a little tense."

"I'd be lying if I said I wasn't."

"You ain't scared of a bunch of upstarts are you?"

Krytien chuckled. "These are more than a bunch of upstarts. They were trained by one of the greatest mages in recorded history. Even their weakest should be well-versed in the basics from a technical standpoint."

Kroke sheathed the blade and pulled out another, switching hands. "So you are scared?" He grunted. "I'll have to remember this day."

"I'm not afraid of spoiled brats whose parents had the money to pay for their education," Krytien snapped. "I've faced off against mages who had twice their talent. They aren't better than me."

Kroke cocked his head. "Never said they were. Just giving you a hard time is all."

"I know. Sorry."

Kroke sheathed the dagger and folded his arms. "So, what's it about this place that bothers you so much?"

Kroke usually wore such an indifferent attitude that the intensity in his stare took Krytien aback.

"It isn't just the people who live here, it's the place itself," said Krytien. "I was once someone with a natural talent and no means to cultivate it. An old mage named Philik befriended me and eventually gave me the robes I wear to this day. He had been schooled on this island and planned to write a personal letter that would have guaranteed me entrance."

"And what happened?"

"He died before he could write the letter. When he died, so did my dreams. This place," said Krytien, gesturing to the ever-growing island before them, "has haunted me ever since. The great unknown of what could have been."

Kroke bobbed his head. "So, that's why you tried to get out of coming?" Krytien nodded.

"And I thought it was because of Kaz."

"What do you mean?"

Kroke pulled out a knife again as the mood of the conversation changed. "I just find it odd that he sent us both along. I mean, I can see why he wanted you to come. Still, Jeldor has a couple of black robes who actually trained here. Why not send them instead?"

"Kaz said it was important for me to come."

"And me? What purpose do I serve here?"

"To watch my back I assume." He smiled. "And to listen to my sob stories."

Kroke flashed a rare grin. "Perhaps."

"What about Drake? Kaz was adamant about him coming along too."

"Somebody has to spy on us."

"What?"

"I don't blame the kid. I doubt he even knows. But I bet Kaz asks Drake his version of what went down to see if we hold anything back."

Krytien chuckled. "And I thought Raker was the paranoid one. So what do you think were Kaz's reasons for singling us out?"

"To get us away from the army. He tolerates me, but there is little love between us. And I think he doesn't like you questioning his decisions."

"That's always been my role."

"Under Ronav? Sure. Jonrell? Yes. Kaz?" He shrugged. "He's a different man than either of them."

Footsteps drummed behind them as the captain barked orders to his crew.

Krytien asked, "Why do you think others follow him so easily?"

"For some, who's in charge matters little. This life is all they know. Others, like Hag, genuinely like him. But I think most follow Kaz out of memory of Jonrell. It was no secret they grew close in the short time they were together, almost as close as Jonrell and Cassus used to be. I think those people hope Kaz ends up like the man Jonrell was." Kroke shrugged. "He hasn't botched things up so far."

"Is that why you follow him? Out of hope for the future?"

"I'm not sure, but that's probably part of it. I guess he hasn't given me a reason not to yet."

Krytien scratched his jaw. "He did the right thing by seeing this through with the queen. Jonrell would have wanted that."

"Yeah. But he didn't have many other options either. He can't exactly go home if he doesn't know where home is."

"Home is where you make it. I've called the Hell Patrol my home and family for most of my life, and you have for over a decade. He doesn't strike me as the kind of man who would just up and abandon those around him on a whim."

"You never know what a man will do until he is presented with the option."

* * *

Drake found a spot on deck away from the bustling activity. He had considered joining Kroke and Krytien at the bow if only so he could catch a better glimpse of Estul Island. But the thought came and went.

He still had yet to feel much closeness with many of the old hands. For those like Kroke and Krytien, he lacked the common ground that he shared with Raker to overcome their age difference. Drake had tried and failed several times over the voyage to connect with the mage and assassin.

I wonder if they blame me for what happened.

His knuckles turned white as he balled his hands into fists. Jonrell had died, murdered by Drake's friend Mal, someone he had known better than anyone.

I saw how unhappy Mal was and I let it go. I should have done something. But, I never thought he was capable of that. He sighed. *That's got to be it. They resent me for my part in taking Jonrell away from them. He was their friend more than their commander.*

Drake realized that he felt the same about Kaz as others did about Jonrell. Training at night when nearly everyone else slept, Drake would see glimpses of the black warrior few others ever saw. Kaz did whatever he could to help Drake succeed, all while listening to the boy's ramblings. At times, Kaz even shared the occasional joke.

But some of the old crew still see him only as Jonrell's replacement. And Kaz isn't blind to that.

Kaz instructed Drake to search the library at Estul Island. He even had the queen sign off on doing so in hopes that Drake would be able to find some hidden bit of information that might help them on the battlefield.

A lover of books, and having devoured a great deal of the queen's personal library, Drake jumped at the chance until he began asking himself why.

He posed the question to Kaz while they sparred. "Why not just ask Krytien or Kroke to look at the library? Raker will be shorthanded if I go."

"Raker can handle things here. You're better suited than the others to decide what's of use and what isn't."

Something in Kaz's tone had caught Drake's attention. "You don't trust them completely, do you?"

Kaz looked off into the night. "No. I don't."

"You don't think they'd do anything to hurt the Hell Patrol?"

"No. Never that. But they have little love for me. They only follow me because I'm finishing what Jonrell started and they don't wish to tarnish his memory." He paused. "They won't do anything that might harm what I'm trying to accomplish. I just wonder how much they would do in order to ensure I succeed."

* * *

Kroke sheathed his knives long enough to grab his bag and fling it over his shoulder. He ran his free hand through his hair, damp from the ocean spray, and brought it around to the back of his neck. Scratching at the stubble on his chin, he stepped off the ship and onto the dock, aware of the looks cast his way from sailors. Most seemed relieved, though few dared to meet his eyes.

Kroke stopped cold as one burly fellow caught his attention, a man he had noticed throughout the journey.

Always eyeing me and then whispering in someone's ear.

The sailor set down a massive crate. He looked to his left and right, gaining confidence from the two at his sides. All three moved toward Kroke.

The man to the right carried a length of chain used to secure cargo while the one on Kroke's left seemed content to trust his fists. The sailor in the center, the largest of the three, held a knife nearly twenty inches long with a pearl white handle.

Of all the times for this.

Kroke dropped the bag from his shoulder and it hit the dock with a thud that silenced the activity around them. The three sailors flinched at the noise, stopping a few feet from him. He felt dozens of curious eyes find them.

"You think you're something don't you?" said the center man. Green as seawater, Kroke saw the doubt hidden behind the man's eyes. The sailor's forehead gleamed with sweat that ran down into his ratty beard. The man spat when he spoke, the spray catching Kroke in the face. "I asked you a question."

A hundred responses ran through Kroke's mind, none was how to nonviolently answer the sailor. Most of his thoughts lingered on what knife to use.

"Kroke, wait!" Drake shouted out.

Kroke never looked away, but the green-eyed sailor did. "Shut your mouth, kid," said the sailor. "I've heard all these crazy stories about the Hell Patrol since I was a boy and then all these new ones floating around since you came to Cadonia, crazier than even the ones my pa told me. Then when I finally see you up close, I see a smooth chested boy, an old man, and this piece of trash," he said, turning back to Kroke. He leaned in. "I hear you're supposed to be some kind of killer." He laughed. "Them little knives you keep playing with don't scare me none." He lifted the one in his hand. "This here is a man's weapon. You're probably too little to even use one of these, huh?"

A small burst of laughter came from those watching.

The man continued. "You know, I've wanted to test you for awhile, but we were at sea and captain's rules are never to kill a passenger at sea. Bad luck and all." He stomped his foot on the dock. "Well, we ain't at sea no more, are we?" He gestured with his head to Kroke's bag. "And you're no longer a passenger."

Drake called out once again. "Don't do it, Kroke. They're who we're supposed to be fighting with, not against."

"That ain't true," said the sailor. "I was born and raised in Tomalt's territory. I just sail with whoever pays best. I could give a lick who wins this war." He stared at Kroke. "So what do you say, little man? Are you gonna prove to me all those fairy tales about your outfit are true? Or are you going to let that little kid up there talk you out of it. Maybe I should've picked a fight with him. He seems to be the one with fire in his belly."

Kroke clenched his jaw. *I promised Krytien I wouldn't do anything. So naturally, they test me.*

He longed for the touch of steel in his hands, but he wasn't one to break a promise. The rest of the dockworkers started to egg Kroke on and as they did, the three sailors grew brasher.

"Kroke!" called out a different voice. Kroke finally turned. Krytien leaned over the railing next to Drake.

"I kept my word," said Kroke. "I ain't killed anyone."

The mage smiled. "I know. But I never said you had to take this garbage." He paused. "Just make sure nothing's permanent. I don't want the captain to be shorthanded. It isn't his fault his men don't have any brains," said Krytien.

"I can do that," Kroke smiled.

Krytien looked to the three sailors. "You might want to ready yourselves." He called over to two others nearby who had come up and joined in the heckling. "And you two may want to give them a hand."

The laughing started up again until Krytien pulled out an apple from his sleeve and nonchalantly took a bite. The mood turned grim and Kroke looked back to the five men before him. The sailor who started it all met Kroke's eyes. The remains of his smile faded as the blades dropped into Kroke's hands.

* * *

Despite being part of the Hell Patrol for well over a year, Drake hadn't spent much time with Kroke. Their areas of expertise lay in two very different areas. During the campaign season, Drake spent his time designing, building, or manning various forms of machinery.

On the other hand, Kroke had been busy doing whatever it was Kroke did. Drake hadn't ever been sure what that all entailed, though he heard plenty of stories. After witnessing Kroke's dismantling of the sailors, Drake finally understood.

He thought about the encounter again and realized that fighting did not accurately describe what Kroke had done. Fighting insinuated that some sort of struggle occurred between the combatants. But there wasn't any real struggle because the assassin had been in control the entire time. What Kroke had done, despite all the spurts of blood flying through the scream-filled air, seemed more like art.

A pretty twisted form of art, but art nonetheless.

Five people had come at the mercenary, brandishing weapons of all shapes and sizes, stabbing and swinging. None of those blows found their mark. Drake could barely follow Kroke's movements, slicing at hands and legs to disarm each person.

And in every instance, the cocky sucker left a paper thin line across each person's throat. Just enough to let them know he could've killed them.

Drake had stood there in awe, as did everyone else who had watched the scene unfold.

All except Krytien. The mage had been busy chomping on the apple in his hand like it was the last one in the world. Drake realized that Krytien had sent his own message to the others watching.

Seem indifferent and let them guess what he's capable of.

Drake had to smile. In those moments, he most enjoyed being a member of the Hell Patrol.

Even still, each step away from the docks eased his worries. Kroke and Krytien may have felt confident in what they could do, but he couldn't say the same. Kaz had taught Drake a lot over the past year, but he still felt far more comfortable behind a catapult than a sword.

They procured mounts from workers near the harbor, which they planned to use to reach the citadel that loomed in the distance atop a small rise in the land. Despite the queen's written orders, none seemed to care who they were.

"This ain't starting out well," said Kroke.

"When does it ever," Krytien said. He struggled into the saddle and clicked the reins. "C'mon we need to get there before dark."

Drake looked to the sky and then the citadel. "That shouldn't be a problem."

"Don't let the landscape nor the size of the place fool you," said Krytien. "In order to make it there by sunset we may have to push the horses."

Drake eyed the sway-backed mount the mage sat upon and the old gray-chinned mare Kroke rode.

I hope we don't kill them doing it.

* * *

The descending sun dipped below thick clouds and bathed the landscape in purple.

Krytien was right.

The blank canvas of rolling hills and open land, specked with patches of tall trees did play tricks on the eyes. After a full day of riding, they finally came upon the school.

Drake thought about how little it resembled what he had always envisioned a school to look like. It had no defensive walls, not even a fence, which struck Drake as peculiar until he thought about the sea surrounding them and realized it didn't need a wall.

The portentous look of the structures made them appear like the giant cathedrals that populated Cadonia. The smoke colored walls of the buildings looked at least six stories high, not counting the towers that crowned the roof every hundred feet. The towers sloped upward and thin metal spires sat on their peaks, each flapping a different flag in the breeze. The highest peak flew the queen's colors. Drake realized the other flags must represent the dukes and lords of Cadonia.

Just like the dining hall in Lyrosene.

Unfortunately, the darkening sky hid many of the school's other details.

Kroke hadn't even raised his head from the saddle, too busy examining the dozens of knives he kept, polishing or sharpening where only he saw the need.

Especially that new one he took from the sailor.

Krytien seemed in his own world. Earlier, Drake had asked the mage questions about the school, assuming that if anyone had the answers, Krytien would. However, the mage seemed distracted, muttering to himself. Drake meant to ask if Krytien was alright, but a shake of the head from Kroke made him think better of it.

Once again no one fills me in on what's going on.

They came to a halt.

As if on cue, a boy appeared seemingly out of nowhere, sporting bone-white robes. "You can follow me. We've been expecting you," he said, and began walking without waiting for a response. Bathed in starlight, his form took on that of an apparition and if it wasn't for the high-pitched squeak to his voice, Drake would have thought the boy had lived and died on the island ages ago.

"How many colors do you sorcerers have for yourselves?" asked Kroke. "Do the women wear pink?"

"The boy's not a mage," said Krytien. "White means that he's still working to master the most basic of concepts. He hasn't even performed his first real spell yet."

Krytien didn't elaborate and ignored the joke about the pink. The mage kicked his horse forward in pursuit of the ghost-like figure while muttering a string of hushed profanity. Drake couldn't make it all out, but what little he heard would have made Raker proud.

Something about arrogant little upstarts?

Rounding the front of the massive building, more of the compound became visible. Complex structures connected buildings through stone pathways on the ground and covered catwalks several stories above.

The boy showed them where to set their horses up in the stable. He let out a huff, apparently dissatisfied by their speed. "You need to hurry. The High Mages do not like to be kept waiting." He started toward a set of double doors across an open courtyard, opposite the stables.

"I think somebody forgot to teach him the basic concept of courtesy," said Drake.

The comment earned him a rare grunt from Kroke, but Krytien stared off at the boy through narrowed eyes, breathing through his nose in a heavy rhythm.

So much for trying to lighten the mood.

As he thought over what the boy said, something struck him as odd. "Krytien, what did he mean by High Mages? I thought there weren't any left."

"There aren't." Krytien stalked after the boy, shoulders bunched.

Kroke looked at Drake with a cocked head. "Well, now you did it."

"Did what?"

"You just made a bad situation a whole lot worse, like rubbing salt into a wound."

"But I just repeated what the boy said."

Kroke didn't say more, following after Krytien. Drake set off after them, fuming. "I hate the way they do this," he muttered. "All the old hands. They all assume that you know what they're talking about."

* * *

The cocky boy swung the great double doors inward. Krytien stepped into a room with high ceilings flanked by twin staircases that greeted the mage like open arms. A bronze statue stood on the floor in the center of the two staircases. The figure held an open book in one hand while his other extended outward as if lecturing a silent audience. Though Krytien had never met the man, he had heard enough about his physical description to recognize the likeness of High Mage Amcaro.

And I guess this is the closest I'll ever come to fulfilling my dreams of meeting the man.

Paintings of mages dressed in dark red robes adorned the walls of the room.

All the High Mages of Cadonia since its beginning.

A throat cleared and Krytien saw the boy standing near another cracked doorway, gesturing for him to follow. "Somebody ought to put that boy over their knee," he grumbled.

With Drake and Kroke at his heels, Krytien walked into a smaller room. A large oaken table dominated the space surrounded by plush chairs of purple cloth and gold trim. Near the back wall a gaggle of mages congregated, wearing various colors of robes, denoting their skill in sorcery.

Sure enough, four had adorned themselves in the dark red of a High Mage. Krytien felt his blood boil.

The young boy cleared his throat again. The mages turned with an air of contempt. One chanced a smirk as he made his way toward Krytien. The others fell in behind.

The assumed leader held his head high, accentuating an already prominent nose that stood out on his smooth, young face. He tossed his head back, flinging his long hair behind him lazily as he extended a hand in greeting.

"I'm High Mage Lufflin and this is High Mage Nora, High Mage Janik, and High Mage Yorn," said Lufflin as he turned to either side. He started on introductions of the others when Krytien cut him off.

"I was under the impression there were no longer any High Mages in Cadonia."

"Well, you're obviously mistaken," said Lufflin, chuckling.

The rest of the group laughed as well. *Almost all.* Krytien noticed a mage in green robes off in a corner with his arms folded. He scowled at the others.

"I don't believe I am," said Krytien.

The young man's smile faded and his voice took on an edge. "Then it appears that your eyesight has faded over the years because what you see before you are dark red robes and nearly a dozen black."

Why do they always act like the robes are what makes the mage?

"Any seamstress can sew a robe."

"And apparently so can an old man like you. Though I think you should have had someone else pick the color, gray means nothing in sorcery except that you're too old to even be worth our trouble."

Krytien's hand came up and across Lufflin's face with enough force to send the young man staggering backward. A sharp gasp among the other mages followed, staring wide-eyed in disbelief that someone would strike their leader. Krytien felt a slight change in the air, the hurried beginnings of a spell.

He had already anticipated their reaction. Krytien had prepared more than a half dozen spells before entering the room. So when the woman introduced as Nora raised her hand to lash out, Krytien pinned her arms at her sides, raised her into the air, and flung her across the room against the back wall. Lufflin suffered a similar fate, more out of principal than any real threat.

Krytien hadn't needed to address the other two leaders, Janik and Yorn. Kroke, as expected, already had the situation under control—daggers pressed firmly into the soft tissue of each mage's throats. Sweat beaded off their foreheads, eyes flicking about in panic.

Janik called out to the others in black robes. "Don't just stand there, do something. He's just some two-bit mercenary with a knife."

"Wait," called out the green-robed mage. He pushed himself off the wall and those in black robes seemed relieved someone else had stepped in. "That two-bit mercenary put a knife to your throats before you could think. He'll kill both of you and likely a few others at the least. And you still have him to worry about too," he said gesturing with a nod to Krytien.

"What about me?"

Krytien glanced to the side and saw Drake looming over one of the black-robed mages, holding a silver candlestick in his hand like a club.

The green-robed mage grunted. "I'm sure you can take out one or two."

"Hey, I could take out more than that."

"Save it for later." Krytien eyed the green-robed figure. He saw a confident man, but not cocky like the others. *Someone with a head on his shoulders.* "What's your name?"

"Tristan."

"Are you the one really in charge here?"

He shook his head. "I'm not ready for something like that."

"You're more ready than these fools," said Krytien.

Tristan shrugged.

"Maybe you should be the one to tell us what's been going on and why no one has answered the queen's messages."

"Don't say anything, Tristan," said Lufflin from across the room.

Krytien slammed his head back against the wall and then flipped him upside down. "Shut it." He looked back at Tristan. "Are you going to cooperate?"

The mage smiled. "You keep doing stuff like that and I'll do whatever you want."

CHAPTER 5

Nareash and his party traveled for weeks down the stone road, passing half a dozen cities along the way. Though each lay as abandoned as Poliktas, the ruins grew more lavish. When they passed a city called Molacat, the stone road changed significantly.

"Absolutely breathtaking." Mizak leaned over the side of his mule, pointing to semi-precious stones scattered over the designs in the black and white marble.

Nareash saw that, among others, topaz, garnet, and amethyst helped create images that told a story.

"Wasteful," said Guwan. "These stones are worth a fortune, but they used them as building material. What does that say about our ancestors?"

Colan spoke up. "It says that they cared little for what we think of as wealth. They'd rather share the beauty of the stones instead of hoarding it for themselves where it can collect dust."

"If they were that weak, it is no wonder they lost everything."

"Weak," Nareash muttered. "Physical prowess is not the only sign of strength. You would do well to take this chance to expand your mind."

"Are you trying to say that I'm simple?" asked Guwan.

"Simple? No. A fool? Yes. You have the ability to become something more than what you are, yet you ignore the opportunity, repeating what you've always known." He paused. "Look at your ruler. He became warleader, and rather than just blindly follow his father, Tobin made his own future. If he hadn't done that, it's quite possible the conflict against the Yellow Plain Clan would have ended differently."

Nareash lengthened his stride without waiting for a response and separated himself from the group.

The flapping of robes from behind caught his attention. "Yes, Colan."

"I think you've finally shut him up. Guwan, I mean. He's wearing quite the expression," whispered the shaman.

"As he should be." Nareash lowered his voice. "Here's the first lesson in your training. Learn people. Listen to every word. Watch every move. Examine every action."

"So you know how to hurt them, if necessary?"

"Yes. That can be important." Nareash smiled. "But it is far more effective to learn how to use them."

* * *

The group entered the mists and walked through them. They could only see twenty yards through the fog, blinding them to the views of sloping hills, deep valleys, and lush cliffs.

Rushing water tickled Nareash's ears though he could not place its location. He swore he felt pulled with each step. He wondered at first whether that faint sensation was simply his mind playing tricks on him or if Quarnoq called to him. It felt oddly similar to how he felt holding Sacrynon's Scepter.

The scepter had never strayed far from his thoughts since arriving in Hesh. Having tasted the power it offered, he longed to possess it again so that he might continue to unlock secrets of the art that had only seemed like legend to him before. Away from the scepter, Nareash admitted that Amcaro had not been completely wrong in what it could do to the one who wielded it.

It began to affect me because I never let the thing go. I allowed it to consume my thoughts, despite all of the warnings left behind in Sacrynon's private journals.

Distance from the weapon had brought him clarity and given him a chance to master the new skills he obtained from it. He would not make the same mistake again. He realized that his former master did have the right of it.

"Before learning how to draw out more of the infinite amounts of power a mage has access to, one must learn to better control that which he already knows. This means that one must use the power he has in ways he is unaccustomed to. Only by perfecting that which is known can one become more familiar with that which is unknown."

The mist fell away and Nareash halted. The rest of the party followed, too enamored with the scene before them to take another step. Unlike the previous cities, Quarnoq did not simply sit atop a rise in the land. It was part of the land, buildings carved into the solid rock of the mountain. Though some distance away, sunlight bounced off the white, red, blue, and green jewels embedded in the outer walls of the structures.

Twin waterfalls flanking the city crashed into a fast river that encircled high walls like a moat before descending the mountainside. The stone road led to a wide, arcing bridge that crossed over the river.

"You were right, Nachun." Guwan's voice held a rare awe to it.

"Hmm?"

"Juanoq is nothing compared to this."

Nareash smiled. "Let's see what else this place has to offer us." He frowned, remembering a passing thought that had tickled his mind since their arrival on this side of the Great Divide.

Kaz. He's probably dead, but it doesn't hurt to be careful. "Tell your men to stay alert. Don't let their surroundings blind them to what surrounds them."

"Do you expect trouble?"

He lied. "No, but I would rather not be caught by surprise."

Does Kaz haunt this place without a memory? That would definitely make things interesting.

They crossed the bridge and passed through the high outer-walls, surprised to see countless rows of fruit trees growing over relatively flat land. The orchard went on for acres before the group reached another bridge over a small canal. The bridge led them to the inner wall and finally into the city itself.

Unbelievably, Quarnoq showed no signs of neglect. Unlike the other cities of the land, plant life had not intruded upon the glorious architecture.

"Do people still live here? The city looks like it was just completed yesterday," said Mizak.

"Sorcery. Am I right, Master?" asked Colan.

Nareash nodded. "Yes. It must have been woven into stone and wood itself." His gaze turned up at one of the slender towers that lined the main road. Cylindrical in nature, it rose twice as high as anything he could recall in Cadonia. "True experts in the art once lived here."

"So, we're here. Now what?" asked Guwan.

"The library," said Nareash. "Mizak?"

The old man flipped through an old piece of parchment. "We stay on the main road. The library is located in the center of the city."

Nareash took off, leaving the others to follow. It took all his will not to break into a run. So focused on what lay ahead, he barely noticed the sights around him. Every spare moment since coming to Hesh he had spent learning about Quarnoq and its mysteries. Previous mentions of the lost continent of Hesh in documents on Estul Island stated that the ancient city contained wonders few could imagine.

Nareash rounded a bend where the jeweled path widened and branched off. At the crossroads of these intersecting streets stood a building, narrow at its base and broadening into an upside down triangle. Unlike the vibrant colors of the structures around it, the black walls of the library stuck out like a storm cloud on a clear summer day.

At first Nareash thought the effect was some masterful trick by the former sorcerers who inhabited the city, but as he neared his goal, his heart sank.

Sorcery had indeed been responsible for the appearance of the library. The stone had been scorched black from an intense heat, disfigured in spots. Though he knew the spell had been performed centuries ago, he could still feel the effects of it, a small hum buzzing in his ears.

Nareash ignored the questions fired at him from behind as he stepped through the splintered doorway. The smell reminded him of Lyrosene and his battle with the other High Mages.

In hindsight, I might have found a better way to seize the throne, but the guard had pushed me into acting sooner than I had planned.

At times, he regretted the lives he took that day, but even at his lowest of moments, he never felt as sick as he did staring at the damage around him. He bent and brushed aside soot from a piece of parchment. It crumbled in his hands. He wiped them, went to a nearby staircase and slowly ascended. Nareash paused at each of the eight floors, satisfied after a glance that its contents had not fared any better. Rage filled him as he reached the top floor. His last shred of hope left him when he saw the damage.

Twisted pieces of metal, wood, and stone littered the floor. The distorted remains told him he would never uncover their secrets. Nareash knew from his studies that the greatest inventions of Quarnoq had resided on this floor—instruments he could have used to regain Sacrynon's Scepter.

He screamed, limbs shaking with anger. Sorcery caused a gust of wind to fill the room, kicking up ash and soot, swirling the debris around his still form. He closed his eyes and calmed himself. After a few minutes, the room settled. The effort took longer than he thought it should have.

What does it matter? The trip was a waste. All the work I did in creating a ship to get us here in order to avoid crossing the Great Divide again was for nothing. I'm stuck here, likely forever. You beat me after all, Master.

A throat cleared behind him and Nareash turned.

"I'm sorry, Master," said Colan. "You've been up here for several hours and night is almost upon us. Perhaps, we should think about finding a place to sleep. The morning may yield better results."

Nareash grunted. He walked past the young shaman without a word.

* * *

A fitful night of sleep spent pondering the struggles of his past did little to brighten Nareash's spirit or restore hope to his mind. Still, he forced himself to rise the next morning and return to the library where the party worked diligently under his guidance.

If I must be stuck on this continent, I cannot let them see me lose control and carry stories back to Juanoq.

He gave specific instructions to everyone on how to handle anything that had been partially preserved, even the smallest scrap of paper containing a single word.

Though Nareash didn't believe they would achieve much success, the group still labored from dawn until dusk each day. With a party their size, they combed every square inch of the library in less than a week.

He suffered through several false alarms after Mizak or even Colan exclaimed at some trivial bit of knowledge—a few sentences on irrigation techniques or methods for breeding superior animals for food and labor. Each time Nareash's stomach would knot in excitement only to twist in disappointment.

He finally had enough.

"We're done," he announced. "Tomorrow we return to the ship."

Mizak blinked. "But we only just got here." The old man had found renewed energy at the prospect of learning secrets from his people's past. "And we've only searched the library. Who knows what else there is to discover—"

"I know what we won't discover," said Nareash, cutting the man off. "We may find more bits of useless information like what we've already unearthed, but you and I both know the true riches were here."

Mizak sighed. "It would be nice to at least learn why our ancestors fled."

"Why indeed?" He lowered his voice and eyed Colan. "You must have figured it out by now."

The shaman cleared his throat. "Master?"

"Have you practiced the art since reaching the city?"

"No. I've been too busy."

Nareash shook his head, disappointed. "Try to do something simple. How is your control?"

The shaman closed his eyes. Sweat beaded on his forehead and he swayed on his feet as a small light formed in his hands. He opened his eyes and steadied himself as the light faded. "What happened?"

"The connection we use to practice sorcery is strained here, changed. It's been difficult even for me." He looked back at Mizak. "The people who once lived here were obviously masters of the art. But something happened. Right here in their library. What exactly? It doesn't really matter. But it destroyed practically all of their records. And in the process, their ability to use sorcery had been severely impinged. So, they left."

"Then why not just fall back to the cities we passed along the way?" asked Mizak. "You didn't notice the effect before, did you?"

"Not to this extent. Perhaps, over time, the ability to use the art has improved there, but enough time hasn't passed for Quarnoq to heal." He shrugged. "The inhabitants must have left their cities and taken a chance to start over because they determined that the farther away they journeyed from Quarnoq, the stronger their connection remained."

"That seems excessive," said Mizak. "Who cares about sorcery when they still had everything else?"

"Spoken like someone who has never tasted true power," muttered Nareash.

"That still doesn't explain why our lands on the other side of the Great Divide aren't filled with cities as extraordinary as those we've come across," said Guwan.

Guwan's observation surprised Nareash.

He faced the Kifzo. "I imagine war had much to do with it. By all accounts the people here were peaceful which was why they prospered. But from the records that were brought over and remain in Juanoq, we know that once Nubinya was settled, things changed. People began to question those in power, thinking they could do better. That's when the various clans formed, each choosing their own little region to call home." He paused. "And they've been at war with each other off and on since. It's hard to create such wonders as what we've seen when people are constantly trying to kill each other. The knowledge to create gave way to those with the knowledge to destroy."

* * *

In the choking blackness of night, Nareash sat alone on the top floor of the library. The rest of the party remained in camp half a block away, preparing for bed. Nareash knew he would regret not doing the same come morning when the journey back to the ship began. Yet, he found it fitting to spend their last night in Quarnoq amidst the ruins of his dreams.

With a few rare exceptions, nothing in life had ever come easily for Nareash. He had been orphaned as a boy after his parents died of disease. Nowhere to turn, he used the talent he had discovered to pick the pockets of Cadonia's upper class in order to get by.

One chance meeting with an advisor to the king had changed his fortune. The noble had been the first ever to catch Nareash. Rather than turn him in, Gauge sponsored his studies at Estul Island.

Nareash had felt as though his dreams had come true until he learned how little natural talent he had. He eventually learned to replicate the lessons Amcaro taught, but only after working twice as hard as the others of his age and class. He made up for his lack of natural ability by spending every waking moment in Estul Island's great library.

With the exception of a few, most ridiculed his serious nature. Nareash mostly didn't care about the taunting of his classmates. He only cared what Master Amcaro thought of him.

"At it late again, Nareash?"

Nareash jumped in his seat and rubbed the sleep from his eyes. "Yes, Master."

Amcaro smiled. "I wish everyone had your dedication. It would make my job much easier." He walked over and patted Nareash on the shoulder. "What are you looking over tonight?"

Nareash's excitement to talk privately with his Master added a tremor to his voice. "Oh, I found this marvelous text written by Sacrynon. I actually believe it may have been a personal journal as it spends a great deal of time discussing his friendship with Aurnon the First."

"I see."

"But the most interesting parts are his thoughts on the scepter he found in the remains of the Quoron Empire before he and Aurnon's conquest of Thurum."

Amcaro hastily removed his hand from Nareash's shoulder. "I'm sorry, Nareash," he said closing the text and picking it up. "I thought this document had been removed. It isn't something that one should study. If you want to learn about Sacrynon, then study my own writings on the man. I've removed the things that are better left forgotten."

Nareash eyed the book with longing and frustration. "But Master, he talks about how to improve a connection to the art through use of the scepter."

"The scepter drove Sacrynon mad. I know. I was there and I had to help Aurnon the First kill my Master. Put it from your mind. Aurnon destroyed it anyway. Study things that will improve your talents, not corrupt them."

Amcaro quickly left the library, leaving Nareash once again alone.

In aggravation, he left Estul Island to visit Gauge. They did not see each other often, but he had become one of the few people Nareash could speak with openly.

"I can't even look at Master Amcaro in the same way now," said Nareash. "How can I respect someone so afraid to take chances?"

"It would be a mistake not to respect the High Mage of High Mages," said Gauge. "But, that doesn't mean that you can't one day be more. I wouldn't have gained you entrance to the school if I didn't think you were destined for great things." He paused. "Amcaro is a wise man, but also an old man. He has no desire to take chances or look for new ways to use his powers because no one has challenged him in a long time."

"Are you saying I should question him openly?" asked Nareash, confused.

Gauge shook his head. "That would be disrespectful. However, if you continued your research in private and then took your findings to him, he might be more inclined to listen to what you've discovered."

"And how am I to do that? He took Sacrynon's journal."

"You've told me how massive the library is. Chances are that if Amcaro misplaced one of Sacrynon's texts, there are others as well. Plus, now that you know a bit about the Mad Mage, you might see things in Amcaro's own teachings that give you more insight. It won't be easy, but that doesn't mean you should give up and leave your studies."

Nareash didn't. Just like Gauge had saved him from the streets and given him a path toward something better, the noble had also ensured that Nareash never lost sight of his goals to be the best.

But now, the path is muddled and there is no clear way to continue on. Do I give up and learn to be happy with what I have in Hesh? No one has the power to stand against me. He grunted. *And at least I have someone to pass the time in Tobin.* He swore.

Nareash had hoped that Quarnoq would give him the answers he sought in order to return to Cadonia. References to Hesh on Estul Island had indicated that the lost continent had a connection to the Quoron Empire.

How?

Faint footsteps jolted Nareash from his thoughts. A light grew as it climbed the stairs. Guwan came into view holding a torch and wearing a troubled expression.

Nareash stood and dusted the black soot from his robes. "Something on your mind?"

"I've been thinking about what you said."

"Oh?"

"You're right. I am single-minded and don't think for myself. It's hard for a Kifzo not to have that mindset." He pulled a worn and slightly singed piece of paper from the inside of his shirt. "I found this the first day we arrived. I've been trying to decide what to do with it since. Its contents are . . . troubling." He extended his hand toward Nareash. "There are places outside of Hesh. I thought you may know something about that."

Nareash accepted the paper carefully and his eyes widened. It was a map of the world at the time people inhabited Quarnoq. Hesh lay clearly in the far south. However, the remainder of the map interested Nareash the most. Though portions had faded or been partially destroyed, the High Mage still recognized the outline of Mytarcis, a few of the Byzernian Islands and most importantly the southern half of Thurum.

And north of Thurum is Cadonia. His face brightened. *One Above, this is a way home.*

Unsure how Hesh related to those lands he knew, Nareash had been unwilling to risk teleporting home. Even with the knowledge in his hands, he would have to take extra precautions in covering such distances.

But I know the spell is possible.

He frowned as a thought struck him. *I still have nothing to counter the scepter.*

Nareash lifted his eyes. "Yes. Hesh is only one of many continents." He paused. "Why did you think I would know this?"

"As you said, I'm not simple. You've never fit in with our clan. I've scouted enough of the Red Mountain Clan in my youth to know you wouldn't fit in there, either. Your mannerisms and speech patterns are too different. You're from one of these places, aren't you?" Guwan pointed at the map.

Nareash nodded. "Yes." He sighed and examined the sea route that would take ships through a space filled with storms and rocks.

The route would not be easy.

He lifted his eyes to Guwan as a thought struck him.

He had access to the greatest fighting warriors currently alive, perhaps who had ever lived. He looked at the map of Thurum in his hands and recalled the jewels all around him in the city. The rest of his plan to bring an army to Cadonia would still be possible.

The scepter would make Amcaro powerful, but not impossible to beat.

"Is there something you want from me in return for the map?" he asked.

"I just wanted you to know that I'm ready to seize the opportunities available to me and that I hope you'll remember this gesture."

Nareash smiled. "I believe I will."

CHAPTER 6

Kaz's gaze shot back and forth across the cylindrical council room. The looks of contempt didn't surprise him. It had been months since he began attending the meetings, yet the attitude of the queen's council had changed little toward him. If they weren't casting stares his way, they were mentioning his name in their childish whisperings.

He thought about confronting some of the worst council members, if only to watch their nerve dribble down their legs and pool at their feet. He restrained himself for Elyse's benefit.

Kaz hated that the nobles found their courage in underhanded remarks and in the company of others. When alone, many of them folded under the pressure. Kaz actually enjoyed being in their presence under those circumstances.

Only a few councilors had the ability to pose any real threat to Elyse and even then, the queen could squash their ambitions if she chose to. However, she remained hesitant at times, not out of the fear she once struggled with, but out of caution. Though Kaz understood her concerns, he had seen her deftly handle a council member in private or manipulate the overzealous Duke Jeldor several times over. He knew she could handle herself and enjoyed watching her do so.

I'm just the reminder to both her and her advisors that her words hold weight.

* * *

In the months that followed the battle of Cathyrium, Elyse had spent little time in Lyrosene. On the advice her brother gave her shortly before his death, she used her time to do something her father had neglected to do for years. She visited the cities and towns still under her control. Jonrell thought such a move would garner sympathy from those commoners prejudiced against the upper class, while strengthening her relationships with the minor lords. Like many of her brother's suggestions, the strategy worked.

As a pleasant side effect of Elyse's travels, her interpersonal skills had improved significantly. She spent so much time in private audience with her subjects that over time the lessons Jonrell tried to instill in her as a child had slowly begun to make sense. She no longer felt intimidated when discussing matters of the kingdom.

While away from Lyrosene, the council regularly sent her word about their doings and urged her to return to the capital to address their concerns.

Where they hoped to push me around again.

Elyse realized her council thought that with Jonrell dead, the threat of the crown held little weight to them. Her advisors had tried to manipulate her immediately upon her return, and Elyse struggled to maintain order in the first council meeting.

That first night back home she cried herself to sleep, not out of helplessness as before, but out of anger. Despite all that she had learned in the months prior, she had discovered that the players in her court had far greater skill than the minor lords of the land.

By the next morning Elyse had calmed herself and stiffened her resolve. She needed someone to take Jonrell's place and help lend weight to her words while she continued to learn the ever-changing dynamics of the counsel.

Kaz had just returned to Lyrosene for the winter, and worked with General Grayer on recruiting and training her army in preparation for the following year's campaign. Elyse had requested that he attend the council meetings with her.

"I wouldn't know what to say," said Kaz.

"You won't need to say anything. I just want you there," said Elyse.

"To scare them?" he asked and Elyse surprisingly saw something almost like hurt in his dark eyes.

She shook her head. "No doubt you will intimidate those who are there, but it isn't your appearance that will scare them," she said touching his arm. "It is what you represent as commander of my army that will give them pause. More importantly, I want you there."

Kaz mulled over her words and after a moment responded. "Whatever I can do to help you, I will."

A thin smile ran across her lips as she looked down at Kaz. She had offered him a seat next to her, but he declined. At each council meeting he stood in front of her, facing outward like a statue carved from granite. She could not see his face, but knew it held the intimidating scowl he normally wore except in the presence of a select few.

Gauge had handled the day-to-day duties of running the kingdom while she was away. However, Elyse had returned to a long list of things they needed to discuss and decisions she needed to make that he did not have the authority to handle. She felt guilty for placing so much on his shoulders while traveling. Since her return, she had done her best to relieve him of some of those duties.

". . . Your Majesty?" asked a voice.

Elyse blinked and her face grew flushed when she realized that she had not been paying attention to the speaker. All eyes watched her. Thankfully,

Elyse could recount Vulira's same tired arguments by heart. "Yes, Vulira, I'm sorry but as I've said before, we will have to put off your pleas for stronger farming research to another day when the war is over." She hadn't meant to sound so put off with the woman, but she grew weary of repeating herself.

Vulira inclined her head with a puzzled look. "Your Majesty, I was not speaking about such matters."

Elyse felt a lump form in her throat. She swallowed.

"Ha," came a booming voice. "I think the queen has become so accustomed to your repetitiveness and lack in originality of thought, that like most of the council here, she has learned to tune you out."

Laughter erupted and Vulira turned red in embarrassment, then anger, as she eyed Illyan. "I have the floor."

"And dare I say, you've had it long enough." He rose from his seat and made his way down to the center of the circular chambers. "You have raised a good point, but perhaps I can do a better job of summarizing your question, rather than making us all late for lunch again." He slapped his thin frame and laughed. "Some of us cannot afford to skip another meal."

Laughter continued and Vulira, thoroughly embarrassed, did not have enough fight left in her to continue arguing. She walked back to her seat, fists tightened into balls.

Elyse noticed the smirk on Phasin's face, but most of all she noticed the ease with which Illyan had handled Vulira and the reaction from others in attendance. The short man had come a long way since that first council meeting after her father's passing. Then, no one had dared to agree with Illyan. But since Adein's and Vicalli's acts of treason, the council had been searching to find figures to lead them again.

Phasin and Illyan had eagerly stepped into those vacant roles. Illyan's rise to power made the queen uncomfortable.

"Your Majesty, I believe the gist of Vulira's question related to some of the crown's plans for the upcoming campaign. There has been an increasing amount of talk that you and your commander," he nodded to Kaz, "plan to bring Olasi's forces into play."

Those plans were not talked about openly. Do we have yet another spy among us? Jonrell suspected as much.

"We could very well be planning for such a thing. But then again, it could all be a ruse to throw off our enemies." She paused, allowing her voice to remain calm and void of the hatred she had for the little man. "Just as my brother once told you, I do not intend to seek military advice from this council."

Illyan smiled in a way that gave Elyse a chill. "A wise policy, Your Majesty. And to your point, I think I speak for all of us when I say that we do not intend to lecture you or your commander on troop placement. However," he said, raising his voice and pausing for dramatic effect, "where policy is concerned, I feel we have a responsibility to advise Her Majesty. And there have been murmurings—"

"I do not care about murmurings," said Elyse, her voice suddenly filled with agitation.

I am tired of these games.

Illyan appeared surprised by her interruption and after a moment to collect himself began to argue. Elyse opened her mouth to fire back, but before the words could come, a gavel slammed onto the black marble. Gauge shot from his seat faster than she thought possible for the older man.

"Is this what you now waste our time with, Illyan? Murmurings? Nothing more than hearsay and gossip?"

The edge to his voice took Elyse off guard. However, once the initial shock wore off, anger replaced it. Gauge seizing control of her conversation with Illyan cast her in an unfavorable light. She calmed herself.

I'll speak with him in private later. He deserves that. Anything I say or do now to address the issue will only embarrass him, and regardless of how I feel now the fact is I would be lost without him.

"I agree," said Phasin. "He is quick to poke holes in the arguments of others, but what proof does he ever bring before the council other than some cryptic message meant to stir us up."

"Yes," agreed Gauge. "What do you have to say for yourself, Illyan?"

Elyse brightened at the chance to see Illyan made to look incompetent.

Illyan remained confident. "My lord, please have your seat. I did not mean to upset you. Or you, Phasin," he said turning. "Make no mistake that the only agenda I push, the agenda that takes precedence above all others, is the one that ensures our great country will be whole in peace once again."

Phasin snorted. "That is debatable."

Gauge leaned forward. "Lord Illyan, I will not allow you to continue without revealing where you've heard this murmured since you only seem to be aware of it."

Not allow? What has gotten into him? I'm sitting right here.

Illyan must have thought the same thing as he cast a look in her direction. "Your Majesty?"

Elyse cleared her throat, forced to go along with Gauge lest she make the man look like a fool. "Please answer the question. Are you withholding information from the crown?"

"Withhold is such a strong word. I simply prefer not to reveal information that might implicate my contacts," said Illyan and for the first time Elyse saw him lose a bit of his composure.

"Since you believe that your informants are better than the crown's, perhaps you could be convinced to bring those contacts in so that Her Majesty might have use of them," interjected Gauge.

"No," said Illyan. His smile had vanished.

"But didn't you just say that you were only interested in the well being of the kingdom?" asked Phasin.

"That is why I refuse to expose them. They might be corrupted or compromised from outside influences."

Elyse felt a shift in the room with those present. Many of those who had in the past several months slowly supported Illyan looked around at each other. Slight nods followed.

They see him struggling and wish to change sides before it's too late.

"Are you making the accusation that the crown's contacts are corrupted?" asked Phasin.

Elyse watched Illyan shrug nonchalantly. She grimaced.

That was the wrong move Phasin. One Illyan expected you to make.

"I would not be the first to make such an accusation. After all, the queen's own brother proposed and proved the same thing just over a year ago," Illyan said.

Elyse quickly judged the reactions of the other councilors and saw that Gauge and Phasin had lost some of their momentum.

I need to do something.

Gauge started to speak again when Elyse reached out to silence him. She had enough. Illyan had made a good point, just enough to save some credibility. She sensed that he was on the cusp of regaining complete control and she did not want that to happen.

He is too intelligent to fall all at once. She stood. "I wish to hear no more about murmurings, whisperings, gossip, hearsay, or anything else unsubstantiated. This meeting is adjourned."

The sound of Gauge's gavel reverberated on the chamber's walls.

* * *

"What did *he* want?" Elyse stared daggers through Illyan's back as he left the chambers.

Trying to smooth things over with Vulira after the meeting, Elyse had watched as Illyan pulled Kaz away to speak in private. By the time she pried herself away from Vulira, Illyan had scurried off.

"He wanted to discuss the logistics involving the army's supplies for the coming campaign," said Kaz.

"Is that all? It seemed more important than that. Couldn't that snake have waited until later?"

Kaz scowled. "Why do you hate him so much?"

"I don't hate him." She suddenly felt embarrassed by Kaz's choice of words. *The One Above teaches us to hate no man. I must be in better control of my emotions.* "I just don't trust him."

"Why?"

"Because he is constantly looking to serve his own agenda."

"Name me someone here who isn't?" said Kaz, folding his arms.

Elyse frowned. "Gauge isn't."

Kaz raised his eyebrows and gestured with a nod. "Then what do you think he's doing now?"

Elyse looked over and several of the council members who had been in support of Illyan clamored for Gauge's attention. Her most trusted advisor smiled as he accepted each compliment for a job well done today. She found herself angered by the scene. She shook her head. "He's only being polite. It comes with a position of power."

"Perhaps you've given him too much power," said Kaz, his voice low.

Elyse whispered. "What? He's served me well since my father's death."

"I'm sure he has."

"That's ridiculous. You tell me I should watch out for Gauge, but you want me to consider the ramblings of a weasel like Illyan."

"Jonrell trusted Illyan. Without him supplying the army, we wouldn't have been nearly as successful against Tomalt," said Kaz.

Elyse's anger grew. "Jonrell also trusted Mal and Glacar. Look where that got him." She regretted her tone immediately, but could not take back the words.

Kaz scratched his goatee. "And he also trusted us."

The remark stung. Before she could apologize, Crusher ducked inside and called Kaz.

"Your Majesty, if you don't need me here any longer, I have other duties," said Kaz.

She nodded. He took a step away and Elyse grabbed his arm, solid as the marble in the room, thick as the branch of a tree. "I did not mean to . . ."

"I know," he whispered.

Kaz hurried from the room. The Ghal followed him.

Elyse stared after Kaz until Gauge came up beside her. "Is everything alright, Your Majesty?"

Elyse blinked. "I was just thinking." She paused for a moment, recalling what Kaz said. "What were you talking about with the others?"

Gauge gestured toward the door and the two started to leave. "Oh, just some gossip. Nothing you need to concern yourself with, Your Majesty."

"I see," said Elyse. His carefree tone reminded her of her earlier thought. "There is something that does concern me."

Gauge inclined his head. "Your Majesty?"

"The way you took over the council meeting in the midst of my discussion with Illyan."

He blinked and sputtered. "I-I'm sorry. I didn't mean to do so. I promise that my intentions were—"

"I know you didn't mean any harm by it, but the fact remains that I can't have that happen again. I'm still trying to erase the impression everyone has of the bewildered queen I was when I took the throne. What you did today makes that harder."

Gauge worked his jaw and frowned. "I understand. I'll be more mindful of my actions in the future."

Elyse touched his arm as they walked. "Thank you. I knew you would understand."

CHAPTER 7

"Will that be all?"

Odala scanned the lavish room she shared with Tobin. Two dresses she selected from the tailor rested on her bed and the third, she wore. An assortment of fruit and fresh bread lay on the table next to her.

"Yes." She responded without looking at the servant, too busy admiring her new dress in the mirror. She loved the turquoise color and the way the fabric accentuated her curves.

The door closed.

Odala broke her fast on a piece of warm bread as she strode to the window and gazed out over Juanoq.

Even in the early hours, the city bustled with life. Wagons rolled down the main thoroughfare and disappeared into side streets. Most people moved in one of two directions—toward the market or the waterfront.

Odala relished the view she knew no other woman enjoyed. She finished her meal, and took one last look over the space and smiled. Tobin took care of all her wants without her ever having to ask.

She left the room, not wanting to waste the beautiful day indoors. Watching people scurry toward the market had enticed her. Though she and Soyjid technically remained captives of the Blue Island Clan, they essentially had the freedom to go where they pleased so long as they took a personal guard along for their protection. The contradiction in freedom no longer bothered her as much as it once did. She understood from the way Tobin treated her that the restriction was more to keep up appearances with his men rather than a lack of trust in her.

Perhaps while I'm at the market I can pick something out for Tobin. He rarely does anything for himself.

Odala made her way through the palace's winding corridors and looping hallways, lost in thought about what to buy Tobin when she heard her name.

Two approached her from the opposite direction. The woman wore a smile. Lucia did her best to dress conservatively, but even the full-length garment could not conceal the woman's shape. Jober flanked her. The stocky man's eyes remained ever alert.

"Where are you off to so early?" asked Lucia.

Odala narrowed her eyes. Though she no longer doubted Tobin's feelings for her, she knew that at one time the Blue Island Clan warleader had eyes for his brother's wife.

"I'm on my way to the market, if you must know."

"Oh, we just came from there," said Lucia. "I'm afraid the selection is rather poor today and most of the best deals are probably gone by now. You need to rise before the sun if you hope to snatch the best wares. I hope you weren't going for anything important."

Odala tightened her jaw.

She talks down to me like I'm a child.

Odala forced a smile. "Actually, I was going to buy a gift for Tobin."

"Oh. How has he been?"

"Wonderful. He told me just the other day that he's never been happier."

Lucia frowned. "I rarely see him anymore."

Because I'm the woman he cares for.

"Well, he's a busy man. If he isn't running his growing empire, then he's showering me with attention." Odala shrugged. "I guess he makes time for what's important to him." She smiled wider at Lucia's wounded expression. "Sorry I can't stay to talk any longer, but if I want to find something in those remaining goods, I need to be on my way."

Odala whisked past Lucia and Jober, feeling proud of herself.

"Odala?" Lucia called her name after less than half a dozen steps.

Odala turned. "Yes?"

"A word of advice. Don't buy anything in turquoise." Her eyes moved up and down Odala's dress. "I guess you didn't know, but Tobin hates that color." She smiled and left.

Odala fumed.

How does she know what Tobin does and does not like?

Odala looked down at her dress and suppressed a scream. She stormed back to her room to change.

* * *

Walking at a brisk pace down the twisting hall, Jober waited until Odala could no longer hear them. "That was very unlike you."

"I know. She brings out the worst in me," said Lucia.

"She's just a girl."

"That's just it. You saw that gaudy dress. She practically looked like a woman working a bathhouse."

"She's not unlike most her age."

"Perhaps it wouldn't bother me so much if I knew she wasn't manipulating Tobin."

Jober sighed. "How do you know she's doing that?"

And who cares if she is. It's not like he doesn't deserve to be taken advantage of after what he's done.

"Intuition. Something just doesn't seem right."

"Well, there's no sense in worrying about it. Tobin is his own man with an ever-expanding set of headaches to deal with. I'm sure he can handle her."

Lucia shook her head. "No. I need to talk to him about it."

He did not understand how she could be so oblivious to who Tobin really was. "He has Nachun to look out for him."

Lucia gave him an odd look. His tone had been more bitter than he intended. "The shaman isn't here. Besides, I've never liked nor trusted him. Kaz never did either."

And for good reason considering what he did to your husband, and what he threatened to do to my family.

"Jober?"

He blinked. "Sorry, I was just thinking on what you said about Kaz."

"You miss him too, don't you?"

"Yes."

Lucia's hand went to her face and Jober saw her wipe away a tear. "Is it crazy that more than a year after his disappearance, I still hold out hope that he will return to me?"

"No. I hope for the same thing."

Maybe then I can be free of my lies.

Lucia reached out and touched his arm. She gestured with her head toward a side corridor. "Come. I've made up my mind. I want to speak with Tobin."

"Now? But he's probably at the training ground."

"I know."

"You can't go there."

"Why not? I've been there before."

"Never at this time of the day."

"I'm sure it will be fine."

* * *

Odala left her room for a second time that morning after hurriedly changing into a violet dress. She quickened her pace. Lucia's comments about the market not having much to offer ate at her mind.

She sighed when her brother appeared from around a corner.

"Ah, just the person I wanted to see."

"I don't have time to talk. I'm on my way to the market."

"Of course. Very important stuff." His voice thickened with sarcasm. "Don't worry, I'll walk with you as we talk."

"Fine. What is it?"

"Well, I wanted to thank you for getting me into Tobin's meetings. It's been invaluable. I see now that you missed a great deal of information before." He eyed her warily.

"You're welcome." Odala chose to ignore his other remark. She did not want him to know that she had purposefully held back information. She was torn between knowing where her loyalties should be and what she feared Soyjid's true intentions were. She stopped. "Why are you here? Tobin should be at the training ground."

"Now is the best time to get word back to Father. Besides, rarely is anything of importance discussed on the training ground and I already know how crazy their methods are."

"How is Father?" asked Odala. She missed him. Her brother said he sent her regards to him, but she didn't know if her father ever got them. Soyjid would not allow her to read their communications.

Soyjid shrugged. "He's growing old and I wonder how much longer he will be able to lead our clan. It's good that he sees the wisdom in my plans."

"Your plans?"

Soyjid chuckled. "Don't look surprised, Sister. Since Mother's passing, Father has relied on me more and more. I'd say I've been quite successful too." He touched the fabric of her dress and then the necklace she had thrown on to match it. "Wouldn't you agree?"

* * *

Tobin dipped his shoulder slightly and then relaxed his front leg. The Kifzo ignored Tobin's first feint, but fell for the second. He lunged. Tobin deflected the attack and disarmed the warrior in one fluid motion. He touched the point of his practice sword against the man's chest.

"Dead."

The warrior bowed. "Well fought, Warleader."

Tobin nodded. "You've improved." He glanced at the three warriors he had already defeated. "You all have." Though Tobin had begun to offer brief bits of encouragement since becoming warleader, many still wore confused expressions when he did so. "Now, pair off and complete the rest of your drills."

They bowed in unison.

Tobin left the practice circle, one of many on the training grounds, and headed toward Walor. Warriors paid their respect to him as he passed, bowing or pounding their chest.

"Well?" asked Tobin.

Walor cracked his neck. "Well what?"

"What did you think?"

"I'd say your improvement has been amazing. You dispatched four seasoned Kifzo in less than a minute. I doubt any other Kifzo could do that, including Guwan."

"Is that enough?"

Walor shook his head. "I know what you're getting at. Let it go."

Tobin lowered his voice. "I need to know. Am I better than Kaz?"

Walor leaned in and whispered. "Who cares? Your brother is gone. You're warleader now, And since you took Bazraki's place, things have never been better. Forget about Kaz."

I can't help it. I have to know if I could best him.

"Just answer the question."

"I can't. Kaz was amazing, but I've seen you do amazing things yourself. I don't think I could say who is better than the other. It would be too close to call now."

Tobin clenched his jaw. *Sometimes I wish he would return just so I can prove myself against him. My ankle is healed and my training has never been sharper.*

Walor used the lull in conversation to change the subject. "Are we still on schedule to leave in three days?"

Tobin gestured toward the barracks and they began walking. "Yes. Today's the last day of training. I'm giving everyone the next two days off to be with family."

"They'll be pleased with that, though I'm sure none will admit it openly."

Tobin sighed. "The old ways of my father are hard to break."

Walor grunted. "It takes time. You've done wonders already without sacrificing the skills we learned under your Uncle Cef. I can't imagine anyone else working so hard to do the same."

"Thank you." Tobin still found it odd to say the phrase to another Kifzo, but in private with Walor and even recently with Ufer, he did so.

Walor changed the subject, looking uncomfortable by Tobin's gratitude. "We finally heard back from Durahn."

"And?"

"He wasn't happy with you telling him how to run Nubinya. And he's angry at being excluded from the campaign. He was already bitter after missing our fight against the Yellow Plain Clan."

"Let him be angry. The farther he is from the Kifzo, the better."

"I agree. It was wise to send him away when you did. He still resents not being made warleader after the Testing when we were boys. Taking orders from you has to be killing him."

Tobin grinned. "I hope it is."

Walor laughed.

"Tobin!"

Activity came to a halt as heads turned to the sound of a woman. Women were not allowed on the training grounds.

A lump caught in Tobin's throat as Lucia came toward him, smiling and waving her arm. He watched her body move, hips swaying hypnotically with each step. He purposefully refrained from spending much time with her, yet she could still take his breath away. A scowl grew on his face as he moved his attention to Jober who flanked her side.

He tried to swallow the anger rising inside as he became aware of his warriors' looks.

Odala would never be so presumptuous.

"You should not be here," he said when she neared.

The edge in his voice caused her to pause, but only for a moment. "I needed to speak with you."

"Then you should have found a better time. The training grounds are off limits to women." He eyed Jober. "He should have told you as much."

"He did," said Lucia. "But I insisted."

"Then what is it?" Tobin demanded.

Lucia glanced at Walor and then to the staring warriors. "Can't we speak somewhere more private?"

"You chose this place, so say what's on your mind."

Lucia straightened. "Fine. It's about Odala."

Tobin's eyes narrowed. "What about her?"

"I think things are getting too serious between you two. I don't trust her and I don't think you should either."

Tobin's voice came out like ice. "Who are you to say that?"

"I'm someone who has your best interests at heart. I'm your friend."

First you deny me by choosing Kaz. Now you question the woman I found to replace you?

Tobin laughed. "Do you?"

"Yes, of course. Why is that funny?"

Because you want to speak to me about matters of the heart when you loved a monster.

Tobin wanted to say that, but still could not bring himself to be that cruel to Lucia. He hated to admit it, but the woman did hold some power over him. His relationship with Odala had taught him something valuable however.

The less I see Lucia, the happier I am.

"This conversation is over. Never speak to me again about Odala. Now go. You're interrupting my training." Tobin glared at Jober. "Do your job and make sure she doesn't come here again. Is that clear?"

Jober clenched his jaw in displeasure, but nodded nonetheless while Lucia looked dumbfounded.

Good. He has not forgotten his place.

CHAPTER 8

Large double doors opened inward and a rush of air exited. The slight chill of the dimly lit room reminded Drake of a cavern. He squinted, but could not pierce the veil of darkness.

"Does anyone have a candle?" he asked.

"A candle? You idiot, you can't bring an open flame into the library. These records are too rare and far too valuable to risk a clumsy boy knocking a candle over."

Drake recoiled at the outburst and outright disdain in the mage's voice. Like the other mages who had decided to promote themselves above their skill levels, Lufflin once again wore his older green robes.

"Sorry. But then how do you see what you're doing?" asked Drake.

"You shouldn't even be here."

"Stop it. We were told to bring him here. He has no way of knowing our methods." Tristan held out his hand and a glowing light formed in his palm. He sent the light out into the gloom where it lit three lamps hanging from hooks on a large stone column.

"But he isn't a mage."

"Others who weren't mages have studied here in the past," said Tristan. "Besides, if you don't like it, take it up with Krytien."

Lufflin sneered. Drake could see that the two mages did not get along and the rift between them had only grown when Krytien had rewarded Tristan's lone adherence to Amcaro's ways.

Lufflin huffed, grabbing a lantern and leading the group down a long hallway. "Let's just get this over with."

The light from the lanterns cast an odd blue glow over the expansive room that dissipated until just enough remained for the shadows to play tricks on Drake's eyes. They walked for a distance far longer than Drake thought possible given what he knew about the depth of the wing. Then he noticed the slight decline in the floor and realized they had descended underground.

Drake had yet to see anything that resembled a bookcase or shelf, or even a discarded piece of paper. Only large columns of stone with the occasional set of tables and chairs occupied the space.

They came to a halt and Drake finally saw several rows of bookcases, about twenty deep, on the edge of the light emanating from Lufflin's lamp. A year ago Drake would have been impressed at so many books in one place, but after looking through the royal library in Lyrosene, he felt disappointed.

It's barely bigger than the queen's.

Lufflin wheeled around and glared at Drake. "What are you looking for in particular? As head of the library, I'll have to help you find it."

Drake glanced at the rows again. "I think I can find it myself actually," he said, hoping to get rid of Lufflin. "It shouldn't take me that long to browse through this."

Lufflin broke out into laughter, his annoying cackle bouncing off the high ceilings. "You fool, this isn't the library. This is simply a reference catalog."

Tristan sighed. "How about you show him where the books actually are? Your braying isn't speeding this up any."

"Come this way," Lufflin said.

Tristan shook his head as they veered to the left. Listening to Lufflin's caterwauling in the eerie place made Drake hate him that much more.

I wonder if he would laugh that hard with a ballista aimed at him.

They came upon another set of double doors, much larger and thicker than the first ones. Lufflin went through and Tristan gestured for Drake to follow. Lufflin allowed his lantern's light to brighten enough for Drake to take in the actual library.

Bookcases and shelves loomed above, over fifty feet high, with ladders, walkways, and scaffolding all around the great space. Doors and staircases led up, down, and out to the sides. Through glimpses of the spanning light, Drake noted even more material in side passages. His mouth hung open, but he couldn't find his voice.

Tristan came up beside him and placed a hand on his shoulder. "So. Where do we begin?"

That's a good question.

* * *

Krytien shuffled along the dark hallway, hand aglow in light. A younger mage told him he could use a lantern, but this worked well enough for him. He reached the second set of double doors leading to the actual library and stared for a few moments at the vast horde of knowledge around him. Books, scrolls, sheets of parchment, and even ancient tablets filled the space. Each contained something of value, whether history, science, philosophy or the art of sorcery. Yet despite the impressiveness of such a collection, something about it felt wrong.

Since reaching the school, that same feeling had been with him no matter where he went. No one could ever call the school plain or uninspired.

However, nothing resembled the visions he had created for himself, and after decades of familiarity with those hopeful dreams of his youth, he found Estul Island depressing.

High Mage Amcaro's death hadn't helped matters. Krytien had never admitted it to anyone, but he used to hang on every word Jonrell spoke about the man, jealous that his former commander had studied with the High Mage. Between Jonrell's stories and the recollections of his old master, Philik, Krytien felt like he almost knew Amcaro.

Krytien yawned and began his search. He had seen very little of Drake since the boy gained access to the library. Krytien had been too busy dealing with personality conflicts to check up on him sooner. Despite the condescending looks most mages gave him, especially those in black robes, he wished that at least one had maintained a residence here. Perhaps he could then lean on them to look after the dozens of students who had stayed after Amcaro's death.

After that initial confrontation with the younger mages, many relinquished their self-promotions with little trouble, but Krytien still saw the resentment in their eyes, especially from those who had awarded themselves the red robes.

Lufflin most of all.

Krytien expected to find Lufflin as he turned into an open doorway and descended a flight of stairs. With each step, the air grew more stale. He entered a dimly lit room and walked past several alcoves of books.

Nora fought sleep with her back against a wall as Drake sat with nose inches from the pages of a large tome while reading.

Krytien put a hand on Nora's shoulder. She jerked her head in surprise. "What are you doing down here?" he asked.

The girl yawned. "Lufflin asked me to give him a break. He said he needed to get some rest and didn't want to spend another night with Drake."

"Don't you have other duties to tend to?"

"I took care of them already."

"Then don't you need your rest?"

"What does it matter to you how much I sleep?" she said, growing defensive. "I could have told Lufflin no."

But you chose not to. I recognize a crush when I see one. "Go get some rest and in the morning I'll talk to Lufflin about this."

"You're not going to punish him, are you?" she asked. Her voice took on a pleading note.

Krytien shook his head. "No." *Not yet, anyway.*

"What about Drake?"

"I'll watch over him."

"Sounds good to me." Nora left.

Steel and Sorrow: Book Two of the Blood and Tears Trilogy

Krytien looked over to Drake. No more than twenty feet away, the boy had barely moved since Krytien arrived. Drake turned a page and his eyes drifted up to the top of the open book.

Good to know he's still alive at least.

Krytien cleared his throat. Nothing. He cleared it much louder, causing a slight echo. Drake jumped.

"Krytien! You scared me." Drake looked up with puffy, red eyes. His expression changed to one of confusion. "When did you get here?" He looked around. "And where's Lufflin?"

"What do you say you take a break? You've been up for a day straight. And before that, I heard you only slept for a couple of hours. You can't keep this up, even at your age."

Drake rubbed his eyes. "But there's so much to learn. They have everything here. I can't go to sleep now." He swayed slightly in his seat.

"Even you will never be able to read everything in this library, especially not in the time before we leave the island. Kroke and I should be finished with preparations tomorrow. We plan to leave the day after."

Drake hung his head. "So soon?"

"Yes. Might I suggest you cut down on the reading and studying for now and instead compile a list of the texts we'll need to take with us."

"Lufflin said that Amcaro never allowed these documents to leave the library, let alone the island. He felt they were too valuable to risk."

"Well, Amcaro is dead and the queen has issued a command that we are obligated to uphold. Besides," he said, patting the boy on the shoulder, "you'll be in charge of their care and I have no doubt you'd rather die than see harm come to them."

Drake chuckled. "Lufflin still won't like it."

"I have a feeling he won't like a lot of things in the coming months. Let's get to bed. I'm not nearly as young as you and my old bones are aching."

"Alright." The boy stood and Krytien steadied him. "I guess I'm more tired than I thought."

They started walking and Drake went on about all that he had discovered. Krytien let him ramble, finding some pleasure in the youth's excitement.

A wonder he's maintained such an attitude after all he's seen.

". . . .besides the books Kaz and Elyse both asked about, I also grabbed a few others that I thought might be of value. I hope they won't mind."

"I'm sure they won't. Elyse did give you discretion to make such decisions."

Drake nodded. "There's a few that I thought you might enjoy too."

"Oh?" Krytien had never been one for books.

"They were written by Amcaro. It's some of his personal thoughts on mastering sorcery, intended for his more accomplished students who—"

Krytien cut him off. "I was not his student Drake."

I was not meant to be some great mage that would live on for centuries. I proved that in Asantia. I don't know what Phillik was thinking when he suggested I study here.

"I know, I just thought . . ."

"I appreciate your consideration, but leave those books here. I'm a mage of a different breed."

They continued in silence.

* * *

The ship had yet to leave the small port and Drake already sat at a desk in a secluded part of the cabin Krytien secured for him. He slid a book from its oiled wrapping with care and delicately set it down. He read the worn cover.

Strategies of War by General Victus.

Drake learned the day before that Victus had been a famed military commander-turned-emperor of the Quoron Empire. Lufflin told Drake that they thought the text had been lost and that it was Drake's dumb luck to discover it while searching for something else. Drake had noted the young mage's emphasis on the word dumb. He sighed.

With Krytien keeping them busy above, I should finally have some peace from him.

A quick pass of the tome's contents back in the library had led Drake to several other older texts that he also packed up for the journey. He hoped that after he had a chance to examine their contents, they might be of some use to Kaz in the coming months.

But first, I need to study the texts I was told to look at.

He turned to the first page.

"What do you think you're doing?"

Drake jerked around and saw Lufflin standing in the narrow doorway. The mage leaned against the doorframe with his arms folded. Drake clenched his jaw. "What does it look like I'm doing?" he said gesturing toward the book. "I'm about to start doing my research."

"And you're breaking every rule to do so."

Drake looked around and didn't see anything particularly dangerous or out of order. "What are you talking about? I'm not even using a lantern for light. Nothing can catch fire."

Lufflin stormed across the room and the mage slammed shut a portal Drake opened earlier for light and fresh air. "No. But you're letting all the salt air in. You'd just as soon burn the books if you're going to do that."

"Well, what do you expect me to do? I need to get through as much of this as I can *before* I reach Lyrosene." Drake gestured to the stacks of texts around him.

Lufflin grimaced. "Then you'll do it only when I'm available to prep the room so the elements won't damage the books." He paused. "This trip is going to be even more miserable stuck with you."

"You could always get someone else to stay with me."

"I'd love nothing better, but I only trust a couple of people to take my place and Krytien has them working on other things. Now shut up, and let me concentrate."

Lufflin closed his eyes and Drake watched in silence. He didn't see or feel anything special except the room filled with the same familiar glow from the library. After a few moments Lufflin opened his eyes. He went over and lay on Drake's cot. "You can start. Be careful. Those books are worth far more than you."

"You know, you could pass the time by helping me."

Lufflin snorted. "Not a chance." He waved a hand dismissively. "Now get to work and don't screw anything up while I'm asleep."

* * *

Estul Island faded out over the horizon and Kroke couldn't be happier. The school had made him uncomfortable, and at least at sea, the upstart mages seemed far less confident in themselves.

Kroke had thought about those mages as he watched Krytien's sullen posture at the stern of the ship. Their trip had impacted the Hell Patrol's mage more than Kroke could have imagined—especially since Krytien insisted on taking most of the mages with them. Many of the obnoxious brats resented the decision, but none did more than vocalize their opinion after the initial confrontation. The ship carried over two dozen green and yellow mages.

At least he left the less experienced ones with Tristan. He's the only one with any sort of head on his shoulders.

Kroke flipped a knife end over end as a light breeze whipped his face. He looked forward to seeing the rest of the Hell Patrol in Lyrosene. Even after all these years, it surprised him how much he could miss them.

Better than any family I ever had. It'll be good to have a drink with Raker and give Rygar a hard time about Yanasi. He flipped his knife again and smiled. *I'll have to get Yanasi to play another round of bow versus knife.*

As he stared out over the rolling sea, he found himself wondering what Elyse had been up to since his departure. Ever since he and Rygar had accompanied her to Ithanthul when she sought an alliance with Jeldor, the queen had regularly stayed in contact with him. He frowned, realizing he missed those casual conversations.

Odd.

CHAPTER 9

Standing near the wheel of the ship, Tobin admired the ease with which the sailor steered the great vessel. He had ridden on Nachun's creations several times over the past year as shipwrights tested each in the bright waters surrounding the Blue Islands. Still, he marveled at their effectiveness.

Tobin looked over his shoulder. Each ship in his fleet held over two hundred warriors. With such a navy, no other clan could ever hope to challenge their supremacy at sea.

He took a deep breath. The coolness and the clean, salty, smell awakened his senses. They would arrive at the Gulf of Eurinul in three days.

Without Nachun's ships, we'd still be marching along the Yellow Plain.

Many things, including his friend, had occupied Tobin's mind since leaving Juanoq. Most he could do without—recollections of his disapproving father, Kaz's ridicule, and Lucia's behavior. Thankfully, he had been able to offset some of those harsh memories by evoking bits of wisdom from his Uncle Cef or through spending long nights with Odala in his arms.

Thoughts of Nachun nagged at him most. He had embarked on the campaign against his friend's wishes. Tobin knew Nachun's power would be a huge boon to their strategy, but as he told others, he could not wait for his friend. Besides the legitimate reasons he had voiced, he also wanted to prove he did not need the shaman to achieve success.

Unlike the fiasco with the Yellow Plain Clan, I cannot blame father's poor planning if things go badly again.

Tobin walked toward the bow of the ship, passing busy crew members and stopped next to Ufer and Walor. They spoke with a young shaman.

"What have we heard from Mawkuk?" asked Tobin.

"Nothing," said Ufer, scowling. "The shaman is useless."

"It's not that, Warleader," said the shaman. "It's nearly impossible to locate men in such a manner, especially an army who wishes to be hidden. Whatever Mawkuk's shamans are doing to mask their presence from the Green Forest Clan is also working against us."

That never bothered Nachun.

"When was the last message we received from Mawkuk?" asked Tobin.

"A week before we left," said Walor. "He understood the plan and should be in place." He paused. "Still, it would be nice if we knew for sure."

"We must have faith in our allies," said Tobin.

* * *

Shortly after dropping anchor, warrior-filled longboats began to fall unceremoniously into the water. Supplies would be transported in later after securing the shore.

Tobin's boat touched the water lightly, swaying gently as rowers moved into position. He took his seat and eyed the twenty Kifzo aboard. Armor sat at their feet and would not be adorned until reaching the beach. He could smell their excitement, their anxiousness to enter battle. He shared those feelings.

Looking for that next challenge has been so ingrained in us.

As paddles dipped in and out of the water, Tobin wondered where he would find his challenges once he united the six major clans under his rule. He did not count the White Tundra Clan in his plans.

After centuries of war, the biggest challenge might be that of peace.

Tobin scanned the dark green forests lining the edges of the lush shores. Starting less than a hundred yards inland, thick evergreens could be seen for miles in either direction, climbing the sloping hills in the distance.

This will be like fighting in the jungles of the Blue Islands when Father warred with the other tribes and seized power so many years ago.

His oldest Kifzo would be invaluable to him now, having greater experience with such conditions.

Longboats slid quietly between protruding rocks, gliding onto the dark sand of the beach. Warriors spilled out of the vessels, their movement masked by lapping waves.

Something isn't right.

He tensed and noticed that others around him did the same. Many ceased with lacing up armor and grabbed for their shields.

"Walor?" hissed Tobin. "Where is Mawkuk? He should be greeting us."

Walor shrugged. "I don't know."

A strange bird sound preceded a hail of arrows that ripped through the air. Two arrows struck Walor, one in the leg, the other in the shoulder. The warriors frantically sought cover, holding up shields while overturning boats. Tobin yanked Walor behind one of the boats as the second flight of arrows sped toward them. One pierced Tobin's left bicep. He ignored the pain.

"You alright?" Tobin asked as blood pumped out of Walor's thigh.

Walor removed the arrow and began a makeshift bandage despite the shaft in his shoulder. He winced. "For now, but it'll need a healer."

Tobin nodded.

Blue Island warriors fired off their own shots into the dense forest. Tobin watched most of the shafts disappear into the foliage or heard them *thump* into tree trunks.

With a grunt, Tobin removed the arrow from his arm as Ufer gathered warriors around him.

"Ufer! Stop!"

Ducking behind a longboat, Ufer raised his hand to steady the men. "Hold!" He looked at Tobin.

"Our losses will be too heavy with a blind charge into the woods. We've barely landed a fraction of our forces unarmored. We need to fall back to the ships."

"We've never retreated," said Ufer.

Tobin paused as doubt crept into his mind. *Neither Father nor Uncle Cef would have been happy with my decision. Kaz would rather have died than give ground. But none of them are here.*

His men wouldn't be happy, but he could deal with their anger later so long as they were alive.

"Fall back now!" he shouted. "Leave behind what can't be easily gathered. Have the shamans focus on covering our withdrawal."

Ufer scowled, but obeyed as he relayed the orders. Tobin turned and waved back those boats eager to reach the shore and help their brethren. He saw the confused looks on their faces as they peeked around the raised shields protecting them from arrow fire. Still, they turned their vessels about.

Boats began slipping back into the water. The Blue Island Clan took heavy losses from the initial strike.

Then Tobin heard it. A giant ram's horn. It sounded like thunder crashing through the air, a low hum in his ears.

The call of the Red Mountain Clan.

Tobin watched warriors clad in bright red emerge from the trees alongside men in deep green. They opened their mouths and Tobin knew they screamed. Yet he could only hear the next horn blast.

He handed Walor off to a retreating Kifzo and ordered the man to get him out of there.

The approaching horde barreled down on him and his men.

* * *

A hand clasped Tobin's forearm, pulling him on deck. Too many of the longboats remained ashore, forcing him to make his escape by swimming.

Dripping blood from multiple wounds, he could only think about one thing. "I want to know how many we lost. I want each and every one of their names," he said in a voice like cold iron.

Ufer nodded. "It will be done. Early estimates are five hundred men, one hundred and fifty Kifzo."

"And theirs?"

"Less than a quarter of that amount." Ufer looked away in shame.

Tobin understood.

He walked past the man and unlaced the sword and shield from his back, dropping them to the deck. He had left his armor on shore.

The water dripping down his face and onto his lips tasted bitter. He strode to the railing and watched as the Red Mountain Clan and Green Forest Clan armies shouted from the shore in defiance. Tobin's mouth filled with the humbling taste of defeat.

When he turned around, men waited for him to give orders. He scanned the other ships in his fleet and shouted. "These are inferior warriors. We grew too confident and underestimated what they were capable of. I take the blame for that. Raise the anchors!" he bellowed at the captain. "We'll begin our assault in a different location than planned and be victorious all the same." He pointed toward the shore. "Look at your enemy! The next time you see his face, your dagger will be in his throat."

The shamans aboard his ship would relay his words to the other vessels.

He made his way below, leaving his men to their anger.

* * *

Pink water lapped against the shore as bodies drifted in and out with the waves. In the distance, countless ships raised anchors and sailed away. The Red Mountain and Green Forest Clan armies raised their weapons high in victory along the beach, taunting the Blue Island Clan from afar.

Though the council of the Green Forest Clan would be pleased by Charu's early success, he knew better than to grow comfortable with the victory.

It's only the beginning.

"Do you want me to stop them?" asked Gidan, his general, as if reading his thoughts.

"No. The Green Forest Clan needs to know that the Blue Island Clan is not invincible. And both armies need to revel in their united effort."

Soft footsteps came from behind. "My congratulations, Warchief."

Charu looked over his shoulder. "I told you to remain back."

Melat bowed her head. "I did, Warchief. But once I heard the thunderous cheering from your men, I knew it was safe to come forward. You predicted the landing site perfectly."

Charu took her meaning. Their informant had given them correct information. He caught Gidan casting a sour look at her. The general did not like him bringing Melat on the campaign. Yet, as warchief, no one would challenge his decision. And he would not deny her company after she had done so much for him already.

* * *

Tobin blocked out the pain as a healer treated his wounds. Walor lay on a pallet next to him, sleeping. The healer said Walor would make a full recovery, but needed his rest for now.

After stitching up the last of his cuts, Tobin rose and made his way out of the hull. Soyjid stood at an open doorway waiting for him.

"You blame my father, don't you?" the boy asked.

"I absolutely blame your father. His orders were to secure the shore and he had more than enough time to do so. Many of my men want him killed."

Soyjid frowned. Surprisingly, the boy seemed calm. "I understand. He did have an obligation to be here."

That had not been the reaction Tobin expected. "So you aren't here to make excuses for him?"

"No."

"Then why are you here?"

"I'm quite certain that his loyalty or intentions have nothing to do with any recent failings. He's an old man, and like many his age, he is prone to mistakes. So, I only ask that you give him the chance to explain himself. And if you decide he's not worthy to lead, still allow him to live."

Tobin considered his plea.

"I know what you're thinking," said Soyjid. "Yes, the line would fall to me. However, I promise you won't be trading one liability for another."

"What do you suggest?"

"I'd like the chance to present some ideas. I didn't want to overstep myself in your council before. But now, it might be the best way to prove my usefulness."

Tobin raised an eyebrow.

"I'll never be a great warrior. However, I can contribute in other ways. All I ask is for a chance."

Tobin felt lightheaded, no doubt from the loss of blood. He too needed to rest, though he hated to admit it.

What would it hurt to listen to the boy? We have time before reaching our next destination.

"Tomorrow morning after breaking our fast you'll have your chance."

* * *

"How well do you know Tobin?"

The question startled Odala from her sleep. She sat up and saw her brother sitting across from her, thin arms folded over his chest. He wore an intense look.

"What are you doing?" she asked, looking around.

"I asked you a question. How well do you know him?"

Odala blinked away the sleep, growing angry that her brother would just barge into her cabin. "I know him better than you if that's what you're getting at."

He laughed. "Do you? He was ready to kill Father after today's fiasco."

"What? No. He didn't mention anything about Father to me earlier."

"Of course he wouldn't. He doesn't want to upset you. But, I overheard him talking to Ufer and had I not stepped in and defended him, Father's life would already be gone. At least now, Tobin will speak with him first."

Odala eyed her brother skeptically. "What do you want from me?"

"I just want you to examine your feelings for Tobin. Ask yourself if the few comforts you enjoy are worth more than your own family."

He stood and left her room.

CHAPTER 10

Drake shuffled across the training grounds and made his way through the armory where the night shift pounded steel between hammer and anvil. His head throbbed from the noise and his red eyes grew heavier from the heat.

Just a few more minutes.

They had arrived in Lyrosene hours before and after ensuring the new mages had a place in the barracks near Krytien, Drake had been dismissed for the night. He didn't argue. Whatever he had to say to Kaz could wait until morning. They had pushed hard since landing in Floroson and the late nights of studying left him feeling ragged.

He entered a set of heavy doors and then another as he walked the length of a short hallway. A plain oak door marked the entrance to the room he shared with Raker.

Home sweet home.

Drake attempted to sneak into the room, but the squeal of rusted hinges betrayed him. He winced at the sound, then doubled over as a stench slapped him in the face. A flickering candle on the table dimly lit the room.

The chamber pot in the corner overflowed with waste near a pile of broken liquor bottles. His nose then caught a different smell, one of death, as he noticed a missile from a ballista imbedded into a nearby post. Dried blood ran along the length of the shaft and a congealed pool of the stuff covered the floor. The ballista against the back wall sat empty.

What in the world happened?

Covers shuffled and a grunt followed. A new smell mixed with the slew of others. He looked over at Raker and sighed.

Passed out and worse than when I left him.

He fumed when he turned his attention to his cot, a place he had been dreaming of for weeks. Raker's dirty clothes and muddy boots rested on his bed.

Drake dropped his bag, walked over to Raker's cot, and kicked the engineer in the rump. Raker didn't budge. Ready for a fight with no one to reciprocate, he took one last look at the room and grabbed his bags. He didn't have the energy to clean up the mess and rest would not come in the sty Raker had made.

All I wanted was one night without Lufflin belittling me at every turn. One night where I could wake up and not have that idiot of a mage in my face. He stormed out the room, making sure to slam the door.

Enjoy your rest, you old fart.

* * *

Exhausted from reaching Lyrosene in the middle of the night, Kroke leaned against a wall and picked at a speck of dirt under his thumbnail.

Despite the hour, Krytien had insisted they meet with Kaz and Elyse right away. Personally, Kroke could not have cared less about giving or receiving any updates at this hour. They let Drake get to bed and Kroke found himself jealous of the boy snoozing away in his cot.

Well, at least one of us will get some rest.

Kroke probably could have gone to the barracks himself, but he thought it a good idea to stick around in case Krytien needed someone to corroborate the state of Estul Island.

Kroke watched the tension in their exchange. Kaz wore a look of quiet criticism. Krytien quickly did the same, probing Kaz for information regarding the coming campaign, then growing exasperated at the vague answers. If Elyse hadn't been there to mediate the exchange, Kroke imagined things might have gotten out of hand.

Elyse had come a long way since those weeks he and Rygar spent with her on the road to gain Jeldor's support, growing into the woman and queen that Jonrell said she could be. Looking at her reminded Kroke about huddling around the pathetic embers of a dying fire, gnawing on cured pork and berries.

He watched her lay a hand on Krytien's arm as his frustration with Kaz grew. The mage's shoulders immediately relaxed. Despite waking in the middle of the night and being forced to throw herself together in a hurry, something about her captured Kroke's attention.

"Hey, Kroke."

Kroke jumped and in the process jammed the point of his knife under his nail, drawing blood. He cursed and stuck his thumb in his mouth. "What's the matter with you, Rygar?"

"Sorry. I didn't mean to startle you."

He sheathed his blade. "What are you doing up this late?"

"I had a late watch. I heard everyone made it back so I found an excuse to get away and drop in. How was the trip?"

"Less than ideal."

"That bad?"

Kroke nodded over to the heated conversation. "Pretty much. Look, how about we talk tomorrow. I'm exhausted."

"That's fine," said Rygar. "I don't want Yanasi to worry about me anyway." He looked down to Kroke's thumb again. "I think that's the first time I've seen you cut yourself. What distracted you?"

Elyse. I was watching Elyse.

He shook his head. "Nothing. Just tired is all. Go get some rest."

"You too. Be careful," said Rygar, walking off.

Kroke turned back to the conversation as it ended. Elyse looked up briefly in his direction and smiled. He felt his stomach tighten.

Be careful, huh?

* * *

With a huff, Krytien passed Kroke and headed out the door. He left the study and plodded down the hallway, taking his anger out on the stone under his feet. He turned back, only briefly, when he saw Kroke catching up to him. The man wore a troubled look and kept staring at his thumb.

Krytien let out a heavy sigh as he descended a set of stairs. He could not figure out why he and Kaz didn't get along. He wondered if it still stemmed from him being a mage, but he thought the man had gotten over such nonsense.

After all, he sent me to Estul Island to bring back more mages. Is that it? He hates mages even more because he has to rely on them?

In the past, Krytien tried to be understanding of Kaz's prejudices. He knew it must be frustrating for those without talent in the art to watch the ability of mages around them, especially in the case of someone like Kaz who prided himself in his physical prowess. Yet, Krytien thought his relationship with Jonrell would have been enough for Kaz to trust him fully.

"He probably only keeps me around because of Jonrell's memory," mumbled Krytien.

"You said something?" Kroke asked, a step behind.

"No." Krytien looked over his shoulder. "Go back to staring at your thumb."

Kroke frowned and did just that as the two continued on to the barracks.

* * *

"What was that all about?" asked Elyse.

"What?" said Kaz.

"That," said Elyse as she pointed to the door through which Krytien and Kroke just left. "Why do you treat him like that? He's only trying to help you."

Kaz grunted. "Maybe. But at what costs?"

Elyse shook her head in disbelief. "Costs?"

"He doesn't trust me. He wants to help, but only as long as I take his advice. He keeps bringing up what Jonrell would have done or the man before your brother, Ronav. I'm not them. I need to do what I feel is best."

"That doesn't mean you need to dismiss his experience or belittle him."

"I treat him the same way that he treats me," said Kaz, scowling. "It's late and you should get some rest."

"What about you?"

"I've got too much to do."

They said their farewells and Elyse watched him stalk from the room, carrying the weight of the world on his shoulders.

* * *

"So you're telling me there was a dead assassin attached to that missile at one point?" asked Drake.

Senald, one of the engineers, had just finished explaining the Assassin's Guild attack on the Hell Patrol.

"That's what I said."

At least I know what all the heads on the city wall are about.

"Then why is the missile still in the wall and blood still on the floor?"

"Raker told me to get the body out of there. He didn't say anything about cleaning up. And he's been too drunk to care otherwise." Senald shrugged.

Drake narrowed his eyes. "I asked you to watch over him while I was gone."

"I really tried at first, but he flips out at any little thing nowadays. About the only thing he stays coherent enough for is drilling us. I can only take so much of him. Besides, he's a grown man."

"Grown man or not, you're going to help me with this." Drake continued before Senald could open his mouth to complain. Second to Raker over the engineers, many still found it hard to take orders from Drake because of his age. "Don't start. Just follow me. This'll be fun."

Not like I find it easy giving orders either.

Drake walked away and listened for the footsteps following. Relief sped his steps when he heard them.

Time to wake up, Raker.

* * *

Surrounded by half-naked women, Raker was loving life. The varied and exotic nature of the bathhouse's workers separated the establishment from any other he had been to.

And I've been to plenty.

A beautiful redhead slipped into the tub after removing the little clothing she wore. A long-legged blonde followed. Both rubbed away the tired aches of his body. He smiled.

A dark-skinned brunette joined them and Raker whispered in her ear. Surprisingly, the brunette's face turned angry. She began shouting. Raker couldn't figure out why she'd be so upset.

After all, she is a whore.

But the brunette only grew more irate and before long the blonde and redhead joined her.

All three repeated the same two words over and over in unison. "Wake up!"

Raker gave them an odd look. *That doesn't make sense.*

The brunette dunked his head under water. He flailed, struggling to breathe until his eyes popped open.

Raker sat up gagging for air. He looked around.

Back in my room. Figures all the good stuff is a dream.

Drake stood a few feet from him with an empty bucket. A few drops of water dripped to the stone floor.

Senald wore a grin. He held another full bucket in his hands. "Is it my turn now, Drake?"

"Not yet. He looks like he's up."

"Yeah, I'm up you miserable pieces of trash." He narrowed his eyes at Drake. "When did you get back?"

"Last night. And I didn't appreciate being welcomed by this mess," said Drake gesturing around the room.

"I'm gonna get you for that." Raker wiped the water from his face. "Senald, hand me my mace." There was silence. "Senald, I gave you an order."

"Drake told me not to listen to you on this one."

"He what?" Raker stood up too fast and pitched to the side, head swimming. He steadied himself on a chair. "Boy, are you crazy? Just wait until this room stops spinning. I outrank you."

"Not like this you don't," said Drake.

Raker heard what sounded like both pity and disgust in the boy's voice. "Don't get all preachy on me again. Save your breath for someone who cares."

"I've got too much to do today to argue with you now. Too much of your mess to fix. In the meantime, Senald is going to help you clean this place up and then get you a bath."

"Bath? What kind of women?" he asked, thinking of his dream.

"None. Not unless you want me to grab Hag."

Raker's stomach lurched. "And what if I tell you to kiss off?"

Drake gestured to the wall. "Senald told me what happened. I can put two and two together. The switch on my ballista worked. If you don't at least do this, I'm hanging that over your head. And I'll make sure Hag is the first one to know. It'll spread like wildfire."

Raker had to hold back a grin. *That boy is growing a bigger pair every day.*

"Alright. You win." He reached out a hand. "You mind?"

Drake set down the bucket and came over to help him. Raker took a few steps and paused as he got his bearings. Then his fist came up and connected with the boy's gut. Raker turned with his other hand and knocked Senald across the jaw. They both crumbled to the ground.

"What was that for?" Drake puffed out as he gasped for breath.

"I said I'd clean up, but I can't just let you forget your place. It's good to see you growing a pair but remember, none are bigger than mine."

"What about me?" said Senald wiping the blood from his lip as he picked himself off the floor.

"That's for not getting that missile out my wall and then telling Drake what happened."

"You only told me to take care of the body."

"Next time, take some initiative. Now, where's my whiskey?"

* * *

Drake's throat burned with each breath. He wanted nothing more than to bend over and retch, but the endless press of Kaz didn't give him the moment he needed. A heavy blow from the blunted practice sword struck the side of his oaken shield and he stumbled back. The vibrations in his arm traveled all the way into his upper back. Drake barely had the chance to wince before the next strike came. He managed to raise his sword in time, deflecting the worst of the attack, but the weapon still managed to scrape across his helm.

"In battle, he might have scalped you, boy," said Crusher, behind the practice area.

Drake jumped over a series of obstacles placed throughout the practice circle, trying to put some distance between himself and Kaz, but the man followed with ease. Drake couldn't see an opening in Kaz's defenses, but he chanced an attack anyway, desperate to do anything to change the course of the fight.

Kaz easily turned away Drake's blows. Drake dodged the counterstrike and crashed to the ground. He instinctively rolled to his feet, but by doing so, left his shield behind.

"Things ain't looking good for you, boy. I thought you'd be better by now." Crusher's mocking laugh followed.

Drake's head pounded to the beat of his racing heart, drowning out all other sounds. He clenched his teeth in anger and charged Kaz, hacking away with every bit of energy he had left.

Moments later he lay on his back again, too tired to move. He stared up at the clear night sky, watching the twinkling stars. Drake rolled over and emptied his stomach unto the ground and coughed.

The laughter continued.

"Enough," said Kaz. "Or I'll have you running laps around the yard until you're puking beside him."

"I was only messing with him," said the deep throated Ghal. "No harm was meant. Right, kid?"

Drake spat the taste out of his mouth and looked up. He nodded.

"See," said Crusher. He got up and walked to the outer edges of the training yard, moving on to torment someone else.

Kaz knelt beside Drake. "You alright?"

Drake breathed several deep, ragged breaths. "I will be eventually."

Kaz looked confused. "You were better before you left. What happened?"

Drake managed a smile. "It's hard to practice on a ship. And once we got to the school, I was too preoccupied with the texts we found to think of much else."

"No doubt. It looked like you took half their library."

"Trust me, that's barely a fraction of what's there."

Kaz tightened his gaze. "Don't spend all your time in those books."

"You're the one who wanted me to bring that stuff back. And I've already shown you some of what I've learned. There are dozens of books I haven't even opened yet. That information could help us win the war."

"It can. But a book will not save you from a sword stroke. You need to get back into a training routine. I don't want to be worrying about you on the battlefield."

Kaz wore a look of concern.

It's too bad so few ever see this side of him. The men know Kaz will fight until his last breath, but they don't see that he does it as much out of compassion for his men as he does for the thrill of battle. He definitely is more like Jonrell than the old crew gives him credit for.

Drake let out a sigh as Raker popped into his head.

"What's wrong?" asked Kaz.

"I'm just thinking about Raker. He's living his life in a bottle."

"Worse than before?"

Drake nodded. "It's hard to notice unless you're around him all the time. Especially because he seems like himself during drills."

"Then maybe things will improve once the campaign begins."

"But what if it doesn't? What if it gets worse and he'd rather hold a bottle than his mace?"

Kaz sighed. "Then I'll have to take care of it. Until then, just keep doing what you can and let me know if I need to step in."

CHAPTER 11

Two days later the Blue Island Clan landed on the edge of the Gray Marshes, near the border of the Green Forest Clan's territory. Tobin's anger raged once the shamans reported that the Gray Marsh Clan still camped in the area, miles from where they should have been.

Longboats came off the ships quicker than before and Tobin felt it necessary to order his men not to take out their aggression on the Gray Marsh Clan. He saw the rage in their eyes, the need to exact punishment on those responsible for their embarrassment at the hands of the Green Forest and Red Mountain Clans.

Tobin stepped out of the boat and into thigh deep water. He strode inland. Walor and Ufer fell in beside him, Walor still limping. Soyjid struggled to keep up with their pace. Physically the boy was still a mess, but he had shown Tobin much in the way of strategy.

A small retinue greeted Tobin on the shore. "Greetings Tobin, Warleader of the—"

"Where is he?" demanded Tobin.

"Mawkuk is waiting for you in his private tent," said the representative.

Ufer spat. "He disrespects you by not coming out to meet you."

The representative shook his head. "No, that isn't it. He became ill and only recently recovered. He's still weak." The man looked at Soyjid and bowed. "Perhaps you can help explain that your father meant no disrespect."

"He can speak for himself," said Soyjid. "I'm not one to put words into his mouth."

The man frowned.

"Take me to him," said Tobin.

The man bowed, as did the others with him. He turned and walked toward camp.

Tobin's temper flared as he passed by roaring campfires where soldiers lounged, gnawing on roasted meat, seemingly oblivious to the impending campaign.

All while we lost hundreds of men.

"I see they are enjoying themselves." Walor's voice dripped with disgust.

"Their lack of discipline will cause us trouble in the future," said Ufer.

"Silence," said Tobin.

Mawkuk's tent stood higher than any other. Guards flanked the entrance to either side. They opened the tent flaps and allowed the party passage.

Mawkuk rose from his hideous, driftwood throne as the group entered. The Gray Clan's council stood around him. Mawkuk lowered his head subserviently toward Tobin and then looked up as he saw Soyjid. His eyes warmed. "It's good to see you, Tobin. And I thank you for giving me the chance to gaze upon my son again." The old man strained to peak around Tobin. "Is Odala also here?"

Tobin ignored him. He looked to Mawkuk's advisors. "Leave us. Now."

The men glanced at each other nervously and turned to Mawkuk for guidance, but the Gray Marsh Clan leader looked equally confused.

Tobin inclined his head to Ufer. "If these men do not leave in the next three breaths, make them."

A blade cleared its scabbard. "Yes, Warleader."

The advisors scurried out of the room without waiting for Mawkuk's answer.

"Sit, Mawkuk."

The old man took his seat. "I-I don't understand. What's wrong?"

"Don't give me that. What are you and your men doing here?"

"Following your orders."

"Liar!" yelled Ufer. "You were supposed to secure the shore a hundred miles from here."

"Ufer!" Tobin shouted. "Hold your tongue."

Mawkuk's brow furrowed. "But we did follow your orders. You specifically told us to be here. I didn't understand why, especially when I learned that you went farther into the Green Forest Clan territory before coming ashore. I supposed we were held back in reserve."

"I never said that. Soyjid. Give your father a copy of my orders."

Soyjid rummaged in a small parcel he held over one shoulder and withdrew a piece of rolled parchment. He stepped toward his father and handed it off.

Tobin continued. "I always make copies of the orders I issue."

Mawkuk scanned the paper and shook his head. "This isn't what your messenger delivered to us."

"Where is the message then? I want to see it for myself," said Tobin.

"I destroyed it, just as your letter said, lest someone see your strategy. But I can attest that your signature matched and the seal had not been tampered with."

"And you think I should believe your story?"

Mawkuk's eyes widened. "Why would I lie? You have my children." He gestured toward Soyjid.

"I don't know. If you aren't lying, then you're making costly mistakes I can't afford to have happen again."

"Tobin? What are you saying?" came a voice from behind.

Tobin whipped his head around and saw Odala standing at the entrance to the tent. "What are you doing here? This isn't your place."

"I wanted to see my father," she said, confused.

"Later," Tobin snapped. "Get back to the tent."

"You're not going to kill him, are you?" asked Odala, horrified.

Tobin clenched his teeth in frustration. "No, I'm not." He gestured to Soyjid. "Escort your sister from here."

Soyjid nodded and made his way toward the tent entrance, grabbing Odala by the arm and leading her outside. Tobin caught the hurt and bewildered look on her face before turning back to Mawkuk.

Mawkuk repeated his daughter's question. "Are you going to kill me?"

"Many of my men would like me to, but there is another option I'd rather pursue."

Mawkuk's jaw tightened. "I see. You and Odala have become close, haven't you?" The old man's voice found a hardness that had been absent. Tobin wasn't surprised.

She is still his daughter.

Tobin ignored his question. "You are no longer leader of the Gray Marsh Clan. You will be watched over by six Kifzo at all times to ensure that you cannot influence the decisions of your clan any longer."

Mawkuk started to argue, but thought better of it and sank further into his throne. "And who will lead?"

"Your son."

Mawkuk sighed. "I can at least find solace in that."

"Good. You will announce the transition immediately after Soyjid returns."

* * *

"You shouldn't have been so accusatory in front of the others. Think what you will of Tobin privately, or with me," said Soyjid.

Odala wiped her cheek. "What did you want me to do? I thought he was going to kill Father like you said he might."

"Now you see why I wanted to be brought into Tobin's circle? I probably saved Father's life by presenting Tobin with an alternative to the one his men wanted."

"What alternative?"

"I've convinced him to let me take Father's place. With me in charge, he will not have to worry about our clan's cooperation following his dismissal.

Tobin can't afford to lose our forces now that we will be fighting both the Green and Red Clans together."

She stopped outside her newly erected tent. *Soyjid taking Father's place? I never expected that to happen so soon.*

"You seem troubled."

Odala shook her head. "I was only thinking. You'll be a good ruler," she added, unsure what else to say.

Soyjid smiled. "I'd like to think so."

Odala sighed. "I still don't know what to think about Tobin though. Before you stepped in, he was ready to kill Father."

Soyjid held up a hand. "I've warned you all along about him. However, you've been happy with him over the last year. That doesn't have to change. He was under a lot of pressure and when I gave him a more suitable alternative, he made the right decision. Forgive him. You must remember his upbringing. It was much different than ours." He paused. "And don't worry about your outburst. I'll smooth things over."

She cocked her head to the side. "Really?"

"Why wouldn't I? I know we argue, but we're still family."

The admission surprised and touched Odala. She gave her brother a hug. "Thank you."

* * *

Tobin left Mawkuk's tent once the six Kifzo arrived to guard him.

Walor cleared his throat. "I don't like your decision."

"I didn't want to kill the old man. His age has more to do with his inability to lead than anything else," said Tobin.

"I understand," said Walor. "I know you want to keep him alive for Odala's sake too. But putting Soyjid in charge is a mistake. He is too sickly to lead from the field."

"He doesn't have to. He has a great mind. You've heard some of his input. Can you find fault with it?"

"Not on the surface. But I still don't trust him."

"First Nachun, and now Soyjid. You're growing paranoid." Tobin glanced to Ufer as they walked. "And what do you think?"

"I agree with Walor." said Ufer. "Something about the boy doesn't seem right." He shrugged. "But just like Mawkuk, Soyjid is a figurehead. You still hold all the power."

* * *

Tobin looked over a large map detailing the terrain of the Green Forest Clan's territory. He had been strategizing with Walor, Ufer, and Soyjid. Most of the plans had been finalized on the ship. However, on one decision they disagreed. Two possible areas of approach existed to reach the Green Forest Clan's capital of Feruse.

Soyjid felt the best course was to approach from the south. Tobin thought that strategy would give Charu, who he had learned led the combined Red and Green Clan armies, a better chance of hindering him. The northern approach, closer to the shore made more sense to him. Soyjid pointed out that the sea would be at their backs again with no ships to retreat to if necessary. Ufer and Walor agreed with Tobin. They took offense at the suggestion that the Blue Island Clan would need to retreat again once all of their forces were ashore.

"I don't understand the reasoning," said Soyjid. "There is nothing wrong with a strategic retreat."

"We don't expect you to understand," said Ufer. "You're not a warrior. There will not be another long swim. We will stand and we will win."

Soyjid threw up his hands. "Warleader, surely you see the value in what I'm saying. A southern route is the most sound strategy for everyone."

Tobin started to speak, but a brief bout of dizziness took him. He steadied himself and blinked. They stared back at him. He turned his gaze down to the map.

"Tobin, are you alright?" asked Walor.

Tobin waved him off. He traced his finger along the southern path that led to Feruse.

Maybe Soyjid is right.

He grunted and raised his head. "The more I think about it, the more I realize this is our best path." He continued before anyone could protest. "Now everyone leave. I have other things to consider."

Soyjid bowed before exiting. Ufer scowled and followed. Walor left after a short pause.

Tobin breathed a sigh of relief once they left. His head pounded inexplicably and he could not imagine carrying on a conversation any longer. He sat in a chair.

Why did I ever want this? To prove I was better than Father and Kaz? He rubbed his temple before relaxing. *I may have been unhappy, but life was simpler when no one cared about what I had to say.*

Despite the light from oil lamps nearby, he closed his eyes and drifted off to sleep, hoping the rest would ease his weary mind.

CHAPTER 12

Elyse stood at the end of a large table. A map of Cadonia lay stretched out on its surface. General Grayer and Kaz flanked her on either side. Kaz refused to allow any others into their meetings as they finalized the coming campaign. He had grown ever more cautious, worried that a spy might be in their midst. Or, just as bad in his opinion, someone who didn't know how to keep his mouth shut.

Grayer read from a stack of messages that detailed recent activity behind Tomalt's borders. Kaz repositioned pieces of varying colors on the map in accordance with the reports. Finished with the first stack, Grayer moved on to less precise reports that had come in about Bronn and Conroy. Using the information available, they brainstormed over the best route to travel in order to meet up with Jeldor's army.

Elyse usually said very little during these meetings. It was not that she was uninformed. She had simply learned that those in charge of her military were more than competent in their roles.

Grayer and Kaz went over their plans for what seemed like the hundredth time, tweaking minor details. The contrast between the two made her grin. Both large men, Grayer was old, fair-skinned, and round, while Kaz was younger, dark as night, and lean. Grayer's thick white hair and beard contrasted Kaz's shaved head and neatly trimmed goatee. Kaz had lost his long braids in a fire at Cathyrium. He had decided not to grow them back.

Kaz stroked his chin while studying the map.

"It looks as though something still troubles you, Commander," said Grayer.

"It's the latest positioning of Tomalt's troops. He's withdrawn a large portion of his army away from his borders. That doesn't make sense when he knows we'll soon be on the move."

"He must think he can't defend them properly and he plans to fall back to more favorable ground." Grayer pointed to a spot in Tomalt's territory. "Here would be his best spot. We'd have quite a time against him, especially if he is able to bring up his other armies. Then he'd control the field and outnumber us in battle."

Kaz scowled. "He'll only outnumber us if Jeldor doesn't meet us in time."

Elyse jumped in. "Let's not forget that he can only bring up so many of his southern forces before leaving those borders susceptible to an attack by Duke Olasi."

Grayer smiled. "Good point, Your Majesty."

Kaz inclined his head. "Your Majesty, what is your opinion on Tomalt's behavior?"

Elyse blinked. Kaz rarely sought out her advice when discussing strategy.

She looked at the map and examined the troop movements. Bits of information she had read from Aurnon the First's early campaigns came to mind. Coupled with what she knew of Tomalt, things just didn't make sense.

"Well, we know that Tomalt rarely does anything that does not follow the rules of warfare. So, for him to abandon his borders, he either feels like his situation is hopeless as Grayer mentioned or he is trying to lure us into a trap." She paused, waiting for Kaz to dismiss her. Instead, he gestured for her to continue. "Tomalt is too proud a man to admit that any situation is hopeless, so I'm willing to bet it is the latter."

"What do you suggest we do?" asked Kaz.

"I'd suggest that we continue with the plan for now. Any changes with so little information could only come back to bite us. However, Aurnon the First believed in having a place for tactical retreat so if he had to face superior numbers, it would at least be on his terms."

Elyse took a deep breath and waited for a response.

A grin crawled across Kaz's lips. "I was thinking the same thing, Your Majesty. As a matter of fact, I have just the place in mind."

A knock at the door stopped the conversation.

Elyse called out. "Who is it?"

"It's Gauge, Your Majesty."

"I thought you told him not to disturb us?" asked Kaz.

Elyse shrugged. "It must be important."

Kaz gestured to a sheet near Grayer. They draped it over the table as Elyse went to the door.

Elyse cracked open the door and saw Gauge's smiling face, creases forming around his old eyes. "Yes?" she asked.

Gauge bowed, "I'm sorry, Your Majesty. I pray I'm not disturbing you."

"We were in the middle of discussing our plans for the campaign."

"I see." He craned his neck down either side of the hallway. "Could I come in and speak with you for a moment? I promise it won't take much of your time."

Elyse opened the door and Gauge stepped in, closing the door behind him. He looked over at Kaz and Grayer as they straightened the last of the sheet over the table. Kaz scowled.

Gauge's eyes flicked back to the queen. He cleared his throat and leaned in close. "The council was upset that you were not at the meeting this morning."

"I thought you were going to take care of their concerns. I had more pressing matters here."

Gauge nodded. "Yes, of course. I was able to smooth things over and we actually got a lot accomplished."

"Oh?"

"It would seem that Kaz's absence put everyone in a more amiable mood. I will fill you in with the details later, Your Majesty."

"Then I don't understand. Why are you here?"

Gauge looked out from the corner of his eye toward Kaz. "It was Illyan. He tried to bring up the same point he attempted to discuss last meeting."

"I see. What's the problem?"

"I'm afraid to say that in the time between meetings, he was able to gain back some of his supporters."

"How?"

Gauge shrugged. "He refused to give any more details without you present. He swears the matter is of high importance." He paused. "And according to Illyan, he spoke with someone high in your confidence who encouraged him to continue digging into the matter."

Elyse leaned back. "Who?"

"I did," said Kaz.

Elyse wheeled around, furious. "We've talked about this several times, Commander. I've told you that it is a waste of time to indulge Illyan."

"Nothing I do is a waste of time, Your Majesty," said Kaz. "If you would listen to him—"

"No," she snapped. "I will not listen to anything that man has to say until he has unquestionable proof and is willing to share his sources. I will not rule my kingdom through hearsay. My father caught himself up in such matters and that is why we're in the mess we are today. You will not change my opinion on the matter."

An uncomfortable silence followed as the two stared at each other.

Grayer cleared his throat. "Perhaps we should get back to strategy."

"No," said Kaz, boring holes through Gauge with his piercing stare. "We're done here." He turned to Grayer. "See that the positioning of troops are shuffled before you leave. Meet me in the barracks tonight if you have any other concerns, General."

"Yes, Commander."

Kaz strode toward the door and halted a few feet from Elyse. He gave her an exaggerated bow. "Your Majesty, may I be dismissed?"

Elyse nodded, too angry to say anything. *Why this sudden act of defiance toward me?*

"About Illyan, Your Majesty," croaked Gauge.

"Later." She said, staring down the hall at Kaz's back.

* * *

Kaz closed the door to his quarters and stripped off his armor. After the last piece came away he sat in a chair, leaned back, and gulped water. He reached across the table, grabbed a heel of stale bread from the morning and gnawed on it between drinks. He had missed dinner again.

The army would leave in the morning and he felt behind after burning off his frustration in the training yard. A few soldiers sparred with him eagerly at first, hoping he would teach them something useful as he usually did. But their attitudes changed when they caught his sour mood. After some time, Kaz dismissed them and continued alone.

When Drake arrived at the usual time, the two trained together. However, both had too much on their minds and neither wanted to talk about it. So Drake went back to his books and Kaz back to his sword, easing their minds in the best ways they knew how.

Kaz forced down the last bite of bread and began cutting up an apple. A lot had changed since Slum Isle. Many of the men who once ridiculed him for his differences regarded him with respect. Some even looked up to him. However, those were soldiers of the royal army. Oddly enough, most of the people he had known the longest in the Hell Patrol still acted put off by him.

They would much rather have Jonrell leading them. He threw a slice of apple in his mouth. *So would I.*

Even though the army now accepted him, Kaz only considered a handful of them his friends. Perhaps that explained why Elyse's tone and expression had bothered him so much.

He understood that politics played a large role in their difference of opinion, an area Kaz knew lay outside his expertise.

Could it be I'm sensitive because I'm such a stranger here? Maybe I should just tell Elyse I will no longer support Illyan, even if it's a lie since I can't ignore his claims. I just don't want to leave on bad terms.

A knock sounded and the door opened before Kaz could respond. A lithe figure glided into the room. Kroke leaned against a wall and whipped out a blade, closing the door with his foot. "You wanted to see me."

Kaz refrained from commenting on Kroke's lack of decorum. He knew the man cared little for Kaz.

Another of the old crew who doesn't understand that I'm doing this to honor Jonrell, not replace him.

"Have a seat," said Kaz, gesturing toward a chair.

"I'll stand," said Kroke. "What's on your mind?"

"Elyse." Kaz saw Kroke flinch slightly at the name.

"What about the queen?"

"With the army moving out tomorrow, she'll be by herself and vulnerable again."

"You mean because you won't be here to shadow her every move."

"Something like that."

"You'll need a few to stay behind and keep an eye on her then?"

"No, just one."

Kroke looked up slowly as realization set in. He scowled. "I ain't no babysitter."

"She doesn't need a babysitter," said Kaz, nodding to the blade in Kroke's hand. "That's what she needs."

Kroke worked his mouth. "You sneaky piece of garbage. I see what you're doing. You're trying to get rid of me."

"What?"

"Yeah, leaving me here means there is one less from the old crew to worry about. Well—" started Kroke, moving forward.

Kaz stood and slammed his fist on the table. One of the legs splintered and the table crashed to the floor. "Stop!" He had enough.

Kroke froze.

Kaz tried to calm himself. He had done his best to lead as Jonrell would have.

But I'm not him.

"I know you hate me. You want to stick that blade in my gut right now and watch the light fade from my eyes, don't you? Well, then do it. You might succeed. Then again you might not. Perhaps we'd both die. But what good would either scenario serve? Whether you like me or not, Elyse put me in control of the army and Jonrell is dead. I wish as much as you do that he wasn't, but neither of us can change that." He paused. "Whether you agree with all my decisions, haven't I at least tried to do the right thing?"

Kroke said nothing.

"Good enough. You know Grayer or Jeldor cannot win Elyse the war. I know you don't want to see her lose. And we both know Jonrell wouldn't either."

Kroke relaxed ever so slightly and put away the blade in his hand. "I'm listening."

"I need you to watch Elyse. Everywhere she goes, I want you there. Whatever we accomplish in the field will be useless if someone kills her first. I know you won't allow that."

"What did she say about this?"

"I haven't told her yet. But I'm not worried about her reaction. I know you get along. It will do her some good to have a friend nearby, someone who is not looking to advance their station like all the other nobles around here."

"No argument there."

"So are we settled?"

Kroke nodded. "We're settled. I'll stay. Just don't screw things up while I'm gone or we may have to revisit this conversation."

* * *

Kroke left Kaz's room confused. He still hated the man, but strangely enough, he found himself respecting him too. That only muddled his thoughts further.

He had been looking forward to leaving Lyrosene in the morning, hoping the distance from the queen would clear his head and allow him to focus on what he needed to do. But now Kaz had taken away that refuge of war, and rather than distancing him from Elyse, he was going to shadow her every move.

To be her friend.

He couldn't decide how he truly felt about those orders.

And that scared him.

Kroke pulled out a knife and flipped it in his hand as he walked.

If I don't kill something soon, I'm going to go crazy.

* * *

"Stay focused, Yorn. Your right side is faltering again."

The green mage cast a scowl at Krytien. "I'm doing the best I can."

"Then you need to do better. I don't have a lot of time to teach you how to fight as a unit in combat." He pointed to a group of yellow mages. "Tighten your circle. There are too many gaps in your formation."

"What do you mean? They're fine," said Janik.

Krytien's hand shot out and tendrils of sorcery snaked toward the various mages on the training ground. It seeped through their defenses and as it did, several forgot themselves and ducked. The sorcery struck Yorn in the chest, knocking him to the ground.

Krytien stalked up to the mages who stared uneasily at him and then at Janik. He reached the green robe mage. "Now do you think they were fine?"

Lufflin came barging up beside Krytien. "What in the name of the One Above is the matter with you? You could have killed him!"

"Yes! I could have! And I could have killed you too as you cowered down next to him. The only one who stood their ground and took this exercise seriously was Nora." Krytien watched Lufflin shoot her a look. The girl averted her eyes, almost ashamed for her efforts.

Too bad that she seeks his approval. There is a lot of potential there. Though they all have potential if they would just listen to me. Lufflin even has a great technical understanding of things. He just has trouble applying the theory.

"Who do you think you are?" asked Janik as he helped Yorn to his feet.

"I'm the one trying to ensure you don't get killed. Tomalt's mages won't be as gentle as I was."

"You never studied at Estul. You weren't a student of Amcaro," fired back Lufflin.

"No, I wasn't."

"Your methods break every rule we've ever been taught," said Lufflin.

"That's because there are no rules in war. You do whatever it takes to get the job done. Amcaro was a great mage who lived for hundreds of years, but he saw very little battle."

"But he studied under Sacrynon before he went mad. Sacrynon helped Aurnon the First conquer all of Cadonia and Thurum. Who else would have been a better teacher?" Janik said.

"Yes, and Amcaro taught us as Sacrynon taught him," added Yorn.

"Theory and practical use are two different things. The sooner you learn that, the better we'll all be. Theory goes out the window when the man across from you is actually trying to kill you. Or when you see the men you were working to protect, die because you failed." Krytien's voice had taken on a solemn tone as he thought over the countless battles of his life. The battle at Asantia stayed with him the longest. "Trust me, you don't want to know that feeling."

An eerie silence hung in the air. Krytien cleared his throat. "Go. Get some rest. But be ready to work on this tomorrow while we travel."

* * *

Alone in his tent, Krytien rubbed the ache out of his tired legs and sipped from a cup of wine. The frustration of dealing with the young mages had worn him down.

And it's only beginning.

He understood their trepidation. After all, they had once studied under the best. Krytien got up from bed and went over to the table in the corner. He opened the bag he had packed earlier and pulled out a small, red leather book.

Despite all he told Drake about not wanting to read anything by Amcaro, he couldn't help himself from taking the private journal of the High Mage. Krytien had discovered Amcaro's personal quarters. It had only taken him a few moments to break down the security wards after figuring out their pattern.

Krytien stared at the book lying flat on the table top. Though he had taken it with the intent to learn more about Amcaro, Krytien had yet to work up the nerve to crack it open. However, he finally had the nudge he needed. He had trained other mages before, but never any so young and stubborn. He wondered if the man he had once looked up to had ever felt as discouraged as he did.

* * *

Drake pawed at his eyes with the palms of his hands, but when he removed them his vision still blurred. He blinked at the pages and slowly the words came back into focus. He knew he should get some sleep. He'd have to wake in a couple hours as the army exited the city. Still, he hadn't gone as far in his research as he had hoped. He had been too busy dealing with Raker's continuing downward spiral to focus on the texts before him.

I hope Kaz is right and he gets better once we get on the road.

Drake had already passed some helpful bits of information on to Kaz, especially a few items related to the works of General Victas of the Quoron Empire. He gave one text that focused less on his military exploits and more on his diplomacy to Elyse. He still had much more to get through in regards to military strategy, general politics, and other miscellaneous items before he would be able to look over the books he took from Estul Island on a hunch. Some of those dealt with ancient sciences, others lost cultures and geography, and a few more random items that just looked interesting.

He rubbed his eyes again. *Just a few more pages, then I'll go to bed.*

The door swung open and sent a gust of wind through the room that rustled the pages. Drake turned as Lufflin barged in.

"You idiot. Be more careful with those pages," he said.

"You're the one who barged in."

"I assumed you had the sense to get some rest for a change. Apparently a lack of brains is common in your little mercenary group."

Drake smiled to himself. "Krytien work you too hard?"

Lufflin growled. "Shut up. Put the book away and leave." He plopped down on his cot and rolled onto his back.

"In a little while. I'm not finished."

"I say you are. This is my room and I'm tired. One Above knows that this is the only chance I have to get any peace from you or that idiot mage."

"Now you know how I feel," Drake mumbled.

"What was that?" snapped Lufflin as he sat up.

"Nothing. Just getting my things together."

* * *

Kaz woke with a start and sat up in bed. Sweat covered his body head-to-toe. The sheets lay bunched in a ball next to him, torn in spots. In a fit of anger, he threw the sheets to the floor.

Glimpses of what had been his past had begun to haunt his dreams more frequently than before. Between the nightmares and the random traces of memories that flashed in his mind during the day, Kaz struggled not to take his anger and frustration out on his men.

He faced pressure everywhere he turned. Everyone counted on him to be an ideal he didn't know if he could live up to. However, Kaz felt no greater pressure than what he put on himself. If the small memories he had could be trusted, he couldn't allow himself to be that man again.

Kaz looked out his window toward the low hanging moon. Dawn was still hours away, but he climbed out of bed all the same. The lingering fears from his dream would prevent him from getting anymore sleep tonight.

I've got too much to do anyway, he thought as he dressed.

* * *

Dressed in full armor, columns of soldiers paraded down the streets of Lyrosene. Crowds of people sent them off with supportive cheers. Children waved at the passing men, some pointing as they recognized fathers or brothers in the ranks. Women watched and wiped away tears.

Elyse could feel her own eyes welling as she sat mounted near the city's gate. She worked to keep her emotions at bay, smiling and waving as the army marched out over the open road. She needed to be strong.

The clattering sound of supply wagons announced the end of the long columns. Kaz had disagreed with the parade, or 'spectacle' as he called it, wanting to move out before dawn in the most efficient way possible.

Another thing we disagreed on. She saw a few soldiers wipe away the redness in their eyes as they passed under the portcullis. *The men need to know how much we care for them.*

She turned out toward the expansive countryside where the army snaked south across the winding road. A lone horseman rode up the lines toward Elyse. Kaz's helm rested on the horn of his saddle and the sun shone brightly off his scalp. She felt her stomach tighten as he approached. They hadn't spoken since Gauge had interrupted them. Kaz had ridden out at the army's head earlier that morning and, other than a formal bow from the saddle, had made no move to speak with her. The gesture had tugged at her heart, knowing like any other soldier he could die and never return.

She held her breath as he pulled in beside her. "Your Majesty," he said, bowing. "Can we speak in private?"

Elyse turned to either side, dismissing her personal guard. Kroke who now accompanied her moved out of earshot with them.

"You wished to say something, Commander?"

"Your Highness. Elyse," he whispered her name. "I didn't want to leave . . ." he started, trying to find the right words.

". . . on such poor terms?" she said, finishing his thoughts.

"Yes."

"Nor did I."

Kaz cleared his throat. "I wanted you to know that I will not support Illyan any longer. I should trust your judgment as you trust mine."

"Thank you. That means a lot to me."

They sat waiting, each appearing unsure what to say next. The last supply wagon rolled by and the roaring crowd quieted. People shuffled along the cobbled streets as they went about their business.

"I don't want to keep you from your duty," said Elyse finally.

Kaz looked around and nodded. "Do you have any last orders?" he asked.

"Yes," she said. "Be careful. And come back. I've already lost so much," she croaked and turned her head away, surprised she admitted such a thing.

Kaz reached out and touched her hand. "I will always come back." He turned her hand over and opened it. He placed the head of a small single flower into her palm and closed her fingers around it. Elyse saw what looked like a smile as he wheeled his mount around and rode back toward his army.

CHAPTER 13

Weeks of traversing the unforgiving southern forests had not been part of Tobin's original plan. Each day his army covered less ground than the day before, fighting for every inch against Charu's staged ambushes and other traps the land offered.

Though Tobin expected the guerilla tactics of Charu's smaller forces, the Blue Island Clan forces still eroded under the constant assault. Even though they inflicted more punishment than they suffered, Tobin knew he could not continue with their current path.

Walor rode up. The horses had once been part of the Yellow Plain Clan and so far had done them little more than suck up resources. The terrain had not been ideal for any extended use of cavalry.

"Charu's waiting atop the next rise with a large host," said Walor.

"He's been funneling us here then." He swore. Tobin looked over his shoulder at the thousands of men behind him and the miles of land they had covered. "And we can't fall back to more favorable ground without him harassing us."

"The Kifzo wouldn't understand another withdrawal, regardless of your decision behind it."

"I know. But winning under these circumstances could hurt us later."

Tobin usually would only be so open with Nachun, but he knew he could trust Walor.

Walor pointed north. "Can we skirt around their position and come at them from a different angle? It would not be a retreat."

Tobin shook his head. "No. The maps show that land isn't suited to handle a host of our size. We'd have to leave most of our mounts and carts behind to make the trip and then split our forces."

"So then we attack?"

"Yes. Let's finalize our plan."

* * *

The place of battle favored the defenders in every way—a wide, gradually ascending mound of rich black dirt, wet from a recent rain. Outcroppings of gray rock and random berry bushes littered the slope. Hard pines with low branches flanked the hill.

Tobin decided that crossbowmen positioned behind several lines of heavy infantry would be effective as the trajectory of their arrows could avoid the hanging tree limbs. He hated how limited his options had become under the circumstances, and wondered why he ever agreed with Soyjid's route to Feruse. He took solace in knowing that Nachun's improvements to their weaponry would make up for his men's vulnerable position.

And then it will just be a battle of wills.

"By your command, Warleader," said Walor.

"Give the signal."

Walor complied and soldiers began a slow, disciplined march up the rise, heavy boots sloshing and popping in the mud.

The enemy waited patiently some two hundred yards away.

"Tell the shamans to begin," said Tobin.

Walor relayed the message and moments later a strong wind pushed against Tobin's back and toward Charu's lines. Fire and some of the more aggressive sorcerous attacks would not do in such a wooded area. Tobin hoped the wind would reduce the effectiveness of Charu's archers.

Shortly afterward, a gust of air pushed against Tobin's face and he knew Charu's shamans now worked against his own. Arrows followed, cascading down toward his men. The Blue Island Clan's shields went up and projectiles bounced away with little effect.

"That was easier than I expected. If the ground were more favorable, we'd be susceptible to a cavalry charge though," said Walor.

"Charu doesn't have horseman with enough skill to effectively take advantage of that in this muck." Tobin glanced over his shoulder where thousands of horses and warriors that had once been part of the Yellow Plain Clan waited. "And given the angle of the hill, we can't use ours either."

The Blue Island Clan's advance continued despite the constant battering of spear and arrow.

"Does Soyjid have the Gray Marsh Clan in position?" asked Tobin.

"Yes. He's leading his men north toward the rock face. If he gets there quickly, he should be able to harass Charu's lines." Walor paused. "I wish you would have let someone else take that role. You admitted yourself that he didn't have to lead his men in order to contribute."

"He won't be at the front, and it was something he desired to do."

Walor did not respond.

The Blue Island Clan's crossbowmen began firing into Charu's lines. They proved more effective than Charu's archers as enemy warriors fell and rolled downhill. Their smaller wooden shields failed to provide the same level of protection as the wider steel-lined shields Tobin's men carried.

A ram horn sounded as the third flight of quarrels sped upward.

The enemy braced as the Blue Island Clan's lines crashed against theirs with spear and sword. Clashing steel rang out. Enemy javelins sailed over the lines and skidded off the raised shields of Tobin's men.

Though Charu's army had flung their weight behind the initial push, they could not penetrate Tobin's ranks.

The Blue Island Clan's lines heaved and took the first step forward. A moment later, they took another. Slowly, his men inched upward.

Tobin noticed a lone figure on horseback at the top of the rise. A personal bodyguard of warriors and shamans surrounded him as the man shouted and gestured wildly with his hands.

"Charu looks upset," said Walor.

Tobin smiled. "He should be. The Red Mountain Clan was said to have better warriors than this."

"They aren't fighting men barely out of the cold waves now."

* * *

Charu swore loudly.

Gidan joined him. "One of your fears has come true, Warchief. The Green Forest Clan's lack of discipline has rubbed off on our men."

Though he never intended on winning the war today, Charu hated seeing his forces beaten so handily. "I knew it was a risk to keep so many of our best units at the Green Forest Clan's capital."

"It was a calculated risk. I too thought our regular infantry could better stand against Tobin's men. Should we bring in the reserves?"

Charu watched his captains work to bring order to their lines. The enemy's weapons, something called crossbows, had been far more effective than his archers.

Just when I think I have their strength gauged, they surprise me.

"No. Have them start organizing a withdrawal. We aren't trying to stop them today as much as we are trying to slow them. Bring up our remaining shamans and their beasts. Tell them to wait for the horn blow to begin their attack."

Gidan's eyes widened. "Yes, Warchief."

Gidan moved to leave when Charu called out. "One more thing, General. Send a small force of Green Forest Clan archers to the rock formation just north of us."

Gidan looked confused by the command, but nodded and set off about his tasks.

Charu grabbed the attention of a half dozen messengers nearby. "Alert the captains to make lanes for the shamans when they hear the horn again. Let them know that anyone in the way will get trampled."

* * *

"What's Charu doing?" asked Walor. He held a hand over his eyes, shielding the rays of sunlight piercing the canopy.

The man and his bodyguard didn't fall back as Tobin would have thought, but instead simply moved off to the side.

A horn blast sounded.

"Must be bringing in his reserves to add weight to his front lines," said Tobin. He smiled knowing he had no need to reinforce his own men.

Deep roars like a blade being raked across rough stone cut through the sounds of battle.

"What was that?" asked Walor.

Tobin shook his head. He watched lanes form in the back ranks of Charu's men. The Red Mountain Clan horn boomed once more and the roars followed, much louder than before.

Massive brown blurs crested the rise, answering Walor's question. Thirty giant brown bears, between twelve and fifteen feet tall at the shoulder, heaved themselves toward Tobin's men. Shamans sat atop each animal, trying to control the beasts.

The bears mauled the staunch lines of the Blue Island Clan, carving through the heavy infantry. Warriors were flung into the air. The Red and Green Clan warriors flowed into the gaps made by the beasts and set to work on Tobin's broken ranks.

Tobin whipped his reins, galloping toward the shamans at the foot of the hill, behind his lines. "Take those things down!"

"Warleader, their shamans have some sort of barrier protecting them," said one shaman.

"Then ignore the bears. Focus on one shaman at a time by attacking in groups," he growled. "Have you become useless without Nachun here?"

"No, Warleader." He quickly relayed the message to the others. Tobin kicked his mount uphill. Climbing toward the nearest bear, he tossed aside his own men to reach the beast. As he unsheathed his sword, sorcery arced over his head. The shaman atop the bear burst apart into bits of flesh and bone.

Tobin brought his feet up and in one fluid motion launched himself forward. He sailed toward the massive creature as it stood on its hind legs. Tobin's blade sank into the creature's chest and a paw swatted him away. His armor protected him from the worst of the bear's massive claws, but he still crashed into the hard shields of the men beneath him. The bear staggered, trying to remove the sword with his mouth, but could not. It collapsed a moment later and warriors hacked away to ensure it would not rise again.

A fierce chorus of elation erupted from his men. He pulled free the throwing axes at his belt, and led them against the next animal.

*   *   *

Charu watched in awe as the giant bears barreled past him. The musk and savagery of the creatures hung in the air. He felt relieved as the last of the beasts cleared the rise and joined the battle. His shamans had managed to cull them two days ago and spent a great deal of energy keeping them subdued.

The shamans maneuvered the giant animals between the opening lanes. As expected, some of his men suffered from their lack of haste.

The Blue Island Clan's warriors did not even flinch as the bears approached. Charu's respect and hatred for them grew. He could not understand how warriors could be trained so thoroughly. Yet for all the Blue Island Clan's skill and courage, they could not withstand the full force of the animals at impact.

Charu's captains followed the beasts' charge and pressed into the Blue Clan forces, finally inflicting damage on the fractured lines. His men died, but Tobin's died in scores. A war of attrition would be his best chance to achieve victory.

And it's working, he thought as blue and gray armored soldiers sailed through the air with each sweeping bear arm.

One of his shamans exploded before his eyes. The riderless bear stood up on hind legs in response, suddenly aware and confused by its situation. A warrior who had worked a horse through the tangled mass of soldiers launched himself through the air.

Tobin.

Against anything else, the man might have dominated the scene, but against the bear, the warrior looked insignificant flying toward the creature like some annoying insect. Tobin managed to impale the beast with his sword a moment before a paw tossed him aside. The animal struggled for only a few seconds and fell dead.

The Blue Island Clan warriors cheered as Tobin fought among them. Two more of Charu's shamans died.

Charu leaned into the shaman next to him. "Tell the others to leave the bears behind and withdraw."

The shaman closed his eyes as he relayed the message to the field. Even without someone directing their movements, the bears would maim and kill. Charu pressed the massive ram horn to his lips and blew four quick blasts to sound the full retreat while the Blue Island Clan reeled.

The shaman next to him opened his eyes and Charu gave him a final command before moving up the trail. "Stay with the others in our rear and mask our retreat. See that we're able to put some distance between us and the Blue Island Clan army."

The red-robed man bowed. "It will be done, Warchief."

* * *

Tobin yanked his sword free of the pungent bear carcass—the first he had killed. The battle had ended and his enemy had retreated, leaving the Blue Island Clan to bring down the massive beasts rather than pursue them. Blood covered Tobin's arms and torso. Sweat hung from his nose.

He tried to wipe the dripping sweat, but the back of his hand only smeared crimson across his face. Tobin took a deep breath, hoping to clear his mind and still his racing heart. He gagged on the smell of fresh gore.

"Warleader."

Ufer favored his right side. Tobin saw a streak of blood near his rib cage.

"Do you need a healer?" asked Tobin.

"It can wait. I have an early estimate."

"How many?"

"We lost two thousand men."

Tobin swore. "And them?"

"Closer to four."

They suffered more and we gained the field. So, why do I feel like we lost.

Tobin gazed out as men searched for survivors. Those too far gone had their screams silenced with a blade to the throat. *An honorable death.*

"We cannot afford to keep fighting like this," said Tobin.

"No. We can't. Not when Charu keeps escaping from us," said Ufer.

Walor walked up scowling deeply. "Where was Soyjid during this? If his men had flanked Charu as planned, they would have been unable to retreat." He gestured with his hand at the bear carcass. "We could have pursued them after finishing off these nightmares. He needs to answer for this."

Soyjid?

In the aftermath of battle, he had forgotten about the boy leader.

"Walor is right, Warleader. How is he any better than Mawkuk? You need to dissolve their army, incorporate those who will not cause any problems into our ranks, and then send the rest back to Cypronya."

Tobin squeezed his hands into fists. "I'll consider the suggestion. Get word out that Soyjid is to see me immediately."

* * *

"You wanted to see me?"

Tobin looked up as the tent flap parted and Soyjid strode through it. A spray of blood caked the oversized breastplate he wore and mud covered his boots. A sheen of sweat sat on his forehead.

So he ended up close to the action after all.

"Tell me everything and do not leave out any details."

Soyjid nodded and began his tale. His regiment circled around north as planned. However, the terrain was worse than originally thought as they climbed piles of rock. Charu had positioned what Soyjid estimated to be a thousand men from the Green Forest Clan at the top of a cliff face. The angle was much steeper than what Tobin had dealt with and Soyjid could do little but wait and avoid the hail of arrows.

Eventually, Soyjid noticed the Green Forest Clan slipping away in pieces and he made his move. They rushed the position in a sweeping mass once they knew it to be undermanned. By that point the enemy's numbers had deteriorated to the point where Soyjid only lost a handful of men. They killed only a hundred of the Green Forest Clan with no prisoners taken.

He had been ready to rip into Soyjid, but after hearing the facts better understood the situation.

Tobin drank from a skin of water during the report and gnawed on a piece of bread. He felt lightheaded for some reason. Even after a day of fighting, the sensation felt peculiar.

When Soyjid finished, Tobin nodded. "You did well, given the circumstances."

"Your commanders don't feel that way, do they?"

Tobin rubbed his temples and then shrugged. "It matters little what they think. They aren't warleader."

* * *

Confident that Tobin would not immediately pursue his retreating forces, Charu finally moved toward the front of his army. He rode past limping soldiers covered in blood who looked up with tired eyes to salute their warchief. He gave each man a small nod or gesture to acknowledge their effort.

He passed shaking supply wagons creaking over the uneven dirt and stone path the army tread upon. Muffled screams preceded carts carrying the dying where healers hacked away at mangled limbs and shamans rushed to close oozing wounds.

Charu found Melat at the head of the column. She had her head down and her face a mask of sorrow. A loud grunt came from one of the carts carrying the wounded, causing her to flinch at the noise.

"Are you alright?" he asked, reining in beside her.

She smiled. "Now I am. You're here." She looked over her shoulder. "It's just a lot to take in. There were wounded before today, but never so many." She lowered her voice, concerned. "Was the latest letter inaccurate?"

"No. The information was helpful. But the tides of battle cannot be predicted. Once the pieces are in place, anything can happen. And you can't have war without dying. Tobin's men suffered as well."

Melat sighed. "Well, I guess that's something."
"No. It's everything."

CHAPTER 14

Elyse scanned Olasi's most recent letter. As usual, the duke began by discussing matters of war. She enjoyed learning from his perspective, and at times found herself rereading his insight. However, it was the personal touch Olasi closed each letter with that meant the most to her. Despite the distance separating them, she felt a genuine connection to the old duke. Just like at her father's funeral, following Jonrell's death, Olasi's concern and sincere condolences helped ease her heavy heart. Since then, their communication included personal matters along with those of the kingdom. He closed this letter with a brief mention of his health.

And even though it seems he isn't feeling well, the emphasis is on his recovery, not on his current state.

She set the letter down as a sigh passed through her lips. She no longer had the distraction of Olasi's letter to take her mind off the morning.

Elyse had given Lobella the morning off and in hindsight probably shouldn't have. Today would be the first council meeting since the army had marched out of Lyrosene several days before. She had wanted time to collect her thoughts alone.

She had plenty of time to think the night before, sleeping little as morning inched ever closer. In the first few days since the army's departure, she had busied herself with meetings and other tasks that needed tending in order to take her mind off her worries. The strategy worked for a time, but by avoiding her feelings, it only made the night before the council meeting that much harder.

She had lain awake thinking of the soldiers she had come to know while making rounds with Kaz, especially Jonrell's Hell Patrol. Lyrosene had been eerily quiet since their departure and it became apparent to her now just how much she missed them. The sun had cleared the horizon moments ago and she realized she also missed the sounds of men and women training in the yard below.

She wondered how long it would be before she'd be able to once again enjoy innocent conversations with Drake, the cackle of Hag, or the sage advice of Wiqua and Krytien. She missed Grayer's stoic nature, the sound of

Yanasi pushing her men to perfection and even Raker's crude comments. Most of all, she missed Kaz.

Elyse's stomach tightened as she finished dressing in a simple gown and did up her hair. She looked herself over one last time in the long stand-up mirror and sighed. Bags hung heavy under her eyes.

But then again, everyone should be used to seeing me like this.

She pivoted on her heel and strode to the door. She opened it to find Kroke waiting in the same position she had left him in the night before.

He inclined his head with a silent question and she answered with a deep breath and a small nod. He set out before her and Elyse followed.

* * *

Kroke glanced up over his shoulder and looked at the queen while she sat behind the raised half-wall of the council chambers. With her head down, Elyse rubbed the bridge of her nose between forefinger and thumb. She looked up and tried to hide her thoughts. But she couldn't hide the flexing cords in her neck or the tension filling her face. He didn't know what exactly ran through her mind, but he had an idea. His own shoulders bunched from the sneers and condescending looks cast his way.

I'd just as soon kill them all.

Only one of Elyse's advisors had even bothered to meet Kroke's eye since he entered the chamber. The short man with curly hair had even given him a slight, sincere bow that caught Kroke off guard. If he didn't know Elyse hated the man, Kroke might have even returned the gesture with a nod.

Nearly two hours into the meeting, Kroke wondered if it would ever end. His head pounded from the commotion of Elyse's advisors as they tried to make their voices heard above others.

Some minor lords near the border of Tomalt's territory raised a fuss over armies decimating their land and possessions in the prior year's campaign. After months of pleading their case, they had finally won a chance to bring the matter before the queen. The lords expected the crown to compensate them for their losses.

As Kroke watched Elyse fight a dreary look, Gauge did his best to handle the situation. "We are at war," said Gauge. "The crown cannot afford to ease the strain of every person affected by it."

"I am not asking that the crown offer aid to everyone," said one of the advisors.

"No," said the other in an accusatory tone to the first advisor. "You only expect our queen to aid the lords you serve while ignoring the others."

"Again," said Gauge. "It is impossible—"

Elyse interrupted in a weary voice. "Gauge, see that we reimburse the lords represented here at half the market value of their land. That should account for any crops or structures lost in the series of battles along the border."

"But Your Majesty," started Gauge. "That is too much."

"I say it isn't enough, Your Majesty," said the first advisor.

Kroke saw that the man would never be satisfied and since Elyse had caved in, he would push for more.

"The lords I represent have contributed twice the amount of foodstuffs and men to the queen's army than anyone else in the area. It only stands to reason that they be given twice the compensation."

"That's ridiculous. The quality of the goods and men the lords I represent provided to the crown were thrice the quality of yours. Should we not then receive three times the amount of anyone else?" said the other advisor.

"Now hold on," said Gauge.

Elyse shot up from her chair like an arrow. "Enough!" A wave of silence washed over the drab chamber. Kroke had never seen Elyse look as she did, nostrils flared and eyes narrowed at the two men cowering below their queen. "How dare you squabble over such things at a time like this? You speak of men that were sent to the army, yet when is the last time that any of you prayed that the One Above might spare their lives and end this conflict peaceably? People are marching to their deaths and you argue over whether you should receive more money than your neighbor? Who gave you the right?"

The question hung in the air for a moment until the first advisor cleared his throat. His whispering voice contrasted to the tone he had used only minutes before. "I beg your pardon, Your Majesty, but in a way you gave us this right. Aurnon the First set up the government to operate in this manner and for generations those in my position have sought to do what we can for those we represent." He looked over to the advisor next to him. "I apologize if we got carried away, but I assure you it was not our intent to disrespect those men who are fighting for the kingdom. I cannot speak personally for the lords I represent but I know that each day I do indeed pray to the One Above for their success and in turn, yours." He paused and raised his head. "Again, I mean no disrespect, Your Majesty, but why should I not fight for the livelihood of the men I represent just as you fight for the livelihood of the kingdom?"

Kroke watched Elyse meet the gaze of the rest of her council. After circling the room, her gaze settled on him and her eyes widened. He flinched and quickly scanned the room, sure he must have missed something. The gasps continued as the rest of the nobles turned in his direction.

"Kroke, please put those away," said Elyse.

Kroke looked down and realized that he held two of his more wicked daggers in his hands. One was the long blade he took from the sailor on Estul Island. The other was a jagged, curved blade with an eagle shaped pommel that Jonrell had given him more than a decade ago. He usually pulled that particular blade when he felt most threatened.

He looked around at the piercing stares and disapproval cast toward him and his hands began to tingle. He gripped the blades tighter as he felt his mind empty. Although he didn't remember drawing the blades, he knew it had to do with the hostile atmosphere of the chamber.

I should just kill them all and be done with it. That would make things easier on everyone, especially Elyse. He seethed in anger.

"Kroke! Put. Those. Away." Elyse repeated.

The queen's voice had taken on a scolding tone and he felt suddenly self-conscious. He sheathed his weapons. Elyse lowered her head as she rubbed at her temple again.

I only made matters worse.

"My lords and ladies, I'm sorry," said Elyse.

The first advisor looked to Kroke and forced a nervous grin. "No need to apologize, Your Majesty. It was just a misunderstanding. That's all."

"Perhaps," came a loud voice. "we can drop this matter altogether for today. We are all obviously distressed. I'm sure others would agree that the best course of action would be to finish these discussions at a later time."

All heads turned to Illyan and Kroke saw Gauge struggle with his words. "That isn't a terrible idea," he said, begrudgingly. "Any opposed?"

Silence.

"Then dismissed."

* * *

Elyse jumped as Kroke cleared his throat. She walked along in such a daze after exiting the council meeting, she had forgotten him.

"I . . . wasn't trying to cause any problems," said Kroke.

He isn't used to this. Kaz was on edge in those meetings as well. Though they were more cautious around him than they were with Kroke. I guess they see the difference in size and assume Kroke is not as threatening. If only they knew.

"I know," she said finally. A sigh followed. "Neither was I."

"I don't understand. I was the one who made everyone uncomfortable."

Elyse shook her head. "No one is completely comfortable in there. Some may seem more at ease than others, but trust me, everyone is working to undermine someone else in an effort to grasp at any morsel of power dangling in front of them."

"It seems like those two men were doing more than that."

"Perhaps, but they weren't anything compared to Phasin or Illyan." She paused. "I overreacted and did exactly what I didn't want to do. Exactly what people like Illyan want me to do as it gives them something else to use against me when garnering support from the others."

They took a sharp right and walked up a flight of stairs. "Do you ever wish you could be doing something else with your life?" Elyse asked.

Kroke flinched at the question. "I'm not sure I understand."

"I guess what I mean is, what would you want to do if you weren't in the Hell Patrol?"

"I'm not sure," said Kroke after a pause. "This life or some version of it is all I've known since I was a boy. I don't know if I'd be good at anything else."

"I see."

"Do you ever wish to be doing something else?"

All the time. But you wouldn't understand. The life I want is probably the farthest thing from your mind.

"Yes, but it doesn't matter, does it?" They turned another corner and she forced a smile as Kroke waited for her to elaborate. "I'm sorry I asked the question. Come, Gillian is waiting for me to discuss matters of the castle." She picked up her pace, hoping to leave her troubles behind.

CHAPTER 15

Elyse walked down the long hallway in anticipation of her next appointment. Kroke walked out front, Gauge at her side. A sense of unease hung over her as she contemplated the most recent council meetings. They had been shorter and less tedious.

Something just seems off, but I can't put my finger on what it is.

"Gauge, have you noticed the change in the council?"

"Yes, Your Majesty."

"What do you think is the cause?"

Gauge cleared his throat. "Well, uh. . . I thought it was obvious, Your Majesty."

Elyse thought for a moment. "Do you mean because I lost my temper?"

Gauge shook his head, then gestured with a nod toward Kroke as they crossed through the long hallway. The mercenary's eyes darted about, searching every passing hallway, door, or window.

"Kroke is the reason for the change?" asked Elyse.

As if on cue, the mercenary whipped out a knife and began twirling it in his hand, seemingly oblivious to Elyse and Gauge's discussion. At one time Kroke's habits had annoyed her, but lately the repetitiveness of his quirks brought her a surprising comfort.

Gauge leaned in to whisper. "Well, many have expressed a certain level of discomfort at having him in council."

Elyse kept her voice low as she responded. "That doesn't make sense. Why would he make anyone more uncomfortable than Kaz?"

"I beg your pardon, Your Majesty, but Kaz kept himself presentable. He had a hard look, but he carried a certain amount of . . ." he lowered his voice further, ". . . civility that Kroke lacks. Frankly, he scares many of the council. Most are worried that if they say something wrong, it could be their end."

"And how do you feel about him?"

"What is there to say? He seems like someone who is good at what he does." Gauge noticeably shivered as if caught by a chill. "Still, he does make me uneasy. And honestly, I don't like the fact that he's always with you. I truly wish you would let me replace him with a bodyguard more trustworthy."

"Absolutely not," Elyse snapped, offended by Gauge's tone. She remembered the hardships she had endured on the road to Ithanthul and knew that without Kroke she would be dead. "Kaz left him to guard me. There are few people I feel safer with than Kroke. And might I add that it was he who protected me from my last set of bodyguards. People you felt were *trustworthy*."

Elyse had done her best to look into Hadan and Willum's betrayal, but even with the help of Kaz, they failed to learn who the two bodyguards had taken their orders from.

Gauge grunted as he tripped over his words. "Yes, of course. I only have your best interests, Your Majesty. And again, I cannot apologize enough for Hadan and Willum's treachery. I'm sorry I was never able to locate who they received their orders from."

They continued down the long corridor in an awkward silence.

* * *

Echoing footsteps and the rustling of Elyse's long gown filled the winding corridor. Elyse and Gauge had assumed Kroke couldn't hear their hushed voices, but they might well have been shouting from the rooftops.

The advisors' worries Gauge spoke of didn't surprise him. Kroke saw every disdainful look and heard every sly comment cast his way.

And he remembered them all.

Kroke privately wished one would be stupid enough to try something against him, if only so he could recount their offenses as he carved them up.

He almost felt sympathy for Kaz after spending the past couple weeks shadowing Elyse.

The confusing emotions he felt for Kaz only escalated when he thought about Elyse's response to Gauge's concerns. Kroke rarely ever heard her use such a tone when speaking to anyone. It held a certain grit, taking on an edge that reminded Kroke of Jonrell. He wondered if her emerald eyes had narrowed and took on a different color like Jonrell's gray eyes so often had when he made a point.

And she did that for me?

He shook his head. Few people had ever stood up for Kroke and all of them had been in the Hell Patrol.

He thought about Elyse as his mind drifted to places he had done his best to avoid in the waking hours.

He cursed, shaking away the thoughts.

* * *

"Finally, a moment of peace," said Elyse as she threw herself onto her bed.

Soft footsteps padded up beside her. Lobella sat on her bed. "Is everything alright?"

Elyse sat up and rubbed her temple. "Yes. It's just been a long day." She stood up and began undoing her dress. Lobella helped her. As she stepped out of her gown, Elyse yawned.

"Will you be going to bed right away?" asked Lobella.

Elyse sighed. "No, I still have some reading I wanted to do. Drake left several books with me before the army left. I'm hoping to find something in them that might help my worries."

Lobella smiled. "If not, I'm sure things will find a way to work out."

"It's what I pray for each night."

"Me too," said Lobella in a distant voice. She put away Elyse's dress. "Will there be anything else?"

"I can't think of anything. Enjoy your night."

"I will."

Elyse sat at her desk and opened a book as the door closed. She found her place from the night before and started to read, but her mind began to wander as she eyed the flower Kaz had given her at the gates of Lyrosene. It sat in a thin vase at the edge of her desk.

"I'll always come back," he had told her.

* * *

Kroke watched Elyse's servant glide down the hall with her head down. The blonde had caught his eye on more than one occasion, though she wasn't really Kroke's type.

Too timid.

He leaned back in his chair and rested his head against the cool stone wall. He'd be stiff in the morning again, but saw little alternative to his position. He wasn't about to stop looking after Elyse simply because of nightfall. Since only one door led to the queen's chambers, he took up residence there.

Besides, it's not like I can sleep in her room.

A flood of thoughts that Kroke had tried to circumvent all day came at him. He swore under his breath.

CHAPTER 16

Even after several weeks on the march, Kaz continued to push the army's pace. In his mind, they were behind schedule. First, Krytien took longer than planned when returning from Estul Island. Then Elyse's grand departure from Lyrosene cost them another day. He understood, but disagreed with her reasons for the fanfare.

The soldiers know they may not make it back. No need to remind them of what they're leaving behind.

He had seen too many hard men shed a tear as loved ones reached out to them during their departure. The images filled him with his own conflicting emotions. Anger, because his men would show their emotions so easily. Sorrow, because Kaz knew they had every right to do that. Jealousy, because they had something they loved so dearly.

To help remove those thoughts from his soldier's minds as well as his own, Kaz maintained an almost frantic tempo for the two days that followed their departure from Lyrosene. By the end of the second day, the army's demeanor changed into the hardness he knew they would need in the months to come.

After they crossed the Tyreseos River, smaller raiding parties began harassing his long columns. The first attack took the army off guard since they were so close to the city of Namaris which was held by the crown. In response, Kaz redistributed his light cavalry with his scouts and moved several companies of Yanasi's bowmen to the back of the columns to better guard the supply lines. At night, he doubled the number of pickets. The attempted raids continued, but never posed any real threat.

Or so I thought.

Kaz called a halt after another attack on the baggage train. From what he gathered, it had been the largest and most calculated strike thus far. He rode to the back of the columns while barking orders to the officers he passed.

Kaz reined in beside General Grayer and Yanasi. Yanasi looked ragged.

"Give me the details," said Kaz.

Grayer saluted. "They had a couple of mages with them this time, Commander. We lost the equivalent of three squads."

"In their entirety?" asked Kaz, his voice rising.

"No Commander, but two of the squads hit will need to be redistributed."

Kaz nodded. He turned to Yanasi. "Captain, what happened?"

"It was like General Grayer said, Sir. We were caught unaware. Their mages concealed their spot in the forest and they waited until the main body passed before striking."

Kaz swore in his native tongue.

Yanasi looked up and cleared her throat. "Sir, I'd like to make a request."

"Go on."

"I want permission to command a platoon of our heavy cavalry along with spare mounts to transport three squads of my archers."

"Is that all?" he asked.

"No, sir. I'll want two of our green mages as well."

"And why should I grant this request?"

"So I can hunt out the remainder of Tomalt's men. I'm sick of them picking us off."

Grayer chimed in. "It's not a bad idea, Commander. The men are growing more frustrated with each attack. They're tired of being targets."

Kaz scowled. "Then I'll need to speak with the officers to get a grip on their men. They can grow frustrated all they want, but they're not to leave the main body and pursue anyone. Not now anyway." He turned to Yanasi. "Captain, your request is denied. Tomalt is trying to hamper our pace and I won't allow him to do so. We'll continue on as before." He met both of their eyes. "I'll see that their raids are taken care of."

Kaz left them without waiting for an answer. The news had put him in a more sour mood than before. He rode to the front of the column where Rygar waited.

"What's your report?"

"All clear for miles around, sir," said Rygar.

Kaz shook his head. "You've missed something. You need to go out again and retrace the same ground."

"But as I said—"

"I heard you. But Tomalt's men just attacked us and used mages to conceal their movements. You missed them, so who's to say you didn't miss anyone ahead? Take Krytien with you and go back out."

"But Krytien's never been very good with a horse. He's liable to slow us down."

"You need his sorcery, not his skills with a horse."

Rygar gave Kaz a hurried salute and left.

* * *

"Pick up the pace, you pieces of garbage! I'm sick of watching each and every one of you move like we're on a stroll through the streets." Raker spat a brown wad and raised the bottle in his hand. He took a long pull at its neck. "Senald! What do you think you're doing? Do I need to put my foot up your rear to wake you up? You know better than to manhandle that piece of equipment."

The mercenary turned, face sour. "I know what I'm doing. We've been running these drills for over a year and a half."

"Then act like it. You look like an amateur. I'd figure by now I could trust you to do something right."

Senald turned back to the equipment and mumbled something under his breath that Raker couldn't make out.

"What did you just say?" asked Raker while taking a step forward.

Senald turned around and threw the rope he held to the ground. "I said I'm surprised you can see anything through that bottle you keep your head in. The only time you take it out is when you're looking to yell at someone."

Raker noticed the sudden silence around them as all eyes turned his way. He spat and took another drink. Raker moved forward, forming a fist. But as he closed in, a hand grabbed him by the arm.

"We need to talk," said Drake.

Raker tore away from Drake's grasp. "Get your hands off me. I'm in the middle of something."

Drake grabbed his arm again. "That's what we need to talk about," he said in a low voice. "Now."

Raker stared down at the kid through narrowed eyes.

Kid's getting too big for himself. I'll humor him this once.

"Fine. Let's take a walk." He turned back to Senald. "Get the rest of the equipment off the wagons. And it better be done right by the time I get back." Senald grunted a response as Raker turned away.

Not even a 'Yes, sir.'

"You better have a good reason for interrupting me like that."

"I do," said Drake. "You need to get a hold of yourself and your drinking."

Raker spat. "You trying to tell me I can't hold my liquor. I can drink anyone here under the table."

"Yeah, that's the problem. You don't know when to stop. All that whiskey is feeding your miserable state of mind."

"Says who? I've always been this way."

"Yeah, but at least before when you'd yell at someone, there was reason behind it. Now, you're just yelling out of spite. Senald's a good soldier and you've got no reason to ride him like you do."

"Don't try to guess the reasons for what I do. You don't know me."

"I know that Jonrell's death affected you harder than you want to admit. His death affected a lot of people, but you don't see others drinking themselves to death."

People cope in their own ways.

But Raker wouldn't admit that to Drake. His eyes narrowed. "Kaz keeps giving you all these projects to do instead of giving them to me. You think that makes you special? I could do most of that stuff too."

"If you weren't always drunk, you could. What are you going to do in the next battle?"

Raker took a drink and pointed at Drake with the bottle. "Don't worry about me. I've been doing this since before you were sucking at your momma's teat. I may drink and I may even be a drunk, but when the fighting starts, I'll be ready."

* * *

Drake stormed off. He just couldn't get through to Raker these days. *Not that it had ever been easy.*

Drake passed by the engineers and gave Senald and the others a word of encouragement. He could see Senald growing more disenfranchised with not only Raker, but the entire Hell Patrol.

I've got to make sure he doesn't quit.

By the time Drake left, the engineers' spirits had lifted, but he couldn't say the same for himself.

He made his way through camp with head down, kicking up dirt with each step. Lost in thought, he failed to notice the giant wall that stepped in front of him until the collision knocked him to the ground.

Drake stared up at Crusher. The giant turned and chuckled. "You need to watch where you're going, kid. You didn't even have a book in your hand this time." The Ghal reached down and yanked Drake to his feet.

"Yeah, yeah. Real funny."

"What's gotten into you?" Drake thought he saw what appeared to be a look of concern on the giant's face.

"Nothing. Look, I've got things to do."

Crusher frowned. "I hope one of them is removing that stick you got shoved up your rear. You're starting to become as sour as the veterans around here."

Drake sulked off without responding.

What do you know? This is all a game to you. You're not even in charge of your own squad. All you have to worry about is taking that big club of yours and knocking over as many men as you can with each swing.

"Drake!" a ragged voice shouted over the noise around him.

Drake saw Hag staring in his direction from the chow line.

"Quit looking at me like I'm a ghost and come over here and get your dinner," she shouted.

"I'm not hungry," Drake yelled back and started to walk away.

Hag pushed aside soldiers in line and waddled into his path, carrying a bowl of stew. She shoved it into his stomach, nearly splashing the contents over him. "I ain't asked you if you were hungry. Now take it and eat! I won't have you lagging behind on the march tomorrow because you're weak from a lack of food."

She left him without waiting for a response and slapped some soldier aside who thought to give her lip for slowing down dinner. Drake's stomach growled as the rising steam reached his nostrils.

I guess I was hungry after all.

He shouted out his thanks, but Hag waved him off and went back to dishing out meals.

Drake ate as he walked to the southern edge of camp, ignoring the bustling activity around him. He settled down on a newly raised mound of dirt. Patrols moved back and forth some hundred yards away. A flickering glow from the dancing campfires behind him cast shadows that stretched into the night. Away from the rowdy games of dice, he finally felt like he had a moment to work things out on his own.

"So, what's bothering you?" asked a voice to Drake's left.

He jumped and whipped his head around. Rygar lay on his back, no more than a few feet away, staring up into the starry sky. "One Above, I didn't even see you there."

"Figured as much. That's why I assumed something was bothering you. This seems to be the place for it."

Drake heard the sad tone in the scout's voice. He reclined on the rough ground and brought his hands over his head. "So, what's eating you?" he asked.

"I asked you first."

Drake blew out a puff of air. "Raker."

"The drinking?"

"It's getting out of hand."

"Yeah, I heard some of the engineers grumbling about him. To be honest, I'm too busy scouting to notice much. Usually when I see him, it's late in the night and he's not the only one drunk then."

"I just wish I knew how to help him get his act together," said Drake. "Since Jonrell died, each day is worse than the day before."

Rygar grunted. "Yeah, Jonrell's death sure made people forget themselves. It wasn't so obvious at first. Everyone was too caught up in the campaign after Cathyrium to dwell on his death, but once we got to Lyrosene for the winter, I guess people had time to think." He sighed. "Now it seems that some people can't stop thinking."

"You mean Yanasi?"

"Yep."

"I was wondering why you weren't with her. No offense, but you two are usually joined at the hip, especially when you make it back to camp after scouting."

"That's generally the truth. Or at least it was. But same as Raker, Yanasi still hasn't moved on from Jonrell's death. She may not be drinking, but I'll wake up in the middle of the night to hear her sobbing next to me. She makes up some excuse, but I'm not dumb. He was like a brother to her. She practically worshipped the man."

"Have you talked to her about it?"

Rygar snorted. "I've tried, but it's no use. One moment she's clinging to me, the next she's pushing me away. Especially since we left Lyrosene. She won't admit it, but I think she feels like I don't understand what she's going through since I didn't know Jonrell as well as she did." He paused. "She's right to a point. I didn't know him as well or as long as others. But that doesn't mean I didn't think he was a good leader or a good man. Besides I've had more than my fair share of losses too. We all have."

"Raker's pretty much the same way when I try to talk to him about it."

"Too bad he and Yanasi can't talk it out themselves," said Rygar.

"I don't know how effective that conversation would be. I'm sure it wouldn't be long before Yanasi would slam her bow between his legs."

The two started laughing. "You're probably right."

Drake felt the weight on his shoulders lighten.

After a moment Rygar asked, "So what are we going to do with them then?"

Drake blew out a chest full of air. "I wish I knew."

* * *

Krytien hobbled through camp. His back ached and so did his rear. The more he thought about it, the more he realized that everything hurt on some level. He wasn't a young man any longer and scouting with Rygar had taken its toll on him.

Kaz did it on purpose just to spite me. Just to make me suffer and just so I'd be out of his way. Well, I've had it with him. We're going to have a talk tonight. Just as soon as I get to my things and take something for this pain.

He headed toward his gear and saw Raker stumble through camp. He had seen the sight many times before, but it struck him that Raker's behavior had grown worse as of late. Krytien debated whether to go after the man when Yanasi's screaming voice caught his attention. Yanasi gestured wildly with her arms as her ponytail whipped about her head. The men of her command stood there with shoulders hunched forward as she carried on.

Krytien glanced back at Raker and saw the engineer sitting at a fire with his bottle as soldiers dealt him into a hand of cards.

He's probably fine.

He turned back to Yanasi as she kicked over a pile a wood.

That situation's a bit more pressing.

* * *

"We're letting too much slip by us. There is no excuse for getting caught off guard like we did today," said Yanasi, pacing up and down a line of her men. She carried her black bow across her back and it bounced against her hip with each step. "We've got to be better. We can't afford any more mistakes."

"But Captain, they had mages cloaking them. There was nothing we could do. Not without a mage of our own."

Yanasi stopped and wheeled on the man. "One Above, Corporal. A mage isn't invincible. And we're no stranger to seeing them in battle. They bleed just like everyone else. We can't use them as an excuse for our mistake. Men died today because we weren't doing our job as we should have. We let our Commander down." Heads dropped as she spoke. Hers did the same. "I let you down. We have to do better and that starts with me. Now eat and get some rest. We're rising an hour before the rest of camp tomorrow morning. We'll run through our drills before hitting the road. It's obvious we're not where I thought we were."

There were several groans as her men shuffled back into camp. Yanasi watched them drudge past. None met her gaze.

"Don't you think you were a bit hard on them?"

Yanasi faced Krytien walking toward her. He brushed back the wisps of white hair that fell into his face. She lowered her face in shame once more. "What do you want me to do? Jonrell always expected the best out of his men."

"Yes, but he also knew when to let up. I think you should do the same."

"But we screwed up today."

"It happens," said Krytien. "And it'll happen again. Learn from it and get better. It won't do them any good to feel even worse about themselves. Nor will it do you any good to keep punishing yourself like you've been doing." He paused. "Maybe I should tell Kaz to redistribute some of your responsibilities to others for awhile."

"No!" said Yanasi, looking up. Krytien flinched which caused her to lower her voice again. "Sorry. It's just that, I want to help. I need to help. Jonrell was finally letting me do more and it felt good. Kaz has done the same. It might sound stupid, but I don't want to let Kaz down. It would be like letting Jonrell down too."

Yanasi started to shake. An arm reached around her and pulled her in tight. She buried her head in Krytien's old robes. "I miss him so much."

"I know," said Krytien. He cleared his throat and she heard the strain in his voice. "We all do."

* * *

"We'll reconvene in the morning then?" asked General Grayer.

Kaz nodded. "I want to talk to you more about the terrain we're heading into. I've noticed some small inconsistencies to the maps we have at our disposal."

"Unfortunately, many are out of date. I'll take a look tonight and make sure there isn't anything that could hamper our plans."

"Until morning then."

Kaz stood at the entrance to the command tent as the old general left. He stared out at his camp. The trenches had been completed long ago and soldiers sat around campfires relaxing and chatting. Grayer had complimented him less than an hour ago on how orderly he ran things. Kaz had simply shrugged. He saw no other way in which a camp should be maintained.

Some of the captains had expressed concern that Kaz had not allowed the normal camp followers to travel with the army. But he didn't care and gave his officers a look that told them the issue had been settled. He refused to allow the whores or sellers of goods to distract marching soldiers.

If they're unable to find comfort in the arms of some whore or the delight in some useless trinket, maybe their frustration will come out on the enemy. The sooner the opponent falls, the sooner they can go back to the real comforts of home.

The thought of home grabbed his thoughts and a flood of small flashes entered his mind. The images remained quick and jumbled.

Pieces of the culture or even a few faces mean nothing to me without any context or understanding.

A group of laughing soldiers around a raging fire caught his attention. He felt alone.

Will I ever learn who I am? Will I ever see my home again? And if so, will I want the life I find waiting for me?

A gray form walked in front of his line of sight. Kaz scowled.

What does he want?

He turned back inside of his tent and closed the flap behind him.

* * *

"That no good piece of horse dung," Krytien mumbled. "I know he saw me." The mage quickened his pace as he headed toward the command tent.

I'm not going to be put off tonight.

Krytien pushed through the tent unannounced. Kaz stood over a table, looking down at a map.

"We need to talk."

"I'm busy," said Kaz without looking up.

"Then make time because I'm not going anywhere."

Kaz stepped away from the table and glared across at Krytien.

"It's Yanasi," said Krytien.

"What about her?"

"She's not handling things well."

"Did she tell you this?"

"Not in those words, but she didn't have to. She's worried that she might disappoint you and let you down. And in her mind, letting you down is just as bad as letting Jonrell down."

"Why would she think that?"

"I don't know, but what happened with the raid today only compounded things. It wouldn't hurt if you told her she was doing a good job."

"She should know that already. I wouldn't be giving her so many things to do if she hadn't already proven herself to me."

"Did you tell her that?"

"I didn't think I had to treat one of my best captains as a child," said Kaz in an exasperated tone.

"In many ways, she still is one. She had a rough childhood before she joined us. And she craves the approval and reassurance from others because she's so worried she'll be seen as expendable. Even the smallest bit of praise, especially from Jonrell, made all the difference to her."

"That isn't the way I command."

"Maybe it should become your way," snapped Krytien. "Jonrell used to—"

"I'm not Jonrell!" yelled Kaz as he took a step forward. "You may be old, but I know you're not blind. I don't look like him, nor do I act like him. I'll never be him. He's dead. I wish he hadn't died, but I can't bring him back! Elyse put me in charge of her army. And for whatever reason the army follows me and is content with my command." He paused. "It seems that most of the Hell Patrol isn't."

Krytien took a step forward himself, releasing his own pent up frustration. "That's because we never made you leader! That wasn't something for Elyse to decide."

Kaz narrowed his eyes and lowered his voice. "Then why has no one brought this up in the year since Jonrell died? Why are my orders accepted?"

There was a moment of silence as Krytien mulled over the questions. He remembered the discussion he and Kroke had on the ship going to Estul Island. "Some of the crew has accepted you as leader. Others just don't know what else to do. The rest know you're doing right by Jonrell so they follow because they owe it to him."

"That's not good enough."

Not good enough? "What?"

"This war is only going to get worse and hard times are coming ahead. I need men who will follow me, not Jonrell's memory. His memory will not keep them alive. His memory will not win this war."

"Maybe if you learned to treat the old crew better. It's like you have it out for many of us."

"Like who?"

"Kroke. Me. I know you hate sorcery."

"Aye, I hate sorcery, but I don't have it out for you. Nor do I have it out for Kroke."

"Then why does it seem like you're constantly burdening us with tasks others can just as easily do?"

"Because I know the Hell Patrol can do it better. It's just like what I said about Yanasi. She's one of the best I have. Kroke is in Lyrosene with Elyse because there isn't anyone better I can leave behind to protect the queen. I sent you scouting with Rygar this morning because I wanted it done right in case there were other mages waiting for us. I'm tired of Tomalt's attacks. They're affecting the men's morale. I needed that taken care of."

Kaz threw up his hands. "And this is what I'm talking about. I was only with the Hell Patrol for a short period of time before Jonrell died and yet I saw him ask the same things of you and everyone else. Often, he asked more. Yet the work got done and no one complained. I see the looks that you and the others give me when I issue an order. You've been around long enough to know that over time your attitude can easily rub off onto the rest of the army, especially if things don't go our way. I can't have that."

Kaz paused again and turned away. "This campaign is too important to risk the backlash of hurting your egos. Regardless of what you might think, I'm not doing this for myself. I'm doing this for Elyse and the promise I made to Jonrell. If you don't want to take orders from me, then leave. Go back to Slum Isle and take the others with you. I have more important things to worry about than hurting your feelings."

Krytien's mouth hung agape, unable to think clearly. "I-I don't know what to say."

"Then go. I have things to do."

* * *

Krytien hated to leave the conversation as he did but left anyway, full of conflicting emotions. He had expected to go in and give Kaz a piece of his mind, but their roles got reversed somewhere.

And he's got me looking at him in a different light now. Maybe even how Jonrell saw him.

The exchange had been the most personal moment he had shared with Kaz since the man joined Hell Patrol. He saw a crack in Kaz's armor. Krytien had been around leaders long enough to realize that the black man was not as sure of himself as he let others believe.

Everyone feels the weight of command at some point. Perhaps he always had and I was too caught up in myself to notice.

* * *

A cool breeze drifted along in the night and Kaz suppressed a shiver. His heavy boots treaded lightly over the open ground of camp as he made his rounds for the evening. It felt good to be out of his tent and walking about. The conversation with Krytien had sent his mind into a dozen different directions. He hadn't intended to air out some of the things he mentioned, but he felt better after having done so. It surprised him that Krytien had not fired back in return.

Maybe he's deciding whether or not to move on. I'll need to reorganize the command if he does. He sighed. *More things to do.*

Kaz walked over to Hag and Wiqua. He passed Yanasi leaving the old woman's tent. She quickly saluted and shied away. He thought back on what Krytien said about her when he heard Hag's voice.

"Late again, I see."

"He has the look of a man troubled by the burdens of command," said Wiqua.

"Burdens? Ha. Try carrying a kid for nine months."

Kaz started. "You have a child?"

Hag waved a hand. "And mess up my figure," she said, grabbing at her wide hips. "One Above, no. I've just heard enough women complain about it over the years. Figure it had to be true." She laughed.

Kaz couldn't help but smile.

"There, now that's better. I thought I might have to show you my teats to get rid of that sour look." Hag cackled louder than before. "Now sit down while I get you a bowl."

Dinner had been dished out long ago, but the two always saved him a portion to eat in his own time. Kaz took a place by the small fire, sitting across from Wiqua. The old Byzernian sipped a cup of tea as usual. He poured another cup and handed it to Kaz. Hag returned a short time later with his dinner. She grunted when taking her seat next to Wiqua.

"What was Yanasi doing in your tent?" asked Kaz.

Hag shook her head. "That's between her and me."

Kaz didn't bother pressing. He knew he would get nothing from her. He resigned himself to his meal.

After a moment, Hag asked. "That conversation with Krytien has got you in a worse mood than usual."

Kaz raised an eyebrow. "What do you know about that?"

"Most everything. I just so happened to be walking by when I heard you shouting."

"So you thought you'd stay and listen?"

Hag shrugged. "Don't give me that look. If you wanted it to be private, you should have had Krytien work a spell over the tent. Jonrell figured that out long ago."

Kaz scowled. "Yes, one more thing that he did better than me."

Hag waved a finger. "Don't you start. You know that's not what I meant. As much as some would hate to admit it, Jonrell was not a god. He made his mistakes like everyone else. I just never would have thought the man's heart would be his downfall. I hope that little snot Mal is rotting down there with the One Below."

"I doubt that Jonrell would wish that on Mal, even now," Wiqua said, clearing his voice.

"Like I said, he wasn't perfect." She lowered her voice. "Now, as far as Krytien goes, you may think the man is always questioning you because he doesn't trust you. Maybe there is a bit of that, but it's more than that. He's been around this group almost as long as I have, and he helped look after Jonrell when he first started out. Ronav before him. They both relied on his council. I'm not saying he's got all the answers, but he's someone you want on your side. Now, don't you go telling him I said that. The last thing we need is for him to get a big head."

He did listen for once rather than push his own thoughts when I exploded on him. "Maybe you're right."

"Of course I'm right. And it's good that you let out all that stuff building up. He needed to hear it just as much as you needed to say it. Maybe now you two can be more civil toward each other."

Kaz watched Wiqua put his arm around Hag. Kaz smiled again while looking at the two. Visiting them always seemed to clear his head.

Who would have thought people old enough to be my parents, or even grandparents in Hag's case, would be the ones I could talk to the most?

He wondered if his own parents still lived somewhere, sitting by a fire and thinking about him.

They would probably think I'm dead by now.

"One Above, what's on your mind now?" asked Hag. Kaz looked up as she glanced at Wiqua. "If he ain't moping, then he ain't happy."

The old Byzernian narrowed his eyes. "You were thinking about your past again?"

Kaz nodded. "It's hard not to."

"And nothing new?"

"Nothing that would give me answers to who I am or where I'm from. They're still mostly flashes and more of the same things. Destruction, blood, war, training. Every once in a while a brief glimpse of a city or a jungle. On a rare occasion even a face. But those are the briefest of all." He swore in his native tongue. "I just as soon not remember anything than be haunted."

A low snore sounded and Kaz saw that Hag had fallen asleep on Wiqua's shoulder. "Sometimes I'm tempted to ask for your help," said Kaz.

"But I've told you the risks," said Wiqua.

"You also said it could work."

"That doesn't mean it will. Your mind could just as easily fall to pieces as it could mend itself." He paused. "For someone who not too long ago abhorred all things sorcerous, I'm surprised you would consider it."

"You don't know what it's like not to know who you really are."

"I just ask you to be patient. It will come." Wiqua smiled. "And I know who you are. Your memories will not change that, for the better or worse."

CHAPTER 17

Elyse's mouth hung open as she read the letter for the third time. She slowly sat in her chair.

One Above, am I dreaming?

"Is it that bad?" asked Lobella.

Elyse shook her head. She had found a letter bearing Olasi's seal waiting on her desk when she entered her room. "Well, yes and no. The letter is actually from Markus, Duke Olasi's son. His father is ill and has asked Markus to oversee his holdings in his stead. Markus is worried that Olasi won't last but a few more months."

"Oh, I'm sorry," said Lobella. "He seemed like a great man."

Elyse remembered the nice old man at the dinner of her father's funeral. Their talk had been the lone bright spot in an otherwise awful evening. "He is." She paused. "But that's not the main reason for his writing. Markus said that he's been in contact with Duke Conroy. Apparently, Conroy is not as interested in the crown as we've all suspected and most of the activity behind his borders has been to prepare for the worst. Markus is trying to convince Conroy to meet with me in order to resolve any of his concerns. He thinks that if I were to travel to Lucartias, it would go a long way in speeding communications."

Lobella's eyes widened. "That's great news! The war would be over."

"Not quite. Tomalt and Bronn are still factors. Of course, Conroy has always been the most dangerous one. If he confirmed his support for me, we'd be able to attack Tomalt from the south while Kaz comes in from the north. And with Tomalt defeated, Bronn would be forced to surrender."

Despite her caution, Elyse couldn't help but feel excited over the prospect of peace.

How often have I prayed for it?

She dropped to her knees. "Lobella, would you pray with me in thanking the One Above?"

"Of course," said Lobella as she knelt.

The two began their prayer.

* * *

Gauge sipped quietly at his tea, eyes cast down toward the scarred white marble of the inner courtyard. Elyse hated the place because of all the awful memories it held. The death and destruction had occurred over a year and a half ago, yet at times she felt like it had all happened just the day before.

Elyse and Gauge spoke prior to her announcing the contents of Markus' letter to the council, but he still asked to speak with her in private afterward. As expected, the council received the news with excitement. However, some remained more reserved than others and Elyse had wondered what occupied their thoughts.

Already thinking of the new possibilities to seize power.

"Obviously, I think your decision to go to Lucartias and meet with Markus is the right one. But I would feel better about it if there wasn't so much danger traveling under these circumstances," said Gauge.

Elyse reached out and touched his hand. *He's worried.* "I'll be fine. I'll have over two dozen of my personal guard with me in addition to Kroke."

"Depending on the threat, those numbers could be inadequate."

"Perhaps. But, the last thing I want to do is take half the city's garrison with me on what is supposed to be a peaceful visit."

Gauge nodded. "Yes, that would leave Lyrosene undermanned and I'll have enough to worry about while you're gone."

Elyse frowned. "Is my absence that much harder on you?"

Gauge leaned back and let out a deep breath. "I'm afraid so, Your Majesty. Since your return, it has been much easier to get things accomplished regarding the day-to-day running of your kingdom. With you gone, I just don't have the authority to make certain decisions, whether or not I know you'll agree with them. Last year when you were traveling the countryside the nobles only grew more hostile. I wish there was a way to solve that situation."

I hadn't considered the impact of my decision on Gauge.

She thought for a moment. "I will sign off on a decree giving you power to make decisions regarding certain matters in my stead."

"Your Majesty, are you sure? There is no precedence for that."

"There was never a need for it either. For as long as I've known you, you've looked after both Cadonia's best interests as well as my own. Why wouldn't I make it easier for you in my absence?"

Gauge offered a warm smile. "Your Majesty, you are too kind." He paused, and when he started speaking again she heard the strain in his voice. "After your father began to dismiss my council all those years ago, I felt so useless and helpless as I watched the kingdom deteriorate. His shunning of me was shortly after my wife's passing and I hit a low I thought I might never return from. But since the king's death, you've given meaning to my life again. I can never repay you for your kindness, except to do the best job I can." He wiped at his eyes.

Gauge's honesty touched Elyse. She reached out and laid her hand on his, trying not to let her own emotions get the better of her. "I would be lost without you, Gauge. Your commitment to the kingdom is more than enough to show your gratitude. I cannot think of anyone more deserving of my trust than you."

"Thank you, Your Majesty." Gauge nodded toward her lap. "Is there anything else I can do for you?"

Elyse looked at the letter resting there. "Oh, this is a message for Kaz to let him know about the news concerning Conroy and my intent to see Olasi and Markus."

"Please allow me to take care of that for you. You have so much to do already for your trip."

Elyse handed the letter off. "That would be a big help."

* * *

A knock at the door sounded, yet Elyse's attention stayed on the letter in her hands. It provided an update of Kaz's position along with a brief overview of several small skirmishes the army had been involved in. Kaz achieved victory in each engagement, but the lives lost put her in a dour mood.

But if I'm successful in Lucartias, the bloodshed should end all the sooner.

The knock came again and Kroke cleared his throat while leaning against the wall.

Elyse called out. "Come in."

The door cracked open and her steward's long face peered into the room. "Lord Illyan is here for your appointment," said Gillian in a low voice.

Time to get this over with. "Send him in."

The door opened wider as the small man strode in. He held his head high, black curls bouncing with each step. Elyse stood. "It's good to see you, my lord," she said, doing her best to remain civil.

Illyan bowed. "Thank you, Your Majesty. I'm pleased that after more than a year of trying to find a place in your schedule, a spot *finally* opened up."

Elyse smiled. At her command, Gillian had been doing his best to put off any appointments with Illyan. However, the stress of dealing with the advisor's daily pressures wore heavily on her steward and eventually she had to concede on a time and place. "I *am* a busy woman." She gestured. "Have a seat and tell me what brings you here?"

Illyan flashed one of his creepy grins that sent a chill crawling up her back. "Oddly enough, the original reason I had set this meeting up so many months ago is no longer important," he said, as they each took a chair.

Elyse started to stand, "Well, then we can adjourn early. Thank you for your time."

"I beg your pardon, Your Majesty. But there *are* other matters to discuss."

Elyse eased back in her seat. "Very well. Go on."

He let out a sigh and seemed concerned. "About this letter you received from Markus. I'd like you to reconsider going to Lucartias."

She raised an eyebrow. "Why?"

"Your Majesty, it's too dangerous to travel."

"By land, yes. But Lucartias is a port city and I'll travel by sea. The waters are most secure since both the royal navy and Olasi's fleets have blockaded Tomalt's ports. Lady Jaendora has done an excellent job of rendering his navy useless."

Illyan puffed out a deep breath in frustration. "Your Majesty, I must tell you the truth of things—what I tried to tell you weeks ago in council before Gauge stepped in."

"I thought I told you that I do not wish to hear any rumors or gossip."

"Your Majesty, Olasi's son, Markus, is a traitor. I believe his contact with Conroy has not been what his letter to you indicated."

Elyse chortled. "Do you have proof of this?"

"Yes, but not the sort of proof I can share with you at this time," said Illyan, almost anxious.

"That is utterly ridiculous. Olasi's family has been most loyal to the crown since the days of Aurnon the First."

"Markus is his own man and it is no secret he is not the same person as his father. Family history means nothing. Otherwise, we wouldn't be trusting Jeldor since his ancestor tried to rebel during Aurnon the Third's reign." He paused. "For that matter, should we judge you based on the actions of your father?"

"You will not distract me from your unsubstantiated rumors by bringing my father up!" said Elyse, voice rising.

Illyan's face turned red. "This is not a rumor, Your Majesty. What I'm stating is true. Markus cannot be trusted. You can do your best to silence me in council, but I will not put the issue off any longer. It is too important to the kingdom."

Why would he want me to stay? With me gone, I would think he'd try to gain more favor among the council.

Elyse's eyes narrowed. "What is your goal? Your wealth has increased dramatically in the past year and your influence grows each day. Are you working for Tomalt?"

"Don't be ridiculous. I have no affiliation with him. You claim to be a pious woman, Your Majesty. When have you ever heard High Priest Burgeone preach that wealth is an evil thing sent from the One Below?"

"Now you bring the faith into this?"

"I'll do whatever I need to do to make you see the truth. Yes, I have prospered. Those tasks Jonrell and Kaz have allowed me to do have all been successful." He threw up his hands. "How could I possibly gain an advantage in this situation with Markus?"

Elyse tried to reason things out, but was too angry to think clearly. She took a deep breath. "Just because there isn't an obvious reason doesn't mean that one doesn't exist. I have far more pressing things to concern myself with than your lies."

"Yes. You must concern yourself with Markus' lies. With losing Olasi's troops and resources if Markus has seized power from his father. Why do you think Kaz did not dismiss me immediately as you do now?"

Because he doesn't understand politics. He doesn't see the games being played every moment of the day, like I do. Spending a few hours in council with me does not make him an expert. It would be like me assuming I could command the army because I read a few books.

Elyse shot from her seat and peered down at Illyan. "What is it going to take for you to drop this issue? Must I command it?"

Illyan stood as well. "Throw me in the dungeons if you must, but I will still tell the tale to the rats if they're the only ones willing to listen. The only way to silence me is to cut out my tongue."

She stared daggers at Illyan until she calmed herself.

"I'm going. I know the kind of person Olasi is and I can't believe that any son of his would do something treasonous. Yes, I will concede that I could be wrong, though because of what I know of the man, I doubt it. I cannot ignore the opportunity to end this war sooner and save the lives of my people."

"Alright. I understand that you feel like someone needs to go. Just send someone else in your stead."

"I will do nothing of the sort. What would Conroy think if I did that?"

"Who cares what Conroy thinks? You shouldn't be allowing him to dictate terms anyway. If he wants peace, let him come to Lyrosene and bend a knee to you here."

"It isn't that simple. He desires peace, but it is not definitive. I won't be like my father and let my arrogance get in the way of making decisions best for the kingdom. Conroy still needs to make the effort to leave his lands too. And by my willingness to travel closer to him, I'll be showing how important his support is as well. If I would have sent someone in my place to meet with Jeldor, I doubt an alliance would ever have been formed."

Illyan ignored her point and grabbed Elyse's hand. His voice took on a pleading tone. "You *mustn't* go! If something were to happen to you, who would take your place?"

Steel touched Illyan's neck and the advisor froze. "Get your hands off of her," said a cold voice.

Illyan removed his grip from Elyse and held up his hands.

I never even heard Kroke move. He was on the other side of the room only a moment ago.

"I'm sorry," said Illyan. "I got carried away."

Elyse was angry at Illyan's outburst, but also elated that Illyan had lost his composure. She looked up to Kroke who waited for her decision. "Please, release him. I'm sure it was a mistake."

Kroke removed his blade with a reluctant pause.

The advisor rubbed his neck. "Thank you."

Elyse sat, smoothed out her dress, and smiled. "I might be willing to consider your suggestion if you admit to me where you got your information on this issue."

Illyan stood for what seemed like an eternity. Elyse saw him struggle to find the words and enjoyed every moment of it. He started to speak twice, thought better of it, and waited again.

Illyan cleared his throat. "I wish I could explain everything to you, Your Majesty. But I can't. And since there is nothing more I can do to convince you of your error, I will leave you. I'm sure you have much to do for your trip. I would ask if you needed my assistance in any way . . . but I have a feeling you would not take me up on the offer." He bowed. "May I be excused, Your Majesty?"

It was now Elyse's turn to stare, dumbfounded.

There was a cough. "Your Majesty?"

Elyse waved her hand. "You're dismissed, Lord Illyan."

He bowed and left.

* * *

"I don't like any of this," said Kroke.

Elyse turned sharply as they walked through the castle, making her way to the armory. Though the bulk of her army marched across Cadonia, she still liked to check in on the progress of the smiths and fletchers left behind and she wanted to do so one last time before leaving. "What do you mean?"

"You shouldn't go to this supposed peacemaking meeting. It doesn't feel right."

"Then why haven't you said anything sooner?"

"Because I only now heard about Markus being a traitor."

"I'm going."

"Why? You could do like Illyan said, stay here where it's safe, but send someone else in your place. They can smooth things over on your behalf and confirm what is really going on with Markus. Why don't you send Gauge? He seems eager to do more."

Elyse shot him a look. "I already went over this with Illyan. I'm not doing it again."

"Look, all I'm saying is that there are better ways to solve your problems without potentially putting yourself in harm's way."

Elyse became flushed with anger. She was already on edge after her meeting with Illyan.

"Did Jonrell ever put himself in harm's way? Even when there may have been other options available?"

"Many times."

"Why did he do it?"

"Because he was in command and felt that the risk should be his to take. He also wanted the responsibility of any failure to fall on his shoulders."

"And why should I be any different? Jonrell commanded a company of men. I rule a kingdom. If something goes wrong, the stakes are much higher. I can't afford to pass off something of that magnitude to anyone else. Even Gauge."

After a long pause, Kroke nodded. "I understand. But I still don't like it."

* * *

Elyse closed the leather bound tome—one of four texts Drake had given her after returning from Estul Island. She had been nervous to openly ask for works about Sacrynon's Scepter, worried that Drake might ask too many questions. But the boy appeared indifferent to the request. Even still, she asked him to keep the matter private and to her knowledge he had.

He's probably too busy to even remember the conversation.

She had hoped the documents would give her some insight on how to destroy the infernal instrument, but so far she had only found more information on the scepter's history. Having been created in the early years of the Quoron Empire by a cabal of mages, the instrument helped construct the ancient wonders of that age. What happened to the scepter after that is unknown, but the instrument was lost for centuries. Sacrynon discovered it by chance shortly before Aurnon the First united Thurum and pushed into Cadonia.

The rest of the story she knew from texts in the royal library. Sacrynon fought diligently with Aurnon during that time. The power the mage wielded through the scepter destroyed many of the mythical beasts that once roamed the land while also humbling the fractured kingdoms of Cadonia. Sacrynon then used the scepter to build many of Cadonia's great cities in a fraction of the time it would have taken to do so otherwise.

Sacrynon held the power for years before becoming the Mad Mage. It changed Nareash in a matter of months.

In a brief moment of coherency which historians contribute to Aurnon's friendship with the mage, her ancestor distracted Sacrynon long enough for his pupil, Amcaro, to wrestle the weapon away from him. Together they killed the Mad Mage. Shortly afterward, Aurnon the First left Cadonia with the weapon, determined to either destroy it or lose it for all eternity.

Her eyes welled up.

Such a tragic tale. And filled with holes. How did the scepter survive? The only two who apparently knew about it were Amcaro and Aurnon. Both dead.

Elyse got up from her desk, checked the lock at her door and pushed a chair against it. She went to her bed, got to her knees, and pulled loose a floorboard nestled against the back wall. The secret hiding spot she used as a girl held a small box. She opened it. Wrapped in cloth, lay Sacrynon's Scepter.

She had no talent for the arts and therefore no desire to brandish the instrument. Still, she refused to take any chances by coming into contact with it again. She only opened the box periodically to make sure of its safety.

She tucked the scepter away and while on her knees said a prayer. She ran through her ever growing list of worries and petitions. As always, the first and the last thing she prayed for was the scepter's destruction.

CHAPTER 18

"This wasn't the plan," said Jeldor as he pushed his way into Kaz's tent, gesturing wildly with his hands. "In fact, this goes against everything we were trying to accomplish in taking the fight to Tomalt. I can't believe you changed an entire season's worth of strategy like this! Do you realize that Tomalt's bringing a massive host in from the east right now?"

The Duke's army had just reached the royal army's camp and though word had been sent ahead that Jeldor was furious, Kaz still fought to remain calm. "I'm well aware of Tomalt's movements. Did you know he is bringing up most of his southern forces as well?"

Jeldor's jaw dropped, framed by his bushy beard. "Impossible."

Kaz walked to a nearby table and grabbed a goblet of wine. He handed it to Jeldor. "I promise you it's not. Now we know why he allowed us to penetrate his lands with little more than some bothersome raiding parties. He was buying time so he could converge on us."

Jeldor snatched the goblet from Kaz's hand and downed its contents. "But where did you get this information?" he asked, wiping his mouth with the back of his hand. "Tomalt isn't the kind of person who would leave his southern border undermanned. Not with Olasi capable of striking at any moment."

"He would if he was certain Olasi's forces would not march against him."

Jeldor cast a confused look and then suddenly as if understanding Kaz's remark, his eyes widened. "The old man turned traitor?"

Kaz shook his head. "No. But shortly before I left, a noble in Lyrosene told me that he believed Olasi's son, Markus, might be working with Conroy."

"Did you get any proof?"

"No. And I told Elyse I'd drop the issue for that reason." He paused. "But something still bothered me so I looked for alternatives to our plan in case the rumors were true. Once I received word about Tomalt's southern armies, it's been all but confirmed in my mind. I've already sent word to warn the queen."

"But why let Tomalt go unopposed?" said Jeldor walking over to pour another drink.

"If he's working with Conroy, it makes complete sense. They let us wear each other down first and then Conroy swoops in and attacks the victor."

Jeldor rubbed at his face. "One Above, we weren't expecting to take Tomalt's entire army at once. With his southern forces, he'll outnumber us."

Kaz nodded. "And he still holds the advantage with mages."

Jeldor let out a sigh. "Can this get any worse?"

General Grayer pushed his way inside the tent. He saluted both Kaz and Jeldor. "Commander. My lord. A rider has just come in from Bronn's territory. He's the only one to make it back to us. Your hunch was right, Commander. Bronn is marching against us with nearly twenty thousand men. From all appearances, it looks as though he's converging with Tomalt's southern army. Based on the other reports, all three armies should be here within two days."

Kaz gave Jeldor a look. "You should have kept your mouth shut."

"We should have gone after Bronn when I wanted us to," said Jeldor. "That pompous fool needs to be taught a lesson."

"He will learn one soon enough. But now you know why I pushed for the forced march. We needed to combine forces sooner," said Kaz.

"But here?" Jeldor walked over to a map sprawled out along a wooden table. He pointed with his hand. "Mountains to our left and the Asycium river skirting around the range, looping at odd angles back onto itself. And you pick the spot where the cursed thing encloses us on the right and from behind. We're blocked in on three sides."

"They have only one path to attack us."

Jeldor grunted. "And we have no place to fall back to."

"We'll dig in here. We don't have enough men, time, or resources to regroup and try again later," said Kaz in a stern tone.

Jeldor downed his goblet's contents again. "Dig in and die."

* * *

"You couldn't have done this earlier?" asked Crusher. "You know how late it is?"

Kaz looked back at the giant as they walked through camp. A cool spring breeze swirled through the air. "I've been busy."

"I've told you before that taking over as commander was a mistake. Too much stress and worry. It's much easier to pick up something heavy and swing it. You don't have to think about that. Just enjoy the moment."

Kaz grunted. "You're whining like a child."

"I'm not whining," said Crusher. "It's late and I'm tired. It's hard to sleep with you staying up all hours of the night pouring over maps and talking to your captains. Ghals never worry about those things. We just go out and kill the man in front while trying not to kill the man next to us." He laughed.

Kaz smiled. "I've told you before, I don't need you watching over me."

"And I've told you before that you'll have to stop me."

Kaz sighed. There was no use arguing with him.

They entered the makeshift forge, walking into a wall of stifling heat. While most of the camp slept, the smiths saw to last minute repairs and worked diligently in preparation for the next day's battle.

Cisod put down a helm as he noticed Kaz and Crusher. He wiped the sweat from his brow with a massive forearm. "Commander," he said, reaching out to shake Kaz's hand. He nodded toward Crusher.

"Is it ready?"

"I just finished the last piece an hour ago. I've been working every waking moment on the blasted thing since Drake brought me the plans. I hope you're happy with it."

"So the technique worked?" asked Kaz.

"Yes. Once Drake helped me translate the old text from the Quoron language, I learned the methods weren't all too different than what I came up with on my own. Though, the end product is lighter," said Cisod.

"Let's see the thing already. It's late and all the pounding in here is giving me a headache," said Crusher.

Cisod raised an eyebrow and looked at Kaz.

Kaz shook his head. "Just leave it alone."

Cisod led them deeper into the tent and stopped near a tarp. He removed the covering and exposed what lay beneath. Kaz heard the quick intake of breath from the Ghal behind him.

"Well, what do you think?" asked Cisod.

The markings of ancient creatures Kaz had never seen before covered the breastplate. Some had multiple eyes, horns, and limbs. They all seemed to be holding their own private wars with one another as the scene connected into the rest of the torso. The surface of the arm and leg braces resembled scales. The boots and gauntlets had been shaped into the head and fangs of giant snakes. Cisod had worked the helm into the head of a panther, the visor an open mouth.

Kaz smiled wide.

"I take it you like it," said Cisod.

Kaz remembered what Jonrell had told him about why the Hell Patrol wore their blood red armor and how the image helped strike fear in their opponents. Jonrell had struck an intimidating figure in his crimson armor, but Kaz wanted something that fit his own personality. "It looks exactly like the picture."

"Almost," said Cisod. "The image from the book was faded so I couldn't tell what sort of cat the shape of General Victas's helm was supposed to be. It might have been a tiger, but I thought a panther more fitting."

Kaz picked up the helm and stared into the gaping mouth of the panther as the dancing flames from the forge changed the armor's color, causing it to shimmer. He ran his fingers along its edges. "It's perfect."

"The color is different," said Crusher. "I understand the red, but what's with the dark blue?"

"Something personal," Kaz said, reflecting on the color of the armor that flashed in his memories. The blue in his armor made him feel closer to his past. "You've really outdone yourself, Cisod."

"My pleasure now that I'm done." He laughed. "Those texts said that only their generals and best warriors had this sort of armor. Now I know why. At my best I might be able to produce four sets a year." He paused. "Oh, before I forget. Wiqua came by with Krytien as I was finishing it up. They put their own *blessings* on it and left looking ragged."

"Sorcery?"

Cisod nodded.

Kaz growled. It was one thing for Wiqua to do something. Another for Krytien. Kaz had taken Hag's words to heart from the other day, but he still felt uncomfortable with the old mage. "Anything else?"

"Not for you." Cisod looked up to Crusher. "My apprentices are done with your request as well."

"Where?" asked Crusher, suddenly eager.

"What request?" asked Kaz.

Cisod led them back a bit more where a six foot long warhammer leaned against a pole. The blacksmith gestured. "You'll have to grab it yourself. I'm not about to kill myself lifting it."

Crusher reached over with one hand and snatched it up like a toy. He flipped it over while inspecting it in detail. "Anyone want to bet how many heads I cave in with this?"

Cisod grunted. "I think you'll be caving in more than heads."

Crusher closed his eyes and grinned as if imagining tomorrow's events. He suddenly scowled. "Now I'll never get any sleep."

* * *

"What did he say?" asked Drake.

"What do you think he said? He cursed me out, ran me off, and told me to tell you to mind your own business. He said he didn't need me, you, or anyone else to watch over him," said Senald.

Drake let out a sigh. "How drunk was he?"

"Plenty."

Drake looked up to the next highest ridge where Raker and his crew had been stationed with trebuchets and ballista.

You promised last night that you'd lay off of the whiskey today. Why did I believe you?

"Alright. Get back to your station, then."

Senald ran off toward the mangonels. Kaz had positioned their siege equipment to the extreme left of the battlefield, on the highest, flattest ridges at the bottom of the bordering mountain range. The engineers would target Tomalt's right wing and rear guard so they'd be unable to gain a strong push against their army's left flank.

Based on the rest of the troops' positioning, it seemed like Kaz would allow the right wing to give ground while the stronger left would push up and around to roll up Tomalt's army. Drake doubted that others saw the brilliance in how Kaz intended to reposition Tomalt against the river, but he recognized it from a book General Victas wrote on tactics. The general used a similar strategy on one of his early campaigns. Oddly enough, Drake hadn't found the time to show Kaz his findings until a couple of hours ago, after the troops had lined up. Kaz seemed surprised and asked if Victas won. When Drake told him yes, Kaz responded. "Let's see if we have the same success."

Drake gazed out over the battlefield. From his high vantage point, he saw captains barking commands at their ranks. The right wing slowly disappeared from view as a low lying fog thickened around it. The fog didn't seem out of place on the unusually cool morning. An overcast sky added to the sullen atmosphere.

Drake watched his crew check over their equipment with care. He and Raker had taught them well, in that regard at least. He looked up to the ridge again, hoping that Raker would hold it together. Drake had voiced some of his concerns to a few of the old crew, but none seemed as concerned as he did.

But then I've held back some of the truth. And Raker's still coherent enough when they come around to check on him that no one thinks it's a big deal. They don't see him late in the night. They don't see him drinking as if he's hoping to drown himself. They haven't seen him look up and talk to the sky. They haven't seen him sob into his hands.

Drake felt his chest tighten as he thought about Jonrell.

I should have known something was wrong with Mal. I could have stopped it.

He cursed his former friend's name as he looked toward Raker's position one last time and saw the man staggering around, gesturing with a bottle as he yelled at his men.

* * *

"Is everyone ready?" asked Krytien.

The four green mages stared back with eyes full of uncertainty and fear. None seemed able to find their voices.

One Above, they're more scared than I would have imagined. And Lufflin for all his talking is white as a ghost.

"If you're not, speak up now. When this starts, you won't have time to say anything then."

Still nothing.

I'll try something different. "Janik, Yorn. What is your responsibility?"

The two looked at each other, hoping the other would answer.

Krytien lost it. "One Above, spit it out!"

That seemed to jar them awake. "We're supposed to fall behind the left wing's first line of heavy infantry. We're to act only as defensive support to the archers and light infantry out front, and then later, support the more experienced mages," said Janik.

"And what happens if it looks like there's an opening for you to attack?" asked Krytien.

"We ignore it unless the ranking captain gives us new commands," said Janik.

"Why is that Yorn?" said Krytien turning his stare to the young green mage.

"Because the safety of the soldiers is most important," said Yorn, gulping at the end of the statement.

"That's right," said Krytien. "You've lived most of your life on Estul Island behind closed doors and safe surroundings. Now each of you will get a taste of what life's really like. You're going to use the arts in one of the ways Amcaro meant you to use them. You will defend the kingdom and support the crown. In doing so, you may lose your life just as he did. If you aren't ready to do that, then run and hide. There is no place for you here today."

Krytien hoped they would remember at least some of what he tried to show them the past few weeks. Although the army nearly doubled their number of mages with those he brought back from Estul Island, many lacked the experience of Tomalt and Bronn's mages.

He was about to quiz Nora and Lufflin on their orders when the sound of approaching hoof beats caught Krytien's attention. The young mages blinked and took a step back. Krytien turned and blinked himself as he took in the rider. If he hadn't seen the demonic armor disassembled in Cisod's forge, he likely would have messed himself. Even without his helm, Kaz looked like he had just crawled out of the bowels of hell.

But I guess that's the point.

Krytien stared at the shimmering armor—blue and red swirling together in a way that made the beasts covering his plate seem alive.

And those snakes! It's like they're slithering along his limbs.

Kaz pulled up and inclined his head. "Are they ready?"

"I was just going over their orders one last time."

"Make it quick. I need to talk to you. Grayer sent word that it won't be long before Tomalt begins his advance."

"I'll catch up to you in a minute then."

Kaz grunted and rode off.
Let's hope this conversation is better than the last.

* * *

Kaz had been in his armor for several hours and still had trouble believing its weight and the ease with which he could move. He reviewed the lines of soldiers as he rode behind them. Captains shouted words of encouragement in earnest. Standing in his saddle, he saw a long black bow rise over the masses at the front of the left wing. Shouts from the archers and light infantry followed. He smiled to himself in approval.

Kaz had taken Krytien's advice and made an effort to speak with Yanasi privately. He could not fathom that someone with so much talent, someone who commanded such respect from her men, still needed reassurance in her abilities. Yet, the old mage had been right. Kaz felt his attempts at praise were awkward at best, but his efforts seemed to work as Yanasi's disposition had changed almost immediately.

Krytien came up beside Kaz. "What did you want to see me about?"

Kaz wanted to yell at the mage for interfering with his armor without his knowing, but he refrained himself. Unable to find Wiqua that morning, Kaz figured that it was all part of the old man's design to get him to talk to Krytien. He calmed himself, remembering his discussion with Hag and recalling the closeness Jonrell had once shared with the old mage. "Are your mages ready?"

"I honestly don't know."

The admission surprised Kaz. "What do you mean?"

"I don't think they understood until this morning the importance of what I had been trying to show them. Several still don't have a clue."

Kaz turned to the formation of soldiers. "They will after today."

"I wish you'd reconsider letting me stay with one of the groups on the left wing."

"They'll each have a black-robed mage with them. That'll have to be enough. Once the battle begins things may change, but to start, I need you and the other mages behind the right wing."

"I understand."

No arguing? No second guessing? No questioning of my decisions?

Kaz grunted. "Jeldor doesn't agree with how I've set up my lines. He thinks it's too much of a gamble to leave the right weaker with Bronn coming in from that direction."

"He would since you've moved him away from Bronn. He hates that man more than any other, I think. The strategy is a risk, but given what Jeldor has told us about Bronn it seems likely that he'll do what you want him to do."

"Do you believe it'll work?"

"I've seen a lot of crazy things work. I'm not saying I would have thought to do the same as you today, but I can see the reasoning behind it. It makes sense."

Krytien's relaxed attitude surprised Kaz. It was the longest conversation the two ever had without one raising his voice to the other.

Krytien cleared his throat. "Something else is on your mind, isn't it?"

"Yes. Cisod said you and Wiqua did something to my armor yesterday. I want to know what and why?"

The mage seemed surprised by the question, at least at first. He gave a slight shake of his head. "I should have known that he wasn't telling me the truth."

"What? Who?"

"Wiqua. He told me that he had talked to you about the armor and that you wanted us to *improve* it. He said you didn't feel right asking me for assistance. So, you sent him instead."

Kaz grit his teeth. "That sounds like Hag more than Wiqua."

"Probably so. I'm sorry. I wouldn't have done anything without your permission had I known."

"What did you do? Cisod said that both of you looked ragged afterward."

"Wiqua found the book about General Victas that your armor was based off of. There were stories that said the armor was even more special than those crafted like it. An older form of Quoron sorcery protected the wearer from certain sorcerous attacks. Wiqua wanted to know more about this, but neither Drake nor Lufflin had seen or heard anything else about that sort of sorcery. Wiqua came to me and told me he had an idea on how to incorporate the Byzernian methods of healing into the metal itself. But to do that, he needed my help to support him during the process and also give him an idea on types of sorcery mages might use in battle."

"So, are you saying that this thing will make me invincible from sorcery?"

Krytien shook his head. "No, it's not strong enough to make you invincible. But to damage you as severely as the mage did in Cathyrium, the attack would have to be extremely powerful. Even still, something that could have been fatal to you before should only leave you with minor injuries now."

"And why can't you do this for others?" asked Kaz, thinking of Yanasi and his other captains.

Krytien shook his head. "It's something about the process used to make your armor that allowed for Wiqua's idea to work." He paused. "And the sorcery wasn't easy on us."

Kaz didn't know what to say. "Wiqua I understand, but why would you put yourself at risk to do this for me?"

"As I said, I thought you wanted it to be done. Look, I know you see me asking questions and offering advice as being a troublemaker, but not once have I ever refused your orders. I also know you talked to Yanasi and are now making an effort to talk to me. You've got a better heart than maybe I gave you credit for." He paused. "I will follow you."

They waited in silence for a moment as the commotion of those around them only quickened. Word reached them that Tomalt was ready to offer battle. Kaz felt relieved, for it gave him an excuse to change subjects.

He gestured. "C'mon."

* * *

"Lose those worried looks. You're ready for this. We're ready for this." Yanasi continued her speech as she walked the line of her men, squeezing the black bow in her hand. She didn't know where the words came from, but she almost felt as if Jonrell's spirit spoke for her.

A few days ago, Kaz met with her in private, discussing not only strategy, but also life in general. She always respected him, but it wasn't until their conversation that she saw why others like Hag or Drake gravitated toward the man.

Or why Jonrell thought so highly of him.

Yanasi and Kaz's conversation eased some of her fears of failing.

Despite having drifted off in thought, Yanasi managed to finish her speech. She assumed it had been effective as her men shouted with an intense fire in their eyes. She smiled and lowered the bow she didn't remember raising.

I wish Rygar were here.

Rygar had left long before dawn on a last-minute scouting mission.

I didn't get to tell him bye or even kiss him one last time.

She realized how much her attitude had affected their relationship.

I dismissed practically all of his efforts to help me and I can't even apologize now for the way I treated him. First Cassus leaves. Then Jonrell dies. Maybe I've been trying to push him away before something happened to him too.

Rumbling hoof beats caught her ear and she glanced to them, expecting last minute orders. Her face lit up when she saw Rygar galloping toward her, his blond hair bouncing atop his head. He smiled as he jumped from the saddle and came up to her.

"What are you doing here?" she asked. "The battle can start at any moment!"

"I know. I begged Kaz to give me this moment before he sent me off again."

"And he allowed it?"

Rygar nodded. "But I would have come anyway." He pulled her away from her men. "I've been thinking. I've been trying to help you deal with Jonrell's loss, but I think I was pushing you more than you're ready for. I'm sorry. I realize the best way to help is to back off and give you the space you need," he paused and Yanasi could see him struggling. He cleared his throat. "I'm ready to do that. I just want you to be happy."

Yanasi's eyes watered. She looked down and blinked, letting the tears fall on the dewy morning grass.

Rygar cursed. "I upset you, didn't I?" He sighed. "I'm sorry, I can't do anything right."

Yanasi looked up. "No, please. You're fine. I was just thinking about how much I needed to apologize to you and how great you've been. I was worried that depending on what happens today I might have never been able to tell you that."

"So, I guess that means I don't have to go anywhere?"

"Of course not."

Rygar grinned. "Good. And don't talk like we won't see each other. I worry about you enough as it is."

"But it's true."

"You'll be alright and so will I."

"So now what?" she asked after a moment.

The ground began to shake some distance away. Tomalt's lines had begun their advance.

"I need to get back to Kaz."

"I need to go back to my men."

Rygar grabbed her by the shoulders, squeezing them through her mail as he pulled her close. Yanasi's breath quickened as their mouths met. Though they had kissed countless times before, this one felt extra special. The circumstances of the kiss weren't like anything her mom had told her about when reciting fairy tales to her as a little girl. Princesses never kissed wearing full armor on a battlefield. But the kiss gave her the comfort and reassurance she desperately needed.

He pulled away. "I promise I'll see you after the battle."

He kissed her again and ran to his horse, riding back toward the rear as he waved over his shoulder. In that moment, all she could think about was following after him and the two running off to some private place where they could be alone.

Perhaps one day.

Yanasi ran back to her men. They all wore grins. She tried to scowl as she looked them over. "What're you all smiling about?"

"We was just wondering if we'd all get ourselves a kiss like that," said one of her men. He was a man from the mountains of northern Cadonia and spoke with a thick accent.

The lines hooted in laughter and Yanasi couldn't help but smile too. A year ago she would have punched him, but now they joked with her not out of hate or resentment, but because they considered her one of them. Still, she couldn't very well let the man get away with such a comment. "Corporal, I didn't think you knew what to do with a female that had only two legs."

The laughter grew louder and the Corporal showed a gap toothed grin of his own as the others heckled him in turn.

Jonrell always said laughter was the best way to ease the tension before a battle. I hope he was right.

* * *

As Tomalt's men advanced, Raker received orders to begin. He took a long pull from his whiskey bottle and turned back to the men busying themselves with last minute adjustments to the nearest trebuchet. Drake had somehow figured out how to get decent range from the smaller piece of equipment. Its size made it ideal for a quick assembly and allowed them more freedom in stationing the devices in odd places like the high ridge they held now.

Drake's getting too cocky for his own good. Thinks he has all the answers.

"Hey! What do you think you're doing?" yelled Raker.

A private called out. "Sir?"

"Don't 'sir' me." He spat. "What do you think you're doing?"

"Making the adjustments Drake showed us."

"That's not how you adjust a trebuchet." He staggered over to the equipment and pushed the man aside as he began to fiddle with the tension.

Drake thinks he knows everything. I'll show the smug little . . .

"But sir, that's not how it's supposed to work," said the private.

Raker turned and sneered at the man. "Boy, I know how to work a blasted trebuchet." He turned and made several new adjustments, cursing as he had to put his bottle down for a second to do so.

"But, Drake constructed this one differently so . . ."

Raker punched the man in the gut. The private fell to the ground, gasping for air. Raker spat near the soldier's feet and scowled at the rest of his crew.

They think they're better than me too.

"Quit standing around!" he yelled. "Get into position."

A minute later he overlooked the battlefield, gulping at the whiskey in his hand. He pulled the bottle away long enough to shout a command.

"Release!"

* * *

A loud crash sounded from behind and Drake flung his head back as the first of the trebuchet buckets came forward. He cursed the second he saw its positioning and the angle the rocks entered into the air.

"What are you cursing about?" asked Lufflin. Against Drake's request, Lufflin and Nora had been assigned to shield the siege equipment, knowing Tomalt's mages would try to go for them as they neared.

"It's off!" Drake followed the high arcing boulders as they fell hundreds of yards short of their target. Their own men, archers and light infantry, ran frantically out of the way. Several rocks crashed within feet of their lines. Yanasi and the other captains did all they could to keep the soldiers from breaking formation.

"One Above!" said Lufflin. "The idiot's attacking our own men."

Lufflin was right, but Drake hollered at him anyway, tired of his constant berating and sense of entitlement. "Shut it and go make yourself useful!"

"Hey, don't think you can boss me around just because . . ."

With no time to argue, Drake gave the green mage his back and ran over to Senald.

"Did you see that?" asked Senald, wide-eyed in disbelief.

"Yes. I'm going up there now. You're in charge down here."

"Wait. I don't know if—."

"Not now, Senald," said Drake, sounding more angry than he intended. "I need you to take over here."

"Go."

Drake climbed the rise and heard Senald shouting orders behind him. Cresting the hill, Drake found sure footing on the flat area the engineers had cleared away to make room for the siege equipment. He expected to see men running around reloading and preparing for the next shot. Instead, everyone had their backs to the battlefield, staring in the same direction. Drake pushed his way through where Raker sat on a small boulder wearing a blank look.

Drake kneeled in front of him. "Raker, are you alright? What happened?"

"I almost killed our own men," he said in a low voice, barely a whisper. "What would Jonrell have said?" Raker put his head in his hands.

Drake shook him. "Get up! C'mon!"

The mercenary didn't budge.

I don't have time for this.

Drake spun and grabbed the closest man. "What happened? I thought I showed you all the changes I made. We drilled on them."

"We tried to explain that to Raker, but he made us change the settings."

"On all of them?"

"No. Just the one we fired."

Drake glanced back at Raker who rocked back and forth. *What's happened to you?*

Drake turned away. "You three, work on getting the settings right while you four refill the bucket." He gestured. "The rest get back to the other two." No one moved. "One Above, now! This isn't your first battle. We got men down there counting on us to do our job."

That seemed to set them off and the ridge became a frantic mess of activity. The other two teams readied their trebuchets in moments. Drake quickly checked the distance with a spyglass and then gave the command. The wooden structure groaned and creaked as stones heaved into the air. This time they found their mark.

* * *

"What in the name of the One Above are they doing up there, captain?" asked a soldier.

Yanasi wondered the same thing. "It was meant to confuse Tomalt's men so they think we don't know what we're doing," she said with a quick lie.

"Then why didn't they tell us?"

"It wouldn't have seemed as natural if we had to fake being scared. Now get back in line and quit asking questions."

I didn't believe Rygar when he told me how concerned Drake was.

She felt a tug of guilt over her selfishness, not realizing how bad the engineer had gotten.

Another rolling thud sounded as the counterweights of the trebuchet slammed forward and echoed over the mountains to their left. Heads went up and involuntarily flinched until they saw the stones continue well past their lines. Tendrils of sorcery from Tomalt's mages went up to meet the rocks, but their mages couldn't deflect all the projectiles in time.

I guess Raker got it together. Hopefully it stays that way.

The discipline of Tomalt's men impressed Yanasi. None broke formation to step around their dead. Soldiers walked on and over the fallen.

Siege equipment from the lower level soon joined the rocking cadence of the trebuchets. Yanasi raised a hand and a young soldier waved a green flag. Archers stepped forward and readied their bows. Tomalt's men marched forward at a determined pace.

"Loose!"

* * *

Krytien moved the spyglass back and forth between the siege equipment and the first lines of the left wing. Arrows, ballista spears, boulders, and bits of metal from the trebuchets and mangonels worked in a steady rhythm. Tomalt's mages worked to shield their men from the falling projectiles, but the sheer volume filling the gray sky overpowered their efforts. Tomalt's soldiers fell like stalks of wheat at harvest.

"They're definitely in sync now since Drake took over."

Kaz grunted. "Raker is a liability. I'll have to deal with that when this is over."

"No," said Krytien as he turned to Kaz. "Please, let me. He's never been this bad before and I should have noticed it sooner. He may be more inclined to talk to me."

"Someone he trusts?"

Perhaps. "Someone he's known longer. Someone he's been through more with."

Kaz nodded. "Let me know what the result is."

"I will."

Kaz pointed to the left wing. Krytien lifted the spyglass to watch as the enemy crashed into Kaz's lines. The two forces heaved against each other and a ripple that shook the ground went out among the ranks. The arrows had stopped and the engineers shifted their focus to targeting the rear ranks of the enemy.

Tomalt's mages went on the offensive, battering Kaz's left wing with wave after wave of sorcery as the two forces clashed. Amid the flashes of light and fire, Krytien struggled to determine who held the advantage. Even through the spyglass, the armies seemed like a giant mass of flailing limbs.

Krytien found a pocket of their mages, several rows behind the front line. Two figures in green robes protected Jeldor's black-robed mages while the latter worked to counter Tomalt's assault.

"How are the mages?" asked Kaz.

"They're holding for now."

"Good."

"We still have to worry about Bronn's mages though."

Tomalt's forces pushed forward and Kaz's right wing purposefully gave ground with the intent to appear weaker than the rest of the formation. Kaz wanted to lure Tomalt in as the left wing then pushed around to encircle him, pinning him against the river.

Krytien glanced over his shoulder at their reserves which consisted mostly of cavalry and light skirmishers. Once the left wing started their move, Kaz wanted the cavalry to sweep behind and support them.

But that all depends on the success of the right. If they fall back too quickly, Tomalt could press us into the mountains. If the right breaks, Tomalt will split our forces. And then Bronn's men will be able to overwhelm our divided army.

The right wing continued their slow retreat into the fog, using the sorcerous cover created earlier to mask Kaz's strategy.

Still visible at the front of the right wing, a tall figure swung out with a giant warhammer, flinging three of the enemy into the air.

"Crusher will take out that whole side by himself," said Krytien.

"Don't tell him that," said Kaz. "His head is big enough already. It took a lot of convincing to get him to leave my side today. The new armor helped. But when he found out I was using him as a rallying point so the wing wouldn't buckle too quickly, he was convinced." Kaz held out his hand. "Let me see the spyglass."

Kaz stood in his saddle searching out Bronn's men. They waited by the river near a spot where it turned back on itself. He grunted. "Bronn hasn't taken the bait yet."

"What do you want to do?"

"Increase the fog as Tomalt's lines advance. Let Bronn think we are close to collapse. Maybe if he believes the battle is decided, he'll be more inclined to act. If what Jeldor said is true, he's only interested in the glory."

* * *

Jeldor's pikemen surged past Yanasi's archers and light infantry, slamming into the wall of Tomalt's spearman. The two groups met with such force that her ears rang from the clashing of steel. Wails of despair and blood-curdling screams of pain drowned out the clanking of shield and armor as the two armies stabbed, sliced, and hacked.

The archers, unequipped for this sort of fighting, fell back behind Jeldor's pikemen. The archers weaved between the lines where possible and loosed arrows as openings presented themselves. She had convinced Kaz to let her try the idea and was surprised he agreed.

Jonrell would have worried too much for my safety.

Yanasi drew another arrow from her quiver and readied it as she moved through the tightening lines. She released her arrow as a pikeman fell. Yanasi made the enemy soldier pay with an arrow to the eye. She got off another half dozen high arcing shots before the constant shoving and pressing became too much. She slithered back through the ranks just as a thrown javelin passed by her head, clipping her helm. She pitched forward and one of her men caught her.

"Captain, we're just getting in their way now. Jeldor sent orders to start wheeling his men to the right."

"See that ours fall back behind the pikemen and heavy infantry. Have them fire over our front lines and into Tomalt's rear, if possible. But under no circumstances is anyone to take chances."

"Captain, where are you going?"

"I need to check on the mages." She heard the lieutenant shouting her orders from behind as she took off.

Sliding through the mass of soldiers gave Yanasi a new appreciation for the infantry. The smell of blood and sweat comingled with fear and death gave the whole affair a personal nature that she only thought she had understood.

Watching from a distance while plucking a bow or defending a wall is much different than this.

A javelin caught a soldier next to her in his chest. She involuntarily let out a yelp at the crunching impact. Soldiers trampled right over the newest corpse with barely more than a second glance.

I guess in the moment you have to be detached. Otherwise you realize the man next to you spurting blood was someone's father, husband, or son.

After more jostling and cursing, she finally reached the small circle where the mages supported the left wing. Two green-robed and a dozen yellow-robed mages aided the two black-robed figures from Jeldor's ranks. The entire group fought against some twisted sorcery she failed to understand. Bursts of lightning, balls of fire and blue light, swarmed around the group.

A sudden gust of wind followed by an intense heat threw her backward. Her helm rattled against her skull as it banged into the ground. She blinked rapidly, trying to clear her vision while ignoring the stabbing pain in her neck. With head swimming, she rolled slowly to her knees. She brought one hand up and touched her face, flinching at the rawness of her skin. She squinted and finally gained some focus.

Soldiers lay around her, chests heaving.

Out cold.

Barely audible above the buzz in her ears, officers bellowed at their men to strengthen the gap as Tomalt's army pressed toward their location. Yanasi staggered to her feet. The ground swayed beneath her as she added her voice to the other officers in order to rally men to their spot.

The lines quickly shored up.

Yanasi shrugged away a hand that tried to steady her as she stumbled over to the group of mages. Soldiers drug away those too injured or dead to be of any use. Three yellow-robed mages and one green had died. Three more yellow-robed mages and one black-robed mage suffered injuries too great to continue.

Blue light swirled around the group as vines of sorcery targeted the survivors. The mages rallied around the lone surviving black-robed mage and held. She ran up to the group. "What happened?"

The black-robed mage glanced at her. "They set us up. We thought we had the upper hand. We weren't ready for their attack."

"What can you do?"

The mage shook his head as another fireball streaked toward them and disintegrated around the invisible barrier above. "Nothing other than this." Sweat poured off his face. "Those who survived aren't strong enough to keep up the defenses while I try to mount a counterattack."

"They're going to wear you down. Why can't someone else attack while you maintain the defenses? Just enough to keep them guessing."

"You need to convince Janik to do that," said the black-robed mage. "The yellow robes aren't strong enough. But I doubt it will do any good."

Yanasi stalked off in the direction indicated.

She almost missed Janik hovering over the lifeless body of his fallen friend. Heat from another fireball radiated against her back. She reached Janik and grabbed him by the arm, yanking the green-robed mage to his feet. "What are you doing?"

"Leave me alone," he said, wrenching her grip free. He made an effort to return to the side of Yorn when she spun him back around.

"What's the matter with you?"

"Yorn's dead!" he yelled.

Something about the way he made that simple statement set her off. She grabbed him by the collar and pulled him in close. "So what? He wasn't the first to die nor will he be the last. You think you're the first person to lose a friend in battle? How dare you act like his life is better than those men still counting on you. Mourn him later. You can't do anything about him now. But you can save dozens, if not hundreds more, by pushing aside your feelings and doing what Krytien told you to do." She glanced back at the group of mages visibly straining under the onslaught of power thrown against them. "One Above! Go help them!"

Janik eyed Yanasi for a moment, turned a last distressed glance on Yorn's body then stormed off toward the group.

Krytien, you better be on your way.

* * *

"Their right wing is falling apart, general," said Bronn from atop his mount. "See how Tomalt is driving them further and further into this blasted fog."

"How do we know it isn't a trap and they aren't trying to draw us in?"

"Don't be preposterous. Draw us in where? They have a river at their back. They're more than welcome to drown themselves if that's their goal. It's time to make our move."

"But sir, Tomalt gave us instructions to remain in reserve in case we have to stop Kaz from flanking his main body."

"Like such a thing is possible," spat Bronn. "Tomalt is almost as much of an idiot as the black foreigner is for choosing this location to meet in battle. They have a river to their rear and right. Low mountains on their left. How could they possibly flank us?" He paused. "General, I won't sit by any longer. Conroy's indecisiveness and unwillingness to commit himself is as ridiculous as Tomalt's risk."

"Conroy did go for your plan to aid Tomalt under the guise of a temporary truce though."

"Yes. He finally realized it was in his best interests." Bronn grinned. *And mine as well. If I can gain the respect of Tomalt's troops now while defeating Kaz and*

Jeldor, I should be able to steal them away after Tomalt mysteriously dies. After all he has no family. His smile broadened.

Bronn cleared his throat. "Pass out the orders. We move in at once."

* * *

The left wing failed to turn as quickly as Kaz would have liked. A massive wave of sorcery struck and the lines buckled. They regrouped in time to avoid disaster, but the damage had been done. His plans to roll up Tomalt from the left looked like they may fall apart. He had sent Krytien and several of the mages held in reserve to bolster that flank.

A runner came up. "Sir, I've got two messages from General Grayer."

"What are they?"

"The center is starting to weaken. He's calling for reinforcements."

"What happened?"

"The sorcery on the left wing disrupted the right's retreat. The lines are off balance and Tomalt's men are flooding over too rapidly."

Horns sounded.

Bronn is advancing.

He cursed. "I thought Crusher manned the center." He could no longer see the Ghal through the blanket of gray, but earlier the man had laid waste to any who had dared come near him.

"He and the squad near him were separated from the lines as we fell back. We don't know where he is since the fog is making it hard for us to see our own."

Kaz swore. "Tell Grayer to do whatever it takes to hold the center and then shift to the right to make room for me when I arrive with our reserves."

The runner saluted and scurried off. Kaz grabbed the other messengers waiting nearby. He instructed one to send word to his cavalry. They were to maneuver around the left wing and disrupt Tomalt's rear. Next, he signaled the remaining mages to lift the fog and focus instead on distracting Bronn's mages. Lastly, Kaz ordered up the few hundred skirmishers he held in reserve. They trotted up to his position, some wearing mail, others only leather and shield for protection.

He dismounted to better lead them and threw on his helm. Looking out from the mouth of the panther's head, he yelled at them to advance.

* * *

Kaz crashed into the center formation with his reinforcements. Bronn's troops had joined the battle recklessly, creating disorder that weakened Tomalt's momentum. Kaz's skirmishers quickly reinforced his heavy infantry and stabilized his lines.

Kaz bullied his way to the front, and sheared the top quarter of a frightened soldier's head with his sword. The man fell, eyes still wide in disbelief. The looks of horror continued as he hacked and battered the interchangeable soldiers that continued to fall before him. His armor seemed to hold the gaze of the first half dozen he killed. Shouts that the One Below himself had taken the battlefield started spreading among the enemy.

The proclamation caused the enemy to find their courage and several rushed him at once. Their foolish prejudice only fueled the fire in his belly. Kaz went about killing like a woodsmen chopping down trees, moving unencumbered as Cisod said he would be able to.

He lowered his shoulder, and barreled into a man with a raised shield. The impact threw the soldier backward into two others. All three fell in a heap of limbs. Kaz sidestepped a thrust from the next attacker. He punched the hilt into the man's face. The edge of the crossguard bit into the man's visor and Kaz tore away part of his opponent's helm. Kaz punched again, jamming the pommel into the soldier's eye. A chilling scream sounded as the man clawed at his face.

Kaz ducked under another wild swing and sliced through his opponent's mail. Entrails spilled from the soldier who dropped to his knees, looking down in horror.

Soldiers came at Kaz one after the other. It seemed to him a line of men waiting death.

Kaz lost himself in the killing as the enemy piled around his feet. He pushed the point of his sword through a gap in an opponent's armor under the armpit. The man collapsed and Kaz yanked his sword free. He looked around for his next opponent and finally found none nearby. He realized then that he somehow had worked himself free of the organized lines and rather than retreating with the right wing as planned, he and his skirmishers had pushed deeper into Bronn's forces.

I couldn't even follow my own orders.

As the last of the fog dissipated, a thunderous scream ripped through the air. Crusher came into focus, standing alone as a pocket of the enemy survivors threw themselves at him. The Ghal's warhammer sent one soldier ten feet into the air while the backswing flattened another. The giant raised the massive weapon overhead in triumph. He roared in defiance.

He'll be talking about this for days.

A burst of fire outside of Kaz's peripheral slammed into the Ghal. Crusher fell.

Three mages, two black and one green, game into view, forming a half circle around the giant. Wisps of smoke rose from Crusher's frame as the fire quickly burned itself out. Kaz would have thought him dead if not for the faint up and down movements of his friend's chest.

One of the black-robed mages spoke, but Kaz only saw the man's lips move. The rage coursing through his limbs and pounding in his heart filled his head. He rushed the three mages, growling. The black-robed mage looked up and smiled. He raised his arm as a bright orange fire exited his hands toward Kaz.

Kaz felt a familiar heat engulf him, reminiscent of the power that struck him at Cathyrium. He tensed his muscles, cursing himself for being so careless. But the fire faded.

The armor worked.

Kaz reached his attacker in several fast strides. The mage's face paled. His sword nearly shorn the mage in half at the waist. Just like at Cathyrium, power exploded from the man. The burst threw Kaz backward, but the armor protected him again and he rose quickly to his feet. Kaz hurried back to the other two mages, dazed from the blast, and lopped off their heads in two rapid strikes.

Horns sounded.

Kaz scanned the field. The remnants of two armies fought their way through the bloody mess of a battleground. To his right, Bronn's battered forces escaped south.

Near what had once been the center's lines, Tomalt's army retreated east.

Kaz's forces hadn't been able to completely encircle Tomalt, but in the end, it didn't matter.

He grabbed the first half dozen men he found and sent orders to Jeldor and Grayer not to pursue the enemy. He didn't want his forces divided.

Looking over the field of death once again, he also knew that his army had not made it out unscathed. Before he pushed on with the campaign he wanted a better assessment of his losses.

He shouted at several of his skirmishers within earshot. "Bring a wagon up and tell the first mage you find to come with you."

"But sir, we'll never get a wagon through all this," the soldier said, waving a hand.

Kaz stormed toward the soldier. "You find a way to do as I say or so help me your corpse will join the others."

The man paled. "Y-yes, sir. I'll be back as soon as I can."

The men ran off. Kaz walked over and took a knee before his friend. He laid a hand on the blackened armor of the Ghal.

"Don't die on me," he whispered.

* * *

Krytien allowed himself to relax when he received word that Kaz wanted no one to pursue Tomalt and that the army should hold its position. Like the other soldiers dragging themselves along, his body ached down to his toenails. He couldn't imagine pushing on in his current state.

I weakened myself too much on that blasted armor yesterday. He blew out a deep breath. *Well, Kaz is alive at least.*

He had reached the left wing just in time to solidify their defenses. Upon arrival, he had been surprised by Janik's efforts in maintaining a steady assault against the enemy. The young mage had worn an intense glare that made sense to Krytien later as he learned of Yorn's death. Krytien tried to comfort the young mage, but Janik said he wanted to be alone.

Krytien didn't press. He understood.

* * *

Janik covered Yorn's head. They had been friends since Amcaro selected them to study on Estul Island as boys.

It was supposed to be fun and games.

He turned his gaze away from his friend's lifeless form and took in the destruction around him as survivors dragged the dead to burning pyres.

It wasn't supposed to be like this.

Yanasi had angered him at the time for pulling him away from Yorn. But in the battle's aftermath, he realized how right she had been. He had managed to pull himself together long enough to help the army's lines hold firm until Krytien and several other mages came to their aid.

He shook his head when he thought about how quickly Krytien had taken over the situation. *He's more powerful than I realized.*

"One Above, Nora was right! Yorn is dead."

Janik turned to Lufflin as the mage approached. He wore a look of dread that turned into anger as he spoke. "We've got to get out of here, Janik. Forget those stupid books. Forget this war and forget this country. Now is the perfect time for you, me, and Nora to sneak off. They won't realize we've gone until it's too late."

"No," said Janik.

"What do you mean, no? We can go to Thurum or even Mytarcis and have some fun there. Their mages aren't as well trained as we are. We can probably be rich in just a few years."

"No. You go if you want those things. I won't ever again see this as fun. Not after today."

"Listen to yourself. You're letting Krytien and all the others change you."

"Yes. And for the better. Yorn died. I can't just walk away while others share his fate. I'm staying."

"This isn't our fight," said Lufflin in a pleading tone.

Janik shook his head. "You're wrong. This is the sort of thing Amcaro had hoped to avoid, yet trained us for all along." Janik met his friend's eyes and for the briefest of moments saw what appeared to be sorrow. But it disappeared and disappointment took its place.

"You're an idiot," said Lufflin. "And before it's done, I'll show you how wrong you are."

Janik watched Lufflin storm off.

I can't believe I ever looked up to you. His eyes drifted down to Yorn's body. *We all did.*

The tears came again as he grabbed the robes of his friend at the shoulders. With a grunt he lifted his torso and walked backward, dragging his best friend toward the blazing fires.

* * *

Krytien breathed heavily as he made it atop the first rise. He spotted Drake and said a quick prayer of thanks if only because he didn't have to climb any higher. Like everyone else, he needed a hot meal and a good night's rest. But also like everyone else, there would be none of that immediately with so much still to do in the battle's aftermath. Kaz had given Krytien permission to check in on the Hell Patrol members before receiving his next set of orders.

Hopefully, I won't be out scouting with Rygar again.

Drake and Senald were wrapping up a conversation. From what Krytien overheard, Drake impressed him. The boy spoke like a veteran, issuing orders after dishing out praise for a job well done.

Drake dismissed Senald and faced Krytien. The mage saw his fatigue went beyond physical. It was stress. Krytien hated to see Drake starting to lose that youthful exuberance others found so infectious.

War will make you grow up faster than you should.

"How are things?" asked Krytien, trying not to let his thoughts show.

"Good. As you probably overheard, Senald did great and the new trebuchets worked. Everyone banded together after an initial misstep, and when the fighting reached us, we kept our heads, made use of the high ground, and defended our position."

Krytien cleared his throat. "About that misstep. Raker?"

Without any further prodding, Drake spilled everything to Krytien. He finished with a heavy sigh. "I just don't know what to do with him anymore."

"Where is he? I was hoping to talk to him."

"He ran off. One Above knows where. He even left his mace behind," said Drake.

His mace? That's bad. "Nothing personal, but I don't think anything you say or do is going to get through to him. Someone from the old crew needs to set him straight. I'll try to talk to him first." He paused. "Who knows, maybe today was the kick he needed to get his mind right."

Drake shook his head. "I hope so."

* * *

The brief moment of security Yanasi and Rygar shared after finding each other at the battle's conclusion ended with the howls of a woman wailing. Other than herself and a few mages, few women populated the army and the cries didn't sound as hard as a soldier's might, but instead seemed frantic with despair.

They followed the sounds and found a pregnant woman on the ground holding the hand of a dead officer in Tomalt's army. Yanasi learned that the man had been her husband.

How did she even find him among all this carnage?

The emotional shock of losing her husband sent the woman into labor. Yanasi sent Rygar off for help, telling him to grab Wiqua if possible. She knew the old man would be busy with their injured and probably exhausted, but if anyone could help, he would be the best choice.

Yanasi knelt at the woman's side while they waited for Rygar to return. The sobs of the woman's physical and emotional suffering brought back Yanasi's own painful memories. She recalled the closeness she once shared with her own mother in Thurum before she died in the plague. Memories of her father's abandonment followed and then finally, the night Jonrell saved her life and brought her into the Hell Patrol.

Rygar galloped up with Wiqua behind him in the saddle. The old man dismounted and hurried over despite his obvious fatigue.

"Rygar told me what happened," said Wiqua as he took a knee beside them.

Sweat beaded on the woman's pale skin and she arched her back with the next scream.

"Please," Yanasi begged after thinking about her mother. "You have to help her."

Wiqua tried to smile. "I will do all that I can. Give me a moment."

Wiqua moved his hands over the woman, pausing at her belly before then lifting the woman's dress. After finishing his examination, he covered the woman's legs and reached out to squeeze her hand. His mouth silently moved and his eyes tightened. The woman's breathing calmed and her pain seemed to subside. Wiqua opened his eyes.

"What's wrong?" asked the woman.

Wiqua spoke in a soft tone. "Your body isn't handling this well and your child's heartbeat is faint from the stress on your body. I've done my best to ease your pain."

The woman began to cry. "Can you help us?"

"Yes. But," he paused, "since you're pregnant and both of you are in poor condition, the situation is complicated. If I attempt to heal you and the baby, it's possible that you may both live, but it's also possible that neither of you will." Yanasi heard the sorrow in Wiqua's voice.

"And what if you heal only one of us?" the woman croaked.

"Then I'm certain that the one I focus on will live."

Without pausing, the woman answered back. "Save my baby."

Wiqua nodded and Yanasi saw a tear run down his cheek. "Of course. A mother will always choose her child. As it should be," he whispered.

Suddenly finding her voice during the exchange, Yanasi blurted out. "Wait. There has to be another way. I've seen you do such amazing things."

Wiqua bowed his head. "It's hard to explain, but the healing process is much more complicated when two are essentially sharing the same body."

Yanasi thought about all the death around her and the anguish the poor woman had already gone through. "It's not fair." She felt Rygar wrap his arms around her.

The pregnant woman smiled at Yanasi. "It's for the best." She reached her hand out and grabbed Yanasi's. "Please, do something for me."

"Alright," said Yanasi in a hoarse whisper.

"I was told by a seer that my baby's a girl. I don't have any other family. Please see that she finds a good home."

"I will."

The woman's body suddenly arched back in pain.

"I have to start now before it's too late," said Wiqua in an urgent tone.

The woman nodded weakly and Wiqua coached her on what to do as Yanasi and Rygar helped where they could. A short while later a baby's cry greeted them.

Wiqua held the baby to the woman. "She'll be just fine."

The woman smiled and whispered, "Thank you," as the light faded from her eyes.

All three figures sat with their heads down, huddled and sobbing, as the baby's cry echoed ominously over the battleground.

* * *

Kaz stared over the flowing river, his back to the field. He had seen enough of it. He had met with his captains, issued orders for the short term, looked over the prisoners, and visited his army's wounded. He thought of those suffering in the infirmary, and those that died.

There will only be more fighting to come. I'm glad Elyse isn't here to see this.

The memories of his past often focused on the heart racing thrill of battle, never on the depressing aftermath. He wondered if those things ever bothered him then.

Fighting with only himself to worry about was one thing, but now that he commanded so many others, he found the feeling of excitement had diminished. Perhaps Crusher's injuries had put him in a foul mood. Kaz had stayed with him until his condition stabilized, only then moving on to his other duties.

Is that how Jonrell felt when I was injured at Cathyrium?

He sighed. *The longer I'm in command, the more I understand him.*

Kaz looked to the sky.

CHAPTER 19

Nareash never imagined that the sight of Juanoq would lift his mood so thoroughly. Since coming to Hesh, all he thought about was returning home to Cadonia. Yet, the distant outline of Juanoq's high walls brought a genuine smile to his face.

He couldn't wait to check on the progress of his projects and eat a well-cooked meal. Most of all, he looked forward to catching up with Tobin. The High Mage had grown up with few friends and most of those he considered mere acquaintances. But over time, he and Tobin had developed a connection.

Nareash squinted as the ship cut through the low waves. With a better view of Juanoq's harbor, he gripped the railing tight. His smile vanished.

"Master, is everything alright?"

"What is wrong with the harbor, Colan?" he asked in a strained voice.

"Wrong? Nothing seems wrong . . . except that it's empty. What does that mean?"

"It means that Tobin grew impatient and has started his campaign early."

"I don't understand. Why would he do that?"

Because he doesn't need me? Or perhaps doesn't want me?

Nareash shook his head and relaxed his grip.

"His reasons are his own," said Nareash.

"The ships!" said Guwan from behind. The heavy boots of the Kifzo clodded up beside Colan. He gestured toward the approaching harbor. "They've left without us!"

"Yes," said Nareash. "They have."

"We need to leave right away to join them."

"No."

"No?"

"We will leave only after I see to other matters first. Three to four days should be enough time. Remember what I said about opportunity."

Guwan took a deep breath. "What am I supposed to do until then?"

Nareash reached into his robes and withdrew a ruby. It was one of many jewels they had harvested in sacks from Quarnoq before leaving the ancient city. He handed it to Guwan. "Get lost in a whorehouse and enjoy yourself. I imagine you could buy a place yourself with that. I'll send someone for you when you're needed."

Guwan eyed the jewel for a moment, then snatched it from Nareash's hand.

After the Kifzo left, Colan asked. "What was that about, Master?"

"You'll have to wait and see."

Nareash gazed over the empty harbor again.

Why, Tobin? Perhaps our connection isn't what I thought it was.

* * *

Nareash's return was met with as much fanfare as a fisherman bringing in the day's catch. The inhabitants of Juanoq apparently could not be bothered with news of the land of their ancestors when life still continued.

Before reaching the palace, Nareash sent word to all of Tobin's advisors about an impromptu council meeting. Back in his quarters, he quickly took a bath and changed his robes. Then he moved to the war room and ate while waiting for Tobin's councilors. Each wore a look that crossed between a frown and a scowl

A merchant whose name Nareash couldn't recall, spoke first. "Nachun, it's good to see you." He bowed and his beaded jewelry jingled. "Was your trip as successful as you hoped?"

"Somewhat."

The merchant smiled. "Please, tell us more."

Nareash sat in Tobin's chair and relaxed. After the long trip, his weary body welcomed the soft cushion. He rubbed his eyes lazily. "I didn't call this meeting for your benefit." He looked up and pointed at the farmer in the center. Another man whose name he couldn't recall. He cared little about names. He knew what mattered most—faces, home addresses, and family details—things that could be used against someone. "You. Tell me what Tobin's last orders were."

The farmer nervously stepped forward. "We were told to continue our jobs as before."

"And none of you thought to go against those orders?" Though Tobin's early departure had upset the High Mage, he still could not ignore their friendship and he wanted to ensure nothing was amiss in the city while Tobin fought, hundreds of miles away. He also needed to minimize any disruptions in the city's government so that his own plans for the future saw success.

The council's faces twisted in confusion. A fisherman gave an answer. "Why would we do that? None of us has ever enjoyed the kind of success we've had since Tobin took over for Bazraki. We would be fools to act on our own."

The other advisors nodded in agreement.

I have to hand it to you, Tobin. You managed to find not only the most competent, but also the least ambitious people I've ever seen. If Bazraki had recognized your potential, perhaps he'd be alive. I don't know why I was worried. This meeting was unnecessary.

"Is something funny, Nachun?" asked Teznak, Captain of the City Guard.

"A private joke, Captain. How are the nobles behaving with Tobin gone?"

"As they should be. They do nothing but indulge their vices. They've learned to be content with Tobin's leadership."

"How do you know this to be so?"

"Because it's my job to know," said Teznak. "Just as it's my job to question why you've called a council meeting without our ruler present, or why you're sitting in his chair. You're not our leader." Like most members of the City Guard, the man had failed as a warrior for some reason or another, but that had not stopped him from holding onto his arrogance and sense of power.

Nareash chose not to answer the man immediately. Instead, he caught the man's eyes and bore holes into him without blinking. He worked a silent spell, difficult to master, but quite effective in its purpose. It raised the man's body temperature slowly until sweat beaded on his face. Nareash saw the man waver in his stance as the heat got the better of him. Teznak's eyes rolled back in his head. "Catch him," Nareash muttered before the man collapsed.

The blacksmith nearby caught him in his thick arms. Nareash rose slowly from his seat and walked over to the man. He carried a cup of water with him and gave it to the blacksmith who poured it into Teznak's mouth. The captain of the guard opened his eyes and stared at Nareash.

"Never question me again, Captain." He looked up to the council. "This meeting is over." He left the war room. Halfway down the long hallway leading to the staircase, an eruption of whispers came from the room.

Nareash grinned. Colan waited for him by the staircase.

"Were you able to get our dinner plans ready?" asked the High Mage.

"Yes. We can go now."

* * *

Nareash savored each bite of the buttery flavor of the fish and the flaky texture of the bread. He finished the plate and continued next with roasted pig. He rolled the meat around in his mouth gently before swallowing. He reached for his glass and brought it to his nose, inhaling the fruity scent before sipping the wine.

Nareash set the cup down. "The rigors of travel seem to dictate that one must eat the same bland and boring food day in and day out." He lowered his head in a small bow. "My compliments, Lucia. This is the best meal I've had in months."

"Thank you." The simple reply had been the first thing she said since their greeting before the meal started.

The small gathering of Lucia, Jober, Colan, and himself had been eerily quiet. Nareash knew he made Jober and Lucia uncomfortable, but he didn't care. After all, few people ever seemed truly comfortable around him. And more importantly, he could not be bothered with their comfort around such gorgeous food.

"What's for dessert?" Nareash asked.

"Cinnamon and honey rolls. A servant should be bringing them shortly. I'll see how much longer they'll be." Lucia rose.

"No. That's alright. Take your seat. We'll use the time to discuss some things." He gestured to Colan and Jober. "Please give us some time alone."

Jober eyed Nareash warily, but after a moment reluctantly agreed. Nareash smiled as they left and the door to the dining room closed.

"He's quite the loyal attendant, isn't he?"

Lucia grew defensive. "He's not just a bodyguard. He's a good friend and a good man."

Nareash smiled, recalling the circumstances of that friendship. "Indeed." He removed the napkin from his lap and placed it on the table. "But that's not why I wanted to talk to you. I've been gone for months and was a bit surprised to learn Tobin left before I returned. Do you know why he changed strategy?"

Lucia blinked, then frowned. "I don't know. Wouldn't it help to ask his council? Surely they would be able to tell you."

"No. Tobin wouldn't have shared that information with them."

"Then why would you think that I might know. He doesn't share information with me either."

Nareash shrugged. "I thought since you and Tobin are close he might have let something slip."

Lucia scowled, but said nothing.

"I take it your relationship has changed."

"It's not important."

"I'll decide what's important. Tell me."

Lucia hesitated, then began. "He's not the same person I once knew. He's changed so much since Kaz disappeared and Bazraki died."

For the better.

"But the biggest change has come since he and Odala began their . . . whatever they have."

If I didn't know the woman clung to the belief her husband was still alive, I'd believe her jealous.

"Are you saying that Odala can't be trusted?"

"I didn't say that."

"Lucia. You and I both know you aren't stupid. You've known Tobin far longer than I have. If Tobin is in a compromising situation, I need to know. Regardless of what you think of me, I do have his best interests at heart."

After a moment of contemplation, Lucia began explaining her misgivings about Odala. Most of her concerns came out of speculation or coincidences, and Nareash felt the entire dinner had been a waste of time. Then something caught his attention. "Wait. What was that about her brother?"

"Oh. Soyjid is just very strange and always hovering over Odala. At first, I thought they were close, but several servants told me that they bicker almost constantly. No one can really make out what is being said, but their behavior together seems so odd."

"I'll need the names of those servants."

Lucia tensed. "Why do you need their names?"

"Don't worry. It has nothing to do with you. I just want to make sure they've been asked the right questions."

"There really isn't much more to say except that shortly before Tobin left, he made Soyjid almost like an understudy and allowed him to sit in on all his meetings."

Now that is interesting.

Following a knock at the door a servant with a tray of rolls poked her head in.

Nareash smiled. "Ah. Perfect timing. We were just finishing." He looked at Lucia. "I hope you'll still join me for dessert."

"Actually, I'm not very hungry."

"I understand. Thank you. You've been most helpful." He took a small bite of roll. "Please tell Colan to come in and see me."

As she strode across the room, Nareash looked up from his plate and watched the sway of her hips. He smiled to himself.

* * *

"Colan. Nachun wishes to see you," Lucia called out from the hall.

The shaman turned at her voice.

Jober tightened his hands into fists as the shaman walked away. He slowly relaxed them as Lucia neared.

She gave him an inquisitive look. "Is everything alright?"

"I'm fine."

"What were you talking about?"

He lied. "Nothing of importance."

Colan had been questioning him about the night Kaz disappeared. Not because he didn't believe the events. He just wanted to hear the story first hand from Jober. Jober had told the story many times and wanted to do nothing more than scream the truth so that he might relieve the burden from his heavy heart. But he couldn't.

Nachun would kill my family without blinking in order to preserve Tobin's position.

Jober redirected the discussion. "Are you alright? You look weak."

Lucia grimaced. "I'm fine. I just loathe that man. He makes me so uncomfortable." She shook her head. "I hate to think about what he is truly capable of."

Jober felt the weight on his conscience again.

If you only knew.

* * *

Nareash rushed over to the stack of papers against the wall near the window and steadied them just before they tumbled to the floor.

"Be careful, you idiot!"

"I'm sorry, but we don't have much room to move around," said the shaman.

"You have more than enough." He gestured to the open space in the center of the room. "Now be more careful and hurry up."

The man lowered his head and slid over to the other two shamans adorned in blue robes working frantically with pieces of chalk on the floor. Nareash finished steadying the stack he held, then moved several other piles toward the back of his room.

A faint tapping came from the door. The shamans paused in their work until Nareash signed for them to continue.

"Yes?" Nareash asked.

"It's Colan, Master."

"Come in."

His apprentice slipped inside and shut the door. He maneuvered around a pile of discarded books and stared curiously at the floor.

"Well?"

"I spoke with the last of the servants today. None can provide any helpful specifics."

"Did you push?"

"Yes. I used the spell you taught me. They weren't holding anything back."

Nareash grunted in frustration. "Did you learn anything of importance?"

"Just that Lucia spoke the truth. Soyjid and Odala were often seen arguing and when they parted Odala usually seemed troubled. I can continue tomorrow though."

Nareash waved him off. "No. We don't have time. I'll just have to deal with it later."

Another knock sounded at the door, this time loud enough to shake the frame and make the three shamans on the floor jump.

"That must be Guwan," Nareash said. "Enter."

The Kifzo strode in, fully armored in blue and gray attire. He walked with a swagger and kicked aside the leg of a shaman that blocked his path.

"You look more relaxed."

"I decided to take your advice," said Guwan, scanning the space.

"Well, I hope you didn't wear the women out too badly."

"They were paid well," said Guwan. "Didn't you get my message about the army?"

"Yes. They're struggling and that's why we aren't waiting any longer to do this. We should be back sometime tomorrow and then we can leave Juanoq the day after."

"I don't understand," said Guwan. "Where are we going? We can't travel far by land or boat in so short of time."

"A city called Asantia. It resides in a country called Thurum on a continent to the north of Hesh. I'll explain everything else once we get there." He looked around at the shamans. "Are we ready?"

"Yes," they answered in unison.

"And you remember my instructions?"

"Yes," they answered again.

Nareash led Guwan and Colan into the circle. "Each of you, grasp one of my arms and do not let go until I tell you to."

They did and Colan asked. "Master, about the shamans . . ."

"Don't worry. While they worked, I created a binding spell which will keep them confined to this room in order to aid us in our return. If they try to leave before then, they'll die."

One of the shamans looked up wide-eyed. "But Nachun, what about our basic needs."

"Food and water are on the other side of my bed. A chamber pot is in the corner. That should be more than enough for the next day."

"What if you don't make it back?" asked another, worried.

"Then the food and water won't matter. Another spell ties each of you to one of our lives. If one of us dies, then so will one of you." He grinned. "So I suggest, you focus quite intently on the task at hand."

The shaman swallowed hard and went back to his work.

"I need complete silence. Do not interrupt me for anything." Nareash closed his eyes and began the teleportation spell.

CHAPTER 20

Nareash had forgotten how much he hated to teleport until the dizziness overtook him after they reached their destination.

Teleportation posed many risks which is why even the High Mages of Cadonia rarely used it. One could potentially arrive in a life threatening situation. Also, the process took a great deal of power to perform properly, especially when trying to transfer more than one person or objects of substantial size. For that reason Nareash had employed the help of the shamans in Juanoq.

The sounds of Guwan and Colan emptying their stomachs to either side of Nareash announced the third reason why many hesitated to use the powerful mode of travel. Teleportation often left the traveler weakened and vulnerable for a time.

Such risks naturally increased when traveling great distances.

Nareash shook his arms free of the two men.

"What did you do to us?" asked Guwan.

Nareash walked over to a pile of tumbled stone and sat. "We teleported. Essentially, we traveled thousands of miles in a matter of seconds."

"Amazing. But, is it always so . . . unsettling, Master?" Colan had taken a knee and his head hung low.

"The first time, yes. It never gets easy, though the sensation does become more bearable. Come and sit. We need to rest before moving on."

Guwan and Colan managed to regain their composure and both took places next to Nareash.

"Master, are we in the right place?" Colan gazed out at the wreckage before them.

"We're where we are supposed to be." Nareash noted the piles of blackened rubble filling the streets and the crumbled remains of buildings in the Southern District. "I specifically chose this location since few residents live here any longer."

"So, you've been here?" asked Guwan, confused.

"No."

"Then how did you know?"

"I've studied Asantia's history. It was once a great city under the ancient Quoron Empire. One of the few places that escaped damage from the great earthquake that struck Thurum some four hundred years ago."

"Then what happened to this place?" asked Guwan.

"Over a decade ago, a famed mercenary outfit named the Hell Patrol made their way through this city while under attack from the province's ruler. The battle was quite epic from what the stories say. Apparently, a mage in their company destroyed a third of the city while the Hell Patrol's survivors made their escape."

"A mage?" asked Colan.

"A shaman if you prefer."

Colan looked out wide-eyed. "The power he must have been able to tap . . ."

Nareash laughed. "Don't spend too much time thinking about it. Something else must have happened to cause all of this. No mage or shaman has called on such power before. If one had, I would know about it."

"So, what happened to this mercenary group?" asked Guwan.

Nareash shrugged. "They took heavy losses, but were able to reform on a distant continent called Mytarcis. It's a place constantly at war with armies and would-be leaders rising and falling like the sun and moon." He paused. "You seem pretty accepting of all of this. You don't question what I say?"

Guwan grunted. "In the past couple of months I've seen the home of my ancestors, set my eyes on wonders few would believe, learned there are other civilizations besides those on Hesh, and have been teleported to one of those places by a man I always suspected was more than what he let on to be. At this point, little will surprise me."

Nareash smiled. "I knew there was something special about you, Guwan." He stood up. "Are we ready?"

The two nodded and left their seats, Colan less steady than Guwan.

"Master, I have more questions."

"And I'll try to answer them, but let's get moving. We've got a long walk ahead of us."

* * *

It took them several tries to find a clear path into the better parts of the city. They passed blackened stone and the remains of wooden timbers torn to shreds. The appearance of such ruin made Nareash wonder if sorcery had at least a small part in the destruction.

A very small part. I would have needed the scepter to accomplish something on this level.

Even the better parts of the city still wore signs of age. To Nareash's surprise, scaffolding hung from the most dire of structures and workers clamored about with new materials in hand.

Hmmm, interesting.

A hand clasped Nareash's shoulder and yanked him backward. Guwan had pulled him and Colan into a side alley.

The Kifzo pointed to a family crossing the street. "Nachun, these people are different. Their skin is pale. We will stick out among them."

Nareash chuckled. "I almost forgot about the glamour." Within moments, both Guwan and Colan wore different faces and the skin on their hands, neck, and face had gone from a deep black to a bronzed tan. "That should do."

The illusion seemed to disturb Guwan while it fascinated Colan.

Guwan touched his face. "Who are we supposed to be?"

"You are still yourself. You just wear the faces of people I once knew. Don't worry, it's only temporary while we walk through the city to the palace."

"Whose face do you wear?"

Nareash shrugged, having dropped his own glamour. "My own."

They reentered the street and headed toward the heart of the city near a large bell tower. Nareash knew the palace resided near there.

Made of white stone, the multi-leveled palace hinted at what the rest of Asantia must have looked like when the lands of Thurum had been ruled by the Quoron Empire. Statues of those ancient rulers still adorned the outside walls. One figure stood larger than the rest. General Victas in his legendary armor. Oddly enough, there was nothing commemorating Aurnon the First's conquering of the city.

Citizens of Asantia dared not pass too close to the palace walls, and outside the gate three dozen soldiers armed in ancient bronze weapons, made sure it stayed that way.

Nareash did not hesitate as he strode up to the gate with Guwan and Colan a half-step behind.

Several of the guards lowered their spears and one spoke. "Turn around. The emperor does not speak with commoners."

Nareash laughed. "Emperor, is it? And what an empire. I assure you the *emperor* will want to speak with us."

More men lowered their spears and tensed. Nareash halted. Guwan held weapons in each hand. Nareash never heard them leave their scabbards.

"Put them away, Guwan." Nareash said over his shoulder. He eyed the guards. "Raise your spears and open the gates."

A mage slid through a side door near the gate and supported the men.

Green robes? That would be insulting if they knew who I was.

The guards stepped forward, spears ready. Nareash knocked them off their feet with a gust of wind. He focused his mind on their spears and lifted them into the air. Wind took the weapons halfway down the street before clacking to the ground.

He used the wind to throw the mage against a stone wall, knocking him unconscious. Nareash pointed to the nearest guardsmen. "Get up and open the gate. And you," he said pointing to another. "Run ahead and tell Hezen that High Mage Nareash will be joining him shortly." He went back to the first guard. "Take me to your *emperor*."

* * *

Nareash strode into the dining hall of the palace. The smell of heavily spiced meats and fresh bread filled the air. Hezen sat in conference with eight other men. Based on the mannerisms of those around the table, Nareash assumed them to be allies or perhaps those newly conquered by the would-be emperor.

Hezen wore a patch over his right eye and a thick beard concealed most of the burn scars on that side of his face.

The guard Nareash sent ahead to announce his arrival stood at his ruler's side. Hezen met Nareash's gaze and pushed the guard away while rising.

Hezen pointed. "Who do you think you are barging into my home?"

Nareash inclined his head at the guardsmen. "I thought I made that clear."

"High Mage Nareash?" Hezen laughed. "Amcaro killed the lunatic over a year and a half ago. You need to come up with a better tale than that."

"It's the truth and I will not be mocked." Nareash eyed the men around the table. "Dismiss your subjects. Our conversation will go much more quickly without them here."

"You dare speak to me in my home like I'm a peasant. I am an emperor—"

"You are the emperor of nothing!" shouted Nareash. His magnified voice shook the walls and cracked the windows of the room. Hezen took a step backward. The others in the room glanced to their leader nervously. Nareash softened his tone. "You may have managed a few victories for yourself, but that is nothing to me. Now send your people away."

A hushed silence fell across the room. After a moment Hezen ordered the others to leave, unable to hide the fury in his voice. One rather large man stayed behind, adorned in high ranking military garb of polished bronze. His hand rested on the pummel of his sword at his waist. He alone seemed unimpressed by the High Mage's demonstration of power.

"Everyone," said Nareash.

Hezen sat down. "No. This is my general. I'm assuming whatever you have to say involves my armies."

"In part."

"Then Benat should stay."

"Without getting ahead of myself, Guwan will command the army going forward." Nareash gestured toward the Kifzo. "Benat will get his own company, nothing more."

Benat looked incredulous. His nostrils flared. "My men will not follow a black-skinned foreigner."

Nareash had dropped the glamour now that they were inside the palace, knowing that Hezen would eventually learn the truth.

"Nor will my men obey anyone who cannot defeat me in combat," continued Benat.

"The first point is irrelevant. I assume the army will do whatever Hezen tells them to do, correct?" asked Nareash.

Hezen nodded.

"And to the second point . . ." Nareash switched to the Heshan language. "Guwan, you may kill him. Quickly please, so we can get on with this."

Benat's eyes widened as Guwan sped across the room without the slightest hesitation. His sword appeared in his hand. Benat clumsily blocked the first of Guwan's strikes, but could do nothing against the second. The general's head fell to the floor and his body followed.

Hezen stroked his beard calmly, watching blood pump from the general's neck. "You have my attention."

"As you mentioned, I do need an army."

"I have five thousand in my own forces plus an additional four thousand men from the allies you just dismissed."

"That's not nearly enough. I need an army twenty times that size."

"T-twenty times? I'd have to pull in troops from all over Thurum."

"Exactly."

"It would take years to conquer that many lands."

"Thankfully, you won't have to conquer anyone. And you have months, not years."

Hezen chuckled. "How am I supposed to do that?"

Nareash pulled a pouch from under his robes and dumped its contents on the table. Hezen's eyes widened as precious stones sparkled in the light shining in through the cracked windows. "Simple. You entice the leaders with the opportunity of riches. This should be enough to whet their appetites. Next time I return, you'll have a sack full of stones to add to these. It will only be a fraction of what they can earn by agreeing to consolidate under one command."

"Am I to presume that you plan to invade Cadonia, High Mage? Finish what you attempted once before?" Hezen taunted.

Nareash ignored his tone. "I'll need a large force to capture the High Pass and then later dispel any resistance as we march on Lyrosene."

Hezen picked at his beard. "The jewels and the common hate of Cadonia should be enough to at least draw interest. But there will be a lot of strong-willed men wanting to take over your conquest."

"Just do your part. I'll handle the rest."

Hezen reached over and snatched up a diamond. A long pause followed as he examined it. "I want Thurum."

Nareash chuckled. "You're in no place to make demands."

Hezen placed the diamond on the table and leaned back in his chair. "I believe I am. Yes, you can kill me now and take my armies, but then what? You have no idea how to handle the personalities of those you want to consolidate and you have no knowledge of this land."

"As I said earlier, money will solve those problems."

Hezen shrugged. "Eventually. But how much longer will it take you to raise an army without me. Don't you care about delays to your plan?"

Nareash tightened his jaw. Hezen was right. He did not want to wait any longer than absolutely necessary to reach his goals. "When I have the throne, I'll see that you rule Thurum as a vassal to me."

Hezen smiled. "I think we have a deal. Will you stay for dinner? I have questions."

"No. We need to be on our way."

Hezen eyed Guwan and Colan. "A pity. I was hoping to hear about where you've been all this time and your thoughts on the turmoil in Cadonia."

Nareash stopped. His killing of the king and the other High Mages would have caused uneasiness in the land. But given the amount of time that had passed since then, Amcaro should have been able to keep things under control. "Turmoil?"

Hezen's brow furrowed. "You don't know? One Above, where have you been?"

"That's unimportant," snapped Nareash. "Now, what are you talking about? What turmoil could there possibly be that Amcaro could not handle?"

"Plenty, considering he's dead. He died shortly after you did." Hezen chuckled.

Dead? That changes everything. The scepter? Is it gone? No. Someone must have it. Elyse? One Above, that's the best news I've heard in some time.

With Amcaro dead, the biggest threat to Nareash's plans had been eliminated. He breathed a sigh of relief. His plan to invade Cadonia seemed even more likely to succeed than before.

Especially if Conroy is involved and has neglected the High Pass's defenses.

Hezen continued. "With no High Mages and an inexperienced queen in power, several of the dukes got ambitious. Most of the land has been at war for over a year."

"A year? I'm surprised the crown held out so long when you consider that Aurnon the Eighth had let his military weaken."

"Well, the prodigal son did return just as Tomalt made his first move."

"One Above, Jonrell?" asked Nareash, surprised.

Hezen spat and his mouth turned up into a sneer. "And he brought the Hell Patrol with him. They managed to work a few wonders against Tomalt."

Nareash hadn't seen the young prince since their time on Estul Island. Jonrell had been the only one in the royal family Nareash had any respect for. As boys, he had stood up for Nareash on one occasion when he saw Rhindora and several others harassing him in the library. The High Mage never forgot that.

Nareash whispered. "So, the rumors were true. He did join them."

"Yes, he did. Those whoresons are responsible for destroying the hold I had in Thurum more than a decade ago. They ruined a third of Asantia and caused this," said Hezen, pointing to his face.

"Jonrell. He could change things," Nareash muttered.

He always had a way of attracting people to his side and he always excelled in his studies.

Hezen started to chuckle. "Maybe he could have, but not anymore. The piece of dung is dead." Hezen wiped his eyes as he laughed. "Killed by a crossbow from some boy he took in. Serves the pompous fool right. I had once offered him a chance at power, not knowing who he really was, and he deceived me." He spat on his own floor. "I hope he's rotting with the One Below."

Nareash's eyes narrowed. "I'll hear no more ill spoken of the man." Hezen looked taken aback by the comment. "Your failings are in the past." He paused. "So, the royal army is barely hanging on again?"

"I wouldn't say that. Elyse managed an alliance with Jeldor. And one of the men from the Hell Patrol, some foreigner many are calling a black demon, stepped in to lead the army after Jonrell's death. Oddly, reports say the man doesn't know anything about his past. Yet, he's committed to the queen." He gestured to Guwan. "The reports actually say he looks similar to him. You should hear the stories. I thought no one could be that good." He looked down to Benat. "But then again . . . ."

Nareash tensed as he listened. "Do you know the man's name?"

Hezen shrugged. "Kaz."

Guwan and Colan both asked questions in Heshan at recognition of the name, but Nareash ignored them, gesturing them to silence.

Impossible. He should be dead. But if I could have been sent to Hesh, then why couldn't Kaz have been sent to another continent. One Above, and he just so happened to cross paths with Jonrell.

Hezen picked up on their change in behavior. "Does the name mean anything to you?"

Nareash wanted to ask a thousand questions, but he needed to get back to Tobin before valuable resources he counted on were lost.

"We can discuss it later," said Nareash. "If there's anything else, make it quick."

"Just that the Hell Patrol also stayed out of memory for Jonrell."

"A few extra soldiers will mean little to me if you hold up your end of the deal," said Nareash as he gestured toward the jewels.

"Yes, but their mage, Krytien, is with him. I don't know why he hasn't done more in the war yet. But he's the one responsible for the state of Asantia."

Nareash grinned. "So you, too, believe this nonsense about one mage being responsible for the city's damage?"

Hezen's expression darkened. "I was there. One of the few who survived. I saw what happened. How do you think I got my scars?"

"I have no doubt you saw something, but I assure you that you're mistaken. I'll be back within a month. See that when I return, there has been progress."

* * *

To Colan and Guwan's credit, neither said a word as they hurried back through the palace and out the gate. Once Nareash restored their glamour and they were lost in the mix of people walking the streets, Guwan finally spoke up.

"I heard Kaz's name . . ." he started.

"Yes. There is a commander in Cadonia by that name."

"Is it . . . our former warleader?"

Who else could it possibly be? One Above, what are the odds he would have turned up in Cadonia? Amcaro dead, Jonrell returned and killed, and now Kaz? So much to consider.

"Anything is possible." said Nareash. "But there are other possible explanations. There is a race of people called Byzernians that live on islands to the east of here. They generally have much darker skin than those you see now. It could be one of their people. And a name means nothing. No one person's name is unique."

"But if it is him . . ." said Guwan, a slight hesitancy in his voice.

"Then we'll deal with him. More specifically, you'll deal with him, General. Will that be a problem for you?"

"No."

"And any of the other Kifzo?"

"Possibly, but not many. Most would like the opportunity to take him down."

Nareash smiled. Kaz had not ingratiated himself with his fellow warriors which had done him no favors in winning their loyalty.

Though it begs the question about how his men perceive him now. He must have changed in some capacity to be awarded command over the royal army. Of course, Elyse was never very bright.

"Master, are we going back to the same site we teleported in from?" asked Colan.

"Yes. It will make things easier for the return trip."

"And the shamans in your room will be able to locate us?"

"I left a trail for them to latch onto more easily. I didn't want to leave anything to chance."

As they reached their location, Nareash took in the devastation around him one last time. He shook his head.

Impossible. I've only heard stories of Sacrynon having this sort of power.

"Grab my arms again. We won't have but a night to rest and then we're leaving to join Tobin's forces."

* * *

"Nachun, please come in." Mizak stepped aside and fully opened the doorway. Nareash entered the old man's simple home. Unlike his room in the palace, Mizak's texts were organized neatly on shelves that lined the walls.

On a table, several small pieces of parchment gleaned from Quarnoq's library had been carefully placed. Nareash saw from the filled paper and half-full inkwell, the old scholar had been busy at work, documenting his findings.

"How are things going?" asked Nareash, tired, gesturing to the table. He had only a couple of hours before leaving to meet up with Tobin.

"Good. There is even more there than I originally thought." The excitement in Mizak's voice drained. "But you aren't here to check up on that, are you?"

Nareash smiled at the old man's sharpness. "No, I'm not." He removed a piece of paper from his robes, the map that Guwan had discovered. He handed it to Mizak.

The old man's brows furrowed. "This looks like a map of Hesh, but this . . ."

"Is the rest of the world," finished Nareash.

The old man's eyes widened as he looked up. "Where did you find this?"

"Quarnoq. It was one of the items I had truly sought." He pointed to a spot on Thurum where Asantia resided. "I'll be going there by ship when Tobin's campaign is done."

"What's there?"

Nareash smiled. "That's too much to get into now. Anyway, I need you to make twenty-five copies of this map for the voyage. I made one myself during our return trip to Juanoq, but it took me too long and you have much greater skill at this than I do. I'm leaving you with the original. Can you do it?"

"Twenty-five, you say?"

Nareash nodded. He expected the old man to ask the question hidden behind his eyes.

Why so many?

But he didn't.

"I want to go with you."

"Why?"

Mizak chuckled. "Why not? It'll be a once in a lifetime opportunity and I'm not getting any younger." His face grew serious. "That's my term of payment. Twenty-five exact copies, and in exchange I'm allowed to join you."

Nareash shrugged. "I can always use another mind as sharp as yours. Done."

CHAPTER 21

"Lucartias is a very different city," said Lobella.

"You'll find that the southern Cadonian cities have very little in common with the northern cities," said Elyse.

"It seems so much darker."

Elyse heard the somberness in her friend's tone as they gazed out from the bow of the ship. Brown, stone towers loomed over the rust-colored mansions that stood out from the black warehouses running along the docks.

"The stones used to build the cities here come from the Cataric Mountains rather than the northern ranges we're used to." She paused and turned to Lobella. "Are you alright? I thought you would have enjoyed the chance to travel by boat for the first time, but you've seemed distant most of the trip."

Lobella forced a pathetic attempt at a smile. "I do like the smells of the ocean. I'm just thinking of mother again."

"I offered to have someone else come in your stead. I knew I should have made you stay."

Lobella put her head down. "No, Your Majesty. My place is here." She shrugged. "Besides, Gauge insisted that you may need me. My duty to you is more important than the duty to my mother."

Elyse tilted her head to the side. "Are those your words or Gauge's?"

"Both. I only needed him to remind me."

Elyse frowned, hurt to see her friend in such a mood. Elyse reached out and placed a hand on Lobella's to comfort her. Lobella tensed slightly.

"May I be excused?" asked Lobella. "I'd like to make sure all our things are together."

"Yes," said Elyse, feeling hurt and confused.

Lobella offered a bow and left.

I'll try to talk to her again later.

Elyse stood alone at the railing, watching the city grow before her eyes, turning her head to take in the expansive view.

It won't be long now. Just a few more hours to dock the ship and make our way through the city. Then, perhaps I can figure out a way to come to peace with Conroy.

Thinking of Conroy led her to recall the conversation she had with Lady Jaendora shortly before leaving port in Floroson. They had laughed and cried reminiscing about the past.

When Jonrell and Lord Undalain were still with us.

The mood soured when they discussed the risks of Elyse's decision to visit Lucartias. Though Lady Jaendora did not like Elyse's plan, she understood that like the queen's risk in obtaining Jeldor's alliance before the start of the war, the opportunity to reduce bloodshed with her visit was too great to pass up.

* * *

"Your Majesty," said Captain Sylik with a bow. "It was an honor and a pleasure to have you grace my humble decks."

Elyse smiled. Lady Jaendora had insisted that Sylik be the one to transport the queen and her retinue. "Thank you, Captain. The pleasure was all mine. Your stories made the trip go that much faster, especially those about Jonrell."

The captain shook his head. "It's a shame what happened to him. He was a good man."

"Yes, he was." She quickly changed the subject. "Will you be staying in port long?"

"If Her Majesty needs me to, I'd be more than happy to wait. Otherwise, I'll try to leave on the morrow. I've got a list of things that Lady Jaendora would like me to check on while in this part of Cadonia."

"Then please, go."

"Thank you, Your Majesty."

They finished their farewells and parted. She disembarked onto the raised docks with Kroke in her shadow as the two dozen men of her personal guard surrounded her. Lobella drifted in behind them.

"This isn't right," said Kroke.

"What isn't right?" asked Elyse.

Kroke gestured with his head at the surrounding dock. "Look around. I know we're at war, but this place is practically deserted."

Elyse scanned the waterfront. "Well, it is getting late in the day."

"Not that late. The sun still hasn't set."

"Sylik didn't seem concerned."

"Yeah, well we ain't at sea anymore. I'll trust his gut while rolling around in the waves. On land, I'll trust my own." Kroke grunted, eyes darting between the heads of the soldiers walking in front of them. "I don't like it. I don't even see the local authority. They should be greeting the ship, especially during a war."

Elyse looked over and saw Kroke tense. She followed his gaze to a small alley on the right. A well-dressed herald stepped into the fading sunlight wearing shades of dark red and bright gold. A dozen armed men wearing brown cloaks over mail and carrying spears followed him.

Elyse touched Kroke's arm gently. "It's alright. The soldiers are with the city's watch."

Elyse called for her guards to halt and they waited at the end of the docks for the herald to arrive.

The herald trotted up, shouting through a scowl. "What is this? Armed men are not allowed in the city, especially not at a time of war."

The captain of Elyse's guard stepped out in front and shouted back. "Open your eyes and look at our colors. You'll want to show some respect when you address your queen."

"The queen?"

Elyse tapped the guards in front of her. They stepped aside, exposing her. The herald dropped to one knee. The city watch followed.

"I'm sorry, Your Majesty," said the herald. "This is completely unexpected. How can I be of service?"

Elyse walked forward with Kroke close at her side. "We would like transportation to Duke Olasi's residence."

Elyse noticed several of the guardsmen flinch, a few exchanging nervous glances.

"Is something wrong?" she asked.

"Uh, no, Your Majesty," said the herald. "It's just that our lord's health is failing." He put on a bright smile. "But let's not talk of that. You must be tired from your travels."

Elyse nodded. The herald turned and quickly sent several men off on errands. After a few moments they returned with a carriage.

* * *

The carriage plodded through empty streets. Elyse's Royal Guard marched alongside her. Intermittently throughout the trip, the number of men from the city watch had grown to over three times the number that had greeted them at the waterfront.

Kroke cursed as he stared out one of the carriage windows. "That's three more."

"So what are three more men?" shrugged Elyse, trying to appear indifferent.

"Three more *armed* men," Kroke corrected.

"I don't understand," said Lobella. "Aren't they just providing us an escort?"

Elyse started to open her mouth, but Kroke cut in with a hushed voice. "You heard that herald. What was his name, Mouse or something? The city is safe and yet hardly anyone is on the streets. Why would we need a small army to reach Duke Olasi's residence?"

"His name is Mase, actually," said Elyse. "And he said that many were in the fields working while daylight allowed, doing their part to provide supplies to Olasi's forces for when they have to take the field. Olasi is an honest man, Kroke."

"What about his son? I was there when Illyan warned you about him. I'm beginning to think that shifty little man is the only one who truly knows what's going on in this country."

"Enough!" Elyse hissed. Elyse glanced over to Lobella who nervously played with her fingers as she watched the twirling blade dance in Kroke's hand. Elyse rubbed at the bridge of her nose. "And please, if you must have a knife in your hand, at least keep it still."

Kroke frowned and shifted in his seat. He began to clean his nails while keeping his eyes on the passing cobbled road.

Elyse sighed. Truth be told, she felt uneasy as well, but the last thing she wanted to do was admit she had made a mistake.

* * *

When they arrived at Duke Olasi's estate, Mase ushered them through the castle and into the duke's audience chamber. He insisted that Elyse's guards wait outside the door, but allowed Kroke and Lobella to accompany her.

A troubled feeling haunted the queen as the door clicked shut behind her. She noticed Kroke's fingers wiggle as he eyed the countless members of the city watch lining the walls of the chamber. The dozens of armored men stood at attention with such rigidness, they resembled the bronze-plated columns supporting the high ceilings. Lobella's heavy breathing sounded over Mase's footsteps as he brought them to the center of the chamber.

Mase bowed. "Your Majesty, I've been told that Markus should be here at any moment. By your leave?"

Elyse nodded. "Yes, of course."

Mase left through a side door and a minute later Markus entered through the same opening. Soldiers clicked their heels together and stood taller as he strode across the space.

In his late fifties, Markus maintained a neatly-trimmed scalp and beard of salt and pepper hair. Elyse had not seen Duke Olasi's son in years, but the man obviously favored his father. He took his seat in a large chair against the back wall. Only after he appeared satisfied with the positioning of his rear did he even look up to acknowledge Elyse.

She spared a glance at the city watch. *This isn't right.*

She remembered the formality and kindness Olasi showed at the dinner following her father's funeral in everything the duke did. Then she looked at Markus and felt angry. Olasi's son wore his arrogance brazenly.

Suddenly he no longer looks like his father.

Elyse started to speak, wanting to voice her displeasure in Markus's behavior when he began.

"Your Majesty, I beg your pardon if I don't kneel or bow, but this old leg injury of mine is acting up and I'd rather not make a fool of myself by tumbling to the floor," said Markus. His tone lacked the sincerity Elyse desired to hear. He continued. "Your visit is quite unexpected, Your Majesty. What brings you to my corner of Cadonia?"

Unexpected? Your corner?

She inclined her head. "My lord, I'm here because of your letter."

Markus blinked. "Letter? I'm not aware of any letter."

"The letter stated that you were in contact with Duke Conroy and felt like my presence would speed up any discussions of peace. It also spoke of your father's declining health." She paused, concerned and frustrated at the lack of recognition on Markus' face. "It bore your seal, my lord."

Markus looked away and rubbed his chin. "I'll have to look into this letter." He turned back to Elyse. "I beg your pardon, Your Majesty. But when may I expect the rest of your escort to arrive. I assume you're bringing in other forces by sea to meet up with your commander as well?"

Elyse looked confused. "No. Nothing like that. The bulk of the army is already with Kaz and Jeldor."

"Excuse me." Markus rang a bell and Mase reentered the room, running past the queen. Markus leaned over and whispered in the herald's ear.

She took a step forward. "My lord—"

He raised a hand and shushed her, stopping Elyse in her tracks, mouth hanging open. Markus then gently pushed Mase away with his other hand and the herald sprinted past her again.

Elyse fumed. "Your father would never dare treat his queen in such a way!"

"You are absolutely right. He would not and that's why you're talking to me rather than him."

"What do you mean? Your father is sick."

"He is. And what better time to make a change in rule that should have happened years ago?"

Kroke cursed.

I was wrong.

"I don't know who sent that letter, but there was some truth in it. Besides my father's health, I have been in contact with Duke Conroy. However, the peace discussed would be of no benefit to you. He and I have formed an alliance. And thanks to your information about Kaz, I know that there will be no reinforcements outside of the army he and Jeldor now field."

Kroke swore again as fighting erupted from the other side of the doors.

Markus motioned with his hands at either side of the room. "Guards, see that they are secured below. Make sure no harm comes to the queen or her servant unless I say otherwise. If anyone else gives you trouble, hurt them, badly."

Elyse noted that he eyed Kroke when he spoke and the queen saw the mercenary crouched with a knife in each hand as the guardsmen approached. "Kroke, put them away."

He didn't move.

"I said put them away. You are no good to me dead."

"And you are no good to the realm locked in a cell," he answered back.

"For my sake, please."

His arms relaxed and he sheathed his knives. The guards rushed in and the butt of a spear crashed into the mercenary's skull.

CHAPTER 22

Odala paced her tent, turning her nose up at the smell permeating the canvas—the smell of an army. She sorely missed the pampered life she knew in Juanoq. Rather than waking to flowers, fruits, and fresh bread, the jarring stench of blood, musk, and greasy stew woke her each morning. Yesterday, she called for a bath to wash away her own foul odor, but her servants explained that they could not waste resources on such frivolous things.

The stink was only part of it. Clanging armor, shouting officers, and cursing warriors led to many restless nights.

She let out a frustrated sigh.

To make matters worse, Tobin spent less time with her as his obsession with the campaign grew. Day and night he drove himself, hoping to find an advantage over the opposition. She couldn't help but feel neglected by his behavior.

Odala jumped as Tobin barged into the tent, seething. Blood ran down his arm and mud caked his chest and face. She ran to him. "Are you alright?"

He pushed her away and began rummaging through a trunk of his personal belongings. "I'm fine."

"But your arm?"

"It's nothing."

She waited a moment. "What happened?"

Tobin stopped and slammed the lid to the trunk. He looked over his shoulder. "What happened was Charu. Somehow he knew our strategy. We still gained the ground, but our losses were great again." He strode across the space to another trunk and searched. "It doesn't make sense."

"How did my brother do?"

"Fine," said Tobin, his tone suddenly morose. "He did fine."

"What are you looking for?"

"A map. It was one of Nachun's and if I remember, it showed the details of the land differently. I need to think of something before this campaign falls apart."

"You're being too hard on yourself." She paused. "Why don't we just go back to Juanoq?"

He slowly turned and stood. He held a rolled sheet of parchment in his hand. "Why would I do something like that?"

The look in his eyes startled Odala. "So we could spend more time together. There is more to life than war, isn't there?"

Tobin narrowed his gaze. "You don't think I can do it, do you? You think I'm going to fail?" He lowered his voice. "I hear the whisperings in camp among some of the men. I know they feel the same." He shook his head. "I thought you understood. I'm Warleader. If I cannot succeed at this, then I am nothing to my people. This is my life."

Odala felt her eyes well up. "What am I then?"

Tobin stared intensely at her. She swore he would say the words she needed to hear any moment. Instead he brushed by without a word, leaving her alone again.

She wept bitterly.

* * *

Tobin's head pounded, muting the sounds of a frustrated army. He didn't have to hear his men's irritation—he saw it everywhere as he strode through camp. He knew they questioned his ability to lead. If he could not find a way to more soundly defeat Charu, he did not doubt his fall from warleader would be more rapid than his rise.

How does he stay a step ahead of me?

Tobin quadruple-checked his plans and tried things he knew no one had ever done before. Yet, without the superiority of his warriors, the war would have already been lost.

And now, even Odala doubts my abilities.

Tobin had enough.

He found Walor in the chow line. Tobin waited for the Kifzo to grab his bowl and then they met in an isolated part of camp, away from prying eyes and ears. He unrolled the map and explained his plan.

Walor listened intently. The surprise on his face grew.

"Are you sure about this?"

"Yes. We need to gain some momentum before reaching Feruse. Do you think he will expect it?"

"I don't think even the Kifzo would expect this."

"Good. I'm telling no one else the plan until we're on our way. I'm beginning to wonder if Charu has found a way to infiltrate our ranks."

Walor nodded. "How many are you taking?"

"Five hundred. Only the best and most trusted. Wait until the camp settles down before you give Ufer his orders. Then we'll rouse the others. I want to wait until the last possible moment before we leave. I'm leaving you in charge."

* * *

Odala woke with a start as she heard her name shouted from outside. She had cried herself to sleep, pondering whether her relationship with Tobin was worth it. She never decided whether she truly had feelings for him or if she had simply been infatuated with the attention and power her position gave her. She felt the cold place next to her and realized Tobin had not come to bed.

Soyjid burst through the tent flaps. "Where did Tobin go?"

"He's probably at some fire with his men," she snapped.

"No, he's not." He cocked his head to the side. "He didn't tell you where he was going?"

She scowled. "No. He tells me less each day. Why?"

"He left with five hundred Kifzo in the middle of the night, but no one knows where he's gone to except for Walor and he refuses to see me."

Odala turned her back to Soyjid and pulled the covers over her head, even angrier with Tobin. "He probably went out on a mass scouting mission. What does it matter to you? He's warleader. Tobin can do as he pleases," she said bitterly.

Soyjid kicked her bed and stormed out of the tent muttering. "Why do I even bother with you?"

* * *

An hour before dawn five hundred pairs of intense eyes stared at the Green Forest Clan village. The company of Kifzo warriors Tobin led had traveled over a day and a half away in order to reach their destination. At his command, the men had left behind all of Nachun's newer armor, opting instead for lighter packs. The Kifzo had not fought this way since their invasion of the Orange Desert Clan.

Seems like a lifetime ago.

Tobin pushed aside the guilt that plagued him for making the same decision Kaz had so long ago.

Kaz would have done this from the start, but this wasn't my first choice. Charu forced my hand.

Tobin noted the eagerness in the eyes of his men.

Ufer crouched beside him. "Warleader, the scouts have returned. They estimate one thousand inhabitants."

"And the warriors using it as a base for scouting?"

"Eight hundred."

More than I thought we'd come against. Nachun's map obviously did not reflect any recent changes.

"Location of the warriors?"

"They're clustered on the far side of the settlement. Those nearest us are the ones living here."

Tobin watched the burning coals from the night's fires glow between the wooden structures and animal pens. His stomach knotted.

"I'll take four hundred men to engage their warriors. Get the rest into position here. When you hear us attack, surge into the settlement. No mercy to anyone except the children. I want them to carry the news back to Charu."

Ufer nodded in what looked like approval. "Warleader, if we are able to finish things quickly, the men will want to enjoy themselves with the women. I know your thoughts, but it would do good to lift their spirits after the past couple of months."

Ufer's words hung in the air.

Tobin looked around at the hungry eyes in his warriors as he considered the request. *I can't believe I'm even considering this. But the whole point of this trip is to solidify their loyalty.* Tobin rolled his jaw. "Just this once, since they'll die soon afterward." Tobin tasted the bile creeping into the back of his throat. "But again, no children."

"It will be done."

Ufer crawled away and spread the word. Tobin glanced one last time at the sleeping village. He selected his men and steeled himself to the grim task ahead.

What's one more nightmare to add to the others?

* * *

The pounding storm hid many things in the murky gray morning. It muffled the screams of women being used. It stifled the celebratory cheers from the Kifzo who, with only thirty-eight casualties, managed to wipe out an entire settlement.

The rain washed the blood from Tobin's skin and clothes while the thunder hushed the wailing cries from the long lines of three hundred odd children fleeing the village in panic. Older ones carried or dragged the younger ones behind them in haste, worried that the menacing warriors would change their mind and turn their weapons on them.

"A great victory, Warleader. The men will spread this tale like fire once we return to the main camp."

Tobin grunted.

"And Charu will . . ."

"Later Ufer. See that the men are doing as they were told."

"Yes, Warleader." Footsteps faded, slopping through the fresh mud.

Tobin stood alone on the edge of the village near the sole road leading away and watched the last of the children run into the trees, thankful that the rain masked his tears.

* * *

Odala left camp and ran into the woods. She slipped and fell on a wet root protruding from the ground. She examined her muddy hands and punched her leg, angry as she huddled near the base of a large pine tree. She brought her knees in close and wept.

Her head jerked at the crunch of leaves and she saw Soyjid round the side of an oak some twenty feet from her.

He glanced her way. "There you are. You know, it's too dangerous for you to run off like that. It's possible that Charu could have someone lurking nearby. They'd snatch you up in a second in order to get to Tobin."

Odala wiped her tears away with the back of her hand. "So? I doubt Tobin would really care."

Soyjid stopped a few feet from her. "So you've heard?"

"Of course I heard. The entire camp is buzzing with what he did."

"Have you spoken with him?"

"No. I saw the men cheering for him and the look of satisfaction he wore. I ran away before he spotted me." Her voice softened. "It reminded me of when he threatened father. I may have actually loved him once." She paused. "But now I hate him. He tries to be good, but any man who could do the things he did is evil." She shook her head. "When you first had me try to spy on him and he told me about some of the awful things he had done, he blamed Kaz and his father for giving him those orders or for putting him in situations where he had no choice. But he had a choice this time."

"I'm sure he'll blame Charu for pushing him into this decision," said Soyjid.

"He's wrong. It's simpler than that. For all his training and physical skills, he failed." She looked up. "Everyone says that you've done well with the orders given to you. Perhaps you should be commander. You wouldn't do something so awful, would you?"

"Never. But watch what you say, Sister. Few outside of our clan would agree with you. His men love him more today for what he's done."

"You were right all along." She sighed. "Too bad we can't stop them."

Soyjid glanced around him and lowered his voice. "Who says that we can't?"

* * *

"That's the last one, Warchief."

Charu rubbed his temples. "You said that last time, Gidan."

"Scouts back-tracked the trails this time."

"What's the final number?"

"Four hundred ninety-eight children. And they're all telling the same story."

So many.

"And you're sure they weren't followed?"

"Positive. I sent men to check the village in order to confirm the story, but given the circumstances I have no reason to doubt what they've told us."

Charu sighed. "Neither do I."

Charu left him and entered his tent. Melat's arms found their way around his neck. Tears ran down her cheeks.

"So you've heard then?" he asked in a heavy voice.

"Yes." She shook her head. "We knew the Blue Island Clan was cruel, but it is still shocking."

He pushed her aside and walked over to a table. "This is part of war."

"Don't pretend to hide your emotions. I'm not one of your men. This bothers you too, doesn't it?"

"Of course it does," he snapped. "Green Forest Clan or not, I wouldn't stoop as low as Tobin did. The men want his blood now and I have half a mind to give it to them."

"But you won't." Melat came over and took his hand in hers. "You're too smart for that. You know he is trying to goad you into making a mistake."

"I know."

Melat pulled out a message. "This came in just a few moments ago. He didn't know Tobin was going to strike. The strategy was a last minute decision that couldn't have been foreseen."

"That means little to the innocents who died."

"I know that, but the letter says more." Melat paused. "He believes that Tobin is so sure the incident in the village will shake you that you should withdraw to Feruse and make him think you're afraid. A strategy was attached to the message detailing the most likely set up of their forces if we meet them in battle there."

"Interesting."

"Do you think it will work?"

Charu examined the strategy and saw that it seemed sound. "It could."

"But?"

"But the closer we get to Feruse, the more likely we might be betrayed." She smiled. "True. So then what do we do?"

"I'll have to think about it before making a decision."

CHAPTER 23

"Get up you worthless piece of garbage. No son of mine would be lying on the floor like that."

Kroke growled as he heard his father's voice inside his head. The man had been dead going on twenty years, yet Kroke's hate for him had never waned. At the age of twelve he had killed his father, tired of the man's abuse of him and his family. The rape of Kroke's older sister had pushed him over the edge.

He rolled himself off the stone floor and sat up in a foul mood. The smell of molding straw from the corner of his cell didn't help his demeanor.

And no one even thanked me. They all thought me the bigger monster for taking his life. He swore under his breath. *I hope they all go to the One Below.*

Kroke lifted a hand to his face, feeling first the dried blood, and then the knot above his eye where the spear butt had struck him.

Against his better judgment he had allowed himself to be captured.

That woman is going to be the death of me. I should have fought them. Better to die fighting than like this.

Three plain stone walls and one of iron bars faced outward to what appeared to be a long hallway. The flickering light provided by torches hanging on the wall sconces didn't allow him to see much else.

He spat. *Worse than Jeldor's dungeons.*

"Psst."

Kroke jumped at the sound and his hand went for a knife. Naturally, he found none.

"Kroke. Is that you? Are you awake?"

"Who's there?" he hissed.

"It's Geran."

"Who?" asked Kroke.

"Geran. I'm a member of the Royal Guard."

"Ah," said Kroke, wishing he had paid attention to the names of the men he had traveled with. "What happened to Elyse?"

"I think the queen is being held on a separate level. I know she isn't down here."

"Who is down here?"

"Four others from the guard. We're the only ones who survived when we were attacked."

"Four? Can any of you still fight?"

"Not all of us. Niken and I are ok. The captain is also with us, but he's still unconscious after Markus questioned him earlier. They're doing the same to Faust right now. It seems like we're going to be next."

"Do you know what they're looking for?" asked Kroke.

"Not specifically," said Geran.

"Were you all awake when they brought us down here?"

"Yes, why?"

"Start giving me details. Anything you can remember. How many floors down we are, the number of guards, possible routes of escape, potential problems—anything you can think of."

"Why? It's not like we can get out of here."

"Just do it," snapped Kroke.

"Sure," said Geran, his voice a little shaky. "But Niken has a better memory for that sort of thing."

"Quit wasting time and someone start talking." Kroke listened intently while he searched himself, double-checking to make sure the guards found all his knives. He had to give them credit. They were thorough.

Good thing I keep more than knives on me.

Out of habit, Kroke dressed in little armor, hating the way it restricted his movements. Yet, he always wore a pair of snug gauntlets to protect his wrists and arms for the close quarter fighting he preferred. The releases for the guards were hard to spot, so he wasn't surprised to find them still on.

He slid two small catches out, twisted them, and then pushed down near his wrist. His right gauntlet opened. Inside, he found a piece of folded leather. He unfolded the leather and removed several pieces of slender, curved metal. He put the leather back and clasped the gauntlet around his arm again.

They should have had the sense to chain me like Jeldor did, he thought while listening to Niken.

Kroke started working on the lock of his cell, reaching his hands through the metal bars and pressing his face against the cold steel as he maneuvered the slivers of metal in the key hole.

Niken wrapped up his description of the dungeon and its inhabitants at about the same time. "That's about all I can recall," whispered the man.

"You did well. Many wouldn't have caught half as much as you did," said Kroke, honestly. The man had a sharp mind.

We could use someone like him in the Hell Patrol.

Geran whispered. "Hey what's that noise? Are you picking the lock?"

"Yes," grunted Kroke as he twisted his arm around to get a better angle.

"Don't bother. We tried earlier. It's newer and one we've never seen."

Kroke ignored the man as he concentrated on his task. Kroke had picked his fair share of locks when he worked as an assassin before joining the Hell Patrol. A target was usually most susceptible when relaxed in their home. Though Kroke practiced his lock-picking skills far less than he used to, he could still recall all his old tricks.

A click sounded and he allowed himself a grin.

"One Above," said Geran. "Did you get it?"

"Yes," said Kroke.

"Well hurry up and get us out of here."

A door slammed from down the corridor and footsteps followed.

"Hurry," added Geran. "They're coming for one of us next."

Kroke swore. "No time. Keep the guards distracted when they get here. I'll do the rest."

"The rest of what?" asked Niken.

"Just do it," hissed Kroke. "And pretend I'm still unconscious."

Kroke quickly removed the small tools from the keyhole and made sure the lock stayed open before he moved away from the bars and settled back on the stone floor in roughly the same spot and position as earlier. He closed his eyes and listened to the distinctive gait of multiple men, their strides out of step with each other. The footsteps stopped in front of his cell.

"He still out?" asked a harsh voice.

"Aye," said Niken. "We haven't heard him budge."

The footsteps shuffled over. "Well, then I guess one of you will have to be next." Someone pulled a sword from its sheathe. "Open the door." Keys began to jingle.

Kroke cracked his eye and saw the shadows of three men silhouetted against the opposite wall, standing in front of Geran and Niken's cell. Kroke slowly eased himself off the ground.

"You. Get against the back wall. You. You're coming with us. And hurry up with the blasted key."

Kroke inched himself closer to the iron bars of his cell as the other guard muttered something under his breath.

"Wait," said Geran. "Where's Faust? How come you didn't bring him back with you?"

One of the guards chuckled. "He didn't make it through the duke's questioning. Let's hope you're tougher, or better yet, more honest. Tell Markus what he wants to know and it'll be a whole lot easier on all of us."

Kroke heard the lock on the cell door next to him click. He rushed to his feet and slammed into the door of his cell. The high pitch squeal of the rusted hinges echoed in the damp underground corridor. The three guardsmen wheeled toward him, shocked. The door of Geran's cell flung open as a set of thick hands pulled the guard carrying the keys inside.

The guardsman closest to Kroke stepped forward to thrust with his sword. Kroke sidestepped and grabbed the guard's arm, using the man's momentum to pull him forward as he jammed a lock pick into his eye. The soldier cried out and released the grip on his sword. Kroke snatched it before it fell, flipped it around, and stabbed it through the man's chest.

Kroke yanked the sword free as he dodged a slash from another guard. Kroke brought his blade up to meet the man's next attack when a Royal Guard charged through the open cell and slammed into Kroke's opponent. The man crumpled to the floor and Kroke finished him off quickly.

The Royal Guard held out a hand. "I'm Niken."

Kroke nodded as he took it. Geran joined them in the hallway with an unconscious body over his shoulder.

The captain.

Niken scooped up a sword. "I'll lead the way."

Kroke grabbed his arm. "No. You'll make too much noise. I can get us out of here. Just don't follow me too closely or say a word. If I get turned around, I'll ask you."

Kroke pushed past Niken before he could respond.

* * *

Elyse paced back and forth in her cell. Lobella sat in a corner near Olasi's family. It seemed that Markus had taken nothing to chance, imprisoning not only his father and mother, but also his siblings, their spouses, and their children. Truth be told, the large room seemed rather small with so many people crammed into it. The only privacy was a half wall which separated the privy. Unlike the hopeless feeling she had when locked in the bowels of Jeldor's castle, rage consumed her.

How could I have been so utterly stupid to fall for this? Even after being warned I took the risk anyway, hoping it would pay off. Now look at me. She dug her nails into her palms. She wanted to scream.

She stopped. *How did Illyan know Markus was a traitor when no one else did? They are half a kingdom apart. And why doesn't Markus remember sending me the letter in the first place? Someone must have set me up. But who? One Above, let me get out of this place and I promise to not only apologize to Illyan for all that I've done, but also get to the bottom of this.*

She glanced over to the back corner where Duke Olasi lay asleep on a pile of hay. Severely ill, the letter had not deceived Elyse about the duke's condition. Arine, Olasi's granddaughter, sat at the duke's side. She saw Elyse watching the duke and came up to the queen.

"How is he?" asked Elyse in a hushed voice.

"Not good. We can only do so much for him here. I'm afraid that unless he receives some sort of medical attention, he'll die." Arine brushed aside her blonde locks and wiped away the tear trailing down her cheek.

Elyse felt a tug in her chest, and put her hand on Arine's arm. She had hoped for a better reunion with her childhood friend. "I don't understand how this all happened. Did no one else see the signs that your uncle could do this?"

Arine nodded. "Many of us did, but Grandfather did not. We tried to raise the issue to him several times, but his biggest weakness has always been his family. He cared too much for Markus to think that such malice could reside in him. He never understood that Markus could not live in the shadow of Grandfather any longer. Grandfather was sick before, but not like this," she said looking back at the frail figure of Duke Olasi. His wife, Ermail, stroked his wrinkled brow. "I think the betrayal has pushed his health over the edge."

Elyse wanted to scream at the unfairness of it all. "Where are all your grandfather's supporters? Other than Master Amcaro, I have never heard of anyone spoken more highly of than him in all of Cadonia."

Arine bowed her head. "My brother would not rest in proving our uncle wrong and he was on the verge of having proof that even Grandfather could not ignore. Yet, he mysteriously disappeared along with several others in his inner circle. Markus seized power shortly after and threw the rest of the family in prison. We found out later that Uncle used my brother's disappearance to threaten many of Grandfather's supporters, using fear to force them to his side. He had also woven in Conroy's men into the ranks of the army. Not a large number, but enough to sow doubt in Grandfather's ability to run his province. Arine shrugged. "The remainder of Grandfather's supporters were too few and simply fell into line."

Unbelievable. If someone as beloved as Olasi can lose his seat than it is no wonder the kingdom is at war.

"My Queen, what will we do next?" asked Arine.

The question caused Elyse's stomach to drop. She looked up, noticing the others in the room staring at her, dozens of hopeful eyes searching for an answer. As their queen, they expected her to have a solution to their problem.

Don't they see that I'm as helpless as they are?

"What about the royal army, Your Majesty?" asked one of Olasi's older grandchildren.

"Yes. Won't your commander storm the city and free us?" asked one of the women. "I hear this mysterious foreigner you have is a force to be reckoned with."

"Yes, Kaz is a remarkable man," Elyse said, sounding distant, wondering if she would ever be able to see him again and tell him as much. "But he is miles away. We'll have to think of something else."

"Don't waste your time," said a tired voice from the back. Everyone faced Ermail, who glanced over her boney shoulder. Her hand stayed on her husband's brow. "I beg your pardon, Your Majesty, but I suggest you get comfortable. My boy isn't likely to free us anytime soon. He won't risk us mingling with the people so soon after taking my husband's seat. If we're lucky, when all is said and done, he may exile us to Thurum or some other awful land." She let out a long sigh. "One Above, how did we go so wrong with him and seemingly so right with everyone else."

"Markus? Markus, my boy, where are you?" whispered Olasi, stirring in his sleep.

Ermail shushed her husband and stroked his face again until he settled down.

The mood of the room grew even more somber.

"I apologize, My Queen," said Arine softly. "My Grandmother is just upset. This is so hard on her . . . on all of us."

"No. There is no need to apologize. She would know her son better than I would. However, I probably will not stay here as long as you. I'd be surprised if Conroy didn't wish to speak with me himself."

It's the least the traitorous devil could do.

* * *

Kroke made a sharp left and spotted a guardsman with his back to them. He closed the distance in three quick strides, cupped his hand over the man's mouth and plunged his knife into the guard's back, angled it upward and pierced his heart in one motion. Kroke eased the lifeless figure to the ground.

He listened for a moment and heard nothing along the quiet corridor. He whispered over his shoulder and Niken came into view, followed by Geran still carrying the unconscious captain over his shoulder.

"How much farther?" asked Kroke.

"Based on what the last set of guards said, they should be just around the next turn on the right," said Niken.

Kroke led the way. He unsheathed another blade, holding two. It had taken everything he had not to search for his knives after their escape, knowing that each moment they wasted heightened their chances of being caught before locating Elyse. As luck would have it, they took a wrong turn and found two soldiers arguing over which of his blades to keep and which to sell.

He had made quick work of them with the sword he had taken from the guard he killed to escape. Securing his knives back had instantly comforted him, their weight reassuring. In the short amount of time since escaping their cells, Kroke had killed six men while moving up two levels within the dungeon.

Kroke peered around the next corner. Two guardsmen stood further down the hallway, outside of a large oaken door. There would be little chance for him to sneak up on them given the distance. Moonlight from a barred window also illuminated the corridor much more thoroughly than the torches lining the walls.

No shadows to take advantage of either. A throw is too risky. Just hope to surprise them in a rush. Need to make it quick though. Who knows how long before someone starts to discover the bodies we left behind.

He turned to Niken and gestured to the keys he held. He signaled with his hands that he wanted the man to follow him. He knew he wouldn't be able to kill the guards without some sort of racket. They had to get the queen out before others came to investigate.

He sprinted around the corridor. Within a few steps both guardsmen turned, far more alert than the others he had killed. In that brief moment of surprise, Kroke took advantage of their widening eyes and flung his arm at the closest guardsman. His blade found its target and sunk into the man's left eye.

One down.

The guard behind him screamed, his face taking on both a look of horror and anger. "Prisoner escape!" he shouted, readying his sword.

The guardsman's raw emotions influenced his attacks and he swung violently in wide slashing motions. Kroke calmly stepped to his right to avoid the first blow and then ducked under the one that followed. The guardsman came back around with a high backswing and Kroke stabbed his dagger into the man's armpit. He finished the job quickly.

Niken was already working at the door's lock, trying several of the keys on the ring stolen from the jailor. Dozens of voices from behind the oaken door had come to life. Worried questions and sobs echoed off the walls.

They probably think we're here to kill them too.

"Quiet," hissed Kroke as he looked into the room through a small window at the top of the door.

"Show some respect and be mindful of who you're talking to," said Geran from behind. "The duke's family is in there along with the queen."

"I don't care who's in that cell. We don't need to be making any more noise than we already have."

"Kroke? Is that you?" came a soft voice.

He saw Elyse push herself from behind several of the people within the large cell who had shielded her. The sight of her caught his breath.

"Finally," said Niken after the key turned.

Elyse ran forward. "Thank the One Above. It is you," she said as the door swung open.

She wrapped her arms around him in a brief hug—much to the surprise of all parties based on several audible gasps. Kroke tensed. It seemed Elyse cared little for the reactions of others as she pulled away. "Can you get us out of here?"

Kroke blinked, thankful for an excuse to turn away from her gaze. He looked at Niken. "You know the way, right?"

"Yes, but it will be tricky to get through the palace once we get to the next level."

"You won't make it and you're liable to get the queen killed in the process," said an old woman in the back.

"We'll make it," said Kroke.

The woman leaned forward and saw the bodies of the guardsmen on the floor. "No doubt you have skill, but you aren't invincible."

"Then what do you suggest?" asked Kroke, tired of the woman already. "We're wasting time."

"There's a back way out of the dungeons that only a few know about. If we make it there, we should be able to escape into the countryside."

"Then quickly tell us. More guards could come at any moment."

"I'll have to show you. Someone will need to help me with my husband," she said gesturing to the body that lay next to her.

Kroke shook his head. "No. You aren't coming with us. None of you are."

Cries of protest erupted and Elyse grabbed Kroke by the arm. "What are you talking about? These people must come with us. That is Duke Olasi and his wife Ermail," she said pointing to the prone old man and the woman next to him. "The rest are his family."

"I'm supposed to protect you. You are this country's ruler. Everyone else is expendable."

Elyse removed her arm and gave him a chilly look. "You can't be serious."

"I am."

Niken cleared his throat. "Perhaps I wouldn't have been so blunt, Your Majesty, but Kroke is right. You are our priority. We can always come back to help the others."

"No," said Elyse, stepping back again. "We must take them with us. Markus is not a calm man and if I escape, he may take his anger out on them."

Kroke grit his teeth. "We have no time for this. I'm not about to get us killed so we can drag along this bunch."

Elyse glanced over at Niken, obviously seeking support. The guard continued to back Kroke. "Your Majesty, he's right. We must go."

Distant shouts echoed, raising the sense of urgency. Elyse folded her arms and glared at Kroke. He swore at everyone in the room and yet she didn't flinch.

He raised a dagger at the old woman Elyse called Ermail. "You, get out here and tell us where to go." He pointed at a few of the younger men. "Take the old man." He gestured to the rest of them. "You will all do as I say when I say it, or I'll cut your blasted throats myself. This is your only chance." He looked back to Elyse. "Satisfied?"

The corners of her mouth turned up slightly. "Yes."

Kroke felt a tug in his chest, only angering him more. "Fine." He brushed past Niken. "You follow the old woman and take point."

"Where are you going?" he asked.

Shouts and clomping footsteps rose in volume from the corridors they took earlier. "To buy you some time. Now quit wasting it."

He paused for a second, waiting for Elyse to call out to him, but Niken and Geran had already rushed her out of view.

Nothing. Just like my family. I do the work that no one has the nerve to do.

His fingers itched, and his head pounded in anger.

He almost felt sorry for the men clamoring toward him as he rounded another turn.

He was in one of those moods.

* * *

After traversing the dark corridors and winding stairs, going up one level and down four, they finally neared the end. According to Ermail, the back exit to the dungeons would be just another hundred feet ahead.

Elyse felt a lump in her throat as she looked over her shoulder. The view was the same as it had been only seconds before. A long line of Olasi's family followed her with Geran covering their rear. The captain of her guard had regained consciousness and Olasi's youngest son helped him along.

And still no sign of Kroke.

She wondered if she had made a poor decision. She knew at the time that leaving Olasi's family behind would have made it easier for her to escape with Kroke. However, she couldn't just leave them to chance.

Ermail and Elyse trailed close behind. A faint bit of light shone brightly from around a bend and Niken doused his torch. The surprise caused several of the men and women to gasp before Ermail shushed them in a harsh manner.

Niken looked back to Elyse. "Stay here, Your Majesty. The exit should be just beyond this turn, but I want to make sure it isn't guarded. Lady Ermail said that though the exit isn't well known, Markus is aware of it."

He inched along one wall, sword in hand. Elyse's eyes began to adjust and she watched him look around the side. He slid back toward them.

"Well?" Elyse whispered.

"Six men," said Niken. He gestured for Geran to come forward.

"Can the two of you take them?"

"Of course, my queen," said Niken, trying to sound confident. Elyse heard the doubt in his voice. "We'll surprise them in a rush."

"Not likely. You'll probably get killed running out there where they have the advantage and are able to surround you."

The volume of Kroke's voice caused her to jump. Someone tried to quiet him, but they stopped quickly when the mercenary glared. Olasi's family cleared a path for him. She gasped as he came into focus. His eyes held a crazed look. Splatters of dark blood covered him.

Her hand went to her mouth.

He frowned, shook his head, and brushed past her. A loud whistle came from his mouth and bounced off the stone walls.

"Are you crazy?" asked Geran. "They'll hear you."

"That's the idea," said Kroke over his shoulder. "I work better in tight spaces." He called out louder. "Hey, anybody out there?"

Men in armor rushed forward. Kroke pushed back Niken who had come up beside him. He growled. "Stay out of my way."

Elyse had watched people fight for their lives before, but she had never seen anything like the graceful brutality that Kroke inflicted on Markus's men. Quick, efficient, and lacking in compassion, he sliced, stabbed, and gorged while spitting half-heard curses at each of them. Several of Olasi's family took the One Above's name in vain at the shock. Arine turned away and threw up. Elyse stared.

She shuddered as Kroke raked his knife across the last soldier's face, cutting into the man's mouth and through both cheeks. The man choked on his own bloody screams as Kroke's other blade pierced his gut. Kroke stood there for a moment seething, seemingly angry about something Elyse could not understand.

"There were seven, not six," he finally said.

No one could find a voice to reply. Kroke bent over and wiped his blades on a dead man's cloak. He stood and started walking. As he rounded the corner, he called out. "Let's go."

Elyse swallowed and followed after him.

CHAPTER 24

Yanasi felt Rygar's stare as she swayed in the saddle, her eyes cast down at the dirt path trailing behind her.

"You did the right thing, Yanasi. You left her with good people and the money we gave them will ensure they don't face any hard times in the next few years," said Rygar.

She sighed. "I know."

"Then why are you in such a miserable mood?"

She looked up and squinted into the sun. "You're going to think this sounds stupid, but I wanted to keep her."

Rygar's eyes widened. "Seriously?"

"Yeah. Her mother wanted me to make sure her daughter was cared for, but all it feels like I did was abandon her instead."

"Don't say that. You had to leave her with that family. What other option did you have?"

Yanasi shrugged. "Raise her myself."

"An army's no place for a kid."

"It was for me."

Rygar shook his head. "You were eight, not a newborn. That's a big difference. Besides, you obviously agree with me on some level."

"I just didn't imagine it would be so hard to let her go after only a few days with her."

Rygar reached over his mount and squeezed Yanasi's hand.

* * *

"I'm worried that we're pushing too hard," said Krytien. The mages words broke the steady monotony of hooves clomping, feet stomping, and armor clanging.

"We are pushing too hard," said Kaz in an even tone. "We need to take Bronn before he brings up other forces. We've talked about this before."

"I know, but the long days aren't doing our men any favors."

"We spent a full day seeing to our wounded. Now, we're just trying to catch up. Bronn is the one setting the pace."

"A day isn't much to get one's thoughts together after the bloodbath we fought."

"That's why it's better to keep moving. I don't want the men to think on what they've been through. I want them angry at being tired and sore, angry from homesickness, and angry at me for pushing them. Let them take their frustration out on Bronn. They can dwell on what they've been through afterward."

Krytien grunted. "Do you think Jeldor is maintaining the same pace?"

"I wouldn't be surprised if he was marching his men harder just so he could try the impossible and meet back up with us before we engage Bronn."

The mage chuckled. "They do have a special hatred for one another." He paused. "It was the right call sending him after Tomalt. He's liable to think more clearly against a foe he doesn't hold a personal vendetta against."

"That was my thought. Let's hope he doesn't make me regret splitting our forces."

Rygar came into view, galloping down the road, riding high in the saddle. Kaz called a stop and sent word to his captains to be on alert. A few moments later, the scout reached them.

"Commander, Bronn's turned his army around. They're marching back toward us," said Rygar, fighting for air.

"How much time?" asked Kaz.

"An hour. Maybe less."

"How do they look?"

"Tired, but determined."

Kaz scanned the terrain. It wasn't ideal by any means, but they had little time to ride ahead or backtrack in order to scout for better land.

No flat place to set up the catapults.

He'd have to rethink how to use the engineers.

He went down the line and gave orders as quickly as he could. Kaz saw the fatigue in the faces of his men. Still, their training kicked in and he watched proudly as they moved at a frantic pace to fulfill his orders.

With his captains taking over, he began his own silent rituals.

* * *

The sun beat down on Drake as he wiped the sweat from his brow. A long march followed by a short battle was not how he had planned to spend the day.

Though who am I to complain? I wasn't in the front lines.

Two men ran past him carrying a stretcher with an injured man crying out for help. They hurried toward the makeshift hospital tent. Other runners carrying empty stretchers pushed and pulled bodies around as they searched for the moans of the wounded among the dead. Drake breathed a guilty sigh of relief, thankful he wasn't one of them.

He had fought hand-to-hand before, but never at the front where men trampled the fallen in front of them.

"Do you ever get used to this?" asked Janik. The green-robed mage seemed to mature rapidly in the short time since his friend Yorn died. Out of the younger mages Krytien whisked away from Estul Island, Janik was becoming someone Drake considered a friend.

"I don't think so." He watched another group of men stripping the dead of their armor as they moved the bodies away from camp. "For some, it might." He sighed. "For me, this only gets harder. It's hard to forget that I'll never again see some of the men I just ate breakfast with this morning."

Janik grunted. "You're talking about the people on our side."

"Well, yeah," said Drake.

"These people aren't just friends or acquaintances, they're my countrymen. Regardless of whether I'm on the winning side or not, it hurts to know that we were responsible for killing so many Cadonians."

I hadn't considered that.

"I guess it could have been worse though," said Drake, not sure what else to add to the conversation.

"Yeah. Kaz's idea to shoot netting with the ballista seemed crazy at the time, but by capturing their officers early, it caused the rest of Bronn's army to turn and run."

"It wouldn't have worked without your help and the others Kaz put with us."

Janik shrugged. "We did work well together." He paused. "I wonder why Kaz didn't pursue the remnants of Bronn's forces though. It seemed like the best time to do so."

"We made out alright, but the left wing got hit pretty hard by their mages. Besides, we caught Bronn. Knowing Kaz, he'll want more information before pushing farther."

Footsteps sounded behind them and the voice that followed caused Drake to cringe.

"What are you two just standing around for?" asked Lufflin.

Drake noticed that Janik's shoulders bunched at the sound of the mage's voice too. Since Yorn's death, Janik hadn't really associated with Lufflin or Nora, spending more time under the tutelage of more experienced black robe mages.

"We were just talking about the atrocities of war," said Janik without turning around.

Lufflin stopped next to him. "Well, all I see is more work. Can you believe Krytien wants me to help them strip the bodies as if I'm some kind of common soldier? I swear he gets some special joy out of riding me."

Janik responded in a low, even tone. "These common soldiers fight a much harder battle."

Lufflin snorted.

Janik wheeled on Lufflin. "You ever thought that Krytien is on you so much because you still don't understand what's going on? We're aren't playing some stupid game on Estul Island anymore. We already lost Yorn. One Above, look around. Who else needs to die for you to take this seriously?"

Lufflin opened his mouth, ready to respond, but was cut off as Yanasi rode up on horseback. Tears streamed down her face and Drake's stomach sank.

Did something happen to Rygar?

"What happened?" asked Drake as she came to a halt.

"It's Raker," she answered in a shaky tone. "He's hurt bad and lost part of his left arm."

Drake felt bile creep into his throat. "How?" he asked in a hoarse whisper.

"He was upset that Kaz told him to stay behind, but he was drunk, as usual, and didn't listen. He went off on his own, and somehow worked his way into the lines. It was pure luck that I noticed him fall. I barely got him to Wiqua in time to stop the bleeding."

Drake swore he heard something like a laugh. A loud grunt followed and he turned. Lufflin lay on the ground holding his gut and Janik stood over him.

"If I ever hear you say anything like that again, you better be prepared to defend yourself," said Janik. His hands glowed in blue light.

Janik stepped over Lufflin and walked toward a group of men searching for wounded.

"Come on," said Yanasi.

Drake grabbed her hand and mounted behind her. He took one last look at Lufflin who lay on the ground staring at the sky.

* * *

Activity bustled around the hospital tent. Drake saw a steady line of runners move with empty buckets down to a nearby creek in order to fetch more water.

Yanasi handed off the reins to one of her men with barely an acknowledgment as she barreled through the crowd and into an open flap. A yellow-robed mage stood near the entrance casting a spell to keep away the flies and other insects eager to feast on fresh blood.

Drake hated the infirmary and had done his best to avoid the injured since the war began. The wounded reminded him, more so than the lifeless forms littering the battlefield, that war was not the game he once thought it would be.

Yanasi led the way past rows of cots and half-dressed soldiers. Some sobbed in pain, others cried out for water or a loved one leagues away. Drake watched Hag move between the wounded, directing others to do what they could to help each soldier.

Yanasi pushed through another flap. Nora worked alongside Wiqua, helping the tired Byzernian stabilize a man's condition. The girl had a knack for healing spells and according to Krytien she had been a blessing to Wiqua.

Wiqua breathed heavily as his eyes opened. Nora did the same and Wiqua dismissed her. "That is all we can do for now. Thank you." He turned his gaze toward Drake and Yanasi. Despite the grim surroundings, he gave a warm smile that Drake needed to see more than he realized.

"How is he?" asked Yanasi.

"He's still out," said Wiqua. "He's lost a tremendous amount of blood. Nora helped me protect the wound from any potential infection. Kaz told me not to do anymore for him right now since I have too many other soldiers to tend to. At this point, it's up to him to get better." He looked down at the cot.

Yanasi took a knee and it was only then that Drake recognized the man as Raker. The lower third of his left arm had been severed, halfway between wrist and elbow. The stump rested on the bone white skin of his bare chest. Small scratches ran across his face and neck. A purple bruise colored his chest.

Yanasi placed a hand on Drake's shoulder and he jumped. She had tears in her eyes again. "I know," she said.

Drake looked at Raker once more as he took a step back. He brushed away Yanasi's hand without saying a word and ran out of the tent, across the camp, over the small creek, and into the woods. He stopped only when he was sure he was alone. Then he cried.

* * *

Krytien slapped the back of his neck with an open hand. He pulled it away and flicked off the red remains of the bug that had attached itself to him. He used his clean hand to wipe the sweat from his top lip.

Ridiculous. Winter lasts forever and now Summer comes early.

He clomped through the small creek, doing his best to avoid slipping on protruding stones. After weaving his way around a hundred yards of trees he finally found what he sought.

Drake looked up at him with red eyes only to put his head back down again. Krytien came up and took a seat on an old stump near the boy. He pulled out a skin of water, took a drink, and passed it to Drake.

"Thanks," said Drake after a swallow.

Silence hung in the air and Krytien waited for the boy to ask a question or say anything, but the boy kept his mouth closed, drawing random shapes in the dirt at his feet with a stick.

"So, do you want to talk about it?" asked Krytien.

"Talk about what?"

"You know what. Wiqua told me you ran out of the infirmary. It took a little while to track you down out here. A lot of people are looking for you. I know Kaz is worried."

Drake threw his stick down. "I don't know why he would be worried. It's partially his fault."

"You mean what happened to Raker? You can't blame him for that."

"Yes, I can. He should have seen it coming."

"Did you ever tell him how bad Raker had gotten?"

"Not specifically, but he's in charge and I know he saw the trebuchet mishap. Besides, I told a lot of people how bad Raker was getting, including you. No one did anything to help him."

"I tried to talk to Raker and I know several others did too. I've known him for more than fifteen years so don't think him turning to the bottle hasn't torn me up—or that it isn't tearing me up to see him in such bad shape now."

"Still, there should have been something we could have done, especially Kaz."

"Kaz did do something. He took him off engineering duty and ordered him to sit out the battle so he didn't get hurt." Krytien sighed. "But I guess that just made things worse."

"He lost half an arm today. And then Wiqua told me that Kaz restricted how much he could heal Raker. He's Hell Patrol, Krytien! Why would Kaz say that? I didn't know Jonrell as well as you did, but I bet he wouldn't have given Wiqua those orders."

"You're right. You didn't know Jonrell as well as I did. He knew how to reach just about everyone, including Raker. More than likely, he would have been able to reach the man long before now and prevented this mess. Though, we both know Jonrell's death is the cause of Raker's issues so the point is moot." He paused. "As far as Kaz's orders are concerned, Jonrell would have agreed with them. Kaz didn't deny medical attention to Raker, he just told Wiqua not to treat him differently than any other soldier. Given the circumstances, I agree with Kaz. Maybe it would have been different if Raker had been his old self and fighting with a level head on his shoulder. But he ran off half-cocked and drunk, endangering the lives of the men around him. One Above, Yanasi put herself and her unit at risk to get him out of there."

"So, you're saying Raker deserved what happened to him?"

Krytien shook his head. "No, of course not. But Kaz doesn't deserve the blame for acting as a responsible commander given the situation and pressure he's under. I used to have my doubts about him, but you of all people should know how much he weighs every decision."

Drake let out a heavy sigh and rubbed the sides of his face with his hands. "I'm assuming Kaz will leave the injured behind again while we continue the march."

"No. I've already talked to him. We're going to stay put for a couple weeks while we rest and let the wounded we left behind earlier catch up. He wants us as close to full strength as possible before we press on."

"So then what can I do for Raker?"

"Spend as much time with him as you can. I know Yanasi's with him now and I'm sure she could use a break. Wiqua and Hag aren't going to let him go anywhere for awhile. Or let him near a bottle. Maybe he'll realize it's time to move on with his life." He paused. "Why don't we go back to camp?"

They got up and started walking in that direction.

"You know, maybe you can use your time with Raker to catch up on your reading. Senald told me you really haven't done much lately," said Krytien trying to change the conversation to a lighter subject.

"That's true. I've just been too busy and tired for it."

"So, have you learned anything useful out of what little you have looked at?" asked Krytien.

Drake brightened. "Actually, yes. Unfortunately, I need to do a lot more studying before I can figure out if we can use any of it. I'll talk to Janik. I think it's something he can help with."

Krytien raised an eyebrow. "Interesting. I'm glad you and he are talking more. I know he took Yorn's death hard and it seems he's distancing himself from his other friends."

"Not all of them. Just Lufflin, which I can't blame him for. I think the only one who still talks to that idiot is Nora and that's because she's too busy making eyes at him to see how self-absorbed he is."

Krytien blew out a big breath. "Yeah, I need to figure out a way to reach him before he does something really stupid."

Drake grunted. "Oh, hey. Since you brought up reading. I wanted to talk to you about something."

"I'm listening."

"Remember when I told you I found some of those books High Mage Amcaro wrote when we were on Estul Island?"

"Yes."

"And remember when you told me to leave them behind?"

"Yes."

"Well, I took those and a few others. I haven't spent much time with them, but they seem full of information that you might find useful. Of course, I don't know sorcery so I could be way off. I was planning on telling you eventually after I studied them, but honestly, I just don't have the time right now. So, if I give the books to you, will you look at them?"

Krytien wanted to kiss Drake. Though he learned a great deal about Amcaro from his personal journal, including just how much the High Mage even doubted his own abilities, little other than his personal life crept into the book. He had just been thinking the other day that he wished he knew a better way to reach the young mages.

This could be my chance.

Krytien did his best to hide his excitement. "Bring them by my tent tonight and I'll give them a look when I have a chance."

Drake smiled and Krytien realized it had been too long since he saw the boy do so.

* * *

Krytien entered the command tent. Kaz sat alone at a table cleaning his armor.

"Did you already speak with him?" asked Krytien.

"No," said Kaz. "I wanted to make him sweat a bit. I just sent Grayer and Crusher to get him. They should be back soon. Did you find Drake?"

Krytien nodded. "Yes, we talked."

Kaz put down the cloth and the helm he worked on. He leaned back in his seat. "Tell me."

Krytien spent the next few minutes going over his conversation with Drake.

"Thank you," said Kaz when Krytien finished. "You probably handled that better than I would have."

Krytien shrugged. "It was nothing. You should still talk to the boy sometime tonight if you can."

"I planned on it. Other than general updates, I haven't talked to anyone on a personal level since the battle ended."

As if on cue, the tent flap pushed inward and Crusher entered. The Ghal walked with a limp, still wearing the scars from his injuries against Tomalt. He flung Bronn to the floor of the command tent. Krytien hadn't seen the duke before, but based on prior descriptions of the man from Elyse, he fit the bill.

Deep blue eyes, fair skin, square jaw. He's definitely got a look I could see the women swooning over.

"Who in the name of the One Above do you think you are, handling me like that, you ape?" asked Bronn.

Krytien could also see what had turned Elyse off about him.

"Sorry, Commander," said General Grayer, coming in behind the giant. "I told him that Bronn should be treated with respect."

"I did," said Crusher. "Where I'm from, we would have already killed him."

Bronn paled slightly before composing himself. He dusted off his clothes as he stood and finally acknowledged Kaz. "So, you're the foreigner then?"

Kaz took a step forward and Bronn shuffled backward. Krytien laughed.

"Your general managed to escape. I want to know the makeup of your remaining forces. I'll need you to draft a letter to him which we'll deliver under a banner of peace. In it, you will acknowledge Elyse as your rightful queen and hand over command of your remaining army to me. They will receive further instructions after presenting themselves to me unarmed," said Kaz.

Bronn tilted his head to the side with a curious look. He exploded into laughter. "One Above, you're an arrogant one, aren't you? I freely admit that I have my own tendencies for such behavior, but at least I have the looks. But you," said Bronn, flicking his hand out, "you're just some black-skinned freak that fell into a position of power after Jonrell got himself killed by a child."

Krytien saw Kaz tense at the mention of Jonrell's name. Bronn must have seen it as well for he stopped then smiled. "Look, why don't you get one of your men to write up a letter to send Conroy. I'm sure he'll be able to work something out in regards to my release."

"You really think Conroy would pay a ransom for your release?"

"Of course. He needs me."

"I doubt it," said Kaz. "There will be no letter except the one that declares your loyalty to the crown."

"Foreigner, I won't do either without speaking to Elyse first." Bronn stared at Kaz as he tried to puff himself up.

"In the field, I speak on her behalf."

Bronn looked Kaz over and snorted. "I see. So now I know why Elyse turned me down. She decided it'd be better to sleep with some black devil—"

Bronn sailed backward into the tent wall, then crashed into the dirt. Krytien leaned over and eyed the duke with raised eyebrows. He lay motionless with a broken jaw and a nose pouring blood.

Crusher let out a roaring laugh and looked at Grayer. "Did you see that?" He slapped the General on the back. "Trust me when I say it's far more fun to be a spectator of one of those punches than to be the one receiving it." He shook his head. "My jaw hurts just thinking about when you did that to me," he finished, looking at Kaz.

"Commander, I know he is the enemy but he is also a prisoner and until Elyse decides his fate, the rightful heir of Asatrya," said Grayer, worried by the scene.

"And he is also a citizen of Cadonia," Kaz replied. "And therefore, will talk about his ruler with the respect she deserves. Crusher, get him back to the prison tent."

The Ghal nodded. "You want me to get Wiqua to look at him first?"

"No," said Kaz. "We're not wasting any sorcery on him."

"But Commander, his jaw may not heal right. It's pretty crooked," said Grayer, making a face as he stared at Bronn.

"Good. Let his face more closely reflect his personality. Everyone is dismissed."

* * *

After looking in on the other mages, Krytien headed toward his tent. The brats he picked up months back on Estul Island had come a long way, especially when working as a group.

All except Lufflin. I hate to just give up on him, but it may be time to cut our losses.

Lufflin still had an influence over Nora and he tended to spend a great deal of time with her. To a lesser degree many of the younger, yellow-robed mages who hadn't yet opened their eyes to Lufflin's bluster also looked up to him.

That's the downside of cutting Lufflin now. Nora is beginning to finally trust me, but the ties aren't strong enough yet. If I get rid of Lufflin, chances are I lose her and perhaps one or two of the yellows as well. We can't afford that.

He would hold off longer and hope that Kaz could convince Bronn to hand over his army and maybe gain a few replacement mages in the process.

Although after tonight, that may take longer than Kaz had hoped.

Krytien pushed aside the flap to his tent and lit a small lamp. A stack of books sat on the table. He sighed and read the names of each one.

Who am I to read something by a High Mage when I've had no formal training?

He pulled from under his robes an apple he had snatched from the supplies and crunched into it while staring at the book on top. He finished the apple, threw the core in a corner, and plopped in his chair. He took a deep breath, flipped open the cover, and began reading.

"Before learning how to draw out more of the infinite amounts of power a mage has access to, one must learn to better control that which he already knows. This means that one must use the power he has in ways he is unaccustomed to. Only by practicing that which is known can one become more familiar with that which is unknown. For instance . . ."

* * *

"So, are you gonna say something and contribute to this conversation or what?" asked Hag before she went into a short coughing fit.

Kaz blinked and looked at the old woman. "What are we talking about?"

"We ain't talking about nothing. That's my point. You sat on that log twenty minutes ago and haven't said a word since. Heck, you haven't even touched your food yet."

Kaz looked at the cold food in his hand. "Has it really been twenty minutes?"

"Close enough. I would have said something sooner, but Wiqua told me to give you time to process things and you'd start talking when you were ready." Hag jabbed Wiqua with her elbow. "If I'd listened to you, we'd still be waiting til the rooster crows."

Wiqua shrugged. "I've never been one to pry."

"At least not in front of others," said Hag with a wicked grin. She started coughing again.

Kaz shook his head. "Are you all right?"

Hag waved a hand. "I'm fine. I'm just old. Now, tell me what's on your mind. I'm assuming it has to do with you ruining that duke's face."

"Something like that." He finally took a bite

"I hear he insulted your woman and you lost it on him."

Kaz started choking. "What? Who told you that? Elyse isn't my woman. She's the queen and should be treated as such."

"Crusher said you punched Bronn after he insulted Elyse. That's all I need to hear to know the truth. I know about these things."

Kaz took a sarcastic tone. "I'm not surprised since you seem to be an expert on everything else."

Hag gave Kaz a look and elbowed Wiqua. "Since he's going to be so thick, you tell him then. He listens to you more anyway."

Kaz rolled his eyes.

"She's right," said Wiqua. "Hag and I have talked in private about the bond you and the queen share." He paused and tilted his head, looking Kaz in the eye. "You really have no clue, do you?"

"What kind of question is that? Of course he doesn't," said Hag. "Otherwise, we wouldn't have to tell him."

"Tell me what?" asked Kaz.

"That the queen shares the same feelings about you as you do for her."

"That's ridiculous," said Kaz, putting his food down. "I'm nothing like the people here. Outside this army, people are frightened by me and think I'm some demon conjured by their crazy religion. Why would she be interested in me?"

Wiqua shrugged. "Hag and I come from different backgrounds."

Hag winked. "If anything, that helps spice a relationship up."

Kaz eyed the woman. "That argument doesn't work. You aren't the queen of Cadonia and you," he said, turning to Wiqua, "remember your past. The few things I do recall I wouldn't want to share with anyone here, let alone Elyse."

"We all make mistakes," said Wiqua. "Relationships work because one person sees who the other really is, despite their shortcomings. Elyse sees who you really are."

An image flashed before his mind. A senseless slaughter in a desert village. He shook his head.

"If she knows who I really am, then I'm positive she doesn't care for me as you say she does."

CHAPTER 25

After weeks of travel, Nareash had the captain drop anchor at the mouth of a small inlet. Longboats lowered. Despite the bright sun overhead, a breeze over the bay gave Nareash a chill as it whipped through his robes.

They reached land quickly.

Guwan stared over the rocky shore and into the woods. "We should cover a lot of ground today."

"We'll go no further than the shore today. And we need to set up my tent as soon as possible," said Nareash.

Guwan turned. He wore a knowing look of dread. "It hasn't been a month."

Nareash lowered his voice. "Close enough." He switched to the common tongue of Thurum to hide their conversation from the others in the longboat. "I'd rather not perform a teleportation spell once we reach the main army. And you have a strong enough grasp of the language now to move to the next phase. You remember all the details we've discussed?"

Guwan nodded and spoke in Thurum's language with a thick accent. "Yes. But what's to stop Hezen from killing me once you're away."

"Colan will be staying with you. He's done well learning the art and is more than capable to watch your back."

Guwan glared at Colan. "He better be."

* * *

The world came into focus and Nareash immediately dropped to the floor of his tent. He had teleported too soon after the previous time and nausea seized him. He crawled over to a skin of water. Leaning on a stool, he took a small sip and swished the water in his mouth before swallowing. After a few deep breaths, the sweating stopped and the inside of the tent ceased its spinning. He finally acknowledged the three shamans warily standing over him. He struggled to his feet.

I have to be me more careful. I can't show myself to be so vulnerable again.

"Nachun, are you alright?" asked one of the shamans in a whisper.

"Yes."

"Where's Guwan and Colan?"

"They stayed behind."

"How does that affect us?" asked another.

"You mean will you still die if something happens to them?"

The shaman nodded.

"Of course."

"But, we can't control what happens . . . ."

Nareash shrugged. "Then you should continue to hope for their success. Now leave me."

The shamans shuffled out of the tent, each wearing a look of their displeasure with the High Mage.

Nareash grinned. No amount of sorcery could tie one person's life to another so the shamans had nothing to fear. Yet, they respected his power too much to disbelieve him. He chuckled and plopped onto his bedroll. He needed to rest desperately.

"Nachun?"

"I said . . ." He stopped short when Walor entered his tent. A guard followed and started to apologize. Nareash stood and waved a hand. "Go."

Walor cracked his neck and watched the guard leave. They eyed each other. Nareash held out the skin of water. Walor refused.

"How did you find us?"

"I had some scouts ranging farther than usual. They reported seeing a small party dressed in our colors. Then one mentioned you."

"Tobin knows?"

"Not yet. I wanted to talk to you alone."

Nareash raised an eyebrow. "About my trip?" He knew Walor had not agreed with his decision to leave Juanoq.

Walor shrugged. "Later perhaps. I'm more interested in discussing how your trip has affected Tobin."

"What do you mean?"

"He's changed. Charu's been difficult to deal with."

"I read the reports in Juanoq. I hurried here to ensure he wouldn't make any other poor decisions."

"His plans were sound and inventive. They should have worked. Something else is going on."

"Sabotage?"

"I think it's Soyjid. Tobin made him leader of the Gray Marsh Clan and the boy is having more success than he should be able to accomplish."

Nareash grunted. "Before I left Juanoq, Lucia told me she thought Odala was the greater threat."

"I wouldn't doubt that she's had a hand in it. I never trusted either of them."

"Have you talked to Tobin about Soyjid?"

"Tobin's not himself. He won't listen to me. He just slaughtered an entire village in cold blood. He left only the children alive to carry the message back to Charu. That's something Kaz would have done. Not Tobin."

"And you think he'll listen to me?"

"Yes."

* * *

Nareash slept hard and woke late the next morning. After a big meal, the party began their trek through the path Walor showed them the day before. Birds chirped in their nests while squirrels and other small critters scampered among the canopy's limbs or across the dirt path. Other than a few difficult climbs through particularly rocky patches, Nareash found the walk peaceful, even relaxing.

In the early evening, the trees thinned and a small, but fast moving stream came into view. On the other side of the stream, just past another line of trees, smoke from cook fires rose into the air. Nareash's stomach growled at the smell of dripping fat.

Blue Island Clan scouts materialized from the brush near the path and folded themselves into the group. Conversations broke out among the scouts and the warriors in Nareash's party of some three dozen men. The High Mage remained quiet as he separated himself from the group, allowing a scout to lead him to Tobin's command tent.

He walked through the camp, aware of the hateful and curious stares cast his way.

Ah, as warm a welcome as I expected.

Nareash felt a difference in the mood in the camp since last time he was among them. The level of malice and intensity that Tobin had dampened since becoming warleader had almost returned to levels from Kaz's command.

The High Mage strode through the opening of the command tent. Heads turned his way. Nareash noticed that all but Walor and Tobin looked surprised.

Good. He convinced Tobin to keep the information quiet.

A scowl formed on Ufer's lips, but Nareash paid it little mind as his attention drifted to the thin boy who looked grossly out of place among the powerful warriors. Soyjid's eyes widened only slightly, but enough to betray that Nareash's presence had rattled the boy.

"Everyone out. I want to speak with Nachun in private," said Tobin.

Soyjid cleared his throat. "But Warleader. We haven't finalized our strategy. I'm sure Nachun wouldn't mind waiting a bit longer while we finish."

Tobin's hand rubbed at his temple. "Well . . ."

Nareash spoke in a hard tone. "Actually, I do mind." He looked to Walor. "Perhaps, you and Ufer can work with Soyjid while I speak with Tobin."

Walor nodded and rolled the map up quickly. "Let's go."

The others filed out of the tent and Tobin blinked his eyes while massaging the bridge of his nose. Nareash poured a cup of water and sprinkled a mixture he pulled from a pouch in his robes before handing it to Tobin. "Drink."

"What is it?"

"Something for your headache."

"How did you know?" Tobin downed the contents. After a moment, he relaxed. "Thank you. I feel better already."

"How long have the headaches been plaguing you?"

"Hmm?"

"How long, Tobin?"

"They started a couple weeks after you left Juanoq. Speaking of, was the trip successful?"

"There are more pressing matters than my trip. When do the headaches generally start and how long do they last?"

Tobin laughed. "It depends, but usually during strategy sessions. Sometimes it's only for a few seconds, other times it can last up to an hour."

"Have they been getting more painful?"

"Yes. Why?"

Nareash walked over and grabbed his head. He pulled back Tobin's eyelids.

Tobin shrugged him away. "What's the matter with you?" he hissed. "I'm fine. I'm sure it's just stress."

"You're not fine. You've had stress your entire life. More than most. When has it ever caused headaches?"

"I've never had this kind of stress before."

"So? You're a more than capable leader. I've proven it to you and you've proven it to yourself and your men. Walor came to me with his concerns. He suspected something was wrong and I think he's right."

"What does he suspect?" said Tobin through clenched teeth.

"That Soyjid's been manipulating you."

Tobin laughed. "Come on."

"With sorcery. That's what the headaches are. He's been pushing on your mind. Poorly, I might add."

"What?"

"I'm serious. Think about it. If he had the means, why wouldn't he? Before I left, you never would have placed so much weight on the words of a boy. Especially over Walor and Ufer."

Tobin stared at the floor. The High Mage knew his friend needed to work things out for himself. Nareash remained quiet, pacing the room and examining other maps where plans had changed several times over. He saw Soyjid's influence as Tobin had always been quick and decisive with his military decisions.

"All this time, my strategy wasn't wrong, was it?" asked Tobin.

Nareash flipped over a map. "Probably not."

Tobin drew his sword and marched toward the tent flap.

"Stop!"

"Stop? I can't let him continue this."

"Kill him now and we won't have the full story. We need to know whether anyone else is involved."

Tobin sheathed his weapon. "What do you suggest?"

"Call everyone back in. Go with his plans and end the meeting quickly. I'll handle the rest."

* * *

Soyjid wheeled around quickly. He concealed most of his surprise, but not his discomfort. "Nachun. I didn't hear my guards announce you."

Nareash secured the tent flap and smiled. "I asked them not to. I hope I'm not intruding on anything of importance?"

Soyjid casually moved a book over a piece of paper and left the small table it rested on. "No. Just preparing for our next battle. We're lucky you could rejoin us for it."

"Lucky indeed." Nareash gestured to a chair. "May I?"

Soyjid nodded and joined him. "What brings you here?"

"I wanted to congratulate you. Prisoner, then assistant to Tobin, and now ruler of your clan. Your father must be proud."

"You'd have to ask him. Is there something specific I can do for you?"

Nareash heard the frustration in Soyjid's tone. "I hoped you could tell me how you did it? How did you turn things around for yourself?"

Soyjid shrugged. "I worked hard. It was no different than how you achieved your own accomplishments."

"Odd that you would make such a comparison. I didn't realize you had become adept with sorcery."

Soyjid blinked. "I don't know what you're talking about."

"Sure you do."

"No, I do not." Soyjid said each word deliberately and Nareash felt the slightest of pushes against his mind. Soyjid recoiled hastily and tried to hide his intentions.

Nareash laughed. "Really? You thought to control me? You don't even realize how insignificant you are to me. Don't get me wrong, I'm impressed you hid yourself for so long and even at the most basic levels, mind control is no easy thing. Perhaps after some training you could have been something more. I'm curious, how did you learn how to do it?"

Soyjid shook his head in defeat. "I knew the basics of sorcery from overhearing the shamans of our clan discuss it. My mother hated the arts so I could never study sorcery openly. I practiced on my own and through a lot of trial and error did my best in piecing things together."

"Interesting."

Soyjid narrowed his eyes. "How did you find out?"

"One, you tried to push Tobin too quickly. Those around him grew suspicious."

"Walor?"

"Two, the headaches. Mind control is something that requires a great deal of finesse and if it isn't done subtlety enough, it can cause irreversible damage to the person who you're using it on. Trust me, I know."

"And now you're going to kill me?"

"After I get some answers. If you're not cooperative, I promise the process will be far more unpleasant than a mere headache."

Soyjid worked his tongue around his mouth and let out a heavy sigh as his body relaxed. "Sure, why not? What do I care? I obviously can't stop you."

"Have you been feeding information to Charu?"

"Of course. He is already aware of the strategy we decided upon tonight, though I'm sure that will now change." Soyjid inclined his head toward the small table. "I was just sending off one more message with a few minor tweaks."

Nareash watched Soyjid's hand slide down his leg where it dangled above the dirt floor. "What was in it for you?"

"Respect and power. Tobin embarrassed my clan."

Nareash felt the slightest shift in the air around him. He seized Soyjid by the wrist as the boy's glowing hand slowly dissipated. "Fool." Nareash's grip tightened and Soyjid screamed. The High Mage's fingers seared the skin on the boy's arm. "Who else knows?"

Soyjid spoke in ragged breaths, as Nareash refused to lessen his hold. "Those Blue Island Clan guards that were assigned to me have acted as runners to Charu."

"And the rest of the Gray Marsh Clan?"

"They don't know any details."

Nareash squeezed harder. "There's someone else."

"Odala. She manipulated Tobin emotionally and physically long before I had the opportunity to work on his mind."

Nareash pushed the boy to the floor.

"You can come in, now," Nareash called out over his shoulder.

Tobin pushed aside the canvas and entered. His face held a plethora of emotions, starting with a depressing sadness nearing misery before shifting to an intense anger bordering on uncontrollable fury.

"Did you hear it all?"

Tobin breathed deep through his nose. "Every word."

He gestured to Soyjid. "Make sure you set an example."

A knife appeared in Tobin's hand. "That won't be a problem." Tobin seethed as he eyed the boy. To Soyjid's credit, he continued to wear a look of defiance.

I have a feeling that won't last much longer. "And the guards who acted as runners?"

"I already called for Ufer to take them away. He'll finish them at my command."

That was fast.

Nareash cleared his throat. "There is one more problem to deal with."

"I know," snapped Tobin. "I'll deal with her later. I have other questions to ask you first. Can he . . ."

"No. I've incapacitated him. And don't worry, I'll have guards posted around Odala's tent."

Tobin rubbed his eyes. "Good. About the campaign. I only meant to take the Green Forest Clan without you. I didn't know Charu had formed an alliance with them."

"It's done. Don't worry about it."

"Really?"

"Yes. We can deal with your other concerns later." He smiled at Soyjid. "You have other matters to attend to first."

* * *

Odala's throat felt like tree bark from her constant yelling. She sensed that something dramatic had occurred in camp, but when she went to investigate, she found her way barred. Guardsmen pushed her back into the tent with little respect. Despite her demands for answers, they gave her nothing.

From all of the movement outside, she had worried that Charu might have taken the offensive against Tobin. Then she realized that the guards would not be so calm.

Then she wondered if Tobin had gone out to wreak havoc on another village of innocents. She decided against that scenario as well.

After Tobin had returned from his recent attack on the Green Forest Clan's village, Soyjid revealed a portion of his plans to her. She knew he kept most of the details hidden, sharing only what he needed her to do. Yet, she didn't feel slighted. She knew Soyjid stood the best chance of stopping Tobin.

But that was before Nachun returned.

She reasoned that the powerful shaman had somehow discovered Soyjid's plans.

I need to finish what he started. I allowed myself to fall for the luxuries and attention Tobin offered me, but now I see the truth. Tobin cannot be allowed to conquer Hesh. When would the atrocities stop?

She wiped the poison she had received from her brother on the inside of Tobin's empty cup. She also hid a slender dagger in the sheets of their bed in case the poison didn't work. One way or another, she had decided that if Soyjid had died, then Tobin would as well.

And they'll kill me afterward.

The sobering thought did not disturb her. Death would be better than continuing her relationship with Tobin after seeing who he had become.

Who he had always been. I can't believe I ever allowed myself to be fooled into thinking otherwise.

Odala went to sleep with those thoughts and dreamed grim dreams.

The light touch of a hand startled her awake. She gasped and recoiled when she saw Tobin leaning over her. He stood and frowned.

Thinking quickly she recovered from her initial shock and sprang out of bed as the sheets fell away from her nude frame. She had gone to bed hoping that when Tobin finally returned, she would be able to distract him long enough to do what she had intended.

Tobin reacted differently than she had expected. For the first time since their relationship began, he did not stare at her with longing. In fact, his gaze shifted only once below her neckline.

He threw a robe at her. "Put this on and sit. We need to talk." He began pacing the small space.

Odala threw the robe on the bed, choosing to stay unclothed. She could tell she wouldn't like what Tobin had to say and wanted to make it as hard on him as possible. "It's Soyjid?"

He looked up and grunted. "Yes."

"You killed him, didn't you?"

The comment halted him. "Yes." He studied her face. "You don't seem surprised."

Odala shrugged and walked across the tent to a small table, mindful to brush up against Tobin as she did so. She poured two cups of water, careful to track the cup she had coated with poison. "No. I'm not. I knew he was up to something and I guess he got what was coming to him."

Tobin snapped in anger. "You knew something, but didn't tell me?"

She turned around and handed Tobin the cup as nonchalantly as possible. "One, I never thought he would succeed, and two, I haven't been particularly happy with how you've been acting. First neglecting me. And then attacking the village. I was frightened."

"You don't seem frightened now."

She shrugged again and went back to the bed. "I've been thinking. I've taken you for granted. I should have supported you more. I'm ready to make it up to you. You are more important than my brother. Now, drink your water and come here, so I can properly apologize."

Tobin eyed the contents of the cup and strode to the side of the bed. He sat lightly next to Odala. It took everything she had not to strike him. He started to laugh.

"What's so funny?" she asked.

"You know, when your brother ratted you out, I was ready to kill you with my bare hands for having betrayed me. I gave everything to you." He paused. "Then I calmed. I wanted to hear your side of things, hoping more than anything for you to give me a reason to believe you."

He snorted. "You must think I'm an idiot. I know you and Soyjid weren't close, but never have you talked about him so coldly. And then this." Tobin raised his cup and showed her the discoloring. "You never let the juice from uliket leaves rest in a metal cup. It causes the metal to change. I wouldn't expect you to know that, but your brother should have. I'm assuming he gave the poison to you." He laughed. "You know that part of a Kifzo's training is to know various poisons."

Odala's hand slid under the sheet. It shot out holding a dagger. Tobin caught her wrist with his free hand and nearly broke it in half as he shook the blade effortlessly from it.

"Did you ever love me? Or was it all a lie?" asked Tobin, his voice heavy.

Odala lied. "Never." She spat in his face.

Tobin's hand seized her by the jaw with such force she saw stars. She pushed air from her lungs in an attempt to scream, but warm liquid drowned her attempts. The liquid ended and she felt an intense pain in her lower abdomen that climbed up to her rib cage. She looked down and saw her insides spill out onto the sheets.

* * *

Tobin stared at Odala's mutilated body. His stomach rolled in nausea. Never had he let his guard down so much with another person.

His rage had surprised him.

The poison would have been enough to kill her, but the blade felt necessary. He had wanted her to feel a small portion of the pain that writhed in his gut.

Except her pain is gone.

He choked on his sobs as he carefully wrapped her body. He hated and loved her all the same.

* * *

Though Tobin wept in private over Odala's death, he managed to pull himself together enough the next morning to burn her body. He watched for hours as the flames danced across her carcass. He finally had enough and spat on her remains.

When he returned to his men, his mind had never been clearer.

Tobin had gained significant information about Charu from Soyjid after Nachun had left them alone. He knew the man's weakness and intended to exploit it through the use of his best and most trusted Kifzo.

Let him suffer.

CHAPTER 26

Conroy walked to his armory with narrowed eyes, carefully inspecting the items his blacksmiths churned out. He ran his fingers over the seams of a newly finished helm, admiring the craftsmanship. He had been careful in hiring men to work his forges and did not consider it boasting to call them the best in Cadonia.

"Good job, Harun. As usual, I cannot find any fault with your work."

The head blacksmith beamed with pride. "Thank you, my lord. The men will be pleased to hear that."

Conroy clasped the man on the shoulder. "Then I'll let you get back to them."

"Same time tomorrow?" asked Harun with a knowing smile.

"Of course. I have to keep you honest." He didn't really believe that Harun's eye for quality would wane if Conroy skipped a day of inspections or even fifty. Yet, Conroy knew how much his approval meant to his men and did not wish to disappoint them.

Harun bowed. "Until then, my lord."

The blacksmith left and Conroy heard the slamming of great double doors on the far side of the armory. His chief aide, Ventrin, hurried toward him. He carried a letter in his hand and a young man with floppy hair followed at his heels. Ventrin wore a look of concern.

"What is it?" asked Conroy as the man neared.

"My lord," whispered Ventrin. "We've received some grave news about Lord Bronn." His eyes flitted around to make sure no one eavesdropped.

Conroy nodded and walked toward a door on the right. They entered a small storage room without windows and home to a lone candle. Though the meeting place lacked comfort, Conroy trusted its security. The door closed, muffling the sounds of the busy forge.

"Did you deliver the message, Private?"

"Yes, my lord" said the man, bowing.

"Let's hear it then,"

"Sir, all of the information should be outlined in the letter."

"I assume you are privy to whatever is in the letter and probably witnessed the events, correct?"

Steel and Sorrow: Book Two of the Blood and Tears Trilogy

"Yes, my lord."

"Then I want to hear it from you. Some things a letter cannot convey. And cut down on some of the 'Yes, my lords.' We're in private now and we both know who I am. But spare no details in the news."

The boy relaxed and told the tale of how Bronn first went to Tomalt's aid as planned, then the details of Kaz's victory, and lastly Bronn's capture. Conroy listened intently, only going back to ask questions after the boy had finished. The private relayed the information well.

"My lord, what shall we do now?" asked Ventrin.

"We'll continue on as before."

"But what about Kaz's victory and Bronn's capture?"

Conroy looked to the private. "You're dismissed. Get some food and rest. I'll have a reply for you in the morning."

The messenger saluted. "Yes, sir."

After the door closed behind the private, Conroy looked to Ventrin and answered his question. "Neither has an impact on my strategy. Though I had hoped for Kaz to take greater losses, I honestly didn't expect him to lose."

The positioning of his forces was ingenious. Strangely familiar.

Conroy continued. "You see Ventrin, it was only a matter of time before Bronn did something stupid and allowed his arrogance to get the better of him. I simply picked the place for him to make a mistake so it worked to my advantage. He helped soften the queen's army, and based on what we heard from the private, his actions likely ended any chance Tomalt had of victory. Best of all, Kaz has divided his army again in order to chase two sets of foes."

"So we won't attempt to negotiate Bronn's release?"

Conroy chuckled. "Of course not. He's served his purpose. I've been in communications with Bronn's general in anticipation of this. He has his orders."

"To join up with Markus?" asked Ventrin.

Conroy shook his head. "No, Markus has his own set of tasks to tend to at the moment. The remainder of Bronn's troops will join up with the foreign army I have coming in from the southeast."

"I don't understand. The only thing to the southeast is the Ghals and they never involve themselves in disputes outside of their lands."

The corners of Conroy's mouth turned up. "Never say never."

CHAPTER 27

Elyse lay flat in the bed of the wagon. Several members of Olasi's family joined her along with barrels of salted pork and a sack of flour. The smell of the pork had already saturated her, and the powder from the leaky bag of flour sent dust into the air with each bump the wagon's wheels struck on the old country road.

Their escape from the back entrance of the dungeon went easily. They made it out of the city and into the woods without any problems. The party came across a family of merchants a mile into their journey and secured three wagons from them. Kroke had been ready to kill the group if needed, but by mere chance, one of Olasi's grandchildren recognized the family.

The merchants fled the city to get away from Markus' rule and were eager to help in their escape. The family threw out much of their goods into the woods so that Olasi's family could hide easily underneath the thick tarps covering the wagon beds. Taking Ermail's advice, Elyse chose to keep her identity a secret and pretended to be a distant cousin.

Kroke, Niken, and Geran pretended to be hired guards.

Elyse winced as the wagon rattled over a particularly rough patch. The last jolt banged her elbow and she audibly groaned.

"Are you alright?" asked Lobella.

Elyse's servant had been more quiet than usual since their imprisonment and other than panicked breathing had said little until now. Lobella's pale face spoke volumes for how the recent events had affected her. Elyse squeezed her hand. "I'm fine."

"If you can't stay silent, then keep your blasted voices down at least," hissed Kroke from above.

Elyse couldn't see the mercenary, but she felt every bit of his displeasure. The jaded bitterness that had lined Kroke's voice when she first met him had returned. She couldn't recall when it had softened and they became friends, but for over a year she had considered him one. His attitude toward her had shifted again and she had no clue why.

Something I did? That look he gave me in the dungeons—it was like it came from someone I never knew.

A touch of Elyse's other arm preceded a hushed whisper from Arine. "How can you travel with someone like that? He is so . . . uncivilized. He actually enjoys killing. And the way he talks to you. The looks he gives all of us. I'm more frightened of him than I was of Uncle Markus."

A day earlier she might have passionately defended Kroke, but after their escape she no longer knew what to do.

He's a good person. I know the kind of person he really is. At least I think I do.

"Everything will be fine," whispered Elyse, unsure what else she could say to ease Arine's mind when her own kept drifting to places she wanted to avoid.

* * *

Kroke stared past the horses and down the dark dirt road. The merchant next to him had tried to make small talk, but after a glare the man got the message. The merchant had been nice enough to give him fresh clothes in order to escape the blood caking his own, but the last thing Kroke wanted to do was talk.

Kroke felt the man's uneasiness at the reins, casting a sidelong glance his way as the mercenary worked his knives methodically over a whetstone. The blades didn't need as much attention as Kroke gave them, but the killer fell back into old habits when he needed to steady his nerves.

Kroke could handle the merchant's unease and even the looks of disdain and horror from Olasi's family. Those he had grown accustomed to over his life. However, he doubted he would forget the look Elyse gave him in the dungeons. Nor would he forget feeling so angry and ashamed at himself when he simply did what needed doing to save their lives.

Maybe I could have killed the last guardsmen quicker, but at that point I didn't care. Maybe Elyse is right for the look she gave me. I'm a cold-blooded killer and I need to get back to those who understand me.

The Hell Patrol would not question or look down upon him for his actions.

They would defend me just as I would defend them.

Kroke strained his ears and listened to Elyse's shaky voice when she addressed Arine's whispered concerns. She didn't stand up for him as she once had.

* * *

After the hopeful first few hours on the road out of Lucartias, the next week turned dismal. The merchants knew of a secret cave used to avoid bandits and the party took refuge there after the first morning. The cave allowed them to avoid notice from the eventual passing of soldiers searching the roads.

Duke Olasi died that first day. Without any healer to treat him, the illness became too much for the old man to fight. All cried except for Kroke who offered to bury the body. Everyone protested at first, saying the former duke deserved much better than to be left in the woods and forgotten. However, Elyse understood that Olasi would not get a funeral befitting of his life, and they could not take his body with him when they finally resumed their travels. She let Kroke dispose of the body so long as he marked it well enough that it could be retrieved after the war. None were happy about the decision, but in the end all consented.

Ermail became almost catatonic afterward, curling up in a ball in the back of the cave, not speaking to anyone. Two days later, she passed. Most agreed that she died of a broken heart. Kroke placed her body next to Olasi's and marked it accordingly.

Little was said in the days that followed until finally Kroke reasoned that the search for them had moved on.

They resumed their journey northwest, traveling at night while Kroke and her guards took turns with watch during the day. Based on information gleaned from random travelers on the road, they steered toward Kaz's most recent whereabouts.

After weeks in the country, they passed from Markus' lands and crossed into Tomalt's territory. Clothes hung loose on their thinner frames. Everyone rode out in the open since few would recognize them this far from Lucartias.

What queen would be stupid enough to travel a war torn land in the back of a beat up wagon? A queen who let her emotions get in the way of the facts around her.

With little else to do but stay alive, Elyse spent her time dwelling on some of her poor decisions—such as her handling of Illyan. She also thought a lot about Kaz. She missed him greatly and hoped that he and the rest of her army had been able to cope with Markus' actions.

Elyse glanced over to Kroke who cleaned his knife while wearing a scowl that would put Kaz to shame.

"I don't understand," said Lobella in a soft whisper.

Elyse jumped. "I'm sorry. What don't you understand?"

"Why you're so concerned with him?"

"Is it that obvious?" she asked.

"Yes. You've been staring at him for quite a while."

"I just . . . he's done a lot for me and I know I've upset him in some way."

"Can't you just ask him?" Lobella posed the obvious question as though the thought had never crossed Elyse's mind.

"It's not something I want to discuss where others can hear and Kroke refuses to speak to me in private. He's even started using Niken as a go-between to avoid even the simplest of contact." She paused. "I wish he would just talk to me."

* * *

After several nights of traveling, a faint light shone out in the distance and at first Kroke thought the night played tricks on his eyes. But the one light doubled, then doubled again, until Kroke realized he gazed upon windows to a large inn situated near a crossroads.

He wanted to push past the inn lest they attract notice. Many who frequented such establishments made note of every passerby, never knowing when that information might be worth a few coppers. Kroke made that point to Niken when the guardsmen asked about stopping.

"You're right, but we could use some news ourselves," said Niken. "We don't even know if we're still heading in the right direction. We need specifics or we're liable to run into real trouble."

"Alright, but we do this my way."

"The captain ain't gonna like that. He already isn't too pleased with you bossing the queen around."

"If he's got a problem with me, he can tell me himself. I ain't perfect, but we've done alright so far. We'll stop just up the road and let everyone out of the wagons except for me and the merchants. I'll scout the place out and if we can, get a few rooms for the night. You, Geran, and the captain can work everyone else through the woods and sneak around back. I'll see about getting everyone in afterward."

Niken nodded.

Kroke liked Niken. He seemed like the kind of man who understood that one had to sometimes think differently to accomplish things, even if that meant getting dirty. "Just make sure you keep them quiet."

"Will do."

* * *

"Can you believe the nerve of him?" asked Arine. "First he makes us climb up a drain spout like common gutter rats. Then he confines us to our rooms, denying us the chance to take real baths."

"He has his reasons. We still can't be noticed," said Elyse.

"So he says. Yet, he is able to drink in the common room and have a hot meal." She inhaled deeply through her nostrils. "One Above, do you smell that? How can you not? Any other situation and the smell might make me vomit, but it has been so long since I've had anything substantial, I might be willing to risk capture simply to try a spoonful."

"Niken said Kroke will bring up a couple of loaves of fresh bread later. He won't be able to do much more without raising suspicion. He can't exactly bring up a pot of stew, can he?" asked Elyse.

"Yes, I suppose you're right, Your Majesty," said Arine, slipping back into the formal address to Elyse since they were away from the merchant family. She groaned. "This is still ridiculous, sleeping so many to a room."

Elyse shrugged, trying to remain positive. "They could only secure three rooms. Even then, they overpaid for them. We should be thankful we have a roof over our heads for once."

Arine sighed. "I don't know how you can remain so positive when so much bad has happened these last few weeks."

Elyse laughed.

"My queen?"

"Arine, I do not mean to belittle your trials," she paused and looked around, "nor do I mean to belittle anyone else here for the losses you've suffered, but honestly, the last few weeks are nothing to what the prior year and a half has brought me. My kingdom is in shambles and I've lost my father and brother, the only family I had left in the world. Men, women, and children alike are dying in this war whether directly or indirectly because of me." She chuckled again. "Sleeping on a hard ground, eating cold food, and wearing dirty clothes seems trivial when you put things into perspective."

An uncomfortable silence hung in the room until Arine's sister-in-law cleared her throat. "I beg your pardon, Your Majesty, but I'd like to apologize on everyone's behalf. It's been hard for us to think how blessed we are to still have each other."

"I apologize too. I'll do my best to stop being so introverted," said Elyse.

"I wasn't speaking of you, Your Majesty." She swallowed. "Kroke frightens us. All of us, including our husbands. Even the captain of your guard has been most vocal about his displeasure with the man. Don't get me wrong, I'm grateful that he helped us escape the dungeons, but frankly we haven't seen any sign of soldiers in days. I beg your pardon for asking, but wouldn't we be better off to move on without him?"

"I understand your concern. I'll talk to him now that there is a place to do so," said Elyse.

The room seemed to noticeably relax.

"I'll need you all to move to another room though and then call for Idouna so that she might ask him upstairs," Elyse continued.

* * *

Kroke nursed the mug of ale in his hand as if it was the last in the world. It was his fourth so far and he had enjoyed each one better than the last after inhaling a trencher of greasy stew. For the first time in months, he allowed himself to relax. No one in the common room posed an immediate threat.

Down on their luck farmers sat at tables, complaining about how much money they stood to lose because of the war. The innkeeper, wearing clothes full of holes, listened to sob stories from passing merchants sitting at the bar. The place had seen better times.

Kroke took another sip and let the warm ale roll around his mouth before he swallowed. He savored the thick, almost chewy consistency.

It's so awful, it's good.

Though he would have loved nothing better than to drown himself in the foul liquid, he couldn't risk being so inebriated he couldn't fight. Not when he still had to look after the queen.

He tried to curse under his breath, but a belch came out instead, filling his nostrils with the stew he ate earlier. Kroke took the last gulp in his mug, ready to call for the bread he had promised to take to the others. He couldn't stall downstairs any longer.

The door to the inn opened and a young blond man came in, casting furtive glances across the room. Kroke grinned and shrunk back into the shadows. When the man took a place at the bar, Kroke slid silently from his chair and slithered toward him as a dagger fell into his palm. He pressed the point into the man's back and whispered. "Get up. Slowly. Now walk back outside with me and if you try anything I'll kill you."

The man complied.

Once outside, Kroke directed the man around the back, near the stables.

"So, are you going to rob me and leave me for dead?"

Kroke sheathed his blade. "I ought to, you idiot. You know better than to sit with your back to an open room like that."

Rygar wheeled around. "Kroke? What in the name of the One Above are you doing out here?" He embraced Kroke with a warm hug and started laughing. "It's good to see you."

All the bitterness Kroke had held in for weeks seemed to melt away as he felt the genuine affection Rygar exuded. He even allowed himself to reciprocate the hug since no one watched them.

"It's good to see you too," said Kroke as they separated. Like Drake, Rygar had that youthful energy that just seemed to lift the dark spirits of the older crew like him and Raker.

"So seriously, what are you doing here? I thought Kaz left you watching over Elyse?" He paled. "Don't tell me you left her behind."

Kroke scowled. "I wished I would have." He saw the confused look on Rygar's face and continued. "She's actually inside."

Rygar's eyes widened. "In the inn? That's crazy!"

"No kidding. Look, it's a long story, but basically she thought by going to Markus she could manage a treaty with Conroy. Come to find out it was all a trap and Markus is a traitor. We got thrown into his dungeon along with the rest of the man's family. We got everyone out, but Olasi and his wife died. We've been on the road for weeks hoping to catch up with the army and warn Kaz."

Rygar whistled low. "That's some story. Don't worry about Kaz though, he figured things out about Markus."

That relieved him. "So how far away is the army then?"

"A few days," said Rygar. "We've been stationary since our last fight. We caught Bronn. Kaz has been sending scouts out pretty far to get more intelligence after Bronn more or less confirmed that Olasi's son was a traitor. He didn't want to walk into anything blind."

"Can you take us there?"

Rygar scratched at the fuzz adorning his chin. "Yeah, as long as we stay off the main roads. Tomalt didn't leave a whole lot of men behind in this area. Jeldor is trying to finish him off in the east. The bigger concern now is what sort of hidden traps Markus or Conroy have set for us."

Kroke grunted. "Do you have any money?"

"Some."

"Enough to buy some horses?"

"Not that much. Maybe two."

"That should be enough."

* * *

Kroke reentered the bar as Rygar went around to the stables to secure horses and supplies for the journey. Kroke wanted to leave that night. Idouna, the merchant's wife, grabbed him as his boots hit the wooden planks of the inn's floor.

"You're needed upstairs."

Kroke gave her a look that begged for more information.

She leaned in and whispered. "The queen wants to speak with you in private. What about, I don't know."

Kroke grunted. "So you knew all along who she was?"

The woman grinned. "Aye. We've traveled all over Cadonia at one point or another."

"Then, I owe you an apology." He normally wouldn't bother saying such a thing, but in light of that information he felt the need to acknowledge the risks the family took without complaining.

She waved him off. "Think nothing of it. We love our country and I doubt you'd find anyone more loyal." She paused. "By the way, I'm not sure what you did to upset them, but you're fine by me."

He moved past her and then up the stairs. His mood had lifted after seeing Rygar and his brief talk with Idouna. He reached the top of the third flight, and walked down the narrow hallway to Elyse's room.

He gave the door a quick wrap of his knuckles and announced himself. A moment later the door clicked open.

Kroke strode in and Elyse closed the door behind him. Despite the state of her clothing and the weight she had lost, the queen still looked beautiful. The fact that he still couldn't help himself from thinking that angered him. Kroke pulled out a knife and tossed it end over end in his hand as they stared at each other.

"I was told you wanted to see me," said Kroke. He hoped that by speaking first, Elyse might soften the piercing gaze of her emerald eyes.

"Yes." She exhaled slowly. "I want to know what happened to us."

"Us? There is no us. There is only Elyse, the queen of Cadonia, and Kroke her hired knife who does all the things that no one else has the nerve to do. Nothing more."

She frowned, looking genuinely hurt by the comment. "Do you really feel that way?"

He shrugged. "Of course. Why should it be any different?"

"I just thought that we had become friends. We used to talk . . ."

"Aye, we did," said Kroke. "But that all changed when you got reacquainted with these prissy nobles you forced me to drag along."

"What is that supposed to mean? Their presence has changed nothing about my friendship with you."

"Yeah, right. I ain't as stupid as you all think I am. I see every sidelong look they cast my way, every nose they turn in my direction, and I hear. Yes, I hear every single thing they've said about me. And you know what, most of them are true. I am a killer. It's what I do. It's what I'm good at and if I wasn't one, you wouldn't even be where you are today."

"Their comments meant nothing to me."

"Then why did you look at me that way in the dungeons?" he yelled.

Elyse cocked her head to the side. "What way?" she asked in a soft voice.

"Like I was the lowest, most vile thing on the face of the earth. Like I wasn't even human," said Kroke. He couldn't believe that he brought the matter up. But it was too late. That look she had given him reminded him too much of the look he saw in his family's eyes after he killed his father. He had once cared about his family just as he foolishly cared about Elyse.

And each time I only receive pain in return.

Elyse's hands went to her mouth. "I'm so sorry. I never meant for you to feel that way. I just . . . I was shocked. I never saw something like that up close."

She stepped toward him and he quickly turned his back to her.

She continued. "Maybe I reacted the way I did because I know just how human you are. You may think you're a killer, but you're not. It's just something you do. That doesn't mean it's who you are."

Kroke hung his head.

"Kroke?"

He cleared his throat while keeping his back to her. "I was just on my way upstairs to see you earlier when Rygar happened upon this place by sheer luck."

"Thank the One Above! That's great news!"

"He's getting mounts for us now. We can meet up with the army in days. We're going to leave in a few minutes. I'll come back and get you then."

"I'll tell Arine and the others."

"No. It'll be just us three. Everyone else, including Lobella, can stay with your guards and travel at their own pace. They're safe and I don't want them slowing us down anymore. On this, I'm not budging. If you don't like it, report me to Kaz when you see him."

Surprisingly she didn't argue. "No. You're right. Kaz was right to leave you with me. I don't know what I would have done without you."

The sincerity in her words cut at him, but he didn't respond. He wouldn't allow anyone else to hurt him again.

"I'll go check on Rygar," he said leaving the room.

CHAPTER 28

Small, dirt hills dotted the field of battle and lines of trees flanked each side of the open space. Tobin eyed the wide clearing of land with a calming numbness he had not felt in some time. His state of mind reminded him of when he would lose himself in archery drills, firing shot after shot for hours.

Only then, my problems seemed so much simpler. I knew what to expect from others. Now, I don't even know what to expect from myself.

The Green Forest Clan's capital city, Feruse, stood in the distance, a shadow of stone and wood that failed to impress. The city supposedly housed a population much larger than Juanoq's, yet Tobin felt that any comparison to his home was an insult.

Lines of figures poured out of the city and marched to join Charu's forces already on the opposite end of the field. Charu's strategy with Soyjid had been to delay the Blue Island Clan's advance in any way possible in order to bring in the remainder of the Red Mountain Clan armies. Scouts estimated that Charu boasted an army of seventy thousand men.

"Impressive," said Nachun.

"We've been outnumbered before and won," said Tobin.

"Yes, but even against the Yellow Plain Clan, we weren't outnumbered by this many."

Tobin grunted. "Charu will be more confident than Sunul was. He sees our men lined up just as Soyjid told him they would be. He also didn't count on you rejoining us."

"I thought you didn't want me to interfere."

"Not directly. But since no one understands sorcery better than you, I want you to manage the shamans. I'll let you know if I need anything more."

Tobin scanned the open expanse. He had placed small squads of men near low mounds that sat on the battlefield in order to set off traps for the enemy. He eyed the tree lines again. For the first time since landing in the Green Forest Clan's territory, he could factor cavalry into his plans. Hundreds of Yellow Clan riders, led by Kifzo, hid in the trees to the west. Tobin did not expect them to take Charu by complete surprise. However, it would be one more thing for the Red Mountain Clan leader to deal with.

"Are you alright?" asked Nachun.

No.

"Of course. Everything's in place."

"That's not what I meant. Are *you* alright?"

Tobin scowled. "You mean, am I thinking clearly after realizing I've been manipulated for months, made to look like a fool, and betrayed by someone I loved?"

Nachun frowned. "I didn't realize it was that serious between you and Odala."

Tobin forced himself not to hang his head. "I thought it was."

"I'm sorry." The shaman cleared his throat. "You know, we never talked about any questions you had over what Soyjid did to you."

Perhaps it's because I don't want those answers anymore.

"It can wait." Tobin chuckled. "I'd hardly call now the appropriate place to begin that discussion. We've wasted enough time here already. Get into position."

An uncomfortable silence hung in the air until Tobin heard Nachun's footsteps drifting away.

* * *

Nareash walked off, leaving Tobin to his thoughts. Warriors moved quickly out of his way as they recognized his mood. Nareash understood Tobin had been through a lot over the past few days, but that didn't make it any easier for him to overlook the brash tone Tobin had used with him.

Nareash reminded himself to be patient. After all, this battle should be the last major challenge. He could talk to Tobin afterward about his plans for the Kifzo.

Walor fell in step with Nareash. The High Mage ignored him.

"Well?"

"Well what?"

"How does he seem to you?"

"Angry, moody, and focused—just as you requested."

"I didn't want to hurt him," Walor leaned in and whispered. "I was trying to help him."

"As was I. But don't tell me you didn't foresee this happening on some level. How would you feel if you learned someone had been playing with your mind? Or your woman had been trying to set you up for failure and eventually death?" He quickened his pace. "I imagine that would ruin your mood as well."

"I understand that, but what about any permanent damage?"

Nareash stopped. "How did you know about that?"

"I didn't. It was just a guess."

"Well, don't talk about it with anyone else. The last thing the men need is to question his sanity."

"So it is a possibility?"

"Yes, but he's been too focused to let me look at him. I won't press the issue until after the battle. Just keep an eye on his behavior."

"I will."

* * *

"Everything is just as you said it would be," said Gidan. He eyed the waves of men pouring out of Feruse to join the thousands already aligned on the field of battle. "And your stalling tactics worked brilliantly. Scouts say we outnumber them by more than two to one now."

Charu grunted. His eyes were not on his own men, but on the enemy's across from him. A lone figure stood out on one of the highest rises. Charu turned to his general. "Have there been any messages for me?"

"Just from Jolnan saying that the council continues to support your command, but wants to see big things from you today. Were you expecting any others?"

Yes.

Charu shook his head staring at Tobin's right wing. He pointed. "They seem thinner there than before. Isn't that where the Gray Marsh Clan is positioned?"

"Yes. Maybe our estimates of their losses were wrong."

"Even so . . . ." his voice trailed off. Something didn't feel right, but the last letter received from their contact assured Charu all was in place.

And Tobin's lines are exactly as the letter said they would be.

Gidan sounded concerned. "Do you wish to delay the battle until we get more information?"

"It's too late for that." Charu pointed. "It's begun."

Gidan shielded his eyes from the sun and followed the line of Charu's arm. "All of Tobin's lines are advancing together."

Charu breathed a small sigh.

Just as the message said they would.

* * *

Tobin checked in with Walor, Ufer, and his other captains before scanning his troop's positioning. Satisfied, he signaled them forward. Thousands of warriors calmly filed past him on the rise. A dozen messengers came up and stood behind him, ready for his orders.

The giant ram horn of the Red Mountain Clan sounded and Charu's forces began their slow advance. The deployment of Charu's men suggested that he believed Tobin still operated under Soyjid's strategy.

Walor moved his men to a sprint. Charu's men sped their advance, and as expected, an enemy unit separated on the left, intending to sweep around Tobin's flank.

Tobin turned to his messengers. A shaman stood among them. "Signal the cavalry. Two bursts, separated by a string of smoke."

"Yes, Warleader." Two small balls of fire shot up into the air, a snaking trail of smoke connecting them before all dissipated.

Tobin trained his eye on the tree line as hundreds of horsemen burst from cover and sped toward Charu's sweeping unit. The enemy had more than enough time to respond, and halted to brace themselves. However, the first wave of Yellow Clan Riders carried short bows. They fired on their targets, softening Charu's left flank. The mounted archer's peeled away as the heavy cavalry swept in behind them and shredded Charu's men.

"Three rapid bursts now," Tobin called over his shoulder.

The shaman obeyed and the cavalry fell back and reformed well outside the battle lines Charu shifted in to support his weakened left side.

In the meantime, Walor had reacted to the mounted charge by slowing his advance to lure Charu's forces in. The enemy's ranks continued their charge and as they approached several small rises, pockets of hidden Kifzo took out their opponent's captains with crossbow shots before sprinting back to the Blue Island Clan lines.

The Blue Island Clan suffered few casualties, and by the time the weight of the two armies came together, they met farther away than where Soyjid had promised Charu, giving Tobin the advantage in terrain.

Now it truly begins.

Tobin sent orders throughout the day. Walor did not gain any ground, nor did he lose any. The Kifzo's ranks stood as unmovable as the walls of Juanoq. The shaman behind Tobin continued messaging hidden cavalry to either side of the battlefield that prevented Charu from mounting any flanking maneuvers.

Charu reacted well to the obvious breakdown in the strategy he planned for, deftly using his shamans to negate Tobin's mounted archers. Nachun stepped in and directed the Blue Island Clan shamans to shift the momentum back to Tobin's forces by focusing their attacks on Charu's center.

The battle raged until shortly before dusk. Both sides agreed to fall back for the day and collect their dead. Tobin hated knowing that he had not finished off Charu on the first day. However, his men did not seem upset and when the estimates of the day's losses came in, he understood why.

Charu's men had suffered four times the number of casualties.

* * *

Once inside the confines of his tent, Charu released the anger he had tried to conceal from his men. He threw his armor down, kicked over a chair, and ripped the letter he had previously received from his informant.

A throat cleared in the middle of Charu's outburst. He wheeled. "What?"

Melat eyed him. "Are you done? Because if you aren't, then finish quickly. Jolnan will be here to see you soon. Of that, I have no doubt."

Charu swore. "Wonderful."

One of his guards poked into the tent. "Warchief. Jolnan from the Green Forest Clan is insisting that he speak with you right away."

Charu eyed Melat. The woman smiled knowingly. Charu turned back to the guard. "Give me a minute and then send him in."

The guard left and Charu took a deep breath.

Melat began straightening up the mess without him asking. He took in her beautiful figure as she did so. She spoke without looking up. "Though I'm flattered that I could distract you so easily, might I suggest you focus on readying yourself for Jolnan." Melat looked up and smiled, taking some of the bite out of her tone.

Such an amazing woman.

Charu sighed. "We've been betrayed."

"Or the more likely scenario is that our contact was found out. You knew both were possibilities."

Charu rubbed his face. "Yet I didn't plan appropriately enough. I knew something felt off, but allowed myself to be deceived anyway. Tobin played me perfectly."

"But it won't happen again, will it?"

"No. It won't."

The guard poked his head into the tent again. "Warchief?"

"Send him in."

Jolnan entered the tent and watched Melat clean up the last of the mess. "Good, you're angry. I take it today's travesty was not part of your plan."

Charu grit his teeth. "What do you think?"

Jolnan sighed. "The council is questioning not only your strategy here, but now everything you've done up to this point. The Green Forest Clan's forces have lost quite a few men in comparison to yours. They are having a hard time understanding why that's so."

"I told you the Red Mountain Clan is better trained," said Charu.

"Not as well trained as Tobin's apparently. What happened?"

"I had incorrect information."

Jolnan raised an eyebrow. "That's it?"

"That's it."

Jolnan grunted. "Well, do you have the correct information now? I have to convince the council to keep faith in you, and to do that I need to have some faith myself."

"From here on, things will be different," said Charu in a flat tone.

"Good. I need to see results and so does the council. Otherwise, we may not be meeting tomorrow under such amiable terms."

The councilor left the tent and Charu stayed his fury over having to placate the elders of a weaker clan.

Melat coolly walked to a table to pour him a cup of water.

Charu got her message. He needed to calm himself. Tobin had surprised him today and he couldn't allow anger to rule his decisions.

Charu admitted that Tobin had done well on the first day of battle.

He must have learned what I had planned, just as before I knew what he would do. Tomorrow we'll see how good a commander he truly is.

* * *

Nareash impatiently watched the second day of battle unfold. Charu had used the night to rethink his battle plan. He placed his shamans within his ranks and battered the Blue Island Clan forces mercilessly. Nareash had done his best to negate the Red Mountain Clan shamans with those Tobin had put under his control, yet Charu still held the advantage. Nareash sent word to Tobin, wanting to step in, but his friend refused him.

He got the message. Tobin wanted to win without his help. His confidence had been shaken after Soyjid's manipulation and along with the lingering doubts instilled in him from Bazraki and Kaz, Tobin needed to win with no assistance.

Nareash watched Charu and Tobin struggle to outwit the other and admitted both commanders impressed him. Charu relied on superior numbers and the prowess of his shamans to counter Tobin's better-trained and better-armed forces.

At the end of the second day, both sides suffered relatively the same number of casualties. The exhausted armies drudged back to their camps and Nareash could not help but notice that even the mighty Kifzo warriors looked weary.

Something must change.

* * *

Only the sentries looked alert as Nareash entered the main camp and slipped between the parting soldiers. He liked to think they cleared a path out of respect, but he knew hate and fear motivated them.

Nareash headed straight to the camp's center. Walor made a move to intercept him, but the High Mage gestured for the Kifzo to wait at the entrance to Tobin's tent as he went inside.

Tobin stood naked to the waist over a bowl of water. The warleader's armor lay on the floor beside him. Tobin ran a damp towel over his skin.

"You must have run to get here so quickly."

The calm tone of Tobin's voice surprised Nareash. "I thought you might be beating yourself up."

Tobin's chiseled torso rose and fell with each breath. "Why would you think that?"

"I thought you might lament over the lack of success or the loss of life, given casualties were great on both sides."

Tobin shrugged his thick shoulders, curling them up his neck until they practically touched his ears. "The lack of success means nothing. Today went as I expected it. Charu impresses me." He sneered. "Even without Soyjid's help, he's a worthy opponent. I knew the battle would not end today, not unless Charu did something foolish. Today was meant to buy time. Tomorrow Charu will make his mistake."

Nareash raised an eyebrow. He thought he had been in on all of Tobin's plans, but it would appear not. *He's lost his trust in me as well.* "And how will you accomplish that?"

"You'll have to wait and see. The men I sent out should be coming back at any moment. If they weren't successful, there are other ways I can achieve the desired result, though none quite so impactful."

Tobin went back to washing.

"What about the loss of life today? In the past, that bothered you."

"I don't want to lose warriors, but I don't take the losses as personally as I used to." Tobin looked up. "I mean why should I? They once hated me. Then they loved me. But, when things started to sour because of Soyjid, some began to hate again. They're too fickle." He shook his head and chuckled. "I've been treated like a tool by everyone I've come in contact with. Why shouldn't I think of others in the same way?"

Nareash's brows furrowed. "You said everyone's treated you like a tool?"

Water dripped from Tobin's arms as he met Nareash's stare. He spoke in a deadpan voice. "Everyone."

Nareash blinked in surprise.

Shouting outside the tent, followed by three Kifzo stepping inside, kept Nareash from asking Tobin for clarification. One carried a sack over his shoulder. Muffled grunts sounded from inside. The three warriors suffered scrapes and cuts all over their bodies. They bowed.

"It was a success, Warleader."

Tobin smiled. "Put her down on my bedroll."

The warrior dumped the sack and unlaced the string. The burlap fell away revealing a beautiful lighter-skinned woman with an olive complexion. She swayed as if in a daze. Her eyes widened, betraying her fear as she saw Tobin. She scooted away.

Nareash waited to ask his question until after Tobin dismissed the Kifzo. "Who is this?"

"Charu's lover." Tobin frowned. "He cares for her deeply and it won't be long before he receives the message I sent him. He'll know who has her." He gestured to the woman's heavily bandaged left hand.

"You cut off her finger."

Tobin grinned. "More effective than a penned note. He'll be enraged and unable to think clearly tomorrow. You approve?"

Nareash grunted an affirmation. Though it seemed very little of the man he first met in Munai still existed, the High Mage could not deny the effectiveness of Tobin's decision. "Cruel, but sound."

Too bad your father can't see you now. Bazraki would be proud.

Tobin faced Melat and stared intently. The coldness in his voice disturbed even Nareash. "I know cruel. Losing a finger isn't cruel." Tobin kneeled down and extended his hand toward her. She flinched away from his touch, but Tobin persisted and ran his fingers gently down her face. "You may leave now, Nachun," he answered without looking back.

Nareash left the tent without a word. He had done awful things in his own life, so who was he to judge Tobin. Still, he found it sad to watch his friend walk such a dark path—especially because it had been Tobin's unwillingness to go to such places that the High Mage had once admired. In a way, Tobin had balanced out Nareash's own tendencies with his desire to avoid inflicting punishment on the innocent.

The damage Soyjid inflicted is worse than I thought.

Walor seized Nareash by the arm after a dozen steps. "I've been calling your name, Nachun. How is he?"

Nareash looked down at his arm. "Don't ever grab me like some child again."

Walor released his grip. "Fine. I'll go talk to Tobin myself." He turned to leave.

"I wouldn't do that if I were you. You won't like what you see."

"Why? What's going on in there?"

"A transformation."

Nareash left Walor to weigh his words.

* * *

Charu awoke drenched in sweat. Light from flickering campfires seeped into his tent through cracks in the canvas. The relative silence of his men made sense given the sun would not rise for hours. Yet, something felt wrong and his stomach twisted in knots as he considered what it could be.

Nerves.

He knew tomorrow would be the turning point in the struggle against the Blue Island Clan and he had gone over his strategy meticulously to ensure he held the upper hand.

That has to be it. Just nerves.

He eased his head back onto his pillow, hoping to snatch some rest before his aids roused him at dawn. The bed felt too large without Melat at his side. He had ordered her to return with Jolnan to the safety of Feruse's walls. She had refused, saying that no place was safer than at his side. Yet, Charu thought that after Tobin's failings in the second day, his enemy might try a night raid. Too many things could go wrong under the cover of darkness and he would not risk the woman he loved.

His eyes shot open as the echoing call of his name cut through the still night. He threw off his sheet, rose, and marched outside.

Gidan sprinted toward him, carrying something in his hand. The man was out of breath and filled with panic.

"What is it? An attack?"

"No, Warchief." Gidan swallowed hard and breathed deep. The man struggled to find the words. "It's . . . a message." He handed Charu a pouch.

Charu opened the pouch and dumped the contents into his hand. A slender delicate finger fell into it. A simple piece of blue cloth had been tied around it at the base, just below a thin gold band.

His chest tightened, and it became hard to breath. He stepped toward a nearby pole to steady himself.

"I'm sorry," said Gidan in a shaky voice. "There were five men protecting her. All dead."

"Five obviously wasn't enough," said Charu, staring at the finger. Melat's beautiful hand would be forever scarred. "I thought she would be safer in the city. I never should have let her out of my sight," he muttered.

Charu swallowed back the emotions coming up from his stomach. He removed the ring and placed it in his pocket. The finger he handed back to Gidan.

"Alert the camp. We attack immediately," said Charu.

"In the dark? I know you're upset, but this is what Tobin wants you to do."

"Then he succeeded. Now go." Charu stood in the gloom for a moment. He looked at the ring again and moved it to a string around his neck. He put the string under his shirt and gathered his armor together, doing his best to fight back the tears trying to spill from his eyes.

* * *

Tobin didn't hear Walor come in. "Warleader. Charu is assembling his men in the dark as you suspected he might do. I have our forces readying to meet him."

Tobin didn't answer. He continued to stare blankly at the woman lying on his bedroll. He had been rough with her, far more than he intended, punching her into unconsciousness when she began to whimper. Her begging had become too much. Hours later and he could still not explain his actions.

What's happened to me? I don't even know myself anymore.

"Is she why Charu is doing this?" asked Walor.

"Yes."

"What happened?"

It was only then that Tobin realized he sat naked on a chair across from the unclothed woman.

"Isn't it obvious," he answered, voice dripping in sarcasm. "I've become the son my father always wanted, crueler even than Kaz who only allowed things to happen, but never participated."

Tobin waited for Walor's ridicule. A hand rested on his shoulder. "Soyjid did something to you. Don't blame yourself. Blame Soyjid. You aren't thinking clearly. You were caught up in the moment. Nothing more."

"Perhaps."

"Trust me. The war will end today. Nachun will help you. And then it's just a matter of putting this all behind you."

Tobin wanted to believe Walor, but he doubted he'd ever be able to put the evening behind him or the hundreds of other nightmares that plagued him.

* * *

Charu changed his tactics completely from what he had originally planned. Tobin would be ready for him so he couldn't expect to catch the man by surprise. He also knew that Melat's life was one of convenience and at any moment Tobin could kill her if he hadn't already. Charu no longer had the patience for a prolonged battle strategy, one that would lessen the deaths of his Red Mountain Clan warriors. He moved his best men to the front lines. He did not have the time to continue to expend the Green Forest Clan warriors.

In the increasing light of the false dawn, Charu lead those front lines, unsurprised to see the Blue Island Clan already waiting for him. The arrogance in their opponent's stance only fueled his hatred. He shouted a war cry that spread throughout his men until each man screamed in unison with him.

They rushed the enemy.

Charu would not stand back and command from a distance. He would make each man in his way pay as though they had been the one to harm Melat.

Charu slammed into the enemy's ranks. Entrails snaked out from the stomach of the first man he killed. His blade sank into the side of another. Charu hacked and slashed his way forward as the metallic taste of blood filled his mouth and the smell of shattered bowels infiltrated his nostrils.

Despite the maelstrom of bodies, Melat remained ever at the center of his thoughts.

* * *

"Well Tobin, you definitely got Charu's attention," muttered Nareash as he watched the epic clash of men. Where the day before, two expert commanders had deftly handled each move of their armies with care and precision, today had brought a savagery pulled from each man's most feral instincts.

"Did you say something, Nachun?"

Nareash blinked and looked down at the shaman. "No. Is everyone in position?"

"Yes."

"Then hurry and take your place. Don't you feel it?"

The shaman looked at him confused.

Nareash scowled as he looked at the gray morning sky darkening once again. Storm clouds had rolled in with little warning. "Of course you don't. It's a wonder Tobin hadn't suffered greater losses before I returned. Now, go," he snapped.

The shaman hurried off.

One Above, what I wouldn't give for even a handful of yellow-robed mages from Estul Island. Amcaro had his faults, but I can't deny his ability to teach the most basic skills.

Nareash felt an intense change in the air, a cool breeze that even the Blue Island Clan shamans noticed. They raised their hands to ready themselves. A moment later, a massive burst of lightning traveled toward the center of the Blue Island Clan ranks, illuminating the battlefield in a burst of white light.

The Blue Island Clan shamans awkwardly deflected the strike, but could not recover to fully deflect the second and Nareash had to act quickly, aiding them even though it went against Tobin's wishes not to directly interfere.

"Pay attention!" Nareash yelled during the brief reprieve. "If one comes so close to hitting our forces again, I will personally kill each one whose concentration breaks!"

The shamans bowed their head in submission and he saw a renewed determination. They blocked the next two strikes followed by several smaller attacks.

Better.

* * *

Tobin thought he had a grip on his emotions after his brief discussion with Walor. However, the hum of battle slowly began to eat away at his sanity. The colliding forces, clashing wills, and guttural screams increased his pulse at such a rate that the pounding blood in his ears drowned out any voice of reason. With each breath, he tried to calm himself, but the fear and excitement only increased his inability to think clearly.

He knew Charu would come at him hard. It only made sense given what he had done to Melat. However, he did not expect Charu's men to fight as fiercely as they did now.

His front ranks are now entirely made up of the Red Mountain Clan. Does he actually think they can defeat my men?

Tobin hurriedly scanned the thin line that divided the blue and red. He knew Charu would be there because at one time Tobin would have likely done the same for Odala.

A brief moment of sorrow consumed him, dulling his rage until several brilliant flashes of lightning illuminated the battlefield. He located Charu's helm among the men. The warchief fought hard and killed two Kifzo in as many breaths. Tobin clenched his jaw and wheeled around.

"Bring her here!" he yelled.

Two men carried Melat. She was conscious, but obviously her wits were not her own as she rocked on her feet, oblivious to the noise around her.

He eyed the shaman next to him. "Make my voice heard."

"Yes, Warleader."

Tobin felt a tingling in his throat. "Charu! Charu, do you hear me?"

Heads turned his way, including Charu's.

Tobin continued, the words falling out of his mouth without thinking. "Because of your deception, you forced me into destroying something I cared for. It's only fitting that I destroy something of yours." He yanked Melat up next to him. He kissed the woman as his dagger slammed into her chest. He felt the impact break ribs. He pulled out the dagger and blood spurted out in an arcing stream. Melat collapsed to the ground. "Now, what will you do?"

Charu raised his head back and his mouth opened. Even without a shaman amplifying the man's voice, Tobin heard the pain in his scream. Charu's sword swung in wide sweeping motions. His men rallied behind their warchief as they tried to carve their way toward Tobin.

"Give him a path to his death!" Tobin called out one last time before jumping down among his men.

* * *

"No!" cried Charu to the sky. Deep down he knew it was likely that she would die, but that didn't make it any easier to witness her death. He felt helpless.

And he kissed her.

His sword came down, snapping the blade of the man in front of him. Then it was as if his men joined him in his pain. They surged forward as one, putting the Blue Clan warriors on their heels.

A victory would mean nothing to him now. Only Tobin's death mattered.

Tobin's voice echoed out again, but Charu did not listen. He only wanted revenge.

A small path opened up among the enemy's forces. Tobin strode forward with sword drawn. The Kifzo moved with the grace of a mountain lion, and up close he saw the power in the man. Yet, none of those things deterred him.

He sprinted toward the focus of his hate. They slammed into each other with a terrible force. Running on pure hate, Charu slashed and stabbed. With anger coursing through his veins, he parried each of Tobin's counters with ease.

He knew he would win.

Tobin's blade slipped and Charu saw his opening. He twisted around the failed strike and slashed upward only to find that Tobin had disappeared. He gasped as his gut spasmed in lancing pain. Tobin stepped into view, wearing a smile. He spoke in a whisper, words meant only for him.

"You weren't even a challenge. What could she have possibly seen in you? At least she knew a real warrior before she died. How does it feel to fail so completely?"

The blade glided up Charu's torso, choking off his response.

* * *

Nareash had watched Tobin's spectacle with interest.

One Above, I hope I wasn't so melodramatic when I confronted Amcaro.

He couldn't see the rest of the details that transpired after Tobin jumped down into battle, but from the outcry among the Red Mountain Clan and the cheering from the Blue Island Clan Nareash knew that Tobin had killed Charu. He expected the enemy's forces to fall apart as the Yellow Plain Clan did after Tobin had killed Sunul. However, the death of Charu did little to dampen the resolve of the enemy, if anything it may have strengthened it.

They know what happened to the Yellow Plain Clan and they've seen what Tobin and his army is capable of. Why would they roll over now?

Though Nareash knew the Blue Island Clan would eventually win he could not ignore the costs of victory. If he let things continue as they were, it would be harder for him to accomplish his own goals.

He calmed himself and narrowed his focus on the enemy's lines. He had never attempted a spell over so large a group before, but it would be the easiest way to ensure a victory for Tobin without anyone realizing he had a hand in the outcome.

Reaching out with his mind, he felt the hate, the rage, and the resolve of the enemy's men. Underlying those emotions he felt their fear as well. He dampened all other feelings except fear until it swelled into doubt and then panic. The enemy lines buckled and the Blue Island Clan pushed forward.

Nareash held the spell as the slaughter began. The outer ranks of the Green Forest Clan and Red Mountain Clan peeled away. Some retreating to Feruse where they hoped to find refuge in the Green Forest Clan's capital. Others, made their way into the trees, knowing the city could not hold out.

Nareash released the spell and let momentum do the rest. His head felt light which he expected, but a sense of pride rose in his chest. He knew that no one, not even Amcaro, had attempted to impose their will on so many at once before.

He headed back to camp with the remainder of the battle a formality.

CHAPTER 29

Tobin waited in the center of Feruse, on the steps of the city's council building, as members of the Green Forest Clan's governing body pledged their loyalty to him. Part of his army filled out the crowd watching the spectacle while Walor led the rest to hunt down those who had fled at the battle's conclusion.

The more affluent members of the Green Forest Clan congregated on the council building's steps. They wore heavy expressions while listening to one of their own speak.

Jolnan had surrendered the Green Forest Clan's capital as a representative of Feruse's populace. The bald man sought to advise Tobin on how best to transition the Green Clan over to his rule while also culling the remainder of the Red Mountain Clan army. The councilor completed his long-winded speech and faced Tobin. "I hope you found my words satisfactory," he said in a low voice.

"It could have been said simpler. You enjoy the sound of your own voice."

Jolnan frowned. "I apologize, Warleader."

Tobin raised a hand to silence the man. He stepped forward and gestured for Jolnan to follow him as he addressed the crowd. "Your councilman has a way with words, yet lost in his self-indulgent rambling is the meaning behind what I asked him to explain." He paused. "You will all submit yourselves to me as your ruler." He pointed to a pile of burning wood and hot metal as his men destroyed the Green Forest Clan's armor and weapons. "Anyone who does otherwise will be destroyed. The clan will pay a tithe to Juanoq four times a year and the representative I leave behind to govern you will speak with my voice. That representative was supposed to be Jolnan, but I see he is a poor choice. He thinks he can persuade me with his silver tongue. He's wrong." Tobin unsheathed his dagger and drove it into the gut of the councilman. Jolnan fell over, clutching his stomach. Tobin pointed randomly to another councilman. "What's your name?"

"H-Hitat," the man stuttered.

"Hitat is your new representative. Is that clear?"

The crowd took a knee and bowed their heads.

***

Nareash examined the deep red walls of the room while waiting for Tobin to return from his rounds of the city. He admired the craftsmanship, but not enough to find the place memorable. Juanoq had been the only inhabited city in Hesh to truly impress the High Mage since his arrival.

Bazraki was an awful military leader, but he knew how to build a city.

The door clicked open and Nareash turned.

Tobin paused at the entrance before shutting the door behind him. "What are you doing here?"

"Waiting for you, of course. We have things to discuss."

Tobin dropped most of his weapons to the floor, keeping only a dagger at his side. "Such as?"

"When we'll be returning to Juanoq."

Tobin frowned. "I assumed you'd want to travel to Guaronope first and at least exact your revenge on the council of the Red Mountain Clan."

"Charu's dead. That's good enough for me."

Tobin gave Nareash a befuddled look. "Why are you in such a hurry to return home?"

"Because I have other goals."

"Are you going to explain them to me?"

"I will once we reach Juanoq."

Tobin tightened his jaw. "And why can't you tell me here?"

"Because I'd feel more comfortable talking about my goals after I've looked at your mind. The more I've thought about what Soyjid did, the more I think you should be in familiar surroundings when I do so. It will keep you focused."

"So there's a risk something could go wrong?"

Nareash nodded. "There's always a risk when dealing with one's mind."

"Then why should I have you look at my mind at all? Since the battle ended, I've felt better. More in control of myself."

Nareash raised an eyebrow. "You call killing the man who had been your representative to the Green Forest Clan in front of everyone, controlling yourself? Or what about the fifty officers of the Red Mountain Clan you hanged *after* they pledged their allegiance to you."

"I didn't want to take the risk they would turn back on their word and stage a revolt."

"Sound reasoning. But before I left for Quarnoq you wouldn't have made that decision."

Nareash watched as Tobin paced the room. The High Mage waited as his friend considered his words.

Tobin rubbed his temples. "We'll leave in two days."

CHAPTER 30

The gray sky of evening placed an ominous feeling over the thin forest. Rygar cleared their passage with one of the hidden sentries and the three riders continued into camp. Elyse breathed a long sigh of relief that they had finally made it safely to her army.

The hard journey had left her saddle-sore. Kroke had forced Rygar into a brutal pace, and a trip she thought would take at least four days only took three.

Elyse glanced over her shoulder. The ride had done little to ease the tension between her and Kroke. In their brief conversations since the inn, she noticed the mercenary's voice had lost the hurt tone it previously held, but that was only because Kroke lacked any emotion at all when speaking with her. She had tried to understand more about what caused the rift between them around the campfire each night, but Kroke had quickly changed the subject and said 'what's done is done.' It seemed that no amount of apologizing on her part could help mend the relationship.

Kroke had claimed the look Elyse wore in the dungeons made him feel inhuman. She could not recall her expression, but she imagined it wasn't pleasant.

He was covered in gore. How was I supposed to react? I'm not a soldier. That's not something I'm accustomed to seeing.

Rygar rode on ahead to announce her arrival. Elyse felt better knowing Kroke appeared more at ease around the young scout.

Maybe some time away from me will help. He needs to be around the Hell Patrol again. Maybe it was stupid to think that I could be friends with someone so different.

She shook her head. Their differences mattered little. After all, she called several other members her friend and despite the differences between her and the others, she couldn't wait to see all of them.

Especially Kaz.

Her stomach fluttered. On the surface, no two people seemed more different than she and Kaz. Yet, since Jonrell's death, she felt closer to no one.

I just dread having to meet him under these circumstances.

The camp quickly came to life and all eyes turned toward her. She spotted runners dash off into camp, spreading the word. Rygar and Kroke cleared a path before the soldiers' excitement got out of hand. Elyse sat taller in the saddle to hide her weariness.

She had worried that they would be bitter toward her, angry to be so far from home and risking their lives so that she could secure the throne. Yet, faces brightened as she neared and soldiers dropped to a knee while bowing their heads. She urged them to their feet as she passed in order to thank them for all they had done while fighting back the urge to cry.

One Above, bless them. They've already been through so much.

To her right, freshly created mounds of dirt caught her attention. Massive graves for the dead.

She halted and tears ran down her cheek unchecked. She felt moved to say something. "I cannot thank you enough for all that you've done for your country. And this is your country, more so than it is mine. You've left family behind to fight for it. You've risked your life for what you believe is the greater good." She paused. "By being in this army you believe that the greater good is for me to rule over this land. It's hard for me to put into words how much that means to me. I don't know if I'll ever be able to repay you for your efforts, at least not like each of you deserve. But I promise only the One Above himself will be able to stop me from trying!"

The soldiers raised their arms and cheered her name.

* * *

Kaz bolted through the entrance of his tent as excited shouts coalesced into one unified cry of "Queen Elyse!" He halted in his tracks, dumbstruck by the outburst, until a soldier ran up to him.

"Commander, it's the queen. She's here in camp," said the private.

"Is this some joke?" asked Kaz. "The queen is in Lyrosene."

The private shook his head. "No, sir. I promise you, it's true. Rygar brought her in and Kroke is with her. She looks tired—like she's been traveling for some time, but I know it's her."

Kaz hurried toward the gathering of soldiers. He didn't want to believe the private, but by mentioning both Kroke and Rygar, he knew it had to be true.

His hands balled into fists.

What were you thinking Kroke? I told you to protect her, not drag her halfway across her country and endanger her life.

He rounded a set of tents where three figures sat atop mounts in the crowd of soldiers. Kroke and Rygar flanked the queen, doing their best to provide her with space. Elyse shouted something to the men, but with the distance he couldn't make out what she said. He doubted that many others could either, but that didn't stop them all from shouting louder when she finished.

Elyse reached down and touched the outstretched hands encircling them as Rygar and Kroke worked to clear her path. Elyse looked up and caught Kaz's eye. The two stared at each other, momentarily oblivious to their surroundings. Kaz swallowed hard as the corners of her mouth turned upward.

Kaz continued walking toward the queen and without saying a word, soldiers parted and lowered their cheers to whispers. He noticed the condition of Elyse's clothes and how much weight she had lost. His eyes shifted to Kroke.

What did you put her through?

He stopped several steps from Elyse's mount and dropped to one knee. "Your Majesty, you honor us with your presence."

The soldiers around him did the same again.

"Please rise, Commander," said Elyse.

Kaz stood. "Your Majesty, I'm sure you're exhausted from your journey."

She smiled again. "I am, but not so tired that I forget my duties. We have much to discuss this evening."

Kaz glared at Kroke. "Yes, I believe we do."

The assassin had the nerve to return the look.

* * *

Only Kroke and Elyse followed Kaz into his command tent. He wanted the full story first before rumors started in order to decide how best to spin Elyse's mysterious arrival.

Kaz gave them a few minutes for food and drink. Once satisfied, Elyse recounted the last few weeks. Kroke said barely a word. Kaz's anger for the assassin subsided once he realized the man did the best he could considering the circumstances Elyse had put him in.

"You did well, Kroke. Go and get some rest. We'll talk more later. I want to speak with the queen in private."

Kaz watched Kroke leave, unsure what to make of the man's behavior. He turned back to lecture Elyse, but froze when her arms wrapped themselves around his neck.

She squeezed him tightly and rested her head on his chest. The desperation in her gesture reminded him of how she hugged him after Jonrell's death. Just as he did then, he put his arms around her, partly because he didn't know what else to do and partly because he realized how much he wanted to.

What's wrong with me? I already told Hag and Wiqua that I couldn't do this.

"I'm so glad you're alright," she whispered. "I've been worried about you."

"I'm fine."

"I knew you would be, but that didn't stop me from worrying." She squeezed him again. "I missed you."

Something about the way she said those words caused him to tense. He dropped his arms.

They were right. She does care for me.

Elyse stepped back. "Is something wrong?"

He walked over to a table, unable to look her in the eye. "No. Nothing's wrong. I wish you had sent word that you were leaving Lyrosene. You could still be in Markus' dungeons and I'd be totally oblivious."

Elyse frowned. "I had Gauge send word before I left. It should have reached you by now."

Kaz shook his head. "I haven't received anything."

"Strange. The messenger must have been overtaken."

Kaz grunted. "Likely. However, I find it more strange that Markus acted as though he never sent the letter to you."

"I've thought about that as well. He had nothing to gain by lying."

"Which means someone set you up."

Elyse nodded. "And whoever that is will likely try to do the same to others while I'm away from Lyrosene. I'll have to send word to Gauge in order to warn him."

"I'll get several messengers ready to leave tonight."

"Good."

Kaz cleared his throat while standing over a map. "Before we do that, we need to determine the best route for you to return home." He started to trace his finger over a road. "I think that if you head east and cross—"

"I'm not going anywhere."

Kaz looked up. "What?"

"I'm staying here with you and the army."

He swallowed. "It's not safe here. You need to go back to the capital."

"If I'm not safe around the thousands you command, then I won't be safe anywhere, let alone on the road back to Lyrosene."

"You won't be alone. I'll send men with you."

"Men you can't afford to lose," said Elyse. "I told you that Olasi is dead and Markus has complete control of the army. He and Conroy's forces are much better trained and commanded than Tomalt or Bronn's. You'll need every man available to face them."

"Jeldor is supposed to meet back up with us once he finishes off Tomalt. Our numbers will be fine then."

"Rygar told me that was your plan. But we both know that you can't sit around forever. Conroy will try to take advantage of your position and you'll be forced to act while undermanned. Besides, the remainder of Bronn's forces are still out there. What if they attack?"

"Then we fight."

"Why not retreat and fight another day?" she asked.

"We'd have to face them eventually. Better to choose the place ourselves. Besides, if Jeldor fails, we will have to deal with Tomalt during a retreat. I'd rather deal with as few obstacles at a time as possible."

"And the more men you have to face each obstacle, the better your chance of success is. My place is here. That is my final word on the matter."

Kaz cocked his head at the strength he heard. "You've grown stronger."

"I've had a lot of time to think and reflect on my mistakes."

Kaz knew he would not be able to sway Elyse's mind and seeing her again, he realized he didn't want to. He missed her as well. And despite her disheveled state, he could not help but admire her beauty.

Kaz nodded. "Is there anything I can do to help you fix them?"

"Yes. I want to send a message to Illyan, apologizing for my mistake and tasking him to start work on certain ideas of his. I also want to send a separate letter to Gauge informing him of my decision so that he can contain any of the backlash my decision might have from Phasin and his contingent in the council."

"Makes sense."

"But first, I want to see Bronn."

Kaz raised an eyebrow. "Now? I thought you might like to rest for the night and do that in the morning."

Elyse shook her head. "No."

"Do you want me to bring him here?"

She grinned slightly. "I'd rather see him as he is."

* * *

Krytien wanted to distance himself from the buzzing excitement surrounding the queen's arrival. He had retreated to his tent, but the noise permeated through the thin canvas and made it nearly impossible for him to concentrate on his reading. Amcaro's writings had not only provided answers to questions from his youth, but also alleviated certain doubts that had troubled him. Granted, he could have continued his studies by casting some sort of minor spell to muffle the outside noise, but doing so would have prevented anyone from entering his tent and he never knew when Kaz might need him.

Despite his progress, he still struggled to grasp certain basic concepts. He had worked off feel for far too long, never having trained in a more structured manner as his own master had urged him to do years ago. Krytien swallowed his pride and sought out help from Wiqua.

The two sat around a fire reading as the hours passed.

"But how do you know you're ready to move on?" asked Krytien.

"You'll just know. At least that's how it is for me," said Wiqua thumbing through the book. "Amcaro did an excellent job of putting some of the basics of sorcery into a step-by-step methodology. I can see why he was a good teacher." He paused. "When I return to the Byzernian Islands, I'll have to take a copy of this if possible. We've taught such things for centuries, but not quite as succinctly."

"Wait. So your people have known all these concepts for centuries?"

"Oh yes. There are some differences here and there since most of what we use our powers for is healing. But when you lay it all out, there isn't a whole lot of differences in the concepts between what I do and you do. We just usually have different goals and therefore different procedures to follow." He smiled. "There are some very strong healers among my people. They make me seem like one of your yellow-robed mages."

Krytien shook his head in disbelief. *Healers who dwarf Wiqua? One Above, I'm already in awe of his knowledge and he acts as though he's nothing but a beginner. With that kind of power, why do his people allow themselves to be taken into slavery?*

He almost said as much, but he knew Wiqua would dismiss the point. The old man had stressed many times before that his people used their powers to heal and nurture, never for harm.

"You know," continued Wiqua, "if you wanted to learn the healing arts, I could teach them to you. You have a vast amount of potential with the power you can access."

Krytien tensed. "What do you mean?"

"Look what we did for Kaz's armor. I tired quickly as we performed the ritual spell, but I easily siphoned power from you to finish the task. In truth, we shouldn't have been able to perform the spell as effectively as we did. The ancient shamans of the Quoron Empire used nearly half a dozen of their most powerful men to do the same thing only you and I performed." He paused. "That was because of you, not me."

Krytien swallowed hard, remembering a dark secret from the Hell Patrol's past. He spoke in a hushed voice. "I've only tried to really push myself once before and I swore never to attempt that again. Plenty of good people died because I couldn't control it."

"Come on, Krytien. Asantia was over a decade ago. When are you going to get over it?" asked Hag. The question sent her into a coughing fit.

Krytien whipped his head around. He had been so caught up in his conversation with Wiqua he forgot she was there. His stomach knotted and his eyes widened. "Jonrell told you?"

"Jonrell ain't told me anything. Nor did Yanasi or Glacar. I don't know the specifics of what happened, but it didn't take long to figure out it must have been bad when you came to the ship looking the way you did. Besides, the mess we left that city in wasn't caused by an earthquake. I knew someone had to work something powerful up for all that to happen. And Hezen didn't have a mage worth his weight. That leaves you."

Krytien sat dumbfounded, feeling sick as he thought about that day. Asantia's skyline, filled with dust from toppled buildings and smoke from raging fires. The stench of death and destruction had been so absolute that he could still recall the sick smell more than a decade later. He swallowed back the urge to retch.

A third of the city gone and on top of that Ronav died.

"Does all the old crew know?" croaked Krytien.

"I don't know," said Hag. "I trusted Jonrell's decision not to talk about it and I wasn't going to be the one to bring it up. But since it's been brought up, you can't let one day hang over your head." She waved a finger. "This war ain't over yet. We're gonna need all the help we can get from you," she added, before coughing again.

Krytien eyed the old woman and noticed just how much older she had been looking lately. "You don't understand. You weren't there."

Hag shuffled toward him and bopped the mage on the head. "You're right I wasn't there. I was safe aboard ship because you stayed behind with Ronav and the others so the wounded and officers could get away. Without you doing whatever you did, I'd be dead." She narrowed her eyes. "I don't know what all happened or how it happened, but I bet if Ronav was here, he'd tell you that you did good. Jonrell too." She threw up her hands. "Jonrell commanded us for ten years after Asantia and the man counted on you just as much as Ronav did. Why would someone do that unless they had faith in you?" She shook her head. "Make peace with Asantia and move on. I don't want to see you lose an arm like Raker because you can't let go of the past." She turned and kissed Wiqua on top of the head. "I'm going to bed. You better get something out of Wiqua tonight since now I'm too tired to enjoy him. I ain't gonna keep making these sacrifices, you know."

Hag waddled away, coughing as she went into her tent and turned out the light.

"Quite the woman, isn't she?" asked Wiqua. The Byzernian wore a soft grin.

Krytien nodded. "She does surprise you from time to time."

* * *

Kroke whipped out a knife and began twirling it in his hand, distracting himself from the thoughts he had after leaving the command tent. After seeing the way Kaz and Elyse watched each other, Kroke couldn't wait to get away from them. Though he had made his peace with the nature of his relationship with Elyse, it bothered him more than he cared to admit to see the looks she gave Kaz.

I guess I always knew they shared something. I just never wanted to acknowledge it.

He shook his head and turned his focus back to the camp as he slid between tents and campfires.

He stopped at the entrance to Yanasi's tent and called out. "Yanasi? You in there?" he asked.

The tent flap peeled back and revealed a pair of bloodshot eyes. A tired smile formed on the red-headed woman's face. "Kroke? Come in." He stepped inside. "You want something to drink?"

"No, I'm good. I actually wanted to see if you were up for a game of knife versus bow, but it looks like I may have come at a bad time."

She gave him a confused look and Kroke gestured to her eyes. "You've been crying, haven't you?"

Yanasi chuckled and plopped into a chair. "Yeah. Seems like I've been doing a lot of that lately."

"Jonrell?"

She bit her lip. "Things have changed so much lately, and little of it has been for the better. Cassus leaves, Glacar betrays Jonrell, Mal kills Jonrell, and now Raker." She wiped her face and sighed heavily. "I just wish there was some normalcy around here again."

"Yeah, I guess everyone felt like the whole world could go to hell as long as our core group from Asantia remained intact. Cassus leaving was one thing, but Glacar's betrayal and Jonrell's death definitely put everything in a different perspective."

"There just isn't much laughter anymore." She paused. "I always knew I could die, but before, it didn't matter. I just figured that Jonrell gave me years I never thought I would have after my father abandoned me. But now I've got Rygar and . . ." her voice faded.

"And what?"

"Well, there was this baby after the last battle."

"Rygar told me about her."

"It just has me thinking is all. I can't die. There are things I still want out of life."

"Then quit," said Kroke, surprised at the ease of his own words.

"What? I can't do that."

"Why not? No one would hold it against you. I wouldn't. And if anyone gave you crap they'd have to answer to me."

The comment put a smile on Yanasi's face. "Thanks. But I really can't, not until I see this through. Jonrell did so much for me. The least I can do is be there for Kaz and Elyse as they try to bring peace to Jonrell's homeland. When the fighting is done, then we'll see."

He sighed. "The fighting is never done. I'm speaking from experience. At some point, you'll have to either walk away or resign yourself to the fact that you'll never stop being who you are. A word of advice, don't wait until you're my age to decide. Chances are it may be too late."

"I won't," she said softly.

Kroke shook his head. "I'm sorry. I didn't mean to come in here and bring you down. I honestly just wanted to catch up."

Yanasi shrugged. "It's fine. I'm really glad you're back. A lot of the old crew is so busy these days I don't get to talk to them as much as I would like. It's not like I can have these sorts of conversations with the men I command, and I put too much on Rygar as it is."

"Rygar's a good man. He can handle it." He paused. "Look, why don't you get some rest and tomorrow, after we've both had a good night's sleep, we'll have a go at that match."

She grinned. "Sounds like a plan."

"Good. I still have to see someone anyway."

Kroke left Yanasi's tent in a much different mood than he expected. It felt good to be back among his friends, but he felt equally uncomfortable at how things had changed. In years past, he would show up after a mission and just fold himself back into the army with little effort.

But that was because Jonrell was the glue holding us all together, making sure things never unraveled. I guess I had hoped that someone would step in to fill that role after his death, but I should have known the man was irreplaceable.

* * *

The tent flap to the hospital burst open. Drake came charging out carrying a book under his arm and wearing a scowl. With his head down, he nearly ran into Kroke.

Kroke stepped aside and grabbed Drake by the arm. "Kid, you alright?"

"Kroke! I'm sorry. I didn't see you."

"I noticed. What's wrong?"

"You can probably guess since I'm sure that's why you're here," the boy said pushing aside the mop of black hair from his eyes. "I'm done with him. I can't keep wasting my time on someone who wants to die. I have too much else to worry about."

"Is he that bad?"

Drake nodded. "You'll see. Look, I hate to just barge off, but I really do have a lot to do and honestly, I just need some time alone right now. Can we talk about this tomorrow?"

"Yeah, sure."

"Thanks. It's good to have you back," Drake called out as he walked off.

Kroke stood there for a bit, puzzled. Like Yanasi, Drake had changed a lot since Jonrell's death, but even more since the army went on the move and he had to stay behind with Elyse. The once bright-eyed boy who seemed to lift everyone's spirits looked older and more solemn than someone his age should.

Kroke walked inside the infirmary. Other than a few dim lamps hanging from the poles supporting the canvas, the place felt like a cave. Most of the wounded slept and he did his best to block out their labored breathing or muffled sobs.

The whole place made him feel uneasy and his hand tickled the hilt of a knife on his belt. Kroke kept his eyes forward.

He found Raker staring at the ceiling, wide-eyed and motionless. The pale face took Kroke off guard, and for a moment he wondered if the engineer had passed. Then Raker turned his head to the side and spat away from Kroke, mumbling something as he wiped away the tobacco juices from his chin with his left arm.

Kroke saw the stump and swallowed hard. He caressed the hilt of his dagger and finished the last few steps, plopping on a nearby stool. "You look like crap."

Raker leaned over and spat again. He grunted. "I figured it would take someone like you to tell me like it is. I get enough lies from everyone else about how good I'm looking. I know it's all a load of garbage to make me feel better."

"Is it working?"

Raker finally turned over to look at him. "What do you think?" He raised his stump and Kroke saw where the tobacco juices had browned the bandages in spots.

"I could see how that might ruin your day."

Raker grunted.

"You don't seem surprised to see me."

"Nah. Hag told me you got in earlier. I figured you had stuff to do and that you'd come and see me when you felt like it."

"You could've looked me up, you know?"

"What's the matter with you? I'm in no condition to move about."

"You're missing part of your arm, not your leg. You can walk."

"Why don't you go fall on one of your knives? I get enough of that from everyone else, especially Drake and Yanasi. I don't need it from you."

Kroke shrugged. "I was just stating the obvious is all. I could care less if you lay here and waste your life away or not."

"Good. The only reason to get up anyway is to go find a drink, but Wiqua's made sure to keep me away from that."

"I figured as much. That's why I brought you this," said Kroke as he pulled a bottle of whiskey from under his shirt.

Raker sat up and stared at the bottle. "I take back every nasty thing I ever said about you. You're an angel! Well, what are you waiting for? Give it here. I might even give you a swig or two in thanks."

Kroke pulled the bottle away from Raker's outstretched hand. "Wait a minute. If I give it to you now, all you're gonna do is get drunk and I ain't done talking yet. I've got some stuff to get off my chest."

"I thought you said you didn't care whether I wasted my life away or not."

"I might not, but others do."

Raker fell back into bed. "If I had both hands I'd strangle you. Go on, say what you gotta say and then leave me alone."

Kroke stood and looked down on the engineer. "I never thought I'd be the one saying something like this, but you need to get hold of yourself. Jonrell was a good man, a great man, and we all loved him. Even me. But he's dead. You know as well as I do that if he saw you acting like a sorry sack of horse dung, he'd be here booting you out of bed himself. But he ain't here. So, I guess you gotta listen to me instead since no one else understands how to talk to a piece of garbage like you."

"I think I like Drake's pep talks better," mumbled Raker.

"I ain't done, so shut it. Now, where was I?"

"Garbage."

"Yeah, garbage. If you stopped feeling sorry for yourself for half a second you'd see people need you. Drake's taking on way more than a boy his age should have to. He might be a genius, but the kid can't even grow a beard. He's been forced to do his job plus yours while working on a bunch of other special projects for Kaz. And he's doing it because you ain't there to help him."

"I got one arm, Kroke. What do you expect me to do?"

"Use your head. You're the one in charge. You don't need two arms to yell. And I know your mouth still works. That kid looks up to you, and seeing you like this is just bringing him down. He deserves better." He shook his head. "And Yanasi . . ."

"What about her?"

"I don't even want to try to understand the relationship you two have, but she cares about you. The girl needs something that only we can give her—friendship. And when I say we, I'm talking about the old crew leftover from Asantia. That means she needs you."

"So two people need me. Big deal."

"More than two need you, but I ain't about to stroke your ego and name off every one of them." He paused. "And I lied. I do care whether you waste your life away or not. Everything I care about in the world is right here in the Hell Patrol."

Raker grunted. "What did that trip with the queen do to you? You sound like a woman with all this emotional crap."

Kroke managed a smile. "I was able to put things in better perspective." He dropped the bottle of whiskey onto Raker's stomach. The engineer winced and coughed. "Do what you want with it. I've said my peace."

Kroke stalked out before Raker could respond.

* * *

Elyse followed Kaz to a heavily guarded part of camp. Crusher greeted them at the entrance to the prisoner's quarters with a bow and a crooked smile. She noticed he favored one side and wore several new scars.

"Shouldn't you be resting your injuries?" she asked.

Crusher's smile grew wider. "Half a Ghal is still better than ten Cadonians, Your Majesty." He stepped aside and held the flap open as Kaz and Elyse entered ahead of him.

Many of Bronn's captured soldiers had sworn allegiance to the queen in order to return to their lands. According to Kaz, most had no real loyalty to Bronn and did not care who won the war. Elyse promised herself that once she secured her throne, she would give each of them a reason to be glad that she ruled over them.

Over fifteen hundred of Bronn's soldiers sought to join her army—some to follow Kaz, some because of their hate for Bronn, some because they just wanted to be on the winning side. Kaz kept nine hundred of those he felt could be trusted.

The few men who had not pledged their loyalties to the queen were imprisoned with Bronn. A row of prisoners sat side-by-side in the tent, chained to each other and secured to the ground. Mostly officers. Some slept and others stared through half open eyes. She crinkled her nose at the smell of the foul chamber pots and the lack of air circulating through the musty space.

Elyse leaned in to Kaz. "This seems harsh."

Kaz grunted. "They sought to kill you and steal your kingdom. They committed treason. They have food, water, and shelter. It's better than many deserve."

"Even still, this is unacceptable."

"Kaz gave them all a chance to talk," said Crusher. "Those who talked moved to better quarters. These are the stubborn ones."

Elyse saw a man with swollen black eyes sleeping against the metal bars. "Did you torture them?" she asked in a whisper, afraid of the answer.

"We tried to encourage them some," said Crusher with a chuckle. "But Kaz hasn't let me do my best work. Most of what you see is due to injuries on the battlefield."

Kaz glanced over his shoulder. "Do you still want to see him?"

Elyse nodded. "Yes."

In the back, Bronn lay on the floor. Grime covered his clothes and blood crusted around his neck. He slept in a ball and with each breath his nose whistled. Crusher took a lantern from a nearby pole and brought it over. The lantern cast just enough light for Elyse to see the rest of Bronn's face. She gasped in surprise at his condition. The whistle made sense based on the angle of his nose. The rest of his discolored face looked like a giant bruise.

"Alright, you pompous prick. Get to your feet," said Crusher.

"Cut it out," said Kaz and the Ghal obeyed.

Bronn balled himself tighter and covered his face when he saw Crusher and Kaz. He let out a girlish yelp as the Ghal stood him up. His eyes opened wider when he noticed Elyse. Immediately, he stood straighter and did his best to appear his old confident and arrogant self.

"Elyse dear, thank the One Above you're here," said Bronn after finally composing himself. His voice sounded more nasally than she remembered. "I understand the need to hire such buffoons for your army, but this is ridiculous. I hope that you will have them punished for the way they've treated me and my officers. I tried to explain our relationship but—"

"Shut up," she said, cutting him off. For a few moments when she had first entered the tent and seen Bronn lying there she felt sorry for him, but in just a few short words old memories returned to her. "We have only one relationship you need concern yourself with. You are my prisoner and I am your jailor. You raised an army against me. I've had enough of you and people like you," she said, raising her voice so all the others detained heard her. "If you thought that by holding out I might save you, you were wrong. Kaz believes you have information we need. You will give it to him." She eyed Crusher. "You have my permission to extract the information from Bronn and his officers," she said louder still, "by any means necessary."

She didn't know who wore the greater look of shock on their face, Bronn or the Ghal. She heard a small chuckle from Kaz that she took for approval.

"I hope that my commander will bring me good news come morning," said Elyse as she turned to leave.

"Wait Elyse!" cried out Bronn. "In the name of the One Above, wait."

She turned, hearing the frightened tone in his voice. "Yes."

"Don't you remember what we had?" he asked, trying to appear confident. "Before your father caught us, I do believe you were screaming in ecstasy," he said, eyes rolling to Kaz as he smiled wider.

Without thinking, she punched Bronn flat on his nose and the duke fell limp. Gasps came from the remaining prisoners.

Crusher's guttural laugh broke the silence. He looked at Elyse. "You keep this up and I may have to apply for citizenship."

Elyse grabbed her throbbing hand and charged out of the tent, both appalled and thrilled by her actions.

One Above, that felt good.

*　*　*

Kaz allowed Elyse to use his quarters for the night until other accommodations could be made. He left the tent with a grin, still thinking of her reaction to Bronn.

She won't be walked on again.

If her assault on Bronn had not been enough evidence of this, the conversation they shared afterward strengthened his opinion. Elyse was stronger, more sure of herself, and Kaz could not be prouder.

She is Jonrell's sister now.

Kaz had learned that as a young teenager Bronn found a way for him and Elyse to be alone. She had failed to see his intentions until he tried to force himself on her. Bronn had managed to get half her clothes off when her steward, Gillian, walked in on them.

Although the king dismissed their betrothal, Elyse said that her father also blamed her for encouraging Bronn's behavior by her constant swooning. Therefore, little happened to Bronn. Adding to her humiliation, Bronn started rumors that she had thrown herself at him.

Kaz's anger had risen until Elyse started laughing.

"If I would have known he would fall so easily from one punch, I would have hit him sooner," she joked.

"I might have struck him harder myself," he answered back.

"One Above, he wouldn't have a face left."

They laughed harder.

Months ago, recalling such painful memories would have likely caused a different reaction from the queen. Kaz realized the queen's newfound strength only heightened the feelings he had for her.

A familiar feeling tugged at his heart and a faint voice whispered in his ear. "I love you, Kaz."

The voice caused his blood to chill and his throat to tighten.

Who was that? His stomach dropped. *Do I have someone waiting for me?* He swore under his breath. *Why can't I just get the answers to these questions?*

Crusher came toward him. He wore a large ugly smile.

"Is he up and ready to talk yet?" asked Kaz.

"Ready to talk? He won't shut up. After he cursed both you and Elyse a few times, he started singing like a songbird when he realized he had no other options. His officers did the same. You want to see him now?"

"Might as well. Though let's take him to a different tent. Elyse is asleep in the command tent."

"No problem. You know, that's quite a woman you got there."

Kaz blinked. "Huh?"

Crusher looked over at him as they walked. "The queen. Women like that don't come around very often. I always thought she was easy on the eyes for not being a Ghal, but after seeing her take out the duke with one punch, well that's just icing on the cake."

"She's not my woman," said Kaz in a tired tone. "She's the queen, and I command her army."

The giant shrugged. "If you say so." He started to chuckle.

"What's so funny?"

"I was just thinking that if the queen can take out Bronn with one punch, it kinda diminishes the impressiveness of yours." The Ghal laughed and nudged Kaz with his elbow.

Kaz grinned. "What does that say about you? Do you mean that the queen could lay you out too?"

The Ghal's laugh cut off. "That's uncalled for, you know."

* * *

The sun shone bright the next day, and in the dead air, Krytien dripped perspiration. Mages of all skill levels sweat right along beside him. He still saw a handful of hateful glares, but they did not deter his actions. He at least had won over the majority.

I only wish I had more sleep. I sure wouldn't have stayed up with Wiqua all night had I known what Kaz wanted today.

Kaz had pulled Krytien aside before breakfast and stressed the need to push the mages harder during drills. Although Kaz had been impressed at their progress, all reports indicated that Conroy's mages would present a tougher challenge than Tomalt and Bronn's mages. Kaz urged Krytien to stop holding back on a lifetime of knowledge.

Krytien hated to admit that he had held back in some areas, afraid that he would have many of the mages picking up his bad habits. He didn't want them repeating his mistakes. But after his discussion with Hag and Wiqua, Krytien concluded that he owed it to the army to do more.

He combined lessons learned from his former master, Philik, and the exercises outlined in High Mage Amcaro's texts, with explanations he received from Wiqua. He then put his own spin on those principles so that he felt more comfortable teaching them. Krytien had trained alongside the mages all morning.

"Lufflin, you've got to relax and empty yourself." He watched the green-robed mage's jaw tighten and his eyes clench tighter as he strained to control the sorcery. The giant boulder swayed in the air, but at a slower pace than what Krytien wanted to see. "Relax. You're trying too hard."

The boulder crashed to the empty ground with a thud as Lufflin opened his eyes and swore. "What are you talking about? How am I supposed to relax when you keep hollering in my ear?"

"You shouldn't be distracted by me. You've done this in battle before."

"Not by myself," said Lufflin as he threw up his hands. "We're supposed to operate in groups. Everyone knows that."

"No. Everyone assumes that we're supposed to operate in groups. That limits what we can do. We don't have as many mages as Conroy and Markus so we need to be able to operate independently."

"You're crazy. We're not ready for something like that."

"He's right," whispered a black-robed mage that came up beside Krytien. "You're trying to teach them techniques they aren't ready for. One Above, many at our level can barely do some of the things you're showing the green robes. And you've got the yellow robes doing things they're still years away from."

"That's ridiculous. I was doing some of this stuff long before I ever got my black robes," said Krytien.

The black-robed mage grunted. "Then you're an anomaly."

"I doubt it. I'm not having anyone do anything they aren't capable of doing."

Krytien faced Lufflin. "Look, I promise that you can do this." He inclined his head. "Janik isn't giving in."

"Don't compare me to your pet," hissed Lufflin.

"I'm sorry," said Krytien, straining for patience. "I didn't mean it like that. Look, how about we alter the exercise and do this together."

Lufflin folded his arms. "Use someone else."

Krytien suppressed an urge to slap him. *Now isn't the time for that.*

He caught Nora watching the exchange. She quickly looked away. "Nora, come here a moment."

"No, that's alright. I'd rather watch."

"No," said Krytien in a stern voice.

"But I've mostly been helping Wiqua in the infirmary. I haven't been practicing battle tactics."

"Even better. Come over here."

Krytien stepped between Nora and Lufflin so she wouldn't be able to see Lufflin's reactions. "Now, we're going to do exactly the same thing as you were doing before with your boulder."

"But I was barely able to swing it with any speed at all," she protested.

"And this time you'll do much more. We'll start the process together, but gradually I'll stop assisting you. Then we'll see if you can keep going by yourself."

She nodded nervously. "If you say so."

"Take a deep breath and let's begin."

Krytien felt her reach out toward the boulder with invisible hands. Having done the exercise countless times over his life, he followed suit. The boulder rose shakily from the ground. "Stop fighting the object," he said softly. "Imagine it's as light as a feather. It should bend to your command not the other way around." He felt her resistance lessen. "Good. Now, let's start slowly. Left to right and back again."

The boulder swung in the air, some twenty feet off the ground. It swayed in a wide, arcing motion, sixty feet to either side. "Alright," Krytien added. "Let's pick up speed."

The boulder increased speed—the whooshing air kicked up dust from the ground. Audible gasps of amazement came from behind.

Lufflin called out in a smug tone. "Let's see what happens when you stop helping her."

"Actually, I haven't helped her since the stone came off the ground."

"What!" the mage exclaimed.

"What!" said Nora.

Krytien felt her lose control and the boulder sailed through the air. Krytien grunted and caught it midflight before it flew into the trees bordering their camp. He eased it down.

"One Above, I'm so sorry," said Nora.

"It's fine. I expected it," he told her.

"You were serious. You weren't helping me, were you?" she asked in wonder.

"No, I wasn't. You just had to get past the mental barrier you placed on yourself."

Nora's face lit up and she hugged Krytien. She stepped away. "I'm sorry. I just can't believe it."

Krytien chuckled as did many of the other mages watching.

Nora looked to Lufflin. "Did you see . . ."

She frowned and her question trailed off as Lufflin pushed through the crowd. No one sought to run after him.

"What do you say we keep practicing?" asked Krytien.

Her face hardened as she watched Lufflin sulk away. "Yes, I'd like that."

Krytien repeated the exercise with her as other black-robed mages did the same with others of lesser skill.

* * *

"C'mon, what is with you? We don't drill for a few days and you forget everything you ever learned!" yelled Drake.

Truth was it had been more than a few days. Drilling had slipped as he spent time with Raker in the infirmary. Senald, who he had put in charge, held a different set of standards than Drake.

A good soldier, but he's not ready to lead.

For the third time that morning, he had the men disassemble and reassemble the trebuchets in a plot of open land he found outside of camp. Their time had suffered greatly since he last ran the drills. Men sprinted between the equipment, stopping only to puke their guts up or gasp for air. Sitting on their rears and drinking each night had done them no favors.

It's my fault. I should have stayed on them rather than worry about Raker.

It was an awful thing to think, but Drake had finally given up on the man. His men needed him too much to waste any more time in the infirmary.

I'm sure Kroke learned the lesson a lot sooner last night.

Four men struggled with a massive beam as another failed to tightly secure the rope. Men scrambled as the beam tumbled to the ground.

Drake opened his mouth, ready to lay into them again when a familiar voice cut him off.

"One Above, you piece of garbage. Who taught you to tie rope like that? It sure wasn't me and I know it wasn't Drake."

Mouths hung open as Raker stomped toward the group. He wore a mail shirt, the left sleeve shortened. He already looked out of breath as he squinted into the morning sun. Raker pushed his way past several soldiers before stopping and spitting at the engineer's feet whose rope skills caused the mishap.

"What's your name, son?"

"Clarnat, sir," said the soldier, confused.

"I know I've been as good as dead, but I don't recognize you or the name."

The soldier looked around for help, but everyone stared at Raker, including Drake, too dumbfounded to say anything. Finally, Clarnat responded. "I came over from Bronn's forces after the last battle. I've sworn allegiance to the queen and to Kaz."

"Ah, that explains it. Well, I could give a horse's backside who you swear allegiance to. All I know is that if you're gonna be working on equipment like this, you better learn how to tie a decent knot." He started barking orders. "You four, close your blasted mouths and pick up that beam again."

Men hurried and obeyed. Within moments Raker worked the rope around the beam with one hand, using his weight and legs to tighten it. Once he got to the end, he looked back at the soldier who watched him.

"Cletan, get over here."

"It's Clarnat, sir," the soldier said as he came over.

"Close enough. You haven't done anything yet for me to remember your name. Here, take this rope."

"What do you want me to do, sir?"

"Listen to me and tie it just how I tell you. I'd show you myself, but I'm missing the necessary tools," said Raker, raising his stump. "Now pay attention, because I hate telling people the same thing twice. Ain't that right?" he called out.

Several grunts of agreement and "yes, sirs" sounded.

Drake listened to Raker explain the knot. It was almost like the engineer had never left.

What did Kroke say to him last night?

Upon completion of the drill, Raker called out, "Now go again. We're gonna drill until dusk unless you get it right."

The men started up again as Raker strode toward Drake.

"Looks like I still got it," said Raker. He spat a wad of tobacco to punctuate the statement.

"So that's it?" asked Drake, staring out at the field. "You act like a mule for months, nearly drink yourself to death, treat everyone who cares about your sorry behind like crap, try to get yourself killed, and you think that just magically showing up one day and doing your job again is going to set things right."

"I guess not."

"No, it won't."

"You want an apology or something?"

Drake turned and jabbed his finger into Raker's chest. "I ought to kill you myself. Want has nothing to do with it. I deserve an apology. Without me, this whole division would have fallen apart. You think you can just come in and take it from me? Well, think again. I've earned the right to lead them."

"Look kid, I ain't here to take command from you, if that's what you think."

Drake glanced back. "Then why are you here?"

"To help you lead. Here's the thing, you suck at being me. Not saying you can't muster out a bit of grit from time to time, but you do better with all that technical mumbo jumbo and being yourself. Face it, there ain't no one here who can do what I can and you know it."

"So, what are you saying?"

"I'm saying you've done good while I've had my head up my butt. But I'm ready to contribute again. Kroke talked some sense into me last night and its time I moved on and lived. I talked to Kaz before I came over here and we're straight too. You and I are going to co-lead the division." His face got sterner. "Now, if that ain't a good enough apology for you, then too bad. I ain't about to get all sentimental with a hard leg like you. Got me?"

"Yeah, I got you. But just so we're clear, you better not have another meltdown. Next time, if you want to die, just let me know and I'll do it. It would save me a whole lot of trouble."

Raker spat. "Fair enough. So, we're good?"

Drake slowly nodded. "We're good."

Raker cupped Drake on the back of his head with his right hand. "Now, I got five gold coins in my pocket that still says I can outshoot you with a ballista."

Drake grinned. "You're on, you old fart." He took off toward the nearest equipment as Raker began a tirade about showing respect for your elders.

Drake felt the weight of the world lift from his shoulders.

* * *

Raker walked back to camp lighter by five gold coins. His old self would have been bitter about the loss, but truth be told, the money meant little to him. The kid had gotten better while he had been in his stupor and it felt good to see Drake win.

He smiled. *Besides, I swiped the coins from Krytien anyway.*

Though Wiqua had healed his arm, the old Byzernian hadn't done much to strengthen his muscles or lungs. Since Raker had lived for too long in his own misery, both had become a shadow of what they used to be. To his surprise, he didn't mind the soreness in his legs or burning in his chest. It made him feel alive.

Raker swallowed hard as he neared his destination. He had not been worried about smoothing things over with Drake. The common ground they shared helped fill in the gaps of their relationship.

But Yanasi's another story.

He took a deep breath and walked through the open tent flap.

Yanasi looked up confused. "I didn't know you were out the infirmary," she said.

"Well, now you do. Mind if I sit down?" he asked.

"Go ahead. I'm glad to see you're doing better. I was really getting worried about you."

"I know." Raker heaved a sigh as the weight came off his legs. "Man, I'm out of shape." He looked her over. "You look too tired for someone your age. Rygar wearing you out?" Yanasi kicked his leg and Raker let out a yelp. "What I say?"

She scowled. "I spent all that time keeping you company in the infirmary and when you get out, the first thing you do is say something like that?"

He rubbed his shin. "Sorry, you're right. Thanks, alright? You know I haven't been in my right mind for some time."

"No, you haven't."

He grunted. "What's today's date?"

"The tenth. Why?"

"Cause I've known you since you were about as tall as my waist and I think that's the first time you ever agreed with me. Thought I should mark the occasion."

She smiled and Raker saw how exhausted Yanasi truly was. He had spoken with some of her men and learned that she had been pushing herself night and day. Rygar confirmed as much, but like Kroke, believed that the real cause for her weariness had little to do with the work and more to do with Jonrell and the current state of the Hell Patrol.

"You know, you don't smile enough. Long as I've known you, you barely ever show those pretty whites."

After a long a pause she raised an eyebrow. "Well?"

"Well what?"

"Well, where's the rest of it?"

"You lost me, girl."

"You never give me a compliment without saying something dirty or sexual afterward."

Raker shook his head. "That's not why I'm here. You saved my life by getting me to Wiqua and I'm here to return the favor." He extended his hand and put it on hers. "We both have some healing left to do."

"Huh?"

"Kroke came to see me last night after he talked to you. I think he helped us both cope a little better with Jonrell's death, but I know I ain't done yet. From the looks of things, I doubt you are either. Am I right?"

A tear fell down her cheek. "Yes."

"Well then. What say you and me take a walk into the past and visit him? I'm willing to bet he's still there waiting for us."

She squeezed his hand. "I'd like that. But you go first."

"Alright." He paused, thinking of a good place to start. "I met Jonrell and Cassus when them two strolled into *The Orchid* on Slum Isle thinking . . ."

CHAPTER 31

Practically alone on deck, with little more than a sliver of a moon to keep him company, Tobin still felt self-conscious. He had rarely shown his face during the trip home, preferring to come out at night as the stars seemed to scrutinize him less than the unforgiving light of day. Other than a few updates from the captain or word sent from one of the many ships sailing in their wake, Tobin kept to himself. Even Nachun disturbed him little, except to ask an occasional question about the Kifzo's strength. Tobin used the extra time alone to question his recent actions, trying to determine how he had become a shadow of his former self.

The more he reflected, the more he questioned his own sanity.

Nightmares had haunted Tobin's mind for as long as he could remember. Acts of violence, malice, and horror had always crept into even his most pleasant of memories. He thought he knew all of those miseries—the viciousness of his father and brother, the ridicule from the other warriors, the atrocities he had unwillingly participated in under Kaz's command, and now the ones he had added since becoming warleader.

But foreign images from his past had also begun to infiltrate his thoughts—images that confused and distorted some of his oldest memories.

The one time Tobin stood up to Kaz, his brother left him for dead after turning him into a cripple. But, new dreams from his childhood showed Tobin as the aggressor. At first Tobin thought his brain had begun to flip the roles of him and Kaz, but then he realized the images were different than those he had known before.

We were just boys then. Yet, I can hear Kaz's cries for me to stop as I beat him. Who would have thought that was possible?

The new memories had one thing in common. Based on the ages of Tobin and Kaz, he knew they all preceded the death of his mother.

* * *

Tobin tried to continue his trend of introspection by ensuring they reached Juanoq's bay in the middle of the night. He knew the thousands of warriors he brought back with him might be upset by not enjoying the city's welcome after a successful victory, but Tobin's guilt would not allow him to suffer through such an event.

After pulling into the bay, Tobin actively sought out Nachun. He found him busy with three shamans.

". . . I don't care what time it is. Make sure everything is ready by the time I get there."

"Get where?" asked Tobin.

Nachun turned, and smiled. "My room. I have something that needs attending to tonight." He gestured to the shamans. "They're assisting me." He dismissed the three men.

"Your plans will have to wait." Tobin lowered his voice. "You'll be assessing the damage Soyjid did to me tonight."

Nachun shook his head, turned his back to Tobin and began walking. "That's impossible. If I do that, I won't have the energy afterward to take care of my own concerns."

Tobin's anger flared. He snatched Nachun by the arm and spun him around. "Then you'll need to reschedule your concerns."

Nachun looked down at his arm. Tobin let go after a moment. The shaman scanned the busy deck. "This isn't the place to have this conversation."

There is nothing to discuss, Tobin wanted to say, but Nachun had already moved away from him. He closed his hands into fists and followed.

When Tobin closed the door to Nachun's cabin behind them, he finally blurted out. "There is nothing to discuss."

Nachun chuckled. "What's your sudden hurry? I had to talk you into returning home."

"I feel worse. I'm having visions of things that I had no previous memory of. I'm struggling to understand them."

"I'm sorry, but one night will not make a difference. We can handle this tomorrow evening after I've done what I set out to do."

Tobin slammed his fist into the door behind him and splintered the wood. "No. That isn't how it works. We will do this tonight. I'm Warleader and you'll listen to me or—"

"Or what!" erupted Nachun. His body glowed and Tobin dropped to one knee, gasping for air. "What will you do to me, *friend?*" He spat the word. "What's happened to you? Have you forgotten all that I've done for you?"

"Have you forgotten all I've done for *you*?" he grunted. "I don't know what's happened to me. That's what I'm trying to figure out." gasped Tobin. He took a deep breath as the air returned.

Nachun sighed heavily. "And we will figure it out. But first you need your rest. You can't be worked up like this when I look into your mind. It will increase any risks associated with the spell." He extended his hand and helped Tobin to his feet.

Tobin did feel tired. Then again, he had felt tired for so long, he wasn't sure how it would feel to be rested. Plus, if he went to his room, the nightmares would find him. Still, he nodded. "Alright. Tomorrow."

* * *

By the time Nareash reached the palace he had managed to forget most of his encounter with Tobin. The voyage home had done little to improve the demeanor of the man he had learned to call his friend. Nareash wondered if he would ever feel confident calling Tobin that in the future. He cast aside the last of his worries as he entered his secluded room. A spell like teleportation needed his complete focus.

Three shamans sat on the floor with their eyes closed. Fresh markings decorated the floor. "I assume everything is ready?"

"Yes, Nachun. We made the adjustments as you specified," said one.

Nareash looked over their work. "You did well."

They opened their eyes at that and bowed at the rare praise.

"Let's begin."

* * *

Nareash opened his eyes to the sound of a woman screaming. Despite his rolling stomach, he instinctively turned toward the piercing yell as a woman quickly dove under the bedcovers to hide her nakedness. The man under her fumbled by his bedside for a sword and climbed out of bed.

"Guards!" the man called out and took a step forward. "Who are you and how did you get in here?"

The man moved into the moonlight coming in from an open window and Nareash chuckled as everything made sense.

"You!" Hezen waved his sword. "What do you think you're doing in my private bedchamber?"

Nareash bowed in a mocking manner. "I sincerely apologize. An honest mistake though one that could have turned out much worse. I tried to arrive in your courtyard, but it appears I miscalculated." A small tightening of his gut reminded him how ugly things could have been.

Tobin distracted me more than I thought.

"Do you have any idea what time it is?" asked Hezen in frustration.

"Yes. It was the first chance I had to check on the progress here." Nareash looked over Hezen's shoulder to the woman who peeked over the covers pulled up to her neck. He smiled. "You have good taste." He cleared his throat and gestured toward the man's naked form. "Do you mind?"

"You're in my bedroom uninvited. I'll stay as I please."

Nareash shrugged.

A loud knock sounded and a voice behind the door called out. "Emperor! Is everything all right?"

"Yes, I'm fine!"

"How do we know you aren't being coerced?" the voice asked.

"I said I'm fine. Leave! And next time get here sooner. I'd be dead by now if I was in any real danger." Hezen lowered his sword and rubbed his temple with his free hand.

Nareash bowed. "I'll be on my way."

Hezen looked up. "You barge in here, interrupt me, and then just leave? I thought you wanted to discuss your plans."

"Well, as I said, my arrival here was a mistake. I need to speak with Guwan and Colan."

"And what about me?"

"Is there something you need?"

"Is there something I need?" asked Hezen, raising his voice. "I'm the one communicating with the other territories!"

"Are you having trouble convincing them to join you?"

"No. Not once they learn what they can gain from the effort."

"Then I have nothing to discuss with you that can't wait until a more opportune time." Nareash inclined his head toward the bed. He patted the man on his shoulder in a condescending manner as he brushed by him on his way toward the door. "Keep up the good work."

"Wait, I . . ."

Nareash closed the door behind him and quickly walked down the hallway until reaching a set of stairs. He slipped by a couple of guardsmen on the lower level and rounded a corner. He wrapped his knuckles against a wood door. The sound carried throughout the corridor.

The door flung open and a half-dressed Kifzo stood with sword drawn.

Guwan's eyes widened. "You're late."

Nareash shrugged. "Yes, well, new developments in Hesh delayed my return to Juanoq. And I've told you before I couldn't teleport while on the water and moving." He raised an eyebrow at the sword.

"I wasn't expecting to see you at this time of night."

"Obviously." Nareash chuckled. "Would an attacker really announce themselves with a knock?"

Guwan lowered the sword and gestured for Nareash to come inside. "I wouldn't put it past them. What's going on in Hesh?"

"We can discuss that later. I take it you've had trouble?"

Guwan lit a small lamp, illuminating the simple room. A large, plush bed, more than twice as large as an average sized one, rested against a wall. Nareash smiled, knowing that out of everything the Kifzo could have, the only pleasure he allowed himself was a better place to rest.

"Not recently," said Guwan. "Colan routed out three poisoners and killed two assassins. I took down four assassins myself. The last three we openly tortured for days where everyone could see. Since then, no one's been bold enough to try again."

"Good. Tell me how things are progressing with my army."

"We're at one hundred and twenty thousand strong. Hezen expects that number to double soon."

"Marvelous. I don't know if there has ever been a host that size in the history of the world."

"I know I've never seen anything like it." He paused. "I'll admit controlling such a force has been . . . daunting."

"Of course it has."

"I need more time. There are a few bright spots here and there, tribes who are more skilled than others, but generally speaking, the men are undisciplined and their skill would pale in comparison with that of a ten-year-old Kifzo."

"Of course they would. A Kifzo is better trained than any soldier I've ever come across. However, I'm not interested in a quarter million Kifzo. Training and maintaining such a force would take too long and cost too much. I need you to instill in them what you can, and learn what each group's strengths and weaknesses are so we can deploy them properly when the time comes."

Guwan nodded. "One thing is certain, even with our numbers, a siege will not be easy. I've studied the material you left behind about The High Pass. It's brilliant in its ugliness. Three curtain walls with killing grounds separating each one. Towers staggered throughout and mountains on the sides so that flanking is next to impossible. And the sorcery used to build it protects it from other spells."

"Yes. Now you know why I need a force so willing to throw themselves against the blasted thing. We'll need to wear down the defenders."

They spoke for another hour, going over strategy, concerns, and the happenings of Hesh before a yawn jarred Nareash. "It sounds as though you have everything under control. I'll let you get back to sleep. I still need to speak with Colan before leaving."

"So you're not staying?"

"No. This is my last visit. The next time I come will be by ship." He grinned. "And I won't be alone."

* * *

Nareash knocked softly on Colan's door. He tried three more times, each attempt growing louder than the last, until a sleepy-eyed shaman stood before him. Colan quickly composed himself and managed an awkward bow.

"Please come in, Master."

Nareash stepped inside. "I'm disappointed, Colan. Guwan was far more alert than you. After what he told me about the failed attempts on each of your lives I would have thought you'd be better prepared when answering your door."

Colan's eyes widened as if suddenly remembering something. "I have wards in place . . . ."

"Which I disabled easily."

"No one here could have done the same, Master."

"That's no reason to grow overconfident."

He lowered his gaze. "Yes, Master."

"It seems that you and Guwan are getting along."

Colan shrugged. "We have our differences, but we understand the common goal. Besides, he's changed a lot since Quarnoq. He sees the bigger picture."

"And have you?"

"I believe so. I've been working diligently on the spells you taught me. I try to push myself more each day."

"Good. Show me."

"Now?"

"Now."

"What would you like to see?"

"Surprise me."

The shaman stood, cleared his throat and Nareash watched the man center himself more easily than before. At first Nareash wondered if Colan had done anything at all, but then he felt a small bite on his arm and then another. The room began filling with mosquitoes. Nareash spoke a quick chant to repel the bothersome creatures from latching onto him.

Colan opened his eyes, smiled at his accomplishment and waited.

"You've improved. Control of a life form, especially a group of insects takes a great deal of concentration and focus. It isn't as flashy as a ball of fire, but malaria will weaken an army more than a brush fire ever will."

"Thank you, Master. Your praise is an honor."

Nareash's tone lowered. "I hope you haven't instructed anyone else in these things."

Colan quickly shook his head. "No, of course not. I've been working with their mages, according to your orders."

"Good."

* * *

The previous few months had been some of the happiest in Jober's life. Juanoq's army had been away fighting and the city practically ran itself. He hated to admit it but the changes Tobin had instituted to the city's leadership were ingenious.

With Tobin and the army away, Lucia had all but stopped talking about the warleader and contented herself with living life. She and his wife, Hielle, spent a great deal of time together that allowed him to see his family more. Lucia had become so much a part of his family that he no longer felt like her bodyguard. He would never say as much to anyone out of fear of what others would think, but he loved her as a sister.

At times, those feelings also caused him an increased amount of grief when he spotted Lucia staring out into the night or going through Kaz's old things. Even after all this time, she still held out hope that her husband would return to her one day. He tried to dissuade her thoughts once and swore never to do it again after he saw how much his words had pained her.

He wished he could ease her mind, but short of telling her the truth, he could think of no way to do so.

"Are you almost ready?" Hielle called out from behind their door.

Jober shook away his thoughts. "Nearly."

"Well, hurry up. Lucia is waiting."

"I'll be right there."

* * *

"Thank you again for coming with me. I know I had told you that I'd give you the day off, but I heard about this new shipment of fabric that arrived from Nubinya and I had to have it," said Lucia. A brightness shined in her voice that lifted Jober's spirits.

Jober carried an arm full of fabric rolls as they entered the palace. "It's no trouble at all."

She smiled and whispered. "Don't tell Hielle, but I'm planning to make her a new gown."

Jober's eyes widened. "But it's so expensive and you've already given us so much . . . ."

"There's no such thing as giving too much to those you care about."

They turned a corner and Jober slammed into a wall that staggered him. The wall stared at him with an incredulous look. Tobin's eyes looked full of venom.

"Tobin! I heard you had returned last night, but didn't expect to see you today." Lucia threw her arms around the warrior's thick neck and Jober watched Tobin's anger melt away. Tobin seemed to forget about Jober as he pulled Lucia in tight and closed his eyes.

Anger gripped Jober and he took a step forward, ready to rip Lucia away, when she started laughing.

"Tobin, not so hard. I didn't think you'd miss me so."

They separated.

Tobin sighed. "It's just good to see you. The last few months have been trying."

The admission surprised Jober.

Lucia rested a hand on Tobin's arm. "I heard rumors. I don't presume to understand anything, but I'm sorry about everything, especially Odala."

Tobin's face darkened and he wrenched his arm away. Jober tensed.

Tobin scowled. "I bet you are. If I recall, you never did like her. I can imagine how happy you must be now."

"No. I didn't mean . . ." started Lucia.

Tobin brushed by her and pushed Jober out of his way and into a wall.

"No one ever means to do anything," Tobin muttered under his breath.

Jober and Lucia stood in the hallway for a moment as Lucia watched Tobin disappear around a corner. She sighed and shook her head.

"Are you alright?" asked Jober.

"I'm not the one to be worried about. Come, let's get this back to my room."

* * *

"You've been talking to my Kifzo."

Nareash had barely opened the door when Tobin's first words hit him. The warrior stood with his back against the window, hands clasped behind his back in a pose that reminded Nareash of the father Tobin had sought approval from for so long. He closed the door.

"So you've been spying on me. When did that start?"

"When you gave me a reason to," Tobin turned around. "Talking to my Kifzo. It has to do with these goals of yours, doesn't it?"

"Yes."

"You aren't from the Red Mountain Clan, are you?"

"No. I'm not," said Nareash, tired of the lies.

"Where are you from?" The steady calmness in Tobin's voice unsettled Nareash.

"Does it matter?"

"Probably not. What's one more lie atop the hundreds of others you've uttered."

"When did you figure it out?" asked Nareash, feeling surprisingly guilty.

Tobin shrugged and turned back to the window. "I think I always suspected something wasn't right about your story, but I was too blind by the friendship I thought we had. Your reaction to this whole campaign, conquering the Red Mountain Clan, and even killing Charu, the man you claimed was your enemy, confirmed my assumptions. Your mind has been elsewhere for too long." He paused. "So what do you need with my army?"

"I need them to help me conquer the land of my birth. It's far from Hesh."

"Is that why you really needed your ships? To transport them."

"Yes."

Tobin chuckled. "Was our friendship anything other than a matter of convenience for you? Or was it all lies?"

"Much of what I said was true. I've tried to look out for your best interests when I could."

"As long as they didn't conflict with yours, you mean?"

Nareash said nothing.

"And if I told you that you couldn't have my men? Would our friendship mean anything to you then?"

Nareash's voice darkened. "It wouldn't be the first time I've killed friends who stood in my way. But I don't want it to come to that. Besides, why would you care? I don't plan on taking your entire army. You'll still have several thousand here and Walor is commanding the main body in the Red Mountain Clan territory. All of Hesh is basically yours." He paused. "I still want to help you before I leave."

"Why should I trust you to look at my mind after your admission?"

"What are your other options?"

Tobin blew out a deep breath. "I have none. The list of people I can rely on seems to dwindle every day." His eyes looked at Nareash and quickly turned away. "If I can't rely on even myself then I have no chance to hold onto what I have. I need to know what's going on with me." He moved from the window and sat in a nearby chair. "I'm ready."

Nareash walked over and stood behind Tobin. He placed his hands on the warrior's head. Since Nareash's time with the scepter, he had used mind control sparingly, only pushing someone in the direction he needed them to go. He had used the method several times on Bazraki to make him appear more incompetent to Tobin and those around him. However, Nareash had never used mind control on Tobin.

I never needed to.

Nareash cleared his thoughts and slowly began examining Tobin's brain, looking for signs of damage. He finished once and repeated the process, reaching the same conclusion. He ran through everything one more time, recalling every detail from the texts he read about the mind in the dark corners of Estul Island's library.

Tobin's brain worked as it should.

What does that mean? Maybe something happened to Tobin in his youth that changed him into the man I knew when I met him. That would explain why he couldn't recall certain memories.

When Soyjid began toying with his mind, he must have removed the block holding the tendencies of his youth at bay.

Soyjid inadvertently fixed him! The lack of mercy, the brutality of enforcing his rule, the lust for blood and war, a desire to inflict punishment. That is who he really is. One Above, Tobin is his father's son.

Nareash frowned.

"Is it that bad?" asked Tobin.

"Hmm?" Nareash stared dumbly at the wall, thinking on the implications of his discovery.

"You haven't said a word or moved in some time. It must be worse than you thought?"

What do I say? Tell him the truth when he wants to believe he's someone better than who he is now.

Perhaps that's it. He's acting this way because he thinks he should. I could try to reinstitute the block, but if I failed, it could make things worse.

Nareash showed one last act of kindness to the man he had once called his friend. He lied. "No. It wasn't bad at all."

"Wasn't?"

"Yes, I already fixed it."

Tobin wheeled around. "You did? But I didn't feel a thing."

Nareash shrugged. "I'm not a clumsy boy like Soyjid. You shouldn't have any more visions haunting your dreams."

Tobin's shoulders sunk in relaxation. He let out a long deep breath. "Thank you."

He looks more like his old self already.

CHAPTER 32

A cool breeze blew across the water and swept along the docks, carrying a light mist that sprayed Nareash's face. He closed his eyes and took in a long slow breath.

This is it.

He looked back through the gate, which led into Juanoq.

After accomplishing his goals, he would send home any Kifzo wishing to return to Hesh. But, he would never set foot on the foreign land again. He had more important things to trouble himself with than revisiting a part of his life he intended to never happen.

First Thurum and Cadonia, then forge an alliance with the Ghal nation.

Once he strengthened the infrastructure of his lands, he would do the one thing that no one had even considered since the Quoron Empire fell centuries before—reenter the lands of the old empire and bring it under the rule of one man again.

Even if I can't find the scepter, no one will be able to stop me.

Nareash knew that Amcaro's death meant his chance of finding the scepter again had only improved.

If Aurnon the First couldn't destroy it, then what could Elyse have done to it?

He turned his back to Juanoq.

Tobin had said his farewell to Nareash the night before. Despite being thankful for healing his mind, he became bitter once again after Nareash told him he intended on taking the Kifzo with him to Thurum. A flash of Tobin's new anger came into his eyes, but he relented if for nothing else out of debt, thinking the High Mage had healed him.

Tobin's attitude and his absence among the curious group of onlookers crowding the docks made Nareash's decision never to return much easier.

Nareash walked over to a group of captains arguing among themselves on the docks. "What's wrong?"

Faces turned sour looks on him that spoke of how little they wanted to embark on a trip into the unknown. Nareash saw they had crowded around a map, one of the copies Mizak made for each ship.

One of the captains spoke. "We were just discussing the risks."

"What about them?"

"We don't like them. We're traveling to a place that none of us has ever seen and may not exist for all we know. And we're following a route that hasn't been mapped in hundreds of years. Who knows what could have changed." He pointed to the section of the ocean that showed the area affected by an abnormal amount of storm activity and reefs. "We may not survive this journey."

"All trips have risks. You have orders from Tobin to comply with my command."

"These risks are too much. I'm not going anywhere until we speak with our warleader in person and voice our concerns." The captain rolled up his copy of the map and held it out to Nareash.

Nareash narrowed his eyes on the parchment, but did not accept it. *I don't have time for this.* "And you speak the concerns of everyone?" he asked, meeting each man's stare.

"I do."

Nareash snatched the map from the captain with one hand and clasped his arm with the other. The captain began to writhe in pain as smoke leaked from his orifices. A foul smell filled the air as the captain voided his bowels. Men heaved, as even the wind could not sweep away the stench of burning hair and searing human flesh. Nareash let go of the captain and he fell to the dock.

He wiped his hand on one of the men standing next to him who flinched at the touch. He cleared his throat. "Does he still speak for everyone?"

Silently the group shook their head. One man had the nerve to ask the question they all wanted to know. "What did you do to him?"

"Heated his blood and boiled him from the inside out," said Nareash in a nonchalant manner. He turned to a nearby captain. "See that this man's first mate receives the map. Let him know that he's been promoted."

The man nodded.

"I'll be in my quarters if anyone needs me."

The group cleared a path for him.

* * *

A cool gust of wind swirled around Tobin as he stood on the roof of the palace. He wore nothing above the waist, choosing to feel every sensation of the air while trying to clear his mind. He watched his ships and the best of his army sail out to sea. It was never said, but he knew that he'd never see Nachun again and likely most of those leaving with the shaman.

Tobin turned away as the last white sail crawled across the horizon and disappeared in the bright sunlight. He climbed down from the roof and went to his room where he finished dressing into his light armor of boiled leather.

Tobin left the palace a short while later and made his way through the city, a guard in tow. Everywhere he went people cheered and shouted his name, thrilled that he had brought success and pride to the Heshan clan that had always been looked down upon before Bazraki began his conquest. Yet, all he could think about were the horrible atrocities he had committed. Nachun may have healed his mind, but he could not take away his memories.

Would they still cheer my name if they knew the things I had done?

He knew the answer.

Of course they would. They cheered for Kaz and they cheered for Father too. They only care that I win.

He paid little attention to them during the rest of his walk to the army's training ground.

Tobin made an appearance and watched over the training exercises led by others he put in charge of the younger warriors. He should have been pleased with their progress and the changes he had instituted since taking over for Kaz, but his mind was still elsewhere.

Can I still be the person I want to be?

* * *

A week at sea in relatively calm waters had eased the worries of many. However, the sun failed to reveal itself on the eighth morning. Dark rainclouds rolled in from the east. Lightning flashed against a horizon as black as midnight, foretelling that the storm would not pass quickly.

For four straight days, the storm mercilessly pounded the fleet. Crews worked around the clock, making repairs and doing all they could to keep their ships afloat. Like everyone else suffering through the weather, Nareash barely slept.

He stood on the sterncastle, next to the captain at the wheel. The High Mage could not trust anyone to maintain the proper course alone in such weather. He squinted into the wind and whipping rain as men fought with a flapping, loose sail. A large gust caused one of the crew to slip. A wave came over the side and washed the man over.

The crew shouted. "Man overboard!"

Others ran over to throw a rope out, but Nareash saw their efforts were useless. The man had disappeared beneath the rolling waves and had yet to surface.

The captain cursed and wheeled on Nareash. "How many more days before we're out of this?"

"There's no way to know. One day. Maybe another four."

"We can't survive that. The crew is running themselves ragged."

"What do you suggest?"

"Turn around and go home. I'm not saying for good," said the captain defensively. Fear tickled his eyes. "But perhaps we should try again in a different part of the year when the waters are better."

Nareash laughed. "So you want to turn around and travel the same amount of time as it will likely take us to push on? No. We succeed now or we fail and die. It's that simple."

The captain sighed. "Can you help us?"

"What do you need?"

"Well, I know you can't quiet the storm. Can you do something to give the crew more energy?"

Nareash thought for a moment. "Yes. It isn't much, but they'll be able to manage on less sleep."

"Please. Anything is better than nothing."

Nareash nodded. "I'll go below and take care of it before sending word to the shamans on the other ships."

CHAPTER 33

Tomalt was dead.

Kaz received word that Jeldor had defeated him. Jeldor immediately headed south but Markus had destroyed bridges along the way, which slowed his arrival. Kaz sent word back to Jeldor on a new meeting point. The commander demanded a brutal pace to ensure all went as planned.

Elyse rode alongside Kaz, surrounded by her three surviving guardsmen as well as several new additions. The guardsmen had made it back with the remaining members of Olasi's family shortly before Kaz broke camp.

He spared a glance at the queen as she scanned the land before them, head high, auburn hair cascading down her shoulders. He quickly looked away.

A lone horseman appeared ahead, exiting the thick forest that bordered the side of the road. The rider leaned forward on his mount and the hobbled animal edged toward Kaz with a limp.

Kaz called for a halt and bid the queen to stay with the army as he took off to meet the scout. Behind him, captains prepared their units for the possibility of an attack.

Kaz dismounted and took the reins of the injured animal. Rygar groaned and fell off his saddle into Kaz's arms. Blood soaked his side. He set the scout down on the ground and lifted his shirt.

"I thought I told you to wear your mail when scouting," Kaz hissed. He grabbed a rag and pressed it hard against the wound to staunch the flow of blood.

Rygar opened his eyes and coughed. "Too cumbersome," he whispered before passing out.

* * *

Kaz issued an order that anyone who caught Rygar not wearing his mail was to tell Yanasi immediately. Based on the tongue-lashing she gave him after Wiqua saved his life, Kaz couldn't think of a better punishment.

An hour later, Kaz had Rygar tell his story in front of the Hell Patrol's old crew, a larger group than what he usually entertained when discussing strategy.

"So after we realized a force waited just on the other side of the bridge, we went down and scouted them from the southeast. But they expected it and ambushed us. Since you said no one else has returned, it looks like I'm the only one who made it out alive." Rygar finished up in a somber tone.

"What the heck are we just sittin' around for then?" called out Raker. A sense of urgency filled his voice. "I know I ain't used to being part of these things, but c'mon Kaz, do you really need someone to tell you we need to get ready for an attack. Rygar said they were half a day's ride away. They could be here any moment and we'll be caught with our trousers around our ankles."

Kaz leaned over a map and looked at the bridge in question. "We won't have to worry about that."s

"What do you mean?" asked Raker.

"Because we have to take this road to meet up with Jeldor. They know what our intentions are."

"And they have the better position too," said Drake.

Kaz looked up and eyed the boy. "Yes, they do."

"According to Rygar's report, we seem to be pretty evenly matched in numbers. We should be able to come up with a strategy to beat them," said Krytien.

"Beat them? Yes. But at what cost?" asked General Grayer. "We aren't facing just the remainder of Bronn's forces. Rygar said they've got nearly eight thousand Ghals with them." The General paled. "Those aren't regular soldiers. They're twice the size of us. Does anyone really want to stand toe-to-toe against an army of people his size?" The General nodded over to Crusher.

Crusher grinned. "Actually, I'm on the smaller side. Most in my clan alone are over ten feet tall."

"Big or small, we all die the same," muttered Kroke.

Grayer bristled further. "If you want to face the army, then be my guest."

"C'mon. Me and the kid got this," said Raker, slapping Drake on the back.

"We do?" gulped Drake.

"Ain't no sweat. We just hit them with a few boulders and they'll be good and dead."

"It'll take more than a few boulders," said Yanasi. "We're talking about eight thousand. And remember, we still got the other ten thousand of Bronn's forces to contend with."

"So it seems that we can win, but our losses are likely to be extensive," said Elyse.

Kaz nodded. "That's the problem. I had hoped that our sorcery might play an advantage. But according to Crusher, an army of Ghals that size would field their own spellcasters. They shy away from using sorcery to attack with since they find it cowardly, but apparently Ghals are very effective in negating the attacks of others."

"I want to know what in the world an army of your people are doing in Cadonia anyway," said Hag to Crusher. "I thought Ghals stayed too busy warring with themselves to bother getting involved in the battles of others."

"Yeah," added Raker. "Don't your people hate our kind?"

"Typically. But, if the price is right, they might be swayed into going against our general beliefs, especially for the right man."

"What does that mean?" asked Grayer.

Crusher shrugged. "Conroy is on good terms with my people. He saved the life of a chieftain's daughter once."

"So this is Conroy's doing?" asked Grayer.

"It would make sense," said Elyse. "We'll be much weaker by the time we meet up with Jeldor. Conroy and Markus's forces would be well manned and better rested than ours."

"Glad you made us a part of this, *Boss*," Kroke said sarcastically. "Better to get all this bad news out of the way now."

Kaz's shoulders bunched at the comment and he saw the glare Elyse cast Kroke. Kaz chose not to respond.

"Well, unless anyone has a better solution, this fight is going to be soldier against soldier. Now, this is what I want . . . ." Kaz began as he went back to his map. Others stepped in closer to see his distribution of forces until a voice cut him off.

"There might be another way."

Kaz looked up and all eyes turn to Drake. "What do you mean?"

"Well, it's something I read the other day on a book I got about foreign cultures."

"What the heck are you reading about that for, kid?" asked Raker.

Drake ignored him. "An ancient custom of the Ghals called a *ribulask* allows for the chief warrior from each side to fight the battle by themselves in place of the armies."

Kaz turned to Crusher. "How come you never told me this?"

Crusher shook his head. "That's not a good idea."

"Even if our side wins, we still have to worry about Bronn's remaining forces," pointed out Grayer.

"They won't dare attack after a battle has concluded," said Drake. "The Ghals take the ritual very seriously and would likely turn on them."

"Sounds like a win-win situation," said Krytien, "assuming we want to go that route."

"I'll do it," chimed in Kroke.

Kaz shook his head. "No, it has to be me."

"No," said Crusher. "You don't want to do this."

Kaz gave the giant a confused look. "What's the matter with you? I have to do this. It will save countless lives. If I had this option on every other battle we've fought, I would have done it then too."

"This isn't like those battles!" he boomed in a giant voice.

The tent grew silent.

Elyse cleared her throat. "These are his people, Kaz. He would know better than us. Maybe we should reconsider. If you lose . . ."

"I won't lose," said Kaz in a curt tone as he stared at the Ghal.

"Don't do this," said Crusher.

"Why?"

Crusher eyed the others in the room. "Just don't."

"That's not good enough."

Crusher swore something incoherent in his native tongue and stalked out of the tent.

"Grayer, get with Drake and send the proper notification to the Ghal army since it seems Crusher won't help.

Conversations broke out but Kaz paid them little heed. He moved to the tent entrance and looked out, baffled at his friend's actions.

* * *

Kaz's shoulder wrenched back and sweat beaded on his brow. "What are you trying to do to me?" he asked, pivoting toward Cisod.

"I'm trying to get your armor ready."

"I thought it was ready."

"It never hurts to make a few minor modifications, especially by the straps. Besides," he said, looking over at Drake. "We consulted the text again and wanted to make sure we didn't miss anything."

"I'm glad you only waited until now to double-check," said Kaz.

"Better late than never. Especially since everything is riding on you this time," said Drake.

"Thanks."

"Quit moving. I'd like to do my job here," said Cisod.

When the blacksmith finished, Kaz admitted the armor did fit better.

"Your sword and shield are over in the corner next to your helm. You need me for anything else?"

"I can't think of anything," said Kaz.

"Good luck then," Cisod said as he left.

"Man, that thing never ceases to impress. It's like I see something new each time." Drake stared at Kaz's breastplate.

Kaz looked down at the symbols on his chest and then at the serpents etched into his arms and legs.

"Oh, Raker told me to give you his best."

Kaz blinked. "Really? He said that."

"Well, not exactly. You know Raker. You have to read between the lines, but I'm pretty sure he would give you his best if he knew how to."

Kaz smiled. Since Raker had gotten his act together, the change in Drake had been remarkable. The boy no longer appeared weighed down by the stress. "And you, do I get your best?"

"I thought that went without saying, though I doubt you'll need it."

"You sound like you aren't worried about the outcome."

"Of course not. I can't imagine anyone defeating you. Besides, you knocked out Crusher before and he's nine feet tall. What's another foot or two?" He paused, his demeanor turning serious. "Are you worried?"

Kaz shrugged. "I don't know. I'm not afraid if that's what you mean. Dealing with the politics and administrative duties of an army and a kingdom frighten me far more than fighting. Still, I haven't seen Crusher since yesterday. That's not like him."

"I'm sure it will be fine."

Kaz noticed Drake fidgeting. "You don't have to stick around, if you don't want to. I'll be making my way over to the bridge soon enough."

"Nah, I'm good."

"Go."

"You sure?"

"Yes, all your jumping around is making me dizzy."

"Well, if you insist. I did want to get a great spot to see it all go down," called out Drake as he sped from the tent and left Kaz to his thoughts.

Kaz walked over to his sword and strapped it around his waist. He picked up the helm and looked it over. The panther's head seemed alive as its metal eyes stared back at him.

"Don't do this," said a deep voice.

Kaz faced the Ghal who walked toward him. At his side, Elyse wore a look of concern to match Crusher's.

"Don't tell me you've taken his side?" Kaz asked her.

"He doesn't think you can win. I don't want to lose you."

Kaz heard the raw emotion in the queen's voice. She met his eyes with an intense look that caused a lump to form in his throat. He swallowed as he looked away to set his helm down, using the moment to gather himself.

Kaz put on a face of stone and eyed Crusher. "I'm assuming you've given her reasons for your lack of faith in me."

Crusher grunted. "It was the only way I could get her to listen to me. She's grown about as stubborn as you."

"So you told her, but not me?" He was surprised how much the slight had hurt him. Besides Jonrell and Hag, Crusher had been one of the first to accept him on equal terms. Here his friend not only doubted his ability to win, but also went behind his back to convince him to stand down.

The Ghal wouldn't meet his gaze. "It ain't like me to talk about my past. It was hard enough to tell her what I did."

"You talk about your past all the time. The cities, the culture, the food, the battles. Half the time, I can't get you to shut up."

"Yeah, but how often do I talk about the people?"

Kaz nodded in understanding. "So, are you going to tell me now?"

Crusher looked at Elyse for help.

"He needs to know," she said.

The giant blew out a deep breath. "The Ghal's champion, the one you're going to face, he's my brother."

I had no idea he had any siblings.

"And you don't want me to hurt him?" asked Kaz.

Crusher shook his head. "That ain't it. I hate that piece of crap. Grin, he . . . ."

"His name is Grin?"

"A name he earned," said Crusher.

"Alright. How do you know I'll have to fight him? You don't have any contact with your country any longer."

"I heard Rygar's description of the colors worn by the Ghal army. Most of those come from the territory I grew up in. That means my brother will be there."

"Another champion might be selected."

"No one is better than Grin. He's never lost. Ever. Look, I kind of fibbed about why I left my country. The reason is I was an embarrassment to my family. I really am small for my people and my brother, well he's been a legend since we were just boys. He's got me by almost three feet."

Kaz's eyes widened. "You're brother is twelve feet tall?"

"And as solid as a mountain."

"That's not going to deter me." Kaz picked up his gear. It was nearing time to head toward the bridge.

A meaty hand jerked him around. "He ain't just big. He's fast, and more agile than a man his size has any right to be. I'm older than him and he used to beat me up. I guarantee you he's meaner than anything you've ever fought."

"That's only because I haven't fought myself," said Kaz, smirking.

"You idiot, I've seen you fight and you can't beat Grin. It isn't possible. Let's find another way."

Kaz broke away from Crusher's hands and grabbed his helm and shield. He also snatched up a long spear. He rarely fought with the weapon, but considering his opponent's reach, a spear would do him good. "Move."

Crusher reluctantly stood aside. He wore a distressed look. The queen waited in Kaz's path.

"Kaz, I hereby command you not to fight their champion in single combat. We will regroup and meet their forces in the field. I cannot afford for you to lose. A kingdom and my throne hang on the outcome of today. Now, quickly prepare your men for battle."

The queen's words would have cut him through the heart if he didn't see the emotion she tried to hold back. The kingdom may have been a concern to her, but he knew that was only part of her reason.

"No," said Kaz.

"No? I gave you a command. You swore your sword to me."

"Yes. I swore that I would solidify your rule and finish what Jonrell started. If I do as you say and we win, our losses will be too great to oppose Conroy and Markus. If I lose as Crusher believes then I've at least prevented the deaths of thousands of men."

"Except your own," Elyse whispered.

"So be it," said Kaz as he walked past her.

"Crusher thought you might say that. I had hoped you would listen," said Elyse solemnly. "Guards, seize the commander!" she quickly shouted.

Kaz whirled around as his sword hissed from its scabbard.

Fighting sounded from outside. It ended in a matter of moments. The three stared at each other, confused, Crusher most of all.

Did he know what Elyse had planned?

Elyse called out. "Guards!"

The head of a grizzled engineer poked through the tent flap and spat. "Sorry, Your Majesty, but your guards have been temporarily relieved of their duties. Don't worry, they're alive. Krytien made sure of that."

"What? How could you know?"

Raker shrugged. "The kid figured it out. Ask him. Don't take it personal, Your Majesty. It's just that the Hell Patrol looks out for each other and we only take orders from our commander." He turned to Kaz and gave him a nod of respect. "Whenever you're ready."

Kaz grinned. "I'm right behind you."

Raker's head disappeared.

"Please," Elyse begged.

Kaz took a deep breath. "Trust me." He left before Elyse could respond.

* * *

Rows of soldiers cheered him on as he walked through camp. Such enthusiasm gave him strength and helped him forget the somber mood he had left behind with Elyse and Crusher.

Kaz took in the moment with a deep breath.

It's as if this is what I was made for.

He thought about the memory flashes of his training as a boy and realized he probably wasn't far off.

Kaz left the fading shouts of the main camp behind and walked alone toward the bridge. Thick rolling clouds blocked out much of the sun. A heavy breeze blew back and forth across his path as if nature could not decide which way it wanted to travel. Orange dirt and pieces of dried grass lifted up into the air and rode the breeze. Closing in on a small hill that led to the bridge, the roar of the fast-moving water in the tumultuous river drowned out the crunching steps of his boots.

When the Ghals had accepted the challenge Kaz offered, their messenger seemed amused. To them, their champion could not be stopped.

According to the rules of *rihulask*, the main body of each army stayed far away from where the fight would take place. Only a few dozen from either side could witness the event. Kaz personally selected those he wanted to attend.

He topped the rise and saw a lone figure, like a giant gray statue, standing in the middle of the bridge. Kaz could not see what Grin held in his left hand, but the Ghal leaned on a giant axe that reminded Kaz of something an executioner might carry.

I need a bigger spear.

The onlookers he had selected stationed themselves near his side of the bridge and shouted out to him. Those Grin brought to witness the battle stood deathly quiet on the opposite side of the bridge.

Drake said that these events are sacred to them.

The witnesses for Kaz did their best to offer a word of encouragement, luck, or advice. Members of the Hell Patrol's old crew stationed themselves closest to the fight.

"I'm not a fighter so I can't offer anything helpful," said Krytien. He eyed Grin for a moment and smiled. "But then again, I would suggest not holding back any. I think he can take it."

"I'll keep that in mind," said Kaz as they shook hands.

Kaz moved down to Raker and Drake. The boy smiled, but Kaz saw his nervousness as he kept looking toward the colossal warrior waiting for him.

Raker spat. "It's been a long time since I witnessed something like this. Before Jonrell, we had a commander named Ronav who used to fight in single combat all the time. The stakes weren't quite as high, but he never lost. Jonrell was from a different school of thought and never did any of that stuff." He eyed Kaz. "But since I've lain off the drink, I can tell you've got a bit more of Ronav than Jonrell in you. And that ain't a bad thing." He paused. "Go make us proud, Commander."

"Knowing how much Jonrell looked up to Ronav, I'll take that as a compliment." Kaz gestured toward the mace hanging at Raker's waist. "You mind if I borrow that?"

"What for?" asked Drake, looking dumbfounded.

"I think it might come in handy," said Kaz. "In certain situations, a sword isn't always the best weapon to use."

Raker smiled and slapped Drake on the arm. "You heard that?" He unlooped the mace and awkwardly handed it to Kaz with one hand. "I don't get as much use out of it these days. Still, I expect it back when you're done. Sentimental reasons and all."

Kaz nodded.

Wiqua stood further down and Kaz stopped in front of him.

"Don't die," said the Byzernian.

"That's it?"

Wiqua shrugged. "I can't heal you if you're dead."

Kaz looked over to Hag, taken aback by Wiqua's unusual bluntness.

"What?" the old woman barked.

Kaz frowned at how tired she looked leaning on a walking cane. Her breathing seemed labored.

"I thought . . ." started Kaz.

"Thought that I might say something to capture this moment?" She waved a hand and chuckled. "You know me better than that." Her face grew stern and she tapped her cane on the chest of Kaz's armor. "Now isn't the time to get soft on me. Go and end this quick. I can't take being on my feet all morning while you dance around out there. So, nothing pretty. Got it?"

Kaz smiled. "Got it."

"Good. Now hurry up."

Yanasi gave Kaz a hug and Rygar a salute and a handshake.

To Kaz's surprise, Kroke waited last in line with his back away from the group. He flipped a dagger in his hand while facing Grin.

I wonder how upset he is for not being able to fight the Ghal himself.

He turned as Kaz approached. Kroke eyed the mace in Kaz's left hand and the spear in his right before moving to the shield strapped to his back and the sword at his waist.

Kroke grunted. "You got enough weapons?"

"If there was ever a time not to be shorthanded, I figured this was it."

Kroke shifted his gaze. "That spear ain't gonna work." He walked over to the side of the road and came back carrying a spear four feet longer than the one Kaz held. "Here. This one should serve you better."

Kaz gave him a confused look. "Where'd you get it?"

Kroke grinned, but ignored the question. "Despite the extra length, it's stronger than what you got now."

"Thanks."

Kroke then unsheathed a knife at his waist and held it in his hand for a moment. Kaz noticed right away that it was the blade he most often saw Kroke using—the eagle-winged hilt and overall craftsmanship unlike anything else Kaz had seen. "This is my best blade. Jonrell gave it to me over ten years ago in Thurum. I've never let anyone else even touch it since then, let alone use it." He extended his hand. "I know Jonrell would approve of you having it today. Just in case."

He and Kroke had never gotten along and the assassin had kept his distance from Kaz since his return to camp. Kroke's gesture shocked him.

He set the mace and spear on the ground and took the blade from Kroke. He hadn't thought about Jonrell during this ordeal, but after Raker's comments and now holding his friend's former blade, he felt the man's presence. He grinned through the panther shaped helm.

"I'll do it proud," said Kaz as he strapped the dagger around his waist.

"You better," said Kroke.

Murmurings caused Kaz to look over his shoulder. Elyse and Crusher came over the top of the hill with several of Elyse's guards.

Kroke thrust the spear and mace into Kaz's hands. "Forget about them for now and go. You don't need any more distractions."

They exchanged a quick look and Kaz stepped onto the bridge.

Gusts of wind blew across the span and Kaz's footsteps thumped on the wide wooden beams beneath his feet. A few rays of sunlight peeked from the thick clouds only to disappear again. Fast moving water roared beneath his feet.

"Are you done preening with your soldiers?" asked Grin. "I can't believe my brother would follow anyone not a Ghal, but especially someone as soft as you appear to be." He made a noise that sounded like disgust. "Armor that fine should have been fitted for someone my size. What a waste."

"Are we going to talk or are we going to fight?" asked Kaz.

"You called for the *rihulask*. That means we must abide by its rules unless you care to disgrace our customs more than you already have by thinking you could challenge one of our kind."

"What must I do?"

"We remove our helms to see the man we are about to face."

Kaz hesitated until Grin dropped his axe, and the morning star he carried in his other hand. They clattered against the wooden bridge. Kaz set the spear and Raker's mace down. He took off the shield at his back as well before unfastening his helm. He removed the panther's head he wore as Grin removed the spike-studded armor protecting his skull.

Grin's dark and narrow eyes grabbed Kaz's attention as he stood in his gray armor mixed with flecks of blue. The pair of colors brought forth images from Kaz's past of warriors he knew he had once commanded. Unlike before, the memories lingered long enough for Kaz to see the warriors' faces. One face stood out from all the others. For a brief moment, Kaz thought he looked at a reflection of himself.

No. It's someone I'm related to. A brother?

The image vanished and Kaz's head throbbed. He blinked rapidly, staring once again at the twelve-foot behemoth some forty feet away. The giant's mouth widened to three times its normal size and the name Grin made sense.

"You look as though you've seen a ghost, little man."

Kaz refocused. "No. Just thinking that Crusher got the looks in the family."

Grin scowled. "I heard you were arrogant, Heshan."

The word rocked Kaz's mind. "What did you call me?"

"That's what you are, aren't you? I thought the stories of the lost continent of Hesh were fables, but apparently there is some validity." He slipped his helm back on. "Prepare yourself."

"The traditions of the *rihulask* are over?"

"They are done."

"Wait. I have questions about Hesh."

Grin ignored Kaz and picked up his weapons. "I'm not here to answer questions about your homeland."

"I need answers," said Kaz, caught up in his emotions. His head buzzed at the mention of his homeland and his heart raced.

Grin chuckled. "Don't tell me the rumors that you don't know where you're from are true too?" He laughed louder. "How sad."

Kaz swore loudly in his native tongue when he realized the Ghal would not cooperate. Kaz secured his helm and picked up the long spear, leaving the other weapons behind for now. He squeezed the shaft. "Before this is done, you will give me answers!"

Kaz charged.

* * *

Kroke watched Kaz and the Ghal remove their helms. From the distance and over the rushing water of the river, he couldn't make out the conversation, but from their body language it seemed like the standard affair of sizing each other up. Kroke had already spent some time taking in the giant and he had to admit that he didn't envy Kaz. That didn't mean that a part of him didn't wish he was out there—if only to knock the giant down and prove that size meant nothing.

Kaz better not lose my knife.

Kroke had surprised himself by giving it to Kaz, but it was the only thing he could think of to make peace with the man.

It worked for me and Jonrell all those years ago in Thurum. Why not do the same now?

The gesture of peace also helped Kroke realize that he no longer harbored any ill feelings toward Kaz in regards to Elyse. He knew they shared something he could never hope to have with the queen.

He grunted. *And that doesn't bother me any longer.*

It wasn't fair to compare her to my family anyway. I just wanted something I've never had. Now I gotta work on mending the rift I put between me and her.

His thoughts drifted back to Kaz. *At least I did something for him.*

Kroke felt a tingle in the tips of fingers. He calmed himself, knowing he could not interfere with this fight even if he wanted to. Still, the sudden shouting from Kaz shook him. A raw pain filled the voice of the normally stone-faced commander. He sounded almost hysterical.

What's going on?

Kroke would have to wait for his answers. The two warriors strapped on their helms. Kaz snatched up the long spear and charged with an uncharacteristic recklessness.

That's about as stupid as something Glacar would have done.

The Ghal moved with surprising speed and evaded the spear with an upswing of his massive axe. Kaz pivoted and ducked under the giant's sweeping counter. The consecutive strikes settled Kaz into a more methodical approach—prodding with the long spear, searching for an opening to slip the point through.

Unfortunately, the spear still looked about six feet too short as Grin's long axe only extended the giant's ridiculous reach. He easily turned away each stab and Kaz spent much of his time rolling and turning away from the giant's counters.

Grin definitely isn't a slouch.

With feet more nimble than anyone could have imagined, Grin stutter-stepped and deflected a quick thrust. The giant swept out a free hand and swatted at Kaz like a misbehaving child. The meaty hand of the Ghal sent him flying backward. The commander hit the bridge hard, but recovered quickly and rose to his feet. Rather than following through with his strike, Grin stood motionless, mocking.

"He could have had him there. Grin was always cocky."

Kroke turned at the sound of the deep voice. Crusher and Elyse had moved up beside him, her royal guards just a step behind. The rest of the onlookers, including the Hell Patrol, had moved up and clumped together as well.

Kroke grunted, "It must run in the family."

"It does," said Crusher in a tone more serious than Kroke expected.

Kaz hurried over to the weapons he had left behind. He put the spear down, strapped on his shield and picked up Raker's mace. He stood there for a moment with arms at his side, shoulders heaving. To some, it must have looked like the commander was already winded, but Kroke knew better.

He's seething in anger. What could Grin have told him?

A guttural bellow sounded from the commander as he pointed the mace at the giant. Grin hadn't moved the entire time. Repeating his reckless charge, Kaz raced toward his opponent. The giant shifted his stance and raised his axe. Kaz gave no indication he planned to turn away from the eventual path of the massive weapon.

"What is he doing?" said Crusher, sounding frantic. "Is he trying to die?"

Yeah, what are you doing?

Kaz flung his right arm forward and Raker's mace sailed through the air spinning toward the giant. Grin's axe crashed into Kaz's raised shield just as the mace collided with the Ghal's knee. Both opponents fell to the wooden bridge.

Elyse's hand flew to her face. Kroke noticed the tears forming in her eyes, lips faintly moving in a silent prayer.

Grin held his knee in pain while trying to stand. He eyed Kaz warily as he too staggered to his feet.

Kaz glanced back at Grin while working the remains of his shield from his arm. The left arm of the commander hung uselessly from his side.

Crap.

"What's wrong?" asked the queen.

"Shoulder looks like it came out of its socket," said Kroke.

"I'm surprised he still has an arm at all after that blow," said Raker from the back. "I can't believe that big ox threw my mace like a stick," he added, voice filled with wonder.

"Save the commentary for later," said Hag.

Surprisingly Raker obeyed and everyone watched as Kaz stumbled back toward his spear, cocking his head back to watch the giant. Grin pulled himself to his feet, leaning heavily on his axe. Kroke's eyes went to the giant's twisted back leg.

"Looks like Kaz traded his arm for your brother's leg," said Krytien.

"I don't know if that's enough," said Crusher.

"You make it sound like the man's invincible," said Krytien.

"Kaz isn't holding back, and he ain't dead yet. That's got to count for something," Kroke added.

The mage grunted.

Kaz reached the spear. His injured arm did nothing more than steady the long shaft while his right arm bore the weight and balance of the weapon. Grin worked his way over to his morning star and snatched it up. The giant looked far less confident, using his axe like a cane—head rammed into the wooden bridge, hand clasped over the end of the shaft. Grin started spinning the morning star with his free arm as Kaz slowly approached.

Kroke heard them shout at each other again. A lull in the roaring wind and crashing water allowed him to pick up a few words.

What is a Hesh? And why would that mean anything to Kaz?

Kroke swore he heard the giant laugh as the morning star whipped at Kaz. Kaz danced away from the strike and the momentum of the swing staggered Grin's balance over his injured leg.

Kaz jabbed repeatedly with the spear, the volume of his voice rising with each stab. The giant struggled to avoid the darting movements.

"What's got Kaz so angry?" asked Drake.

"My brother has that effect on people," grunted Crusher.

Kaz lunged and the chain of Grin's morning star wrapped around the spear's shaft. The giant pulled his arm back, ripping the weapon free from Kaz's grip. Rather than stepping back, Kaz drew his sword and jammed it through an opening in the giant's leg guard. Grin immediately fell to his knees, letting go of both morning star and axe. He grabbed Kaz by the throat with one hand and ripped the sword free from the commander's grip with the other, flinging it aside. Blood poured from the giant's leg, but still his massive hands worked to squeeze the life out of Kaz, covering not only the commander's throat, but his entire head.

Lifted off the ground, Kaz kicked at the giant but could not reach him. His arms came up to try and work themselves between Grin's hold.

Crusher took a knee and bowed his head. "It's over."

"What? No," Elyse choked. Kroke heard the anxiety in her voice. "This is ridiculous. I've had enough of this. Someone has to save him." She looked around. "Krytien? Crusher? Kroke? Please, help him," she said staring into Kroke's eyes.

He shook his head. "This was the risk."

Elyse wore a look of betrayal. "How can you be so cold?"

"No. He's right," said Krytien.

"Yes, this is *rihulask*. One dies so others can live and fight again," said Crusher

"One Above, I've had enough of this! Guards . . . ." Elyse started.

"Look!" Kroke pointed.

Grin dropped to the ground and clutched at his wrist. Blood squirted into the air. Kaz fell and rolled. He held a dagger in his hand.

'Bout time he used the thing, though Kroke, relieved.

Kaz rushed in one last time and after a flurry of quick slashes and stabs, slammed Grin backward.

Better with a knife than I thought. He cut the tendons on the Ghal's arms.

Kaz sat on top the giant, mere inches from his face, yelling once again. Kroke saw him work the dagger under the Ghal's armor. Grin screamed.

"What's he doing?" asked Elyse. Kroke heard the strain in her voice. It reminded him of her reaction in Markus' dungeons.

"I'm pretty sure he has to kill him to win," said Krytien.

"That sounds like more than just killing," said Raker.

"You don't have to kill your opponent to win," said Crusher. "Death is an option, but if either combatant is unable to continue, the battle is considered over. By *rihulask* standards Kaz has won."

Kroke heard the sorrow in the Ghal's voice as Grin's agony sent a shiver up the killer's spine.

Regardless of their relationship, that's still Crusher's brother. What has gotten into you, Kaz?

Another scream echoed out over the span of the bridge and Kroke caught another look of horror on Elyse's face. Kroke whipped around and pulled Drake by the collar in close. He whispered. "Is it alright to interfere now?"

"What do you mean?" asked Drake.

"Can I go out there or will it disqualify Kaz?"

"Like Crusher said. It's over. The Ghals aren't doing anything because it's the right of the victor to do as he pleases," he said with a hard swallow.

Kroke let the boy go and sprinted across the bridge. As he approached he heard the questions Kaz asked, but their meaning still meant nothing to him.

"Kaz! Stop! It's over," said Kroke, finding it almost ironic to be so worried over one man taking another's life.

Under any other circumstance, no one, including me, would even care. But Grin is Crusher's brother and Elyse knows it. Kaz has too much to lose to continue this.

Kaz wheeled around and through the panther's mouth of his helm, Kroke saw a pair of crazed eyes. Kroke's hands went to his daggers, worried what Kaz might do next. The commander blinked and Kroke saw recognition return to him.

He looked down at his blood soaked hand and Grin's motionless frame. "I didn't mean to go that far . . . I just wanted answers."

Kroke frowned. He looked over his shoulder as the others made their way toward them. "And so will they," he whispered.

The Ghals on the other side of the bridge had no desire to come near their former champion.

Kaz slowly stood, dizzy on his feet. "What will the others think? Crusher and Elyse . . ." his voice trailed off.

Kroke put out his hand, eyeing the dagger Kaz held.

Kaz extended his arm. Kroke snatched Jonrell's old blade and immediately plummeted the knife into Grin's throat. The giant's body arched back and went still. Shouts of shock from Elyse and her guards erupted. Kroke looked up to Kaz. "They'll think I'm the same cold, heartless killer I've always been and that I ended the life of a man you granted mercy to and had tried to save. I do the talking and you just nod."

Kroke wheeled about and put on a crooked grin as he headed toward the group. He headed straight for Elyse, certain that convincing her would be easiest of all.

So much for mending our relationship.

CHAPTER 34

Conroy threw his glass across the room where it shattered against the stone wall.

"I'm sorry, my lord," said Ventrin, head bowed. "Lord Markus feels awful for his error."

"He feels awful?" said Conroy, his voice rising. He began pacing his study. "He should feel like an idiot. The queen was foolish enough to walk right into his home and he let her and his entire family slip through his fingers. This entire war could have ended all the sooner. Think of the lives that could have been saved." He took a deep breath. "How far away is he?"

"Lord Markus should arrive within the week."

"We'll leave the moment he gets here, day or night. He needs to pass this way before we meet at the place of battle anyway and I want our forces together when we do so. See that word gets out."

"Of course."

"Go. I want to be with my thoughts," said Conroy as he walked to a window.

"Yes, my lord."

The door clicked shut.

Conroy gazed out over the courtyard and into the clear horizon where the Cataric Mountains loomed. A fortress stood out guarding the High Pass. Strange reports of activity in Thurum had come in recently, armies on the move.

More petty leaders squabbling over the same tracts of land. Let them kill each other down to the last man as long as they stay away from Cadonia.

Conroy went back to his table and opened the book he had been reading before Ventrin disturbed him. He flipped to a bookmarked page and compared it to the details in the letter received earlier that morning. He had heard rumors about the beastly armor that Kaz wore, but now he had a more detailed description after the commander's battle with Grin.

He beat a Ghal in rihulask *and I've lost their support because of it.*

That thought alone caused his stomach to tighten. He would have thought it impossible if not for receiving the news from a trusted source. As startling as that news had been, the armor's appearance troubled him most. He looked down at the faded image of General Victas of the ancient Quoron Empire.

One Above, they are almost identical.

He broke out in a cold sweat and for the first time doubt crept into his mind.

Victas never lost a battle in his life.

CHAPTER 35

Though they had spotted land days before, the captain didn't express his wonder until the ships neared the docks of Asantia.

"All this time, there was a whole other world."

Nareash nodded. "Many would say the same if they saw Hesh."

"Good point." The captain's words hung in the air. The destruction near the docks distracted him. "What happened to this place?"

"Some natural disaster. Do we have enough room for all twenty-five ships?"

The captain eyed the harbor with a hand over his eyes. "It looks like we do."

"Then lead the way."

Nareash glanced back at the ships gliding along in their wake. He had to give the Blue Island Clan people credit. They had become masters of their craft at an alarming pace. The journey had been hard, but every ship made it safely, only two dozen men died from disease or drowning.

Nareash left the captain. He wanted to enjoy the moment of docking in Asantia alone.

* * *

His face soured when he saw that only Guwan and Colan welcomed him. If word had reached them about the strange fleet arriving in the harbor, it should have reached others just as easily.

Ignoring formalities, Nareash asked. "Where's Hezen?"

Colan cleared his throat. "One of the tribal leaders is trying to throw his weight around and undermine the current authority. Hezen didn't feel comfortable leaving the palace while the man continued to politick with other leaders. He hoped you would understand."

Nareash turned to Guwan. "Why did you let this happen?"

Guwan scowled. "I wanted to kill him, but Hezen said he wanted to take care of it himself. He was meeting with the main instigators when we left."

"I still would have killed him. But good for Hezen," said Nareash.

Kifzo had begun to form ranks on the dock, fully armed and wearing a look of disgust for everything around them. As their gaze settled on Nareash, their loathing only deepened. He turned back to Guwan. "They have been ordered to listen to no one but you or me. They know many of the basic commands in Thurum's common tongue for now. I'll make sure they become more adept at the language when we're on the march. Are you ready to lead them?"

Guwan stood straighter and nodded.

"Good. Then let's get moving."

Nareash walked past Guwan and Colan without waiting for them to respond.

Within minutes they entered the city. The pounding steps of soldiers followed at his heels. Citizens and local soldiers stopped to stare at the passing army making their way through the narrow streets.

Nareash thought that the people of Asantia would be accustomed to soldiers traversing their streets with tens of thousands camped outside their gates. Yet, he forgot just how unique the Kifzo warriors appeared. The black warriors stood out as much from their clean lines and armor as they did from the color of their skin.

Nareash leaned over to Guwan. "What are our most recent numbers?"

"Two hundred forty-five thousand as of yesterday. Others came in this morning with more still on their way."

Nareash smiled in satisfaction.

Guwan led them quickly through the city and to the palace. He settled the Kifzo in Hezen's personal barracks. The general selected a half dozen Kifzo immediately to act as his next ranking officers. They joined Nareash, Colan, Guwan, around a large map of Thurum and Cadonia. Hezen met them shortly afterward. The map focused on the land around the Cataric Mountains, the mountain range itself, and the High Pass.

Hezen first explained that the issue with the disgruntled tribal leader had been handled. He then explained the route he had plotted to move their massive force and how he planned to supply such numbers.

Nareash pointed to a spot suggested by Hezen for the army to make camp. It bordered a lake. Yet, the rest of land seemed barren. "How plentiful are the trees in this area? We'll need them for siege equipment."

"Not good," said Hezen. "We'll need to bring logs with us. Guwan and I sent a group of men ahead to begin clearing trees. We'll meet them along the road and pick up their work along the way." He sighed. "Too bad you couldn't just transport the army by sea and skip the High Pass."

Nareash shook his head. "We don't have enough ships."

Hezen shrugged.

Nareash looked at the map. "You've done well. Tell me about Cadonia."

Hezen grunted. "It looks as though you'll be conquering a land already ravaged by war. The good news is that the casualties have been high and it's likely the High Pass will be undermanned by the time we arrive."

"So Elyse has not lost the throne yet?"

"No. K—"

Nareash cleared his throat as Hezen started to utter Kaz's name. "Her commander," he said. If this Kaz was indeed Tobin's brother, he would deal with him at the appropriate time. Until then, he didn't want rumors to spread that the Kifzo's former warleader lived.

Hezen gave a confused look, but continued. "Yes. Her Commander is as skilled a strategist as he is a fighter. No one has been able to defeat him yet."

Hezen described the queen's forces and the strategies employed by Kaz. He also commented on the numbers of Conroy's men. None were of substantial size, yet Cadonia didn't need to have two hundred thousand men to meet Nareash's army. The High Pass could be held with far fewer if led by a competent man.

Nareash adjourned the meeting. They still had much to do before leaving in two days.

Guwan followed at Nareash's heels. "We need to talk."

"I thought you'd want to start integrating your men."

"This won't take but a moment."

They stopped, alone in the hallway. "Yes?"

"It is Kaz, isn't it?"

"What do you mean?" asked Nareash, trying to feign indifference.

"I saw you wave off Hezen from saying his name. You think he's alive, don't you?"

"The similarities are remarkable. Do you think it's him?"

Guwan nodded. "I know it is."

CHAPTER 36

The wagon bounced along at a brisk pace and each bump jarred Drake from his attempts at sleep. The army was on the move once again, making their final push toward Conroy and Markus.

Grayer and Elyse said the duke's intelligence could rival only his patience. Drake understood the truth in that. Conroy had allowed others to take the most risks and do all of the work up to this point.

It feels like we're marching into a lion's den.

Drake rubbed his eyes and sat up. There would be no chance at a nap with such thoughts on his mind. He eyed Raker who examined rope for the siege equipment.

It's good to have him back. A few weeks ago, he'd have a bottle in each hand.

Drake swallowed as he eyed his friend's stump.

"Quit staring, kid. I already know it's not there," said Raker, looking up.

"Sorry. I didn't mean anything by it."

"Yeah, I know. It's just driving me crazy. Thing won't stop itching."

"Maybe Wiqua can help?"

"Nah, just gotta stay busy with something to keep my mind off it. That's why this is the third time I've checked over this same rope."

"We've got time to kill. We could do something else."

"Like what?"

"I don't know. Talk."

Raker shrugged and put the rope down. He leaned back. "Alright, kid. Talk."

"About?"

"You're the one who brought it up. Something's gotta be bugging you."

Drake didn't want to talk about Conroy. They had covered him enough.

Just like we argued enough about whether Kaz should have allowed Bronn's remaining forces to disband after the rihulask *and return to their lands so easily.*

Drake had supported Kaz's decision to allow the soldiers to go home after disarming them. Though they could have used the numbers, too many would wonder whether they could trust them in a battle with Conroy.

A thought struck him. "We never talked about what happened during the *rihulask*?"

"There ain't much to talk about. We both watched the thing happen. Great fight and Kaz won."

"Well, I meant more about what happened after the fight. What Kroke did."

"What about it? You were next to me when Kroke came back and told us what happened. Kaz had been trying to save Grin's life for whatever reason, but couldn't get his armor off and ended up making things worse. Kroke saw the Ghal nearing death and put him out of his misery. What else is there to say?"

"Lots. I've heard some people talk about how shocked they were when they learned about the brutality of it."

"Like who?"

"Not any of the Hell Patrol," said Drake, lying about his own discomfort. "I heard a couple of Elyse's royal guards talking about it. I can understand what they're saying. I mean, Kroke just stabbed him right in the throat in front of everyone, including Crusher and Elyse."

"Death ain't ever pretty. You know that. And few know the nuances of it better than Kroke. It may have looked ugly, but he put an end to the Ghal's suffering rather than drag it out as Kaz had been doing."

"But Wiqua was right there with us. He could have done something to heal him."

"Maybe. But the old man said he lost more blood than I did when I got this," said Raker raising his stump. "And I barely made it. Wiqua might have just prolonged the inevitable too."

"We don't know that."

"No, we don't. But it's in the past and although Kroke can be a killer with ice in his veins, there ain't many men better than him. He rarely loses his head and he's more loyal than an old dog. Crusher is upset because it was his brother, even though a few minutes before he would have killed the man himself. And Elyse is upset because she doesn't understand this sort of thing like we do. But me, I trust Kroke's decision completely and if anyone has a problem with it, they can come see me about it," said Raker, tapping the hilt of his mace next to him.

"One arm is going to make it difficult to use that thing," said Drake.

"Nonsense. It just means I have to hit everyone twice now." Raker's mouth widened into a yellowed grin.

* * *

"You wanted to see me, Boss?"

Kaz turned in the saddle as Kroke came in next to him. He had wanted to see the man, but once alone, Kaz found himself struggling with what to say.

He hadn't spoken to the assassin once since the *rihulask*, yet those moments had occupied nearly all of his free thoughts.

"Yes," said Kaz finally.

"This about the business at the bridge?"

"Yes."

Kroke grunted. "I figured you wouldn't be able to just leave it alone." Kroke flipped the blade in his hand one last time and slipped it into his sheathe. He looked Kaz in the eye. "I'm ready."

"I wanted to explain my actions."

"You don't have to."

"I feel like I need to."

"Alright."

"I don't like to talk about my memory with anyone except perhaps Hag or Wiqua, but it has started to come back more substantially. It's still far from complete though." He paused. "One of the things that bothered me above all else since I woke up on Slum Isle is that I have no idea what family I may have abandoned. On the bridge when I faced Grin, an image sprang into my mind and lingered. I realized I was looking at someone I think was my brother. I felt an intense emotion toward him, almost like he needs me and I need him. Only I don't know how to return home or even where home is."

Kaz turned away to stare at the road. "Grin used a word I hadn't heard since I lost my memory. He called me a Heshan and referenced a lost continent of Hesh. I begged him to tell me more. How did he, of all people, know about the place? Where could I find out more? But he was tight-lipped and taunted me with the knowledge. That's when I lost it. I'm sure you saw how I fought him. The rage I felt was . . . immense."

Kaz paused after finding the best word to describe what he felt, knowing it didn't do his anger justice. He had felt like a completely different person fighting Grin, one built completely on hate.

"So, when you got Grin on the ground, you set to work trying to get the information you needed," said Kroke.

Kaz hung his head. "Yes. I couldn't help myself. All I could think about was that he was keeping the truth from me."

Kroke grunted. "I'd have done the same thing in that situation. I think most of the crew would have also."

"Would Jonrell have done that?"

Kroke chuckled. "Jonrell did do that."

Kaz's eyes widened.

"Are you really surprised?" asked Kroke.

"A little," admitted Kaz.

"Don't be. Jonrell was a great man, maybe the best man I ever knew and he held a high set of morals. But, he would do whatever it took to make sure we were cared for. If he needed information that would save our lives, he got it, by any means necessary."

"But I tortured for selfish reasons. If I had the same mindset that Jonrell had, I wouldn't have done that, especially to Crusher's brother."

Kroke shrugged. "We can't all be Jonrell. Honestly though, it still wouldn't matter to the rest of the crew."

"Then why did you kill Grin and spread the lies about what I was doing?"

"Because I've made my own share of mistakes and I could tell you instantly regretted what you did. I saw the look on your face when you realized that Crusher and Elyse would learn what happened. But I don't care if they hate me."

"Why would you take the blame though? You always had issues with me."

"True. But I realized that part of why I didn't like you was because we're a lot alike. In many ways we're both outsiders trying to fit into a world where we don't belong. The only place I've ever felt at home is with this group of people. I didn't want you to ruin that for yourself by damaging the relationships with your friends. No one needs to know the truth except me and you."

Kaz shook his head. "I have to tell them, even if Crusher turns his back on me and Elyse never speaks to me again."

Kroke sighed. "I recommend you don't. Elyse is a good woman. Don't lose her." He flipped out a knife. "Still, the decision is yours."

* * *

Elyse rode at the back of the army. She had been neglecting Olasi's family for some time and felt an obligation to ease their fears about the uncertainty of the upcoming battle.

Lobella still shadowed Elyse, but it seemed that her friend had grown more introverted since their capture, regressing back to the shy servant of years ago. Elyse had tried to pry Lobella into talking, but their conversations held little weight. In the end, Elyse decided that Lobella would probably not open up again until she was safely behind the walls of Lyrosene.

Though I rarely got any sleep there, it will be good to lie down in my own bed. A soldier's life is definitely not for me.

She managed to hide her weariness as she listened to Arine drone on about nothing in particular. Elyse decided that they would have to part ways after lunch. She needed a break from the ridiculousness of their conversation.

"It's still bothering you, isn't it, Your Majesty?" asked Arine.

The question caught Elyse off guard as she had been paying little attention to the woman. "I'm sorry, what's still bothering me?"

"What Kroke did," said Arine.

The simple statement said it all. Despite fighting for his life and the life of an entire army Kaz had tried to save Crusher's brother. Wiqua had said afterward that Grin likely would not have survived, but to Elyse that did not excuse Kroke's actions. Up until that moment, she had hoped they could mend their relationship and become friends again.

Arine continued. "I heard what happened from the others. He'll keep the One Below company at the end of his days."

Elyse's heart tugged for the fate of a man she once called her friend. It hardened.

We all must pay for the consequences of our life's choices.

They rode a bit in silence. Arine made a questioning sound with her throat.

"Is something wrong?" asked Elyse.

"No, Your Majesty. I was just thinking about Kaz."

"Really?"

"Yes, for better or worse most everyone thought making a foreigner your commander was a grave error. Then the rumors of him fighting like a man possessed and that devilish armor he wears." The woman shuddered. "But he went to such trouble trying to save a man who moments before wanted to kill him. That says a lot about who Kaz really is."

* * *

"Well?" asked Drake.

Janik wore a big smile as he came walking up. "He said he'll think about it."

"He'll think about it? What does that mean? The way you're grinning, I thought Krytien had said yes."

"Not yet. He actually freaked out at first. But once I explained everything to him, he calmed down. Don't worry, he just has to think about it and he wants to look at some of the texts you gave him to verify how we treated the chemicals," said Janik.

"So, you think he'll come around then?"

"Definitely. Apparently, Krytien actually used Nitroglycas before, so he is familiar with it. However, his experience with the stuff has only been in the form that requires a High Mage to create. The fact that you found a way to better make and store it, reduces its risk and the need for a High Mage's involvement. He's going to want a small test tomorrow."

Drake jumped. "Yes!" He froze. "You told him we don't have much of the stuff, right? It's taken me months just to get the little bit of the ingredients I have, especially while we've traveled."

"Yeah. He knows. But he'd rather be safe than screw it up in battle."

Drake sighed. "I can't argue with that." He grinned and slapped Janik in the arm. "We did it!"

"You did it. You found all the references in the books about Quoron's war strategies."

"Yeah, but you provided the advice about whether my theories would work from a sorcery standpoint."

"Call it even."

"Deal," said Drake. "Let's go check everything over again for tomorrow. If Krytien gives us the go-ahead to show Kaz, imagine how this will help against Conroy."

The two quickly ran off to Drake's personal supplies, eager to review their handiwork.

* * *

"How are you holding up?"

Yanasi turned and came to attention. "I'm doing better, General."

Grayer smiled. "You look better. More rested. And I can tell Rygar is less worried than before. He's a good man."

Yanasi blushed. "Yes, he is."

"Seeing you two together brings back memories of my own family, you know."

"I've never heard you talk about them, sir."

The general's eyes took on a distant look. "Yes, I have a son. My dear wife, Helneth, died giving birth to our second—"

Yanasi reflexively cupped her mouth. "I'm so sorry, sir."

He waved her off. "No, it's fine. Even though it was over twenty-five years ago, I rarely talk about it. She was an amazing woman. After she died, people urged me to take another wife, but no one else could meet the standards she set. I eventually stopped looking."

"Is your son well?" she asked.

The general frowned. "Last I heard, yes. He moved away several years back, seeking to make his fortune elsewhere. We write each other every now and then, but nothing more. The boy never understood my loyalty to the crown during Aurnon the Eighth's reign." He paused. "It's hard to explain to my son that after his mother died, my duties are what kept me sane. You could say that Cadonia became my wife after Helneth. And just like my dear wife, I'd gladly lay down my life to see Cadonia safe again."

The general cleared his throat and ran his hand over his mouth. "Yes, well I'm terribly sorry, Captain. I came over here genuinely interested in your well-being and somehow turned the mood sour."

"Nothing to apologize for, General. I'm honored that you would share your wife's memories with me." She looked down, trying to think of something better she could say to Grayer. "I know where Hag has some wine hidden. Would you care to have a cup with me? You know, for those we've lost."

"Yes Captain, I believe I would."

* * *

Krytien let out a yawn as he drifted through camp. He had called for all mages to work on the lessons he had developed from his studies of Amcaro's work. Things had clicked for many of the younger mages thanks to Nora and Janik's examples.

Those two have come so far since Estul Island. I think in the long term, each has the potential to become a High Mage one day.

A few others also showed flashes of brilliance, but one in particular still caused Krytien fits. Although Lufflin finally began to put more effort into his training, it was obvious that he did so begrudgingly.

What a waste. He has the most potential of all but is too hard-headed to listen to what I have to say. If it wasn't for Nora and the fear of being on his own, I think he would have left already.

Krytien yawned again. He couldn't wait until the campaign ended, if only so he could sleep for a week. The long days had grown longer as summer arrived. Unfortunately, dusk did not mean he could rest, especially not as the end seemed so close. He wanted to spend some time in the books Drake had given him in case there was something he could use in the near future.

I need to thank the boy for his stubbornness as well.

Someone coughing, hacking with enough force that the sound carried throughout the night gave Krytien pause. Heavy gasping for air and the mumbling of voices followed. He located the source and walked toward Hag and Wiqua's tent. As he neared, he heard Wiqua speak in a soothing tone.

"Please, rest," said the Byzernian.

"I still need to see to a few things," said Hag.

"Tell me and I'll see to them then."

"Don't be ridiculous."

"Woman!" said Wiqua, raising his voice. "I am more than capable of doing your work if it is needed. You will lie down and get some rest or so help me I'll strap you down myself." Krytien had never heard Wiqua speak in such a harsh tone and though he felt odd for prying, he came around to the front of the tent where the flap had been pinned open.

"Is everything alright?" asked Krytien.

They both turned. Hag sat on the edge of a cot, sweating. Wiqua stood over her with a hand on her shoulder.

Hag did her best to straighten and collect herself. "Everything's fine. You just heard a little foreplay is all," she said with a half-hearted attempt at a grin.

"We usually keep that stuff a little more private, but we got caught up in ourselves."

She finished the last word and went into another coughing fit. Wiqua closed his eyes and Krytien saw the Byzernian move his mouth. Slowly the fit subsided and Hag eased down in the cot.

"Maybe I'll just rest a bit after all," she said in a hoarse whisper.

Krytien frowned at Wiqua. "How long has she been this bad?"

"It started months ago and has slowly gotten worse. The last few weeks have been particularly rough," said Wiqua.

"Can't you heal her?"

"I do what she lets me, which is mostly easing her pain."

"You can't heal old age," said Hag.

"Is that true?" Krytien asked.

Wiqua shrugged. "More or less. If she was younger or took better care of herself, it might be possible to extend her life. But she's lived hard. It's taken quite a toll on her. Extending her life would not ease any of her pain."

One Above, not her too. I guess it makes sense given her age, but then again, she's always been old. And she's always been here.

Krytien cleared his throat as he felt a lump form. He and Wiqua talked over Hag's ragged breathing. "How long does she have?"

"Months. Weeks. Days. Hours. I honestly cannot say," said Wiqua. Krytien saw how much the old woman meant to him.

"And when in the name of the One Above were you planning to tell someone?" said Krytien with more grit in his voice than he had intended. He couldn't help himself. She was the longest standing member of the Hell Patrol. He couldn't imagine her not around.

"It was her wish to keep it secret. There has been too much turmoil in the ranks since Jonrell's death and she didn't want to add any more stress."

"One Above, you at least have to tell Kaz."

Hag's eyes shot open. Krytien thought she had fallen asleep. "No! Not that. Most of all do not tell him."

"As commander he has the right to know," said Krytien.

She tried to sit up, but a coughing fit took her back down to the cot. She collected herself quicker this time. "Because he is commander, that's why he shouldn't know," she finally managed. "He's got too much troubling him already. I know you can see it. The last thing the big softie needs is to worry about me too. Please Krytien, don't say anything to him until this is done."

The honest plea took Krytien by surprise. Hag rarely ever let her guard down, but the mage saw that the last thing she truly wanted was to burden anyone.

Krytien slowly nodded. "I understand. It's for you to tell."

"Thank you."

"Just make sure you stay alive long enough to do it. It's the least you owe him and everyone else for that matter."

"Then drop all this mushy stuff and let me get some rest."

Krytien smiled. "I can do that."

He exchanged a look with Wiqua and left the tent, wiping his eyes.

* * *

Kaz looked up as Elyse entered his tent.

"Working late again, I see," she said.

Kaz grunted. "Of course. We'll end up converging with Jeldor sometime in the next two days. Based on reports, we're likely to face off against Conroy and Markus by the end of the week."

Elyse walked over to him and rested a hand on his shoulder. Her touch caused him to flinch, but she did not remove it.

"I hope you know just how much your effort means to me. I nearly gave up after Jonrell's death. Without you, this war would already be lost."

Kaz turned away from her intense gaze. His guilt over Grin's death weighed on him too greatly. "I wanted to talk to you about something," he said.

Elyse grabbed his arm and pulled for Kaz to turn back and face her. "I wasn't finished," she said.

Kaz found he couldn't speak as he stared into her emerald eyes.

"Not only would the war be lost but so would my kingdom. Most importantly, I would be lost. You have been the rock in my life. It is because of you that I'm stronger. You've given me everything." She paused. "I know the mysteries of your past bother you more than you let on. I just wanted to tell you that I don't care about your past, I care only about the man you are now. You are a great man and someone I am proud to know."

Elyse's words bit deep into his flesh as he thought about his conversation with Kroke. He knew the right thing to do would be to tell Elyse the truth. Yet, he found himself conflicted after hearing her open up to him.

"The decision is yours," **Kroke had told him earlier.** *He doesn't care, so why should I? What's one secret? No. I can't do that.*

He opened his mouth to tell Elyse the truth, when she did something he would not have expected in ten lifetimes.

She wrapped her arms around his neck, pulled him close, and kissed him. He forgot his guilt as her soft lips pressed into his and his arms found their way around her waist. They held each other tightly and Kaz did not want the moment to end. Yet, his past haunted him.

As he kissed Elyse, a vision entered his mind of a beautiful woman with soft skin, the color of polished onyx. In the vision, he caressed her cheek and stared into her deep brown eyes.

"I love you, Kaz."

He started to respond in turn, except he blinked. And when he did, he saw that it was Elyse who had spoken those words. He had caressed her cheek.

Who . . . who was that?

Intense emotions for the woman in his vision coursed through his mind as he pulled away from Elyse.

She was someone I loved.

"Is everything alright?" Elyse asked. She looked alarmed.

Kaz looked up, realizing he had dropped to his knees. Elyse wore a look of confusion.

"I'm sorry," she continued, her expression turning to one of hurt. "I shouldn't have overstepped myself."

Kaz opened his mouth, trying to find the words to explain what happened, but the more Kaz fought, the more impossible it became to do so. Slowly, the image of the woman faded.

"Kaz, please. Speak to me. Are you alright? What happened?" Elyse asked. She knelt down in front of him.

"I don't know," he whispered.

CHAPTER 37

"They would be an impressive host if we didn't outnumber them two to one," said Markus, shielding his eyes from the blistering sun.

Conroy's mount shuffled restlessly in place. His squinted eyes never left the enemy's lines when he answered. "Numbers don't mean everything."

"As Kaz has shown before."

"We will win," said Conroy, sweat beading on his brow. "But it will not be easy. Kaz's men have become hardened veterans. Just look at their lines. Those are well-disciplined soldiers. He's done wonders when you consider the state of the queen's army before this began. Even though we have every advantage, I expect this to still be a hard fought battle."

Markus grunted and Conroy almost chuckled to himself. Olasi's son liked to think himself a man capable of ruling as well as his father had, but Conroy knew he was but a shadow of the former duke.

Even in old age, Olasi's mind was sharp. He would have looked over our enemy and offered some sort of insight rather than restating the obvious. He wouldn't have let Elyse slip through his fingers and he would have done a much better job of delaying Jeldor from meeting back up with Kaz. Granted, the old man would never have bent a knee to me either. I guess you take the bad with the good.

"My lord," said Ventrin, pointing. "It looks as though they accepted your offer to parlay."

Conroy did his best to conceal his excitement as he watched three figures separate themselves from the ranks. He had hoped the foreign commander would be willing to meet before battle if only so he could see Kaz in person. Conroy wanted to hate the man for making his path to the throne more difficult than it needed to be, but he could not.

"Let's go," said Conroy, clicking the reins of his mount. Markus and Ventrin fell in behind him.

Conroy had forced Kaz to meet him on a field of his choosing. Long ago after King Aurnon the Eighth's death, Conroy had planned for this day, knowing that this location would be the most ideal for him to achieve victory. Every lie whispered, gold piece spent, and decision made since the king's death had led to this battle.

Other than a few low hills spread haphazardly over the land, the terrain was mostly flat before them. Tall grass and small patches of trees lined the sides of the open space.

Conroy slowed his mount as he neared the three men. Duke Jeldor and General Grayer accompanied Kaz. He would have considered them more, but Conroy found himself captivated by the foreigner. He closed his jaw, realizing that his mouth had started to gape. The reports had been true after all. Kaz wore a suit of armor reminiscent of what the great General Victas had worn.

How is that possible? He would not have access to such texts. And who among his ranks possibly has the skill to craft such a thing.

Only after composing himself over the shock of the elaborate armor did he realize that Elyse had not joined the party.

Interesting.

Their groups came to a halt some ten feet from each other. Neither said a word. Conroy watched Jeldor and Grayer eye their commander.

One Above, I didn't think anyone could make Jeldor hold his tongue.

Kaz carried himself in a way that demanded respect. He sat rigid in his saddle, holding the famed panther helm under one arm. The sun shone bright off the black man's shaved head, a thick goatee and furrowed brow added to his intense demeanor.

Conroy felt a slight twist in his gut. Never had any man's gaze intimidated him, yet something in Kaz's stare unnerved him. He caught himself.

He is but one man.

"Where is your fair queen? Did she not have the nerve to meet me face-to-face?"

"She did not want to give you the wrong impression," said Kaz.

"And what impression is that?"

"That she would accept any of your terms."

"I'm not surprised. Her rule has been plagued by foolish decisions."

"If you suspected her response, then why call this parlay at all?" asked Jeldor.

Conroy ignored Jeldor and spoke to Kaz instead. "You know Commander, I've been impressed with your ability. I hoped that if we had a chance to speak in person, I might convince you to leave Elyse and join me. Together we could not only secure Cadonia, but tame Thurum once again and unite the kingdom as it had once been under Aurnon the First."

"What are you talking about?" said Markus in a hushed whisper.

Conroy glared at the man, refusing to elaborate further.

"I will not turn traitor," said Kaz.

"Traitor," repeated Conroy, the word sour on his tongue. "I'm sure you've heard of General Victas, later Emperor Victas of the Quoron Empire. After all, you wear armor almost identical to his. Many thought he was a traitor at first when he seized the throne, yet most historians agree that without him the empire would not have survived as long as it had." He paused. "Like Victas, I know that it is my duty to Cadonia to take the throne from Elyse. Call me a traitor now or perhaps a villain, but in time, history will prove that my actions saved Cadonia."

"And I thought Bronn was arrogant," said Jeldor under his breath.

Conroy glared at the duke, but did not allow his emotions to get the better of him. He gave Kaz one last chance. "You have proven yourself a worthy commander and I'll admit your armor is quite the sight to behold, but you are not Victas. You will not win today."

Kaz grunted. "You're right. I am not Victas. I know a little about the man. Unlike you, I don't idolize the ghosts of the past."

"The man was the greatest general to walk the face of this earth, undefeated in his lifetime," said Conroy, terser than he intended.

Kaz's stare intensified and his voice took on an edge that Conroy felt crawl up his skin. "Victas may have been undefeated in his lifetime, but that is only because he did not live long enough to face me in battle."

* * *

Elyse paced the hospital tent, waiting for it all to begin. She had decided not to meet Conroy. She knew that it may come across as a sign of weakness to the duke, but her real purpose was to show that she only wore one face today.

Not the young princess. Not the unprepared queen. Not the stubborn woman. Let Conroy see Kaz up close to know the kind of man who commands my army. Let him understand better than before that I will not be pushed again.

In the meantime while the parlay took place, Elyse felt the need to stay busy. So, she helped Wiqua with any last minute preparations he needed in the infirmary. The beds were empty now, but Elyse knew it wouldn't be long before each would be filled with the moans of the wounded and dying.

One Above, let this be the last time. Win or lose, please no more death.

"Thank you again for your help, Your Majesty," said Wiqua, bowing.

Elyse smiled back at the Byzernian as she finished organizing fresh linen. "It's nothing. I just want to do my part."

"It's a rare thing for someone of your station to even be seen talking to us, let alone pitch in and do some real work, you know," said Hag. She sat down as she talked in order to catch her breath. "Your brother surprised us all in much the same way. He'd be glad to see you here."

"Thank you. I try to learn from the best," said Elyse. "Unfortunately, I can't stay much longer. I do need to witness the battle."

"Of course," said Wiqua. "Please, go on now. I believe we're as ready as we can expect to be."

Elyse understood the solemn tone of the man's voice. She parted after giving him a warm hug and then walked over and did the same with Hag. The two could not be more different and yet Elyse saw the genuine love they shared. Their relationship had encouraged her to express her feelings for Kaz.

She left the tent with guards and Lobella at her side. Kaz's reaction to her advances and their kiss confused her at best. At first, he seemed to reciprocate and his warm embrace filled the gaping hole in her heart. But then, he had tensed and pulled away, wearing a look of distress before sinking to the ground.

Elyse had tried to learn what had happened, but all Kaz would say is that certain memories came back to him. He would not elaborate. And since then, Kaz grew increasingly distant.

Their conversations since had been about general strategy and reviewing information Elyse obtained from Bronn in regards to Conroy's tendencies as a person and leader.

Perhaps he has too much on his mind and will not allow himself to open up until the battle is over.

She said a silent prayer as she walked, praying to ease the stresses of Kaz's mind as well as the worries of her own.

* * *

The three men headed back to camp and Kaz eyed the formation of his soldiers.

"That went better than I thought it would," said General Grayer.

"His offer to you took me off guard," said Jeldor, looking at Kaz. "Conroy isn't known to hand out compliments. You've earned his respect and apparently his admiration."

Kaz shrugged. "I could care less what he thinks of me. His meeting was a mistake on his part."

"How so?" asked Grayer.

"He's more enamored with Victas than what Elyse learned from Bronn."

"He certainly wasn't happy about how you diminished the greatness of Victas," said Jeldor.

Kaz smiled. "Of course he wasn't. And because he strikes me as the kind of man who's unaccustomed to being challenged, I'm willing to bet his emotions will influence his decision-making and battle strategy."

"So, how will that affect our plans?" asked Jeldor.

"It won't," said Kaz. "You will still take the right, and Grayer the left. I will command the center. We've already positioned ourselves to look like we might be susceptible to a wedge attack. I was worried he might have seen through our deception and change formation, but now, I think he'll use that strategy no matter what."

"What makes you so confident he won't change?" asked Jeldor.

Kaz saw Grayer grinning. "Tell him."

"Kaz had Drake look up tendencies in Victas's strategies. It took him awhile to cross-reference all the accounts, but apparently in a situation similar to ours, Victas always preferred a wedge formation. He practically invented the strategy," said Grayer.

Jeldor chuckled. "Conroy would know that too. And since you downplayed your knowledge of Victas, he'll be bent on proving to you the man's genius."

Kaz nodded. "Let's just hope I haven't out-thought myself."

"I doubt it," said Jeldor. "I haven't agreed with everything you've done, but I'm not ashamed to say that I can't imagine we'd have been as successful without you."

The three stopped fifty yards from the first line of soldiers. They said their farewells and wished each other luck. Kaz had a great deal of respect for both men. He hoped this wouldn't be the last time he'd see them.

Jeldor rode left while Grayer peeled away toward the light infantry on the right. Kaz dismounted, handing the reins to an aide and walked toward the front lines of his men. Krytien awaited him.

"How'd it go?" asked the mage.

"About how I expected," said Kaz.

"Any changes?"

"Nothing for now. Any adjustments will have to happen once we're engaged."

"So, you still want me out here then?" asked Krytien.

Kaz heard the nervousness in the mage's voice. He put his hand on his shoulder. "I need you here. You're the only one I trust to get word to Drake and Janik. Besides, you and the other two are crucial for keeping the center from falling apart. We can't give away ground too quickly which means we'll need to suffer a lot of abuse until the wings fold around Conroy."

Krytien sighed. "Let's get this over with then."

"Good. Take your place in the third line, directly behind me. As long as you don't stray, I promise no one will get to you."

Krytien met his eyes and nodded before easing into the ranks. He took a place next to Nora and Lufflin.

Crusher came up beside Kaz. "They're ready. Did you want to say some words to them?"

Kaz shook his head. "They know who they are. They know what this means. If they don't, then I've failed them as a commander."

Crusher grunted. "Are you ready?"

Kaz thought about that for a moment. He still hadn't admitted the truth to either Crusher or Elyse. The weight of the image he still held in his mind of the black-skinned woman had distracted him too much.

Besides, now is not the time for such a discussion.

He wondered what kind of a man he was to hide the truth. He picked up his helm and secured it over his head. Looking out through the panther's mouth toward Conroy's lines, his heart raced and his hands twitched. Whether in the glimpses of his distant past, or the newly formed experiences of his time in Cadonia, he had always been ready to fight.

It may be the only thing I truly know.

"Absolutely," said Kaz finally to the Ghal.

Crusher slapped him on the back and grinned. "So am I."

The two fell into ranks and watched as Conroy's troops came forward in a tight wedge, just as Kaz had predicted. The weight of the world trickled off his shoulders and he grinned.

I may have been born for this.

* * *

"Are you sure those things are going to work?" asked Drake.

"For the fiftieth time, yes they're going to work! You need to put some trust in Krytien," said Janik.

"Oh, I trust Krytien. It's just this is all new to me."

"Are you trying to say that I have experience hiding in a concealed pit in a battlefield?"

Drake sighed. "Point taken." The confines of their temporary home had begun to wear on their friendship.

Drake watched Janik check the small, smooth stones on the floor for the tenth time in as many minutes. Places in the false ceiling allowed small rays of sunlight to accentuate the various colors of the multi-sized rocks. The mage looked as nervous as Drake felt about their task. Krytien would activate certain stones based upon Kaz's orders. Then it would be up to them to set off the containers of Nitroglycas that coincided with the stones that flashed.

Kaz had wanted to send someone else in Drake's place, but Krytien supported Drake's assertion that they couldn't let just anyone handle the Nitroglycas, regardless of the modifications they made to it. Actually, the mage still wasn't a fan of anyone handling the stuff.

Drake and Janik had left the main army days before and ridden out ahead to the battlefield. With the help of Janik's sorcery, they constructed a foxhole in the middle of the flat land. They built a solid roof and camouflaged the entire place to blend into the landscape. Since then, neither had been in contact with the rest of the army, though they had been able to sneak the occasional peek at the surface through a lookout hole. They heard and saw when both forces arrived.

"Man, I wish we could just get this over with," said Drake.

A sound reminiscent of rolling thunder shook the ground, causing bits of loose dirt to slide down the walls. Drake shot up and peeked through one of the openings. Janik squeezed in behind him.

"Looks like you're going to get your wish soon enough," said the mage.

Conroy's army advanced.

* * *

The arm of the mangonel slammed into the crossbeam, sending reverberations through the entire piece of equipment. Another went off to Raker's right, followed by two trebuchets and then every other piece of siege equipment they had. The engineer smiled wide.

It feels good to be doing this again.

He watched the stone and debris sail through the air, grimacing because part of Kaz's strategy was to have most miss, thus making them appear inept at first.

"We're going to run out of rocks real quick at this rate," said Senald.

"We're going to spread them out going forward. I just wanted the first round to look more impressive in order to add to the illusion."

"What a waste."

"Yep," said Raker. He hated holding back, but he reminded himself it was for good reason. "But our orders are to appear like we're having trouble sighting our targets. That's what Conroy would expect given the spy he used to infiltrate our ranks and try to sabotage us. We don't change our approach until we hear from Kaz. Besides, the real damage this time is supposed to come from Drake and the mage. At least for now, we're more of a distraction."

Senald grunted. "How'd you sniff out the spy anyway?"

"During the last set of drills, I noticed Cletan . . . ."

"Isn't it Clarnat?"

"Who's telling this story?" said Raker as he gave Senald a look. "Anyway, Cletan had caught on too quickly once he came over from Bronn's army. He just seemed to have a knack for how the equipment should operate. I figured he was either some overachiever like the kid is or he was hiding something."

"And you chose the latter?"

"You should know by now, I'm too cynical not to."

A trebuchet bucket whipped off to the right. Both watched the contents miss Conroy's advancing army by nearly twenty-five yards.

"You're worried about him, aren't you?" asked Senald.

"Worried about who?"

"Drake. I can tell by the way you're scanning the field. You're trying to find their hiding spot. And well, this is the most you've talked to me without an insult since I've known you."

Raker chuckled. "Yeah, the boy grows on you." He whipped his head around. "Don't go telling him I said that. The kid is already making me soft."

"Don't worry, I won't."

"Good." Another trebuchet groaned as the wheel rocked. "You're alright, Senald. I'm hard on you and the others because I want us to be the best. It's not personal. If I didn't like you, I would have dropped you off the wall at Cathyrium."

"Thanks. I guess."

Raker's attention went back to the slowly disappearing field. Conroy's forces marched in one of the tightest lines he'd ever seen.

I hope you keep your head on straight, kid. We're counting on you to be the ace in the hole.

* * *

Kaz braced himself as Conroy's heavy infantry collided with his center with the force of a giant wave pushing against a mountain. The lines buckled under the impact and faltered back several steps before digging in to counter the tide of men.

Conroy had used Markus's spearman to form the point of his V formation. The men stabbed with the heavy shafts methodically. Kaz had positioned his own spearman across the center as well. The losses he initially suffered made him wonder if he should have placed Jeldor's better trained pikemen at the center.

No. We aren't trying to push through the center. We just need to hold.

Jeldor's pikemen would be far more effective on the flank as they sought to encircle the enemy.

Kaz felt the shift in the air and the resolve of the men to either side of him strengthen. The spear points of the enemy missed their mark more frequently than before. He didn't need to look over his shoulder to know that Krytien and the two mages had lent their support. His ragged lines tightened against the enemy's onslaught. Kaz grunted out a command and stepped back, deflecting the spears thrusts lancing out at him. Another step slowly followed the first.

The enemy pushed harder once they saw Kaz's lines give way, but to his men's credit, they held lines as they lured their opponent in.

* * *

Yanasi's bowmen had harassed the enemy forces on their approach, but the tight shields of the spearman ensured little of her company's shafts reached their targets.

"Captain, General Grayer is calling for you to pull back," said a private that materialized beside her.

She tightened her jaw in frustration, but gave the orders to her men.

They retreated out of the back rows of light infantry and reformed outside of the lines. Yanasi found Grayer atop a mount near a small company of light cavalry. He watched the battle intently.

"General, permission to return to the ranks," asked Yanasi. "I was about to bring up the crossbowmen. I think their added strength is more effective against the enemy's armor."

"Permission denied," said Grayer shaking his head. "I need to tighten my lines."

"Then what do you need me to do, sir?"

"Nothing, for now. Return to your men and stay ready."

"But sir, what about. . . ."

"Captain, those are my orders. Stay safe."

"Yes, sir."

Yanasi begrudgingly returned to her men as the sounds of the battlefield reverberated around her.

So that's it? He's trying to protect me?

"Where is he sending us next, Captain?" asked one of her men, eager to do his part.

"We're to remain in reserve until we receive further instruction."

"But—" started the man.

"Your instructions are to sit tight, soldier," she snapped. "I'll let you know if they change."

"Yes, Captain," said the man as Yanasi drudged past.

She stood at the front of her men and watched the battle rage on. They couldn't fire from this distance without the risk of striking their own men. Essentially, they were birds whose wings had been clipped. Her knuckles turned white as she tightened the grip on her bow.

* * *

Kroke huddled behind the trunk of a thin tree. Rygar lay on his stomach somewhere in the tall grass about twenty yards away. Though Kroke couldn't see the battlefield from his position, the rattling noises traveling across the land permeated his senses. He closed his eyes for the smallest of moments, trying to picture the scene in his mind.

Weapons clashing. Men shouting. Blood spurting. Soldiers dying. Survivors crying.

He wished he was there.

Jonrell had always given him special missions so what Kaz had in mind did not surprise him. Still, he wished to be fighting at his friends' sides.

They better not die on me.

Rygar's head popped out of the tall grass and with the slightest of hand gestures signaled Kroke forward. Kroke sprinted low and joined Rygar on his stomach.

"Fun, isn't this?" whispered the scout.

"No."

"But I thought you did this sort of stuff all the time when you had to do your assassin work."

"You mean sneaking around? Yeah, but that was usually indoors or in some sort of city where there are more places to hide. I don't like being this exposed. Besides, sneaking around wasn't the fun part of a job."

Rygar eyed one of his blades and nodded. "Got it."

"Are we clear to move?" asked Kroke.

"As far as I can tell."

"Then let's move," urged Kroke. The sounds of battle made Kroke anxious. Their efforts could either solidify Kaz's victory or possibly end the battle early.

They snaked through the tall grass, sometimes crawling. They ducked around the occasional tree or small hill while moving quickly. They had been at it since late last night when Kaz tasked Kroke with sneaking behind enemy lines.

"Try to cause some disruption. Even if you only take out a few random soldiers, preferably officers, and then cut out of there, you'll cause just enough problems to make Conroy wonder what we're up to. Anything to distract him will work in our favor," Kaz had said.

Kroke had bigger plans than just simple distraction.

I'm coming for you, Conroy.

"You know," whispered Kroke. "I'm surprised Yanasi allowed you to come along. It's one thing to go scouting, but to actually infiltrate their camp is something I never thought she'd let you do."

Rygar noticeably swallowed.

"She doesn't know?" asked Kroke, much louder than he intended.

"Shhh," said Rygar. "What's the matter with you? You know better than that to raise your voice. I can't see everywhere."

"What's the matter with me? You better not die out here because I sure don't want to be the one to explain to Yanasi what happened." He shook his head. "Unbelievable. What were you thinking volunteering for this?"

"I knew you needed the quickest and safest path to their camp if Kaz's plan was going to work. Like it or not, I'm the best at what I do. Kaz knows it." He paused. "I sorta lied and told him Yanasi said it was fine."

A distant voice shouted out. "I think I heard something, Sergeant."

"Then let's go check it out," came the reply. "Private, do a quick sweep of the area."

"I told you to keep your voice down," hissed Rygar.

Kroke put a hand up to silence him and peeked over the grass. Half a dozen soldiers came over a small rise in the land. Another three joined them from the left. They began to fan out.

Rygar tapped Kroke's leg and gave a questioning look. Kroke held up nine fingers and Rygar's face paled. The kid swallowed and made a move to go for his sword, but Kroke grabbed his hand and steadied it. "Like I said, I'm not going to have that talk with Yanasi," whispered Kroke.

"But there's nine and they're getting farther apart."

Kroke flashed a rare grin. "I like a challenge. Besides, this is what I do best."

Throwing knives slid from Kroke's sleeves and into his palms. He stood and in one fluid motion whipped his arms forward and took out two soldiers carrying crossbows. The rest froze in surprise and he snatched two more blades at his waist and took off in a sprint. Kroke threw another blade, taking out the man farthest to his right. As he did so, one of the other soldiers found his nerve and a crossbow quarrel whizzed by Kroke's head. Kroke sidearmed his next throw at that man as the soldier nervously tried to reload. The knife ended his efforts.

Four blades, four throws, four kills.

The sergeant lit a fire under the other men. Three brandished spears. The Sergeant and another held swords. Rather than call out for help which Kroke thought would have been the wiser decision, the men closed in.

Confident.

Kroke enjoyed the looks of surprise when he continued to run toward them. His two favorite knives materialized in his hands—the bone-hilted weapon he took off the sailor on Estul Island and the eagle-hilted dagger Jonrell had gave him long ago. The spearmen tried to position themselves strategically to encircle him, but they didn't expect Kroke to be so fast. He slipped under the first two stabs they aimed at his head and chest. He deflected the third attack and slid on the grass under one of the spearman's legs. Kroke's arm thrust upward and his blade sank into the soldier's groin. The spearman dropped his weapon, gagging on an attempted scream, as his hands went between his legs.

Kroke spun away from a slashing sword and rose to his feet. He did the injured spearman a favor and finished him quickly.

Kroke knocked aside a darting spearhead and used the curved hilt of Jonrell's old blade to hook another spear coming at his stomach. He twisted his wrist and wrenched the weapon from the soldier's hands. Kroke stepped forward while driving a knife into the man's gut. Kroke used the soldier as a shield, blocking a slashing sword. Kroke let the man fall and took out the last spearman with two quick dagger punches to the throat and sternum.

Kroke pivoted to face the final two more heavily armored soldiers. Just as he got into a crouch, Rygar came up out of the tall grass swinging wildly. The outburst distracted the swordsmen and Kroke went after the closest of them. Trying to recover, the sergeant swung high, but Kroke ducked under the cut and slid his blade into the officer's chest. Kroke twisted the blade and finished him.

Rygar stood over the dead body of the last man, wearing a satisfied grin. "See, you needed my help after all."

"I didn't need anything," said Kroke, quickly sheathing his blades. "I had both of them."

"Maybe. But now I can go back to camp and brag about what I did."

"You mean without lying."

"Oh, I'm still going to lie," said Rygar as he put his sword away. "It's just now there will be a bit of truth to it." He started stripping the closest soldier, then stopped and looked up. "You gonna help? We don't have much time."

"What are you doing?"

"Someone is going to look for them eventually and it will be even harder to sneak around then. Disguises would help."

"You think we can pull that off?"

Rygar shrugged. "We have a better chance of doing it this way than trying to crawl in the grass." He stopped a second. "Uh, what're you doing?"

"Stripping the body."

"No offense, but how about you try to grab someone closer to your size like that one over there. Besides, it would probably be smarter to pick someone with less blood on them."

Kroke grinned and moved to the body Rygar pointed out.

Nothing like killing and good-natured ribbing to lift your spirits.

* * *

Krytien swore loudly as a heavy boot from the man in front slammed down on his foot. It had been the third time in less than a minute and he could feel his toes going numb. Mages didn't generally wear standard issue foot coverings, but after today he'd change that.

As long as I make it out of this.

Kaz wanted him as close to the front of the army's lines as possible in order to maximize the protection he could provide the men. Nora and Lufflin flanked him. Soldiers jostled the three mages as the men did their best to both fight the enemy and protect them. Krytien knew it had been a risk to include Lufflin in their strategy, but given the other details of Kaz's plan, he had no other option to turn to.

The three mages worked a series of spells that helped the soldiers become better versions of themselves—adding strength to their limbs, making it easier to breath, increasing their determination. Krytien had only recently picked up the new spells from notes he found in Amcaro's writings. He had worked diligently over the last several days trying to perfect the sorcery, pushing Nora and Lufflin to do the same in order to cover a larger area than the original spell intended. The young mages helped him greatly, but he could feel them beginning to waver under the resistance of both physical and sorcerous forces around them.

The sound, smell, feel, and even the taste of such close-quartered fighting strained Krytien's concentration. He spared a glance to the two green-robed mages next to him.

An invisible gust of power assaulted Krytien's senses and he fell into the soldier next to him. Thankfully, the large man caught him before he hit the ground where even among allies, he would surely be trampled. Nora and Lufflin suffered similar fates—the girl most of all. Her eyes rolled back in her head and Lufflin squirmed his way over to her as he tried to stand her up.

He shouted at Krytien to be heard over the chaos around them. "What just happened?"

"We've been targeted," said Krytien. "Conroy's mages must have found us."

"How can they worry about us? The others have been dropping stones over them the entire time."

Krytien hadn't been able to see what else had been going on. However, it was hard to miss the boulders flying through the air that proceeded the pounding rhythm of the engineers' machines. He had worked with Raker to time the shots with the other mages so they could catch the airborne rocks and redirect them midflight if necessary. Krytien had hoped that such swift changes of trajectory would keep the enemy's mages too busy to pay Krytien, Nora, and Lufflin any mind.

"Apparently, they're even stronger than we thought," said Krytien as he tried to refocus.

"What are you doing?" Lufflin called out again, his voice sounding frantic. "Nora's hurt bad. We need to get her out of here."

He glanced down and saw her coming around.

She shook her head. "No, I'm fine."

"Don't be crazy," said Lufflin. "You need medical attention."

"No," said Nora. "Our orders are to stay here."

Krytien didn't catch the next series of exchanges as Kaz turned for a moment and yelled. The commander had been blessed with the voice of a leader and even over the cacophony of battle, Krytien could hear him. "Krytien, we're losing ground too quickly."

The attack from Conroy's mages had broken his spell. Fatigue had returned to the battered soldiers and they struggled under the full might of the enemy's disciplined forces. The grunting strain of the men around him drowned much of the clashing steel.

Steel and Sorrow: Book Two of the Blood and Tears Trilogy

Another wave of sorcery struck, but thankfully Krytien had some protection this time and wasn't affected by the worst of it.

Lufflin cried again. "One Above, Nora!"

Krytien looked over and saw Lufflin holding the young woman's body. Blood dripped from her eyes and nose, over her cheeks and lips. A solider next to Lufflin tried to take the body away from him.

"Drop her to the ground! She's in our way!" the gruff man shouted.

"Get your filthy hands off her. She's not dead, yet!" Lufflin yelled back.

"Lufflin! Control yourself!" called Krytien. He saw the young mage's hands had begun to glow as if ready to attack one of the men he should have been protecting.

"Then help her! She's dying." The arrogance had dropped completely from the young mage's face as he pleaded with Krytien. Another wave of sorcery struck and this time he felt the power permeate through his body and into his bones. His very bowels twisted. Unlike before, the soldiers around them felt it too and buckled under the weight. Conroy's troops surged forward.

"Krytien!" yelled Kaz again.

"I'm working on it," he shouted.

"Work faster," came another voice. This one much deeper and Krytien saw the Ghal looking back at him.

During the brief exchange with Kaz, Lufflin continued to plead with Krytien while the gruff soldier howled at him to drop the woman and get out of the way.

Three short rapid blasts from Conroy's mages struck their spot again. A rush of the enemy followed and the army was flung back a solid ten feet before the men slowed the retreat.

Now the yelling came from everywhere as soldiers around him began to panic. He smelled their fear.

"Just give me something," cried out Kaz. "I need to reestablish our lines."

Images flashed in his mind and suddenly Krytien relived his nightmares. *Glacar and Ronav fought near him as the few remaining members of the Hell Patrol defended the narrow street in Asantia while the others escaped. Sorcerous assaults blasted into him and blood sprayed across his black robes from a man his commander, Ronav, killed.*

Death knocked at the door. He had to do something. He tried to access more power. It worked initially, but when he needed to access more as The Hell Patrol's odds worsened, he found the power too much to control.

He panicked while fighting to control the swelling sorcery. His limbs shook and the air changed.

An explosive blast erupted as the power slipped from his grasp. Bodies flew up into the air from both sides. Despite his best efforts to shield the Hell Patrol, many went up in flames. The ground rumbled and buildings crumbled. The pain nearly drove him insane.

Then it was over. Death and destruction were all around him. He spotted Glacar kneeling over Ronav's lifeless body.

Jonrell seemed to materialize from nowhere and dragged Krytien safely out of the city.

Krytien's gut wrenched. That had been the last time he stood so close to the physical fighting. And just like then, he felt the pressure all around him. People begged for his help and he had a responsibility to act.

I swore never to access such power again.

He recalled his recent readings. Amcaro's writings and ten years of practice had greatly improved his control.

Kaz said he doesn't need me to stop the tide by myself. Just enough to stabilize the army.

Krytien calmed himself and despite the jarring motion from the men around him, he blocked out the sounds of battle. The roar faded to a dull hum. Sweat poured from his body, but none of that mattered. He recited a small cant and slowly opened himself to the natural forces of the world. He felt it almost instantly—a well of power ready for him to do as he pleased. As Phillik once told him and Amcaro's writings confirmed, a mage must learn how to break down the barriers separating him from each level of power and control what is given to him.

Since the sorcerous attacks from Conroy's mages had first struck him, all his efforts went to defending himself rather than helping the army's resolve. Now, as he dipped into the energy waiting for him, he recast the original spell to support the soldiers while also maintaining his own defenses. Conroy's mages must have felt him try to do two things at once. They pressed him harder. Krytien accessed just enough power to accomplish what he needed.

He felt the sudden shift in the lines and heard Kaz shout out orders to the men. He opened his eyes and saw that the army's confidence had returned and though the retreat of the center continued, it did so on their terms.

He spared a glance over to Lufflin where the young mage stared teary-eyed at Nora. Krytien knew he shouldn't push things, but he did so anyway.

Just a little. Never again will I be so greedy.

Krytien had never been much of a healer, but the few spells he knew could at least return Nora to consciousness. He worked the spell quickly so he wouldn't be tempted to hold onto the power longer than he needed to. The girl opened her eyes and he saw Lufflin's face light up. Lufflin embraced her and then turned to Krytien and mouthed, "Thank you."

"She should be able to walk on her own. Get her out quickly and return to me. I still need help."

Lufflin nodded and hurried Nora through the ranks. Krytien winced as Conroy's mages sought him out again. He felt their frustration by his ability to turn them away. He was on the edges of power so immense he wondered if he could turn the battle solely by himself.

No.

He shook the thoughts from his mind.
I will not make the same mistake again.

* * *

Elyse watched the battle from a small hill. She wiped at the tears streaking down her face. The tears had come when she saw Conroy's men surge forward. She knew that could not be part of Kaz's plans.

Her army seemed to find itself again and the center retreated in a much more deliberate manner. She clung to the small amount of hope that remained.

Bloodied men with limp limbs dangling from stretchers passed by her on the way to the infirmary. Their moans added to her distress.

When will this end?

Conroy and Markus were her enemies, yet she felt no ill will toward the men they commanded. They simply followed orders. If only she could destroy the leaders and leave the innocent alone. Those thoughts reminded her of the naivety she once had. Life was not fair and war was part of life.

Blue tendrils of sorcery arced across the battlefield, boulders smashed in the air, and fires burned in small patches.

There are so many ways for a man to die today. Yet, none would be as they had hoped. In their home of old age.

"Your Majesty."

"Yes, Arine."

"I know this might not be the right time, but have you heard any news from the capital?"

Elyse turned in her saddle, incredulous.

"It's just that, there have been some strange murmurings that we've picked up from the locals a few days ago. I wanted to bring it up earlier, but you've been obviously busy."

"And you thought *now* would be the best time to do so?" snapped Elyse. "People are dying in droves. Whatever nonsense you've heard can wait until the day is done. Show some respect to these soldiers. One Above, if we lose today, you'll be taking your concerns to your Uncle Markus anyway."

Arine bowed her head. "I'm sorry, Your Majesty. I only thought—"

"No, Arine, you did not think. Leave me. I'll find you later," said Elyse, appalled at the woman's lack of sensitivity.

"Yes, Your Majesty."

After the woman left, the guard to Elyse's right cleared his throat. "Your Majesty?"

"Yes, Captain."

"I beg your pardon, I just wanted to say thank you"

"Thank you?" she asked, turning.

"Yes, Your Majesty. For caring," said the man as he gestured out to the battlefield.

Elyse nodded and returned to her thoughts.

* * *

Kaz knew immediately when Krytien had regained his control for he felt the change in the attitude of the men around him.

Quickly, he and Crusher solidified ranks, killing in droves. The Ghal's sweeping cuts knocked men sprawling as he shouted orders. Since they had regained their footing and settled in, Kaz continued the retreat in a more calculated manner.

He called out to flag bearers several rows behind to raise the blue flags on outstretched poles. It was time for the flanks to encircle Conroy's men.

* * *

Conroy wore a smug grin as he monitored his troops through the spyglass. He reasoned early on that his plant among the engineers had been caught. They tried to fool him with their misses and it would have worked if he hadn't recognized the pattern in their attacks. He had to give them credit, the men working the equipment were skilled, perhaps better than his own, yet even with the originality of how they employed their mages and engineers together, Kaz would not gain an advantage there.

Ingenious nonetheless.

The unique strategy had neutralized a bulk of his mages as they worked to deflect the attacks. His scouts had underestimated their engineers' strength. The battle would be decided man against man.

Kaz's overconfident demeanor had bothered Conroy. The commander actually believed himself to be a superior commander than General Victas.

No one could compare to him. Or if anyone could, it would be me. I know the man inside and out.

Conroy had employed a V formation with his infantry and through the spyglass he saw that Kaz's center had given considerable ground. Conroy's troops could be slowed, but not be stopped.

Simultaneous movement from Kaz's left and right wings caught his eye. The wings began to fan out and creep around Conroy's formation. His grin disappeared.

He's more clever than I thought.

"Ventrin!" he yelled.

"I'm here, my lord," said the man to his left.

"Signal the cavalry. Full charge on Kaz's right wing. Immediately."

"Yes, my lord," said the man as he rode off, shouting orders.

"What's going on?" asked Markus.

"Kaz baited us. He wanted us to use a V formation."

"What are you talking about?"

"During the latter half of Victas's years, a way many tried to counter the great general's infantry was to allow their center to purposefully collapse and then encircle the enemy. The formation falls apart when attacked from so many sides." He paused. "But Victas had already determined his formation's weakness before his enemies had and kept a reserve of cavalry behind. If encirclement occurred, he attacked the weakest wing of his opponent which would prevent them from completing the encirclement."

The ground shook behind them and the beating of hooves drowned out all other sounds. Over a thousand heavy cavalry rushed past Conroy and Markus.

"So, you're attacking the wing commanded by the old general."

Conroy nodded as the dirt-filled air settled and his ears picked up other sounds again. "I'd rather not have my cavalry face Jeldor's pikemen. He's a pompous fool, but his men are far more competent than most give them credit for."

* * *

Raker's heart raced, his head pounded, his eyes blurred, and he felt ready to vomit.

And I ain't even drunk.

He huffed and grunted alongside his men as he leaned into the trebuchet with his shoulder. His feet slid on the grass with each step, but finally they got the thing turning.

We're going too slow.

"Put your back into it," he yelled to the panting engineers.

"Sir, they're closing in too quickly."

"Shut up and push, Private, or I'll strangle your scrawny neck with my good hand."

The man put his head down and with another big shove Raker called for them to stop.

"Load that thing up, men. Triple time!" He looked over his shoulder. "Senald, what are we waiting on? Get those things going."

"We're trying."

"Try harder," he shouted. "It ain't gotta be perfect. We need to get something in the air to give those horses something to think about."

While the rest of his men focused on working with the mages, Raker had noticed the cloud of dirt off in the distance, and the cavalry in the midst of it. They charged toward Grayer's lines, but the old general was too caught up in the battle before him to notice. Raker sent a runner down to give him word.

In the meantime, he made a judgment call to change strategy, hoping to soften the eventual clash.

"What are you doing?" said a black-robed mage, charging up the small rise. He pushed Raker square in the chest. "Get these things turned back to the way they were. We haven't been given orders to do otherwise."

Raker fumed and closed his hand into a fist. Then he realized that hand wasn't there anymore.

Stupid mind playing tricks on me. No matter, I've still got the other.

He took a step forward and the mage's hand glowed as if begging Raker to do something to defy him. The engineer didn't care.

One hand or not, I'm king here.

A fist came in from the side and connected with the mage's jaw. The black-robed figure dropped to the ground. Senald then kicked the mage in the rump. "Get your behind back to your people. You mind your own and we'll mind ours." He pointed. "Conroy's mages are attacking the rest of yours now."

Shocked, the mage scurried off, holding his jaw and wearing a scowl.

Raker gave Senald a look and opened his mouth.

Senald held up his hands. "I know. That's your job. Well, I was tired of you having all the fun. You can get the next one."

Raker spat and held back a grin. "Fair enough." He paused. "But next time, twist your hips. You'll put more into it."

Senald smiled. "I'll keep that in mind."

The first of Senald's trebuchets rocked forward, sending stone into the air. It looked like most of it would miss their target, but at the least Raker saw the cavalry's lines disperse which would lessen the impact of the charge.

The siege equipment began to release in rhythm.

Unfortunately, we'll only be able to get in a few more rounds before the cavalry gets too close. Let's hope it's enough.

He spotted Yanasi's company sweeping around the rear, armed with bows and crossbows.

Crud. You better not do anything crazy, girl.

Raker swallowed when he saw what she intended.

Too late.

* * *

Crusher's roaring voice filled Kaz's right ear while pain exploded in his left from the sword that struck him. Small white dots appeared before his eyes, staggering him. He did his best to fight off the dizzy nausea. Without Cisod's armor, the blow would have ended him.

The soldier who struck him came around again with his sword, sensing Kaz's moment of weakness. Kaz got his own sword up in time and the blades clanged together before sliding apart. Another soldier attacked Kaz in the brief moment the two separated. Kaz deflected the blow off his shield.

Kaz hated to admit it, but Conroy's men had the upper hand and they were too well-disciplined for Kaz to make up for his lack of numbers.

He caught a glimpse of the flag bearers. They had not changed to the gray color signaling the completion of the encirclement. Jeldor and Grayer were taking too long and the center would break without something to ease the continued push of Conroy's soldiers.

He ignored the splitting pain in his head and squinted through his clouded vision. Kaz took the offensive against his opponents, hacking away in the close confines, alternating strokes between both men. The sword arm of one collapsed under the force of Kaz's strikes. Kaz readied himself to finish the man, but the head of a warhammer descended before his eyes. A sickening crunch followed by a spray of blood through the soldier's visor came next. Crusher's swing had caved the man's head in. Kaz killed the other man a moment later. In the distance, he caught sight of a rising cloud of dust.

Cavalry.

Kaz noticed then that the barrage of stones had moved away from the center of Conroy's forces and now targeted that distant, but fast approaching, charge.

Raker saw it before I did. I'm glad he's sober.

He had wanted to avoid signaling Drake and Janik, hoping to win this battle man to man, but he remembered a saying he heard muttered among members of the Hell Patrol's old crew.

When in doubt, cheat.

Kaz called out to Krytien and gave the orders. He finished just as a morning star swung toward him.

* * *

Drake peeked through the opening of their underground hideout. In the heat, he sweated like a pig. His whole body quivered along with their little shelter as the horses rode over. He swore.

"How about now?" he asked.

"I told you, I'll tell you when we've been given orders. Until then, we have to just wait," said the mage in an exasperated tone.

"How can you be so calm? Our men are dying out there and Conroy is sending in heavy cavalry." He paused. "We should do something."

Janik shook his head. "What's the matter with you? You heard Kaz specifically say that we were not to act on our own, only by his command. If he hasn't called us, then maybe he doesn't need us."

Drake resumed his watch of the battle. Unfortunately, from his position he saw very little except the backside of Conroy's lines and now the rumps of what he estimated to be a thousand armored knights.

He turned at Janik's gasp. In the mages palm glowed six stones of various colors and brightness. Janik looked up at Drake and swallowed. "We've got the orders."

"Quit gaping then, and let's go," Drake said as he left the lookout spot and went over to a crate filled with small vials of liquid packed in straw.

* * *

Yanasi thanked the One Above that Raker had seen the cavalry too. The falling stones, played havoc on their formation, and slowed their approach enough for her to position her men. Grayer had told her to stay out of the fighting, but she quickly defied his orders when she saw the horses.

She commanded a company of just over four hundred men, mostly bowmen and crossbowmen. When she saw what the wing would face, she ordered her bowmen to drop their weapons and pick up spears. These weapons were not their customary choice, but she had made sure that her men knew how to use them.

One hundred crossbowmen knelt on the grass before her while an additional one hundred stood behind the spearmen positioned between the two groups. Both lines waited for her signal. A spear rested on the ground in front of her. She stood by her men. Despite the slim chance of survival, she would not let them die alone.

* * *

Even though the partially mixed chemicals were harmless in their current state, Drake had not wanted to take any chances with their safety. Janik conveyed the locations of each strike as Drake adjusted the strength of the mixes based on previous instructions. Janik would be the one directing the charges to their destinations.

Quickly and carefully, Drake mixed the amounts into small clay containers. When he finished, eight balls of Nitroglycas lay on the dirt before them.

"They're ready."

Janik nodded and set the glowing stones down. "Move them to the edge of the opening and then call the distance for me."

"Anything else?" asked Drake.

"Say a prayer to the One Above."

* * *

The flash of blue and red light preceded the first explosion by half a breath. Even the air shook from the blast. Pieces of earth, horse, and man sailed skyward.

Raker's jaw dropped. The survivors of Conroy's cavalry continued, but raggedly and much slower than before.

Another explosion erupted in the center of Conroy's V formation. It knocked more than half the men on the field to their backs. A dull ring buzzed in Raker's ears from the thundering sound.

Dark smoke enveloped the battlefield, yet he could still spot bits of flesh and battered armor raining down.

Six more successive blasts followed in the distance. Raker followed the bright light and billowing smoke, realizing it formed a line between Conroy's reserves and the main battle.

"Is that the stuff Drake had been working on?" asked Senald, voice filled with wonder and dread.

"I reckon so," said Raker.

A second passed.

"I believe he got it right," said Senald.

"He definitely didn't have it wrong."

Raker couldn't help but grin.

That's my boy.

* * *

The explosion came from nowhere and everywhere at once. Others followed, one close by and then several off in the distance. But to Yanasi, the only one that mattered was the first. The remaining cavalry that emerged from the cloud of smoke and dust looked like a unit sent from the One Below. Five hundred knights, covered in black dirt and bits of bright red flesh and blood from their fallen brethren, barreled down on her position.

Their discipline is amazing.

She waited until the last possible moment before giving the orders to her men. As she yelled the command, crossbows fired low and high from in front and behind her. The quarrels ripped through the air and sped toward the enemy. Dozens of knights fell, but far too many continued. Her men picked up their spears while the crossbowmen moved back and drew swords.

She and her men butted the spears into the ground and waited less than two full breaths as the wave of knights crashed into them. Her spear broke in half as it sunk into the exposed chest of a horse. The impact threw her backward, slamming her into the ground. A hoof stomped her leg and she screamed as the bone cracked. The leg of another mount kicked her in the helm and she rolled.

Yanasi's head swam and she struggled to focus. A warmth flowed down her face, over her left eye, and into the corner of her mouth. She tasted blood. Through her blurry vision she saw her men fight valiantly, even killing many of the mounted knights. Despite being at a disadvantage, they refused to give in.

She crawled to her knees, the pain from her leg coursing through her body. She bit her lip and tried to ignore it. She had an obligation to her men.

Her bow had fallen off her back, but it lay a few feet away. She half-crawled, half-dragged herself to it. Despite the rush of horses, and the careless trampling of animal and men, it remained unscathed.

She drew an arrow from her quiver, and with the bow in her hand, the pain subsided. Hobbling on one leg, her focus returned. She knew at any moment a sword could swipe her head off, but she didn't care.

One. Two. Three arrows. Three kills. Several more followed all within a matter of seconds. A blood curdling scream came from her right and she turned as a mounted knight charged her while swinging a mace over his head. Yanasi raised her bow, but froze. In all the excitement, in her need to exact punishment on others, she had forgotten about Rygar.

A lump caught in her throat and her arms shook. She didn't want to die. She wanted to be with Rygar. Yet as the knight grew closer, all she could do was stare death in the eyes and wait.

Another horse slammed into the knight and the two riders tumbled to the ground. The collision jarred Yanasi from her stupor.

Grayer rolled around with the much younger knight.

He saved my life.

Yanasi watched as the knight pulled a dirk and stuck Grayer through his ribs before rolling the old general off him. She reached back for an arrow, but found her quiver empty. Yanasi hobbled over and swung her bow out, cracking it on the side of the knight's face. She came back around and did it again, this time breaking the black wood in half. Without his helm, the knight's eyes rocked backward and he fell to the ground. She picked up the mace the knight had dropped, almost collapsing under its weight with just one leg to stand on. She redistributed her load and with one heave, destroyed the man's face.

She knelt next to Grayer as the old general clutched at his chest. Blood seeped through his fingers. His breathing was short and rapid.

He looked at her sternly. "You didn't follow my orders, Captain."

She started to cry. "No, sir. I didn't."

His expression softened. "I'm glad for it. You bought me enough time to bring up our reserves."

She looked around and saw Conroy's cavalry overwhelmed with Grayer's reserves.

"You saved the wing, General. You're a hero."

He chuckled and winced. "On a day like today, there are many heroes. My name doesn't need to be one of them. I'm just a soldier doing his job."

The general's hand went limp and his eyes faded. Yanasi started to sob as the sound of battle faded.

* * *

"One Above!" cried Markus. "What sort of sorcery was that?"

"That was not sorcery," answered Conroy, his voice barely a whisper.

"Then what was it?"

Conroy swallowed. The explosions had shaken more than just the land. They had shaken his soul. "Nitroglycas. An extremely rare and volatile compound. Only a High Mage has the power to work the stuff."

"Then how could they have it? There aren't any more High Mages."

I don't know. With one explosion, I could have believed that they somehow discovered something that had belonged to Amcaro. But eight? The High Mage would have never been so careless to make so many.

"Are you listening to me? What do we do?" asked Markus.

Conroy blinked away his thoughts and raised the spyglass once again. Through the dust and smoke, he saw glimpses of the battlefield. His cavalry charge had been turned back and Kaz's wings had closed in on the sides of his troops. One of the explosions had rocked the center of the V formation, turning it into shambles. He could not blame his soldiers for breaking. No one had used Nitroglycas in hundreds of years. He never thought to prepare them for that possibility. In fact, if he hadn't read so much history, he would have been as shocked as Markus.

"Conroy! We have to do something. Should we send in our reserves?"

"No," he said in a heavy voice, still scanning the struggle through his spyglass. Parts of his army had begun to flee or surrender. He couldn't send in his reserves even if he had wanted to. The last six explosions destroyed much of the terrain and a giant crevasse separated his position from the main battle.

Even if I tried to march our reserves around that, we would be sitting ducks for their engineers. And then what? By the time the reserves reached the main engagement, it would be too late.

"We can't just give up."

"We can and we will." Conroy handed the spyglass over to Markus. "See for yourself. Kaz has seized control of the battle."

"What is the matter with you? You act as though the devil has won," said Markus. "We still have time to retreat to your palace in Segavona where we could hold out during a siege."

"No. He's won. Don't you see? If he has any more Nitroglycas, our walls would be useless. We would only prolong the inevitable." He let out a heavy sigh. "He is the better commander." *He is Victas come again.* "We need to give ourselves over to the queen."

Markus threw down his spyglass. "Are you mad? We'll be hanged for treason!"

"So be it," said Conroy. "We must accept the consequences."

"No. You can accept the consequences. I'm taking the rest of my men and leaving. I'll leave this dump of a country if I must, and carve out a kingdom elsewhere. But first, I'll burn Lucartias to the ground, if only so no one can have it."

Why am I not surprised? Perhaps I could have won if I had stronger allies. But then, no one else understood what I meant to do.

Conroy frowned. "I can't let you do that."

Markus withdrew his sword as did the two aides who flanked him. "You don't have a choice." Markus nodded behind Conroy and when he turned saw that two of Markus's men had moved up behind him. One held a crossbow in his hands. Olasi's son smiled. "I never did trust you."

To Conroy's surprise, one of the men whipped out two knives and felled the aides flanking Markus. The man with the crossbow aimed it at Olasi's son.

The soldier who threw the knives had another in his hand that he pointed at Conroy as a warning. Conroy understood with one glance he had little chance of taking the man. He recognized a professional when he saw one.

"You ain't going anywhere," said the man with the knife. "Rygar, shoot Markus if he does anything other than drop his sword to the ground. Aim for his gut. The duke thinks death by hanging is bad. A rope is a blessing over a wound to the stomach that takes hours to bleed out. You can trust me on that," said the man as he eyed Markus.

Markus dropped his sword.

"Good," said the man with the knife. "You ain't as dumb as I thought you were last time we met."

Markus's eyes widened. "The queen's bodyguard?"

"Former bodyguard. I've got my old job back."

"And what's that?" asked Conroy.

"Professional killer," said the man in an icy tone. He nodded to a group of soldiers heading their way with weapons drawn. "I'd call off your men if I were in your position. Things usually get ugly when I feel threatened."

Conroy signaled his men to stay back. Markus did the same.

"Why not kill us now?" Conroy asked.

"If I had it my way, I would. But, I'm sure certain people would like to have a word or two with you. But if you'd like to try your luck, go for it." He grinned. "Now stay still. This'll be over soon enough."

The man gestured toward the battlefield where shouts of victory replaced the cries of battle.

CHAPTER 38

Tobin listened half-heartedly as each of his councilors gave their reports. Still reeling from the impact of Nachun's words weeks ago, he had been going through the motions of being a ruler since his return to Juanoq. Thankfully, he had done well in choosing the men around him, and at least in the near term, his lands ran themselves.

A messenger relayed a report from Walor that arrived earlier that morning. The rulers of the Red Mountain Clan had quickly sworn fealty to Tobin. However, pockets of resistance in both the Red and Green Clan's territory remained. Walor would need time to eliminate those factions before returning to Juanoq.

The messenger finished the report, then pulled out another. "Warleader, we also received more word from Nubinya."

"Save it for our next meeting."

The messenger cleared his throat. "Warleader, this message is over a month old. You've put it off for some time already."

"Fine. What does Durahn want?"

"He assures you that Nubinya is stable. He wishes to return to Juanoq."

Tobin chuckled. "I'm sure he does." *Getting him out of Juanoq was one of the best decisions I ever made.*

"Shall I write up a reply?"

"No. It won't be necessary. Anything else?"

"No, Warleader."

"The meeting's adjourned."

* * *

Tobin woke up screaming. When he stopped he could barely swallow through the rawness in his throat. He sat up and tears flowed uncontrollably down his face. He had lain down on the palace's roof to examine the stars and had fallen asleep. He dreamed of his mother. For the first time he saw her face—every detail, including the hollow eyes staring back at him and the small trickle of blood at the corner of her mouth. Her neck was angled in an awful way as her body rested on the ground, arms to her sides.

He had no idea how she had gotten like that. Everyone in his personal life had refused to discuss her with him and he quickly learned not to bring up her memory.

All his life he tried to remember his time with her and never could.

For the first time since Nachun had healed him, Tobin dreamed of his early youth. He was foolish to think that the shaman had rid him of his nightmares.

He sobbed. *How did she end up like that?*

He screamed again, angry that he didn't know the answer to the question.

Lucia's voice called out from behind. "Tobin? Are you alright?"

He wheeled as she hurried toward him. He quickly turned away and wiped frantically at his face with his palms. "What are you doing up here? It's well past midnight."

Her footsteps slowed. "I couldn't sleep and thought I would grab some fruit from the kitchen. I heard a scream and recognized your voice." She knelt beside him and rested a hand on his shoulder. He tried to avert his gaze, but she urged him toward her. "Please. Tell me what's wrong."

He looked up, feeling ashamed. "It's nothing. Just a bad dream."

She cupped his face with her hands and stroked his cheeks with her thumb. Tobin saw the tears forming in Lucia's eyes as she did her best to smile.

"Why do you cry?" he asked.

"Because I understand."

Lucia's hands slid behind Tobin's head and she wrapped her arms around his neck. She leaned in and kissed him with the tenderness he had always dreamed of. It happened so suddenly that it took Tobin a moment to respond. His arms enveloped her, pulling her tight against his frame. He felt her take a quick intake of breath and for a moment worried that he had gone too far. But Lucia's kisses grew more passionate. Tobin's heart raced in the still night air.

Am I still dreaming?

* * *

The heat of the warm morning sun tickled Lucia's bare skin, causing her to stir from her slumber. Her head rose up and down on her husband's chest with each breath he took. She grinned and opened her eyes.

No. Not Kaz.

She looked up at Tobin's peaceful face as he lay asleep.

What have I done?

Lucia had lied to Tobin the night before. She had not been hungry. It had been the anniversary of her first meeting with Kaz and she couldn't bear to look at his empty place in their bed. When she had heard Tobin's screams and later saw the pain in his face, her heart had ached to help him. Of all people he understood her own loss better than anyone, having lost all that had been dear to him.

Friends. Family. And a lover.

The helplessness in Tobin's eyes had also reminded her of the part of Kaz that no one else ever saw. Seeing Tobin do the same had raised emotions she hadn't felt for him before.

The sun shone brightly over Tobin's dark skin as her eyes ran down and back up his nakedness.

He is so similar to Kaz. Is it wrong to be doing this?

She sat up slowly and moved away from Tobin as she dressed, careful not to wake him. She struggled with a whirl of emotions.

Lucia couldn't deny that she felt something more for Tobin than she had before, but Kaz's presence still hung heavily over her.

But everyone keeps telling me he's dead. I need to move on. And Tobin is a good man. She watched a soft smile form on Tobin's lips as he slept. Even such a small gesture reminded her of Kaz. *Is that it? Do I only care for him because he reminds me of Kaz?* She shook her head, confused.

Before they drifted off to sleep last night, Tobin mentioned them having an early dinner together today.

Lucia tiptoed away from Tobin with that on her mind. She needed time to sort through her feelings.

* * *

Jober opened his eyes to a harsh beam of sunlight striking his face. He sprang out of bed, panicked. He was late.

His wife sat up as he began to frantically dress. "What's wrong?"

"Something's not right. Lucia's usually here by now for her daily trip to the market."

Hielle patted the cushion beneath her. "Come back to bed and enjoy the extra rest."

"What do you mean? She's your friend. Aren't you worried?"

Hielle shook her head. "Last night was the anniversary of her first meeting with Kaz. She told me that she would probably sleep in and wanted to be alone."

Jober stopped. "Why would she tell you and not me?"

"I'm sorry. She wanted me to wait until morning to tell you. She loves you like a brother, Jober. The last thing she wanted was for you to worry."

Loves me like a brother, yet I can't stop living the lie.

He started dressing again.

"What are you doing?"

"I should be there for her. It's the least I can do."

"No!"

Jober stopped. His wife rarely raised her voice.

"If she wanted you there, she would have requested it. Give her this time alone. She needs it."

Jober sighed. "Alright." He stripped off his clothes and crawled into bed. Hielle wrapped herself around him and they held each other close in bed. "I just wish I could make things right for her."

Hielle hugged him tight. "I know you do. You're a good man."

So I hear.

* * *

Two boys fought in a small circle with wooden swords—their movements anything but fluid. They looked to be no older than seven or eight and yet bruises and small cuts covered their torsos. Around the circle, other trainees cheered the youths on while older warriors who had long since completed their training took wagers.

Despite the beautiful day, Tobin could not focus on the sparring. His thoughts kept returning to the previous night. Her absence when he awoke had been unsettling at first, but then he recalled their plans for an early dinner and he had to suppress a childish smirk.

She's probably gone to the market to cook something herself. She's always thinking of others. And she's finally mine.

The combatants separated and slowly circled. Hate shone bright in their eyes.

"What do you think, Warleader?" asked the Kifzo overseeing the training.

"They have potential."

"Yes. These two are the best by far in their age group."

Tobin raised an eyebrow. "What makes them so much better than the others?"

The Kifzo shrugged. "Physically, they're stronger and quicker, but above all else it's their relationship to each other."

"What do you mean?"

"They're brothers, Warleader. I thought it was obvious. Have you ever seen such hate in ones so young before?"

The warrior laughed and if it wasn't for the innocence in his mirth, Tobin would have thought the man had meant something ill by the comment.

The two brothers did hate each other and though they did not resemble each other as much as Kaz and he had, the boys greatly reminded Tobin of the relationship he once shared with his brother.

Have you ever seen such hate in one so young? Tobin repeated the question in his head. *Yes, I have. Only I never realized that my hate for Kaz had been nearly as great as his hate for me.* Tobin wondered what had changed him into the person he was before Soyjid tampered with his mind.

And why are the memories of me and Kaz so clear while the rest are still muddled and in pieces? Especially those of my mother.

In his happiness over Lucia, he had almost forgotten the images of his mother's dead body.

"What do you think of these, Warleader?"

The question jarred Tobin. He blinked and realized two older participants had entered the circle. They looked fifteen or perhaps sixteen. They moved with the fluidity that Tobin would expect after years of training as a Kifzo.

"They fight well."

"Yes. They may be a little young, but I think they're ready to fill in our ranks."

Tobin turned. "Fill in our ranks?"

"Well, I know we lost a lot of men during this year's campaign and Nachun has . . . borrowed many of our best. If we are to go after the White Tundra Clan next, then we'll need to replenish our numbers, correct?"

Tobin had not considered the White Tundra Clan, as they had never been part of his father's plan. However, they remained the last unconquered clan in Hesh.

The people of the White Tundra kept isolated in the far south. Little was known about their land or their people. They could have a populace distributed among various villages or be completely isolated in the capital of Erundis and no one would know. The thought of such a test ignited a fire in his belly.

"Yes. We'll need to replenish our numbers." Tobin grinned. He welcomed the challenge.

* * *

Tobin returned from his appointments, bathed, and dressed in his finest attire before moving to the dining room. He entered to a cornucopia of sights and smells. The table displayed enough food to feed an army, yet only two place settings had been laid out.

Lucia stood at the head of the table wearing a flattering deep blue dress. "Dinner is ready," she said simply.

Tobin walked over and took her in his arms. It had only been hours since he last saw Lucia, yet their time apart had felt like years.

Now that she's mine I never want to let her go.

So caught up in the moment, it took Tobin several seconds to notice the difference in Lucia's behavior. Though she allowed Tobin to pull her in close and her arms rested on his shoulders around his neck, she seemed tense, her body rigid.

Tobin pulled back. "What's wrong?"

Lucia looked up as tears streaked down her cheeks. "I-I tried. I really did. I thought if I came here tonight things would fall into place. But it's not."

Tobin blinked. "I don't understand."

She cried harder. "After last night, I wanted this to work. For both of us. But I can't do it. I still love Kaz too much and if I was with you, it would be for all the wrong reasons. That isn't fair to either of us." She pulled away from Tobin and whispered. "I'm sorry. I'm truly sorry."

Lucia sped out the door as Tobin sank to his knees in a daze.

CHAPTER 39

Conroy surrendered himself and his army to Elyse.

Krytien had been around enough war to know that once the fighting ended, the real work began. Soldiers saw to their wounds and officers determined who should be held accountable for treason. Kaz ordered Krytien to evaluate Conroy and Markus's mages closely in that regard. Afterward, Krytien spent much of his time assisting Wiqua heal the injured from both armies since everyone was on the same side again.

Kaz ordered a southward march to Segavona immediately. Elyse wanted to return to Conroy's former residence while trying to determine who would be best suited, at least in the short term, to oversee the former duke's territories.

As they settled behind the thick gray walls of Segavona, Krytien seized the first chance he had in weeks to speak privately with the mages from Kaz and Jeldor's armies. It felt odd to open up and show his gratitude, but once he started to speak, he found that the words simply flowed out of him. He wondered if Jonrell and Ronav had ever experienced a similar feeling.

He started to leave, but surprisingly many of the mages wanted to shake his hand and personally offer their own thanks, knowing how difficult his task had been. Even the black-robed mages, who once had looked down on him for his lack of education, paid Krytien some of the highest compliments he had received.

Krytien smiled, feeling vindicated.

Maybe Philik was right in giving me the black robes after all.

Many of the green and yellow-robed mages showed appreciation for what they had learned from him. They didn't know what the future held for them with the war over, and since Amcaro could not continue their education on Estul Island. Several hoped that once Elyse made a decision regarding the school's future, Krytien might stay on and help with their development.

He was speechless.

After everyone else had left, Krytien noticed that one mage remained. He hadn't spoken to Lufflin since the battle. Lufflin wore an intense look that worried Krytien.

"What's on your mind?" he asked, trying to feel the mage out.

"I wanted to talk to you in private. It's been hard to get you alone since the battle," said Lufflin as he walked over.

"Yes. Kaz keeps me quite busy."

Lufflin stopped a couple of feet from Krytien and stared into the mage's eyes. He extended a hand.

Krytien looked down warily and accepted the gesture.

"I wanted to apologize. For everything. I'm yours now."

After exchanging nods, Lufflin walked away. Krytien shook his head. *One Above, will wonders ever cease?*

* * *

Yanasi and Rygar sat at a clearing in the inner courtyard of Conroy's home. She looked up at the night sky and watched the bright stars twinkle.

"What are you thinking about?" asked Rygar, putting his arm around her.

Yanasi sighed. "A lot of things. But mostly General Grayer."

"He was a good man."

"A hero," corrected Yanasi.

"Without him I would've lost you." Rygar pulled her close and wrapped both arms around her. "Look, the war's over now and I've been thinking about us and our future."

Yanasi blinked. "What?"

"I can't imagine living my life without you, Yanasi. I want you to marry me." He smiled. "Who knows, maybe we can have a family? What do you think?" he asked, suddenly nervous.

Tears streaked down Yanasi's cheeks. "Yes," she whispered. She leaned in and kissed him. They held each other while sitting silent in the night. Yanasi pulled away and wiped her face. "So, what do we do tomorrow then? I mean we have to tell Kaz, right? And I guess we need to find someone to do the ceremony. And . . ."

"Yanasi."

She stopped and looked up at Rygar's smiling face. "Yes?"

"Tomorrow will work itself out. How about we just enjoy tonight?"

She nodded and put her head on his shoulder.

* * *

Drake would miss dinner if he didn't leave, but that didn't stop him from turning another page. He had only been able to read in short bursts while the campaign was in full swing. Having finally reached Segavona, Conroy's seat, he hoped to make up for lost time.

The door swung open and Raker called out. "C'mon kid, we finally got a chance to breathe. Get your head out of that book."

Drake marked his place and turned. "You're back early. I thought you were going to play cards."

"So did I, but it's a lot harder to cheat than it used to be. You try palming a card without your hand." He spat.

"Then why come back here?"

Raker grinned. "Me and Kroke are going to this bathhouse I heard about. You wanna come? I hear they got women of all shapes and sizes. I'm sure they've got one close to your age. If not, there ain't nothing wrong with an older woman."

Drake tried to hide his nervousness, but still heard his voice quiver. "Nah, I've got too much to do here. I planned on staying up all night reading."

Raker looked at him incredulously. "What would you want to do that for when you could relax in a hot bath with a beautiful woman? Maybe even two?"

Drake turned back to the book. "Kaz asked me to look up what I could about some place called Hesh. He thinks it has something to do with his past. I want to help him if I can. Besides, I like doing this stuff."

Raker raised an eyebrow. "I never thought I'd see a boy your age choose a book over a woman. You're starting to worry me, kid."

Drake chuckled nervously. "It's nothing. I'll come with you some other time. I just want to clear my head tonight."

Raker mumbled something about priorities. "Suit yourself." He opened the door. "Don't wait up."

The door slammed and Drake heard fading sounds of Raker whistling down the hallway.

* * *

Kaz barreled through the tent flap and stopped in his tracks. Wiqua turned his head around and met his gaze with red eyes. "Good, I was worried the messenger wouldn't find you in time," he said.

Kaz hurried to the small cot Wiqua knelt beside. His voice was dry when he spoke. "I was on my way to meet with Elyse and Jeldor when I got word. I came over as quickly as I could." He swallowed hard as he saw Hag's current state. "What's going on?" he asked, dropping to a knee beside Wiqua.

Hag opened her eyes. "I'm dying," she whispered. "I thought that would be obvious." She started coughing and Kaz heard the air rattle around her lungs.

"How?"

"I'm old as sin, that's how," she answered.

"You told me you were just battling a chest cold that wouldn't go away." She smirked. "I lied."

Kaz's stomach tightened. "Why would you hide this?"

"I did what I thought was best." She looked to Wiqua. "I'm sorry I made you keep it secret for so long."

Wiqua patted her hand, but otherwise said nothing as he fought with his emotions.

Hag continued. "The last thing I wanted was to be another distraction. In case you forgot, we just fought a war." She paused. "But it's finally over and we won."

"But . . . why would you keep this from *me*?" he asked, suddenly angry despite his sorrow. "I thought we were close." Kaz hung his head, surprised at his own admission.

"I'm close to a lot of people. Each soldier is almost like a child to me. I've watched them live and I've watched far too many die." She took Kaz by the hand. "I kept my health from you because I knew that you were the best chance for my kids to live. You didn't need to worry about me." She sighed. "Out of all the Hell Patrol members I've known, you're the only one I truly wish was mine, Kaz."

Kaz's throat caught. He started to speak, but Hag reached up and squeezed his jaw.

"No. I don't know how much time I have left and I need to say what I have to say. I know what really happened in your duel with Grin and I know that Kroke covered it up for you. He's got a bigger heart than many give him credit for. But that's not my point. I can tell that it's been weighing on you. You need to let it go. Things happen. People make mistakes. Learn from it. Don't let one screw up or even a hundred screw ups define who you are or prevent you from being the person you want to be." She cleared her throat again. "And one more thing. Whether you find peace from your past or happiness in your future, know that you made this old woman's life brighter and that she's proud of you." She finally lowered her arm and sank into her pillow. After taking a deep breath, she closed her eyes and whispered. "There, I'm done. You can stay if you like, but I need to rest a few moments."

Kaz did stay, but only after sending messengers out to find members of the old crew who would want to see Hag one last time.

The messengers struggled to find anyone.

They're all off in the city enjoying their first night off in months.

Kaz and Wiqua knelt in silence. He thought about asking Wiqua why he didn't heal her, but he already knew the answer. Either there wasn't anything the Byzernian could do, or Hag had warned him not to.

Kaz could not recall weeping in his past life, and prior to seeing Hag in her current state, he could not imagine doing so. Yet, every few moments he felt a tear fall from his eyes.

When Hag's breathing stopped he put his arm around Wiqua and the old man sobbed.

They stayed that way for some time. The weight of the situation put a new perspective on his life. Since waking up on Slum Isle, Kaz had lost acquaintances, friends, and someone he thought of as family.

The loss of so many lives solidified his decision. If he could feel such pain over those he knew for only a short time, how could he not do everything in his power to reconnect with his past? What if he left behind people who grieved him? He may have lost much more in his former life.

"Wiqua?" asked Kaz.

The old Byzernian looked up.

"I need to ask you to do me a great favor."

Wiqua wiped away his eyes with the palms of his hands. "I'll do what I can."

"I need you to fix my mind."

Wiqua's eyes widened. "But . . . the risks . . ."

"I know the risks. You've explained them to me before. I could gain nothing. I could lose what little I have. I could become a simpleton. Or I could die. I don't care. I need to know."

"But why? I mean, why now?"

Kaz looked at Hag. "I need to know if anyone is waiting for me. Every moment I'm here means that I could be missing the last moments of someone's life who was once dear to me. I don't want to risk that."

He looked down at Hag. "There is a chance I could lose focus."

Kaz shook his head. "I've watched you work. When you heal, the rest of the world doesn't matter." He paused. "I'll have to talk to Elyse again soon and I'd like to be able to tell her what my plans are for the future and see if she can help me accomplish them. I've got Drake working on the smallest of leads, but that's all. I need more."

Wiqua rubbed at his face, mulling over Kaz's words. "I understand. The decision is yours." He grabbed a sheet and gestured. "Let's cover her out of respect and then we'll begin. The last thing she would want is to be the cause of us waiting any longer."

* * *

Elyse impatiently paced Conroy's private study as she and Jeldor waited for Kaz. Jeldor contented himself with relaxing in a plush chair while thumbing through one of the large volumes that adorned the wall. The queen had to admit that Conroy's tastes impressed her. She always heard he was an intelligent man, but his library dwarfed her own in Lyrosene. She would have to ask Drake to select the more important works from it to take back with her to the capital. She shook away those thoughts, remembering her aggravation.

"You're certain your messenger spoke with him?" she asked.

"Yes, Your Majesty," said Jeldor looking up from a page. "Kaz told the boy he would be on his way."

"Then what is taking so long? Do you think something has happened to him?"

Jeldor chuckled. "Not likely." He closed the book. "Relax, Your Majesty. Enjoy our surroundings. Neither of us has seen these comforts in some time. In my case, I've never had these sorts of comforts," he added bitterly.

Elyse continued to pace. "I don't wish to wait. We've waited long enough to speak with Conroy. I know the goal was to make him sweat and think about things since his defeat, but One Above knows it's made me as anxious as it's probably made him."

Jeldor stood. "Well, then let's begin now."

Elyse stopped. "Without Kaz?"

"You rule this land, Your Majesty. Not him. I'll have someone keep an eye out to let him know we began without him."

Elyse shrugged. "He hates politics anyway."

"That he does."

I'm doing him a favor.

Elyse gestured to Jeldor. "Then let's see what Conroy has to say for himself."

* * *

Once they cleared a space, Kaz sat on a chair and bowed his head. Wiqua stood over him and Kaz felt the old man's hands wrap around his shaved skull. The faintest tingling sensation rippled across his scalp.

"Interesting," said Wiqua. "I don't think blunt trauma caused your memory loss at all."

"What do you mean?" asked Kaz.

"An advanced form of sorcery was the cause." Wiqua grunted. "I guess that's why you have such an aversion to the stuff."

"Can you undo it?"

"Yes, but the risk will be even greater."

The statement hung in the air and Kaz knew Wiqua waited for his response. "Do it."

"Relax as best you can. This will hurt quite a bit."

Those words were the last Kaz heard. His entire body shook, pains shot from the base of his skull through the rest of his body. His skin crawled and his eyes burned. His nostrils flared and his mouth watered. Bile crept into the back of his throat.

I'm going to die.

His head pounded and his ears popped.

But his mind began to feel less muddled.

The memories returned in waves, some short, others long.

Some were from his childhood while others as recently as a few years ago. There seemed to be no order for how his memories returned, and he struggled to process the massive influx of information.

One memory lingered long enough for him to relive it. He was still a teenager and he and several others had been given a task by his father to determine who would become the warleader of his father's army. He watched his younger self order the death of another Kifzo to claim the prize. Afterward he fought his brother, Tobin. Kaz broke Tobin's ankle and left him for dead. In the aftermath, he allowed his men to do unspeakable things to an innocent family in order to reaffirm their support.

Try as he might, Kaz could not recall why he would do such things. He only knew the intense hatred he felt for Tobin grew with each year that came after that memory. Kaz's mind would not allow him to search further back in order to learn where such hatred began.

How could I do that to my brother? And how could I allow a family to suffer for my own gain? What would Jonrell say? Or Elyse? What would anyone say?

Kaz realized that his biggest fear had been true. He had been an animal. Merciless killing, ruling through fear and intimidation, allowing atrocities to occur in order to further his own goals.

He wanted to kill himself right then, but the bombardment of awful memories kept coming. Women raped, children mutilated, villages burned. He never participated, but he allowed it to happen over and over again. Oddly enough, in each memory Tobin stared at Kaz with a disapproving scowl that only angered him more. Eventually Tobin would turn away. *He never participated either. What drove me to do such things?*

Finally, when he thought he couldn't take anymore, the atrocities stopped. A petite woman with skin as beautiful as polished onyx stood before him in a dimly lit room. She wore a sly grin and her inviting lips called his name. He became lost in her deep brown eyes and suddenly nothing else mattered. They embraced. He knew instantly the woman was his wife and that when he was with her, he could be the man he desperately wanted to be.

They lay in bed, entangled in each other's limbs. He stroked her cheek and she smiled. "I love you, Kaz," she whispered. He felt his cheeks tighten as he smiled back. "I love you, Lucia." In that moment, he had never been happier.

Then her face disappeared and the image vanished.

Kaz blinked and stared dumbly at his surroundings. Wiqua stood before him, yelling, trying to get his attention.

"Kaz, are you alright? Speak to me."

He cleared his throat. "I'm alright."

"Then it worked. You remember?"

Kaz nodded and slowly rose to his feet. He took a deep breath. "Yes."

"Is it as bad as you feared?" Wiqua asked hesitantly.

"Worse."

"Remember what Hag told you. She spoke for both of us. You are a good man . . ."

Kaz raised his hand. "Perhaps one day, but not yet. I've done things I dare not speak of." He rubbed his eyes and fought back the emotion in his voice. "Wiqua, I have a wife and she's the most amazing woman. She kept me sane. She saw me for who I could be just as you and Hag did. Just as Jonrell did. Just as Elyse—" He cut himself off. "I have to tell her."

Wiqua frowned. He patted Kaz on the shoulder. "If you feel as though you must tell her, then go now. This is news that can't wait."

Kaz glanced back to Hag. "But what about . . ."

"Go. I want some time alone with her before we perform the burial."

"I'll return when you're ready." Kaz turned to leave and stopped. "My oldest memories haven't returned yet."

"They will," said Wiqua. "Even though the path is now open, it will still take some time for your mind to reorganize itself."

Kaz walked over and hugged the old Byzernian. "Thank you."

* * *

After descending several flights of stairs, Elyse's Royal Guard escorted her and Jeldor down the long corridor that led to Conroy's cell. Elyse spared a glance at the bushy-bearded duke and thought their situation odd. A small part of her still resented that time in Jeldor's dungeon, but she understood Jeldor's trepidation in forming their alliance. Since then, the duke had done all in his power to ensure she held the crown.

It isn't for completely selfless reasons though. I must never forget that. I trust Jeldor, but then again, my father trusted Conroy.

They waited as the jailor opened the door to the cell. The tumbler clicked and the hinges squealed. The high-pitched grinding seemed louder in the damp underground, and her teeth hurt from the effect.

Conroy looked up as they entered the room and to his credit dropped to a knee. "Your Majesty."

Elyse had him stay in the position while her guards brought in chairs for her and Jeldor. They sat down and Elyse finally spoke. "You may have a seat."

Conroy complied and sat uncomfortably on a small stool. He looked calm. They waited for nearly a minute in silence.

"Do you have anything to say for yourself?" Elyse finally asked.

"I'm sorry, Your Majesty, but could you be more specific?"

Elyse dug her nails into her palms. "Why did you take up arms against me? Why would you bring war to my kingdom? Is that specific enough for you?"

"Does it matter any longer? You've won. Your commander has defeated me when I thought myself undefeatable." He paused and looked over Elyse's shoulder. "I had hoped to speak with Kaz."

"Kaz is not here. And you will answer my questions."

Conroy massaged his temple. He let out a sigh. "No, Your Majesty. I don't believe I will. There are more important matters to discuss right now."

"How dare you speak that way to the queen? Even after losing, you manage to be just as obnoxious as ever! What can be more important than answering the queen's questions?" asked Jeldor.

"The High Pass. We've been away for some time and I think it is in everyone's best interests to get an update on its status."

"The High Pass will care for itself as it has for hundreds of years," said Elyse.

Conroy shook his head. "That is my sole request, Your Majesty. I must know the current status of the High Pass before I answer any of your questions."

Elyse calmly rose from her seat. "Conroy, I will not have a prisoner dictate terms to me." She looked to Jeldor. "Let's go. I had assumed so much time alone would loosen the duke's tongue enough to explain why he thought it wise to commit treason and tarnish his family's name after centuries of loyally serving the kingdom, but it appears I was wrong and more drastic measures will need to be taken."

"Treason?" Conroy said the word like a curse. "Is that what you think? I never stopped being loyal to my kingdom, Your Majesty, only to the one who wore the crown. I promise you that I only had the realm's best interests at heart."

"Yes, just like Tomalt, Bronn, and Markus did, I presume?"

"Do not lump me in with them."

"Why not? You even allied yourself with two of them."

"A means to an end. Nothing more."

Elyse narrowed her gaze. Her voice took on an edge. "Your means caused the death of thousands of people who live in the kingdom you claim to care about. And you accomplished nothing." She chuckled. "You claim that you would have been the better ruler." She shook her head. "How can you possibly say you did what was best for Cadonia when you allowed her to bleed?"

"Say what you want. I no longer care. I was too cautious, too worried about leaving the High Pass undermanned for too long because of the responsibility of my family. If I would have left it sooner, things would have ended differently. But, it doesn't matter. You have my army, my lands, and my home. Decide my fate and let me die."

Elyse took two quick strides over to Conroy and slapped him across his face. The force knocked him from the uneven stool. He looked up at her, shocked.

"You will hang, Conroy. But until then, you will show me the respect of my station. Next time we meet, I promise you will remember that."

She spun and left the cell, noticing the slight smirk on Jeldor's face as he followed.

She stormed down the long corridor. She heard the jailor lock up behind them. At the far end of the corridor, she saw Kaz round a corner and walk toward them.

Her anger only increased because he had not bothered to join them. She realized that Conroy's words cut her. Without Kaz she would never have won the war. Such a thing shouldn't matter, but it did.

She quickened her pace, ready to lay into her commander for skipping their meeting and disobeying an order when he walked under a lit torch hanging from the wall. The look of sorrow and pain he wore caused her to pause before she hurried toward him. Her anger vanished.

"What happened?" she said.

Kaz's head hung low. "Hag is dead."

Elyse gasped and her eyes welled up. *One Above, she meant so much to him.* "How?"

"It was just her time," he said. "Wiqua and I were there with her when she went."

Elyse's chest tightened. She wanted to wrap her arms around him, but she had never done such a thing in front of others. *Still, who cares. I am queen after all.*

She stepped closer and almost as if sensing her decision Kaz stepped back and put his hands up.

"There's more. A lot more," he said.

She raised a hand to her mouth. "Is everyone else alright?"

"Yes, as far as I know. What I need to say is unrelated. I have my memory back, or most of it at least." He looked up and suddenly straightened, standing taller as he realized they weren't alone. He cleared his throat. "Can we continue this in private?"

One Above, he's going to leave me.

"Yes, of course," she said, trying to remain calm. "We can return to Conroy's study and—."

"Your Majesty! Your Majesty! Urgent news!"

Elyse heard the shouting and subsequent footsteps before the young messenger cleared the turn ahead. The boy sprinted down the dark corridor. Several guardsmen followed behind. He came to a stop and nearly fell over trying to take a knee.

"Your Majesty, urgent news from the High Pass," he managed between breaths.

"What is it?"

"A large horde in Thurum is massing near the fortress."

"A horde?" asked Jeldor. "The High Pass has never been assaulted by anything that would be described as a horde. The petty lords trying to conquer Thurum have trouble getting more than a few thousand men together at best."

Elyse turned back to the messenger. "Do you have a letter?"

"No, Your Majesty. There was no time to write one. I nearly killed my mount getting to you. Captain Samhan just told me to do the best I could. He had too much on his mind to write anything official. When I left, there were already an estimated fifty thousand men making camp, and he was scrambling to shore up our defenses. He needs reinforcements right away. We were undermanned due to . . ."

"Conroy committing treason?"

The boy bowed his head. "Yes, Your Majesty."

"How long is the ride to the fortress?"

"If we leave now and push through the night, we can make it by dawn."

"You can't be serious, Your Majesty. I find fifty thousand men hard to believe. This could be a trap," said Jeldor.

Elyse looked at the pleading messenger's eyes. "I need to see things for myself." She turned to Kaz who still appeared distracted. "Can you get the army ready to move?"

Kaz wore a confused look. "No. It will take much longer to break camp. Many of the men are probably drunk or in the city enjoying what they thought was a night without worry."

"Then grab all that you can now, even if it is only a few hundred." She turned to Jeldor. "You stay here and organize the rest of the army. Bring them up as soon as possible. I'd rather be safe than sorry. If we are indeed facing fifty thousand, every man will matter. Oh, but we need to leave an occupying force as well and trusted men to watch over Conroy."

"I'll handle it, Your Majesty," Jeldor said.

She nodded. "Then let's not waste another moment."

* * *

Elyse stood next to Kaz and Captain Samhan on the outermost of the fortress' three high-curtain walls that guarded the High Pass. Elyse had ridden through the night in relative silence with over a thousand soldiers. They arrived just before the false dawn.

As the rising sun slowly illuminated the land before her, the weight of the messenger's words sunk in.

Can this really be true? Cadonia is barely one nation again. And a battered nation at that.

"I obviously can't be certain, but that appears like more than fifty thousand men," she said aloud, unable to hide the awe in her voice.

"Your Majesty, they've been bringing in men and supplies all night. The last estimate I had from one of my scouts was over four times that number. And somehow, I don't believe they're done." He shook his head. "We heard rumors of odd movements over the last few months, but we dismissed them. No one believed anyone could manage an assault of this scale. Only the One Above knows how anyone organized this."

As the sun rose higher, Elyse saw that Captain Samhan's new estimate of two hundred thousand men made more sense. A wave of nausea hit her as she thought about the death that would come because of the impending clash.

Kaz scanned the opposition next to her with a spyglass. She couldn't imagine what he must be thinking. She had asked him to save her kingdom once already, and it looked as though she would have to ask him to do it again. He hadn't said more than five words as they traveled through the night, and most of them had been single syllables.

He wanted to talk to me about regaining his memory in private. And rather than grant that simple request, I bring him to this.

"What are your thoughts?" she asked.

"Jeldor better not dally with the rest of the army," Kaz said without dropping the spyglass. A sudden gasp came from his mouth as he froze. "It can't be," he whispered. "It's impossible."

"What? What is it?"

He lowered the tube and shook his head in disbelief. He handed it to her and pointed. "There."

She looked through the spyglass and saw several thousand warriors dressed in menacing gray and blue armor. They stood out not only because of the quality of their attire and the manner in which they carried themselves, but also because each warrior's skin was as black as Kaz's. Her mouth hung open as she lowered the tube.

"Are they . . ." she started to ask.

"Yes. They are from my homeland. A continent called Hesh, though I have no idea where it's located. Before your brother found me, I acted as warleader of my father's army and commanded those men. The ones you're looking at are Kifzo, an elite force, trained since boyhood for war," said Kaz. He turned to Elyse. "I don't have all my memories back yet, but I do recall a great deal." He looked back out toward that group.

Elyse blinked. "Can you get word to those you once commanded?" she asked. "Perhaps you can persuade them to join us or at least remove themselves from Thurum's forces."

"It's possible. But I wouldn't know who to send word to. I do not see my father nor others I thought may have taken my place. I don't know who commands them or why they're here. My father wanted to bring all of Hesh under his rule. We never even knew about these lands."

"That's because your father wasn't the visionary that I am," said a mysterious voice that seemed to call out from all directions.

Everyone on the wall looked around, unable to find the source of the strange voice.

"Down here, Kaz."

"Nachun?" said Kaz, voice full of both anger and confusion.

"One of my names," said the voice.

A chill crawled up Elyse's back.

No.

She raised the spyglass and honed in on the figure standing a hundred yards away. She saw dark red robes, like those of a High Mage, except with small blue designs embroidered throughout. Elyse held her breath as she focused on the man's face. In a shimmer, his skin lightened and his bone structure changed. The spyglass fell from her hands and shattered against the stone merlons.

"Nareash," she whispered.

"Yes, Elyse. I've come back for what you took from me."

Her stomach dropped.

The scepter.

He presented his back to the fortress and walked back to the enemy's camp. Her eyes widened as she watched the massing army grow in size.

EPILOGUE

As twilight bathed the swamp in a metallic gray, a Marsh Clan warrior bowed. "This is the last one."

Mawkuk stared out at the men, women, and children discovered as spies from the Blue Island Clan. They kneeled on the soft ground of the swamp, heads hung low. Behind them burned a massive bonfire—its flames rising thirty feet into the air. "How many in total?"

"One hundred and twelve."

Mawkuk leaned forward. "Are you sure that none have been missed?"

"I swear it on my life."

Mawkuk stood to address the thousands of citizens who called Cypronya home. Some joined him on the ground while others gazed down from suspension bridges and lower level buildings in the trees. He nodded to a shaman next to him. "My people," he started, voice amplified by sorcery, "we have been wronged in more ways than I can count. Tobin has used our warriors while ensuring we received none of the glory that comes with victory. I take full responsibility for that as I let the love of my children get the better of me—the very children that Tobin defiled and murdered."

He hung his head and fought back tears. "I will not throw away the second chance you've given me to restore our clan's pride. I have nothing left but all of you, and I will die before I give in to that tyrant!" He paused. "The past year's campaign caused the Blue Island Clan to suffer heavy losses and on top of that, much of their army is still trying to bring peace to the territories of the Red Mountain and Green Forest Clans. We know that Nachun has set sail on some strange mission with more than four thousand of their Kifzo. Some speculate those men are likely lost forever. This is our chance to exact revenge!

"Durahn has agreed to our terms. He's raised an army of his own and will stand with us against Tobin. We just received word that the alliance with him has convinced the survivors of the Yellow Plain Clan army to take up arms against the Blue Island Clan as well. Yesterday we were all enemies and tomorrow we may be enemies again, but today we will stand as one to bring down the Blue Island Clan!" He pointed to the spies. "Give them to the flames." Soldiers dragged men, women, and children into the blazing bonfire without hesitation. Their chilling screams sought to drown out his voice. He shouted louder. "All of Juanoq will burn because of what they've done to us!"

The swamp came to life as the roars of his people sent wildlife running for cover.

They shouted his name as one. "Mawkuk!"

Thank you for reading my story. If you enjoyed it, please consider leaving a rating or review at the site of purchase as well as other places such as Goodreads and Librarything. Like many other indie authors, I do not have a marketing team working for me and a positive review (even if only a couple of sentences long) can go a long way in enticing others to give my works a try.

Thanks again for your support.
Joshua P. Simon

ABOUT THE AUTHOR

Unlike most authors, Joshua did not immerse himself into the world of books as a child. After finishing graduate school, he quickly made up for lost time by buying and devouring countless graphic novels. Remembering his love of the original Conan movies, he moved on to the fantasy genre with the compilations of Robert E. Howard. He was hooked.

Since then, he has moved on to other authors such as Glen Cook, Joe Abercrombie, George R.R. Martin, Steven Erikson, Paul Kearney, Steven Brust, Peter V. Brett, Patrick Rothfuss and many more.

Joshua was inspired to write and create his own fantasy world after reading Glen Cook's Black Company series. Thanks to a vivid imagination, he soon found himself with more ideas than he knew what to do with. After some prompting by his wife, he took the plunge.

When not writing, Joshua lives a life devoted to God and spends time with his beautiful family. He is employed as an accountant.

Contact Joshua through any of the following:
BLOG: www.joshuapsimon.blogspot.com
EMAIL: joshuapsimon.author@gmail.com
FACEBOOK: www.facebook.com/JoshuaPSimon
TWITTER: www.twitter.com/JoshuaPSimon

Sign up for Joshua's newsletter to be the first to hear about new releases and receive exclusive content.
http://joshuapsimon.blogspot.com/p/newsletter.html

Printed in Great Britain
by Amazon